Praise for

HOUSE *of the* HUNTED

"Picture it: An Art Deco villa on the French Riviera in 1935. A witty crowd of expats caught up in a mad whirl of dinner parties, tennis parties, boating parties and scavenger hunts. . . . Mark Mills has chosen this seductive setting for *House of the Hunted*. . . . Mills is a polished stylist with a singular talent for capturing the defining moment when something precious is about to be lost forever. Here it's that sliver of time between the wars when cordial relationships were still possible among civilized people of all nations."

—*The New York Times Book Review*

"Mills's story is suspenseful and romantic, vividly drawn and engaging, reminiscent of some of the best spy novels of the past. Readers will recognize echoes of Eric Ambler, Graham Greene and Alan Furst, but *House of the Hunted* stands on its own."

—CNN.com

"Mesmerizing . . . [Mills's] best work in an already accomplished career."

—*The Independent* (UK)

"Written like a wild-fire hybrid of John le Carré and Ernest Hemingway, this highly literate thriller goes deep into the inner workings of the spy game circa 1935 and accurately depicts the fractured relationships between all the countries involved. . . . An excellent read for those who enjoy both espionage and literary thrillers."

—Bookreporter.com

"Mills, with a preternatural skill at making times past feel like lived experience, has set *House of the Hunted* in 1935. . . . Layers upon layers of dissembling deceit are slowly unpeeled . . . [with] a haunting force."

—*Houston Chronicle*

"Summer on the French Riviera: long swims, sailing jaunts, wine-soaked dinners on stone terraces—and an attempted assassination. So begins Mills's delicious *House of the Hunted*, a terse, carefully plotted journey through the precarious world of pre–World War II Continental politics that'll have you guessing until the very end."

—Oprah.com

"Mills takes a cliché of espionage fiction . . . and overhauls it in this lush, atmospheric thriller. . . . Mills struck gold with his earlier novel *The Savage Garden* . . . [but] *House of the Hunted* is even better, with a vivid sense of place, character and the geopolitical complexities of the period."

—*The Guardian* (UK)

"Plenty of twists and turns . . . The book paints a convincing picture of a man whose past returns to haunt him and who must face it while he keeps his wits and protects the people he loves. . . . A lot of atmosphere complements the excitement."

—*Kirkus Reviews*

"Bloody brilliant . . . Mills has crafted a masterpiece of espionage fiction that fully thrills. . . . Beautifully crafted, breathless and immensely satisfying. Do not miss this one."

—OLEN STEINHAUER, *New York Times* bestselling author of *The Tourist* and *The Nearest Exit*

HOUSE *of the* HUNTED

HOUSE
of the
HUNTED

A Novel

Mark Mills

Random House Trade Paperbacks
New York

2013 Random House Trade Paperback Edition

Published in the United States by Random House Trade Paperbacks, an imprint of The Random House Publishing Group, a division of Random House LLC, a Penguin Random House Company, New York.

RANDOM HOUSE and the HOUSE colophon are registered trademarks of Random House LLC.

Originally published in hardcover in the United Kingdom as *House of the Hanged* by HarperCollins Publishers, London, in 2011.

LIBRARY OF CONGRESS CATALOGING-IN-PUBLICATION DATA
Mills, Mark.
House of the hunted: a novel / Mark Mills.
p. m.
ISBN 978-0-8129-8021-9
eBook ISBN 978-0-679-64424-8
1. Soviet Union—Fiction. 2. Political prisoners—Fiction. I. Title.
PS3613.I569H98 2011   13'.6—dc22   011024449

Printed in the United States of America on acid-free paper

www.atrandom.com

9 8 7 6 5 4 3 2 1

Book design by Virginia Norey

For my mother

Man is neither angel nor beast; and the misfortune is

that he who would act the angel acts the beast.

—BLAISE PASCAL
(1623–1662)

HOUSE *of the* HUNTED

1

Petrograd, Russia. January 1919.

The moment the guard called her name she felt the weight of the other women's eyes upon her.

It didn't make sense, didn't fit with the grim clock that regulated their lives. Too late in the day for an interrogation, the usual hour of execution was still some way off.

"Irina Bibikov," snapped the guard once more, his silhouette black against the open door of the darkened cell.

She was hunched on her pallet bed, her back against the wall, her knees pulled tight to her chest for warmth, as tight as her new belly would permit. Unwinding, she rose awkwardly to her feet, her palm pressed to the damp stonework for support.

The guard stepped away from the door. She knew better than to meet his gaze as she passed by him and out into the corridor.

Blinking back the ice-white light from the bare electric bulb, she briefly heard the murmur of prayers on her behalf before the guard pulled the steel door shut behind them.

Tom fought the urge to hurry ahead. *Nothing to arouse suspicion,* he told himself. His papers, though false, were in good order, good enough to pass close scrutiny. He knew this because he'd been stopped by a Cheka patrol earlier that day while crossing Souvorov Square.

There had been two of them, small men in shapeless greatcoats that reached almost to their ankles, and they had enjoyed their authority over Yegor Sidorenko. The name was Ukrainian, to account for the faint but undisguisable hitch in Tom's accent. He had called them "Comrade"; they had called him "Ukrainian dog" before sending him on his way. More than a year had passed since the Bolshevik coup, but evidently the spirit of brotherhood so widely trumpeted by Lenin, Zinoviev and the others had yet to reach the ears of their secret police. So much for lofty ideals. So much for the Revolution.

Tom knew that he couldn't bank on being quite so lucky if stopped again, but only as he drew level with no. 2 Gorokhovaya did it occur to him that he might actually find himself face-to-face with the same two Chekists as they entered or left their headquarters.

There were patrols coming and going, passing beneath the high, arched gateway punched into the drab façade. Beyond lay the central courtyard, where the executions took place, where the bodies were loaded into the back of trucks, their next stop, their terminus, some nameless hole hacked out of the iron-hard ground beyond the city limits.

At least the sharp north wind sluicing the streets of the Russian capital permitted him to draw his scarf up over his nose, all but concealing his face. As he did so, he cast a furtive glance through the archway, past the sentries shivering at their posts.

What was he looking for? Signs of unusual activity, some indication that the plan had already been compromised. He saw nothing of note, just a courtyard shrouded in the gathering gloom, and the dim outlines of men and vehicles.

Trudging on past through the deep snow, Tom silently cursed the fact that Irina hadn't been transferred by now to one of the state prisons, Shpalernaya or Deriabinskaya, where security was considerably more lax and bribery endemic. Instead, his only option had been to try to spring her from the beast's lair.

In spite of all the planning, all the precautions, it suddenly seemed too much to hope for, and that unwelcome thought chilled him, far more than the raw wind that slammed into him at the end of the street. He bore left, hugging the shadows.

He couldn't quite see St. Isaac's Cathedral up ahead but he could sense its brooding presence in the darkness.

It was a cellar room, small and all but empty. There were some mops poking from their pails in one corner and a few large cans of cleaning fluid stacked up in another, but Irina's eye was drawn to the wooden stool standing alone in the middle of the room. On it were some clothes, neatly folded, with two pieces of paper resting on top.

One was a visitor's pass made out to Anna Constantinov. On the second was scrawled *St. Isaac's Cathedral.* The words were in English, and she recognized the handwriting.

"Quick," said the guard. He was the youngest of the three who oversaw the female prisoners, not much more than a boy, his mustache a tragic overture to manhood. "Get changed."

Irina stared at the slip of paper in her hand, not quite believing that it had happened, trying to picture what Tom must have put himself through, the dangers he had faced, the border crossing from Finland . . .

It was almost inconceivable.

"Hurry," hissed the guard.

His ear was pressed to the door, but his eyes remained fixed on her—eager young eyes, hoping for a glimpse of female flesh.

She was happy to oblige. It might provide some scrap of comfort at the end of his short life. She wondered how much money he'd been promised. More than enough to see him safely away, out of the country. To stay would mean certain death before a firing squad. She looked down at her belly, the still unfamiliar bow, the tautness of the pale skin around her navel.

Dressed now, her soiled clothes heaped on the floor at her feet, she wrapped the shawl around her head and turned to the guard.

"I'll get rid of that," he said, taking the piece of paper from her.

Young, yet sensible. It wouldn't be wise to have details of the rendezvous about her person if she was stopped while trying to leave.

"Good luck," he said.

"You too."

They parted company wordlessly in the corridor outside, the guard pointing out her route before vanishing into the darkened bowels of the building.

Irina passed by the steps leading up to the interrogation rooms, silent at this hour, making for the stone staircase at the end of the corridor.

She was curious to see how far she would get.

On the floor above, she ran a short gauntlet of offices flanking a corridor before finding herself in the main lobby. There was a guard on duty at the big desk by the doors, bent over some paperwork. When she stopped to show her pass he waved her on, almost irritably, and she wondered if he too was in on it.

Outside in the gloomy courtyard, no one paid her a blind bit of notice, not the troops huddled around the brazier, not the officer berating the two mechanics poking around in the engine of a canvas-covered truck.

Was it really that simple? A mere slip of paper?

There were still the sentries at the main gate to get past, but she could see freedom looming ever larger beyond the tall archway as she approached. A quick glance over her shoulder confirmed that she wasn't being followed.

One of the sentries unshouldered his rifle, keeping a close watch on her while the other checked her pass against a ledger in the small cubbyhole that served as their guardhouse. A bitter blast whistled through the archway, stinging her eyes. Then suddenly everything was in order. The pass disappeared into a drawer. Anna Constantinov was free to go.

How had Tom done it? No one had really expected him to try, let alone pull it off, least of all her. He had outwitted them all and she knew what she should now do, but she found herself thrusting her hands deep into her pockets and setting off up the street. She needed time to think, to work it through in her head.

She had taken no more than a dozen tentative steps along the icy pavement when she heard the teasing drawl of a familiar voice behind her.

"Going somewhere, Irina?" it said in Russian.

Tom lit another candle, an excuse to stretch his legs and warm his fingers over the bank of flickering flames.

He had spent almost an hour in the Alexander Nevsky Chapel, most of it on his knees, head bowed in a show of prayer. A pew would have been nice, a stool, anything, but seating had never figured large in the thinking of the Russian Orthodox Church. It allowed them to cram the people in. Fourteen thousand souls could fit into St. Isaac's Cathedral; at least, that's what Irina had told him when she had first taken him there, soon after his arrival in Petrograd, his raven-haired tour guide skipping her classes at the Conservatoire to show him some of the sights.

It had been a bright June morning, the sunlight flashing off the vast gilded dome and laying bare the fussy opulence of the interior: the intricate patterning of the marble floor, the steps of polished jasper, the columns of green malachite and blue lazurite, the walls inlaid with porphyry and gemstones, and the gilded stucco and statues wherever you turned. A blaze of fragmented color, had been Tom's first impression, like stepping inside a child's kaleidoscope.

He had made the right noises, but Irina had read his thoughts, sensed his reservations.

His church, the church of his youth, was a humble ivy-tangled affair in a village on the outskirts of Norwich, where the damp rose in waves around the bare plaster walls, and where Mr. Higginbotham, the churchwarden, had once threatened to resign his post because the new altar frontal sported an embroidered hem. Tom's father had seen that the offending article was returned to Wippell's, who had promptly dispatched a suitably chaste replacement.

"Your father is a priest?" Irina had asked.

"A vicar."

"Is there a difference?"

"I suppose not. Only I've never heard my father refer to himself as a priest."

"I'm surprised," Irina had said, tilting her head at him.

"What, I give off an unholy glow?"

It was the first time he had seen her laugh, and he could still recall how his heart had soared at the sound of it, and at the sight of the curious new look in her eyes that seemed to hold the promise of something more than mere acquaintance. He hadn't been wrong. The invitation to dinner at her uncle Vladimir's dacha out on the islands had followed a few days later. It was one of many little wooden villas huddled along the shore, with wide, open verandas on all sides and a rambling garden running down to the Neva. It was also theirs for the weekend. Vladimir, a lawyer, had been held back in Moscow on urgent business at the last moment, but they were to make themselves at home. They did just that, helping themselves to a bottle of white Burgundy from his cellar and taking his fishing rod to the end of the stumpy jetty, where Irina pulled their supper from the river—four perch, which they gutted then grilled over a fire at the water's edge. It was a warm evening, humid and close, and the sounds that came to their ears seemed muted by the heavy air: the distant whistle of a passenger steamer, the bells of a church on the mainland, the bark of a neighbor's dog, a snatch of song from a passing barge. They sat out there for hours, bathed in the strange, eerie radiance of the long northern night, talking effortlessly of their lives and the upheavals of recent times. And well after midnight, when tiredness finally began to get the better of them, Irina showed him to his bedroom, only to return a short while later and slip silently between the sheets. They didn't make love, not that first time out at the dacha; they held each other close and they fell asleep to the sound of the polecats scampering about inside the wooden walls and in the roof over their heads.

How had they gone from that to this in little more than six months? He knew the answer, of course. A few weeks after that dreamlike introduction to the islands, Czar Nicholas and the imperial family had been murdered, slain by the Bolsheviks (in the basement of a house in Ekaterinburg, if the intelligence report that had recently passed through Tom's hands in Helsinki was to be believed). The real turning point, though, had been the attempt on Lenin's life at the end of August—two bullets, one to the chest, one to the neck—as the leader of the Bolsheviks was leaving a rally in Moscow. No one had expected Lenin to survive, but even before it became clear that he would, the Red Terror had been unleashed: a brutal crackdown intended to turn back the rising tide of anti-Bolshevism in the country.

Suspecting British involvement in the assassination plot, the Cheka had stormed the embassy in Petrograd. It was a Saturday, and Tom hadn't been in the building at the time, but Yuri, the porter, had been. It was Yuri who had searched Tom out at the English Club and described to him the death of Captain Cromie, chief of the Naval Intelligence Department, dispatched with a bullet to the back of the skull after a fierce firefight on the main staircase. Tom's boss, Bruce Lockhart, head of the special British diplomatic mission to Russia, had been taken into custody, and the Cheka had issued a warrant for Tom's arrest.

Yuri had been accompanied by a tall and taciturn Finn assigned to spirit Tom away that same evening. In spite of Tom's protestations, the Finn had not allowed him to see Irina before leaving. Evil was in the air. And besides, there was no time. The last train from Okhta station left at seven o'clock.

Tom's summer in the Russian capital had ended abruptly with that journey northward: by rail to Grusino in a boxcar crammed with silent refugees, then a sapping foot march through the forests and bogs, dodging the patrols, tormented every weary step of the way by thoughts of the woman he had been forced to leave behind. Even when they had slipped past the border post on their bellies into Finland and freedom he had experienced no sense of elation.

The dread prospect of repeating that same perilous journey—not only in the dead of winter, but with Irina in tow—brought Tom out of his reverie.

His eyes darted to the bag of clothes he had secreted in the corner of the chapel, just beyond the glow of the candles. He couldn't make it out in the shadows, but he sensed that it was there, just as he sensed the presence of someone standing behind him.

His head snapped around expectantly.

It wasn't Irina; it was a young priest, not much older than Tom, and yet there was something haggard and careworn about him.

"If He hasn't heard you by now, then I doubt He's listening."

Tom returned the faint smile, but said nothing.

"Bad times."

"Yes, Father."

"*Vade in pacem,*" the priest said softly before retiring into the gloom shrouding the main body of the cathedral.

Maybe it was the young priest's depleted air, but Tom felt a sudden shiver of unease pass through him. He now noticed that some of the icons were missing from the walls of the chapel. Stolen, or removed for their own protection? Either way, their absence pointed to an ominous shift in the natural order of things. A story blew into his mind, something Irina had once told him. She had been present when two hundred victims of the so-called Bloodless Revolution had been laid to rest on the Champ de Mars. Apparently, no crosses had been carried in the procession, and no priests had been allowed to officiate at the burials.

Irina. Was she trying to tell him something? He would normally have dismissed such a thought as superstitious claptrap, but by now the fear had lodged itself in his chest. Why had he even chosen St. Isaac's? Because it was safe? Nowhere was safe in the new Russia. There was certainly no place for obsolete notions of religious sanctuary.

He was a fool. At the very least, he should have remained outside the cathedral, whose thick walls rising into the darkness were beginning to feel more like those of a prison than a place of worship. Even the mosaic saints set in the marble iconostasis towering before him seemed to look down on him now with a certain disapproval, reproaching him for his stupidity.

He hurried over and recovered the bag from the shadows. The park directly across from the north portal would give him a view down Admiralty Prospekt of Irina approaching. More important, he would be able to see if she was being followed. He refused to consider the possibility that she wouldn't show at all. If the mission had failed, there would be no second chances.

He was ten yards shy of the north doors when he saw them enter the cathedral directly in front of him. They weren't in uniform—they didn't need to be. The way they were moving, the arrogant purpose in their step, marked the pair out as Chekists. Tom's instinct was to turn and flee, but he knew they would have the south and west doors covered by now.

Extending an upturned hand, he carried on toward the two men.

"A few rubles, comrades," he pleaded pathetically, "for a veteran of Tannenberg."

Mention of the bloody battle didn't curry any sympathy.

"Papers," snapped the smaller of the two Chekists.

"I haven't eaten in days."

Not so far from the truth, but Tom found his hand slapped aside.

"Papers!"

"Leave him," growled the other. "You heard what Zakharov said— he has a beard."

Zakharov. There was no time to process this news—or to give thanks for the last-minute precaution of changing his appearance—as two more men bowled into the building through the north doors. They were wearing leather jackets crossed with cartridge belts. The taller of the two Chekists turned to them.

"Neratov, you guard the door."

Any suspicions that Neratov might have had of Tom were dispelled when the smaller Chekist shoved him dismissively aside. The scruffy man with the bag in his hand had evidently been checked and cleared. While the three other policemen fanned out into the cathedral Tom crept sheepishly past the glowering Neratov and out through the doors.

In his haste to put the danger behind him, he slipped on the icy steps leading down from the pillared portico. Falling hard, he felt something go in his wrist. He bit back a cry, not wishing to draw attention to himself.

He glanced up and down Admiralty Prospekt: the pavements were deserted, just an *isvochik* heading toward him, drawn by a shaggy white horse. It was free, and Tom waved it down, almost laughing at the absurdity of his good fortune.

The coachman, muffled in furs, was bringing the small sledge to a halt when Tom heard the shout.

"Stop him!"

It came from the cathedral. The tall Chekist stood dwarfed between two pillars of the north portico, waving furiously.

"Stop him!" he bellowed again. "He's an enemy of the Soviet!"

With a flick of the driver's reins the sleigh took off. Tom stumbled after it, unable to get any meaningful purchase on the compacted snow, falling quickly behind as the horse's trot became a canter. Realizing the futility of the pursuit, he cut left across the street and disappeared into the park on the far side.

Overhead, a half-moon hung in a cloudless sky, and even beyond the pool of light thrown by the streetlamp he could still pick a route with ease. Unfortunately, this also meant that his pursuers would have no trouble following his deep tracks in the snow.

That first lone shout had now become a chorus at his back. Outnumbered, the only thing he had in his favor was that he had prepared himself for such conditions. The snow in the park was deep, thigh-deep in places, just as it had been in Finland. Before leaving Helsinki, he had trained hard in anticipation of their flight from Russia, pushing himself on occasions to almost masochistic extremes. Not only was he in better physical condition than he'd ever been, but he had also accustomed himself to the hunger and the cold until his mother would barely have recognized the lean, gaunt specter of her own son before her. He had grown a beard, and he had learned to stoop convincingly, knocking a few inches off his height, making him one of the crowd.

"Come on, you bastards," Tom muttered to himself. "Let's see what you've got."

What they had, it turned out, was guns. And they weren't afraid to use them.

The first few shots ripped through the skeletal branches above his head. He assumed they were warning shots until he heard something whistle past his left ear, death missing him by a matter of inches.

Crouching, he drove his legs on, knowing that every hard yard gained now would equate to three or four when the snowbound park gave way to Admiralty Quay. He lost a little of his advantage when he was suddenly pitched forward into the snow, as if shoved hard in the back by a phantom hand. Scrabbling to his feet, he figured the bullet must have struck the bag slung over his shoulder, embedding itself in the jumble of clothing he'd put together for Irina.

A primeval impulse to survive, to live beyond his twenty-two years, took complete possession of him now. He plowed on like a man sprinting through a waist-high sea to save a drowning child. Pleasingly, the shouts of his pursuers had dimmed almost to silence by the time he finally broke free onto Admiralty Quay.

He knew that the frozen stillness of the river lay just beyond the low wall ahead of him. Should he risk it, skittering across the ice, out in the open? No. He bore left, away from the Admiralty building, his legs burning, but with a lot of life still left in them.

Run, he told himself. *Settle your breathing and stretch out your stride.* He would take the next street on the left, head south, lose himself in the backstreets around the Mariinsky Theatre.

Tom glimpsed the revolver in the other man's hand a split-second before they collided. Both had been slowing to make the turn, but the head-on impact still sent them sprawling in a tangle of limbs.

The gun. Where was it? No longer in the man's hand, but within reach. Tom lashed out with his foot, slamming the heel of his boot into the man's head, catching him in the temple. This bought him a precious second, enough to give him a fighting chance. The two of them scrabbled and clawed for possession of the weapon, the lancing pain in Tom's damaged wrist numbed by the panic.

The moment he realized he'd been beaten to the prize, the Cheka man froze. Keeping the revolver trained on him, Tom scrabbled to his feet.

"Please . . ." said the man, raising a futile hand to stave off the bullet.

Tom glanced down Admiralty Quay: vague smudges of movement in the distance, drawing closer, but too far off yet to pose a threat.

Tom looked back at the man. He was young, Tom's age, his lean, handsome face contorted with fear, and in those pitiful eyes Tom saw everyone who had ever been cruel to him, everyone who had ever hurt him, deceived him, betrayed him.

"*Vade in pacem*," he said, backing away.

Go in peace—the same parting words of Latin that the priest had offered to him in the chapel at St. Isaac's just minutes before. He didn't know why they sprang from his mouth; he didn't care.

He was gone, disappearing down the darkened street, flying now on adrenaline wings.

The apartment building was a drab five-floored affair on Liteiny Prospekt, near the junction with the Nevsky. The gray morning light didn't do it any favors.

Tom watched and waited from across the street, one eye out for Cheka patrols, or anyone else showing undue interest in the apartment building. He had got rid of the bag, abandoning it in the coal cellar where he'd passed a sleepless night, swaddled in the clothing intended for Irina. The bullet that had knocked him flat in the park was now in his hip pocket. He had tried to think of it as his lucky charm, but how could it be? If Irina wasn't dead by now, she would be soon. He was too much of a realist to believe otherwise.

He knew how the Cheka operated; months of tracking their working methods from the safety of Finland had introduced him to the brutal truth. In Kharkov they went in for scalping and hand flaying; in Voronezh they favored rolling you around in a barrel hammered through with nails. Crucifixion, stoning and impalement were commonplace, and in Orel they liked to pour water over their victims, leaving them to freeze outside overnight into crystal statues.

This is what the Revolution had brought out in men: not the best, but the very worst, the stuff of bygone eras, when Genghis Khan and his bloodthirsty hordes had run merry riot through the steppes.

In no way could Tom be held accountable for the dark state of nature that lurked in men, but he was to blame for choosing to gamble with it, and losing. How would things have turned out for Irina if he hadn't tried to intervene? She might have weathered the incarceration, the torture, and been released. What if he had underestimated her? Should he not have had more faith in her resilience?

These were the questions that had kept him awake in the coal cellar, and he couldn't imagine a time when they wouldn't plague his thoughts. If he had come here to this grim apartment building on Liteiny Prospekt, it was only with a view to dragging some small consolation from the disaster.

He had a street number and an apartment number, but no name. Markku had told him that the name was of no importance; the one he knew her by was probably false anyway.

"It's a woman?" Tom had inquired.

"It's something close," had been Markku's enigmatic reply.

The problem lay in slipping past the concierge unnoticed. It was well known that the building caretakers of Petrograd were rapidly becoming the unofficial eyes and ears of the Cheka. It was even rumored that some made false denunciations of their residents, leaving them free to pillage the apartments once the "counterrevolutionaries" had been carted off.

Seeing an elderly woman rummaging for her key at the entrance door, Tom hurried across the street, arriving as the door was swinging shut behind her. He stopped it with his hand, waited a few moments, then slipped inside.

The cavernous entrance hall was dark and deserted. He heard the woman puffing her way up the stone staircase, and through the glazed doors directly ahead of him he could see a man shoveling snow in the courtyard.

The apartment was on the third floor, toward the back of the building. He knocked, and was about to knock again when he heard a female voice.

"Who is it?"

"Markku sent me," he replied, in Russian.

"I don't know anyone called Markku."

"He told me to say that you make the best *pelmeni* in all Russia . . . after his mother's."

Three locks were undone before the door was opened as far as the guard chain would permit. A small woman a shade over five feet peered up at him defiantly. Her black hair was threaded with silver strands and pulled back tightly off her lined face. Her dark eyes were clear and hard, like polished onyx. They roamed over him from head to toe, then past him, searching the corridor behind. Only then did she release the chain.

Tom followed her along a corridor into a large and extravagantly furnished living room. The rococo divans, Persian rugs and gilt-framed portraits—one of a booted general, another of some high-bosomed ancestress—had obviously been intended for a far nobler space than this; here they looked awkward and overblown, eager to be elsewhere.

Tom turned and found himself staring into the barrel of a handgun.

"Take off your coat," said the woman. "Take it off and throw it on that chair there."

There was nothing strained or hysterical in her voice. She might just as well have been a doctor inviting him to remove his clothes in a room.

Tom did as she requested, unquestioningly, watching while she searched the coat, knowing what she would find. Her eyes left his only momentarily, to glance down at the revolver as she pulled it from one of the pockets.

"This is a Cheka weapon," she said, leveling her own gun at his head.

Tom barely flinched, beyond caring. "It was. Until last night."

"You're not Russian."

"I'm English."

She switched effortlessly to English, with just the barest hint of an accent. "And where were you born?"

"Norwich."

"A flat and dull county, Norfolk."

"You obviously don't know it well."

"Sit down. Hands on your knees."

Tom deposited himself on a divan. The woman remained standing.

"Who are you?" she asked.

"Tom Nash. I was part of the Foreign Office delegation sent over here last summer."

"A little young for that sort of thing, aren't you?"

"It was my first assignment after joining."

"You knew Bruce Lockhart?"

"Of course. I worked for him here."

"Lockhart was lucky to get away with his life."

"So was I. It was Markku who got me out of the country after they stormed the embassy."

"And how is Markku?" she demanded flatly.

Tom and the tall Finn had become fast friends since their escape from the capital. They'd had little choice in the matter; the consulate in Helsinki had lodged them in the same room at the Grand Hotel Fennia.

"Stuck in Helsinki," said Tom. "Frustrated. Drunk most of the time."

"He's still one of the best couriers we've got. So why, I'm wondering, do they send us a boy from the Foreign Office?"

"I'm with the Secret Intelligence Service now."

"Is that right?" She made no effort to conceal her skepticism.

"I was transferred when I got to Helsinki."

This wasn't quite true. Tom had pushed for a transfer to the SIS in Helsinki, anything that would keep him close to Petrograd, to Irina. A desk job back in London hadn't been an option in his own mind, and he had managed to persuade others that his skills as a Russian speaker would be best served closer to the front line.

"Prove it," said the woman.

"I can't."

"I suggest you try."

Tom hesitated before replying. "ST-25."

"That means nothing to me." She shrugged.

But she was lying; he had seen the faint flicker in her obsidian eyes. She knew as well as he did that ST-25 was the code name for the sole remaining SIS agent in Petrograd. The Bolsheviks had brutally broken the American spy network over the autumn, and they were close to achieving the same with the British. The elusive ST-25 remained a thorn in their side, though. The Cheka had even set up a special unit devoted to hunting him down.

"You want his real name?" said Tom. "I can give it to you if that will help."

"She doesn't need to know my real name."

The voice was low and steady, and it came from behind Tom.

He turned to see a man of middle height step into the room. It was hard to judge his age—early thirties, maybe—the thick dark beard blunting his handsome features showed no signs of gray.

"Katya, I think our friend here could do with a hot drink . . . and maybe a piece of bread, if you can spare it."

Katya eyed Tom with all the warmth of an attack dog called to heel by its master. Handing over the two guns, she disappeared into the kitchen.

"Paul Dukes?" asked Tom.

Dukes nodded and settled into an armchair. It was a moment before he spoke. "What happened to your wrist?"

It was tightly bound with the leather belt he'd brought along for Irina. "I think it might be broken."

Dukes released the barrel of the revolver and checked the cylinder. "She's right," he said. "Why did Leonard send you?"

Leonard Pike was chief of SIS operations in northern Russia, calling the shots from the embassy in Stockholm. Although Tom had never met him, it was Leonard who had agreed to take him on in Helsinki.

"He didn't send me," Tom replied. "I'm sailing under my own colors."

Dukes snapped the barrel shut and looked up, intrigued. "Go on."

Tom told him everything: of his relationship with Irina, his forced flight from Russia, and his work for the Secret Intelligence Service in Helsinki, which had involved deciphering many of Dukes's own intelligence reports. Helsinki was a mess, a sinkhole of desperation and duplicity, swarming with émigrés and spies. Information and disinformation were the twin orders of the day in the Finnish capital, and Tom's other duties had entailed trawling the city's restaurants, hotel bars and drawing rooms, keeping an ear out for anything of value.

This wasn't how he had got wind of Irina's arrest, though; that news had come to him via Markku, who had heard it from one of the other couriers, along with the small but devastating detail that Irina was pregnant. Tom didn't reveal this to Dukes, if only because the notion that he'd fathered a child was still too big to grapple with on his own, let alone share with a stranger. Besides, at the time it hadn't colored the decision he'd arrived at with Markku's encouragement and assistance.

Both men knew that Bayliss, the SIS station chief in Helsinki, would never have sanctioned a rescue attempt, so the plan had been hatched in secret, with Markku providing false documents, detailed instructions on a number of routes in and out of the country, as well as the names of a few reliable contacts in Petrograd. The sixty thousand rubles that Markku estimated would be required for bribes had proved much harder to come by. In the end Tom had been left with no other choice but to "borrow" it from the SIS slush fund.

Dukes had been listening attentively throughout, but now broke his silence with the bleak observation "That's going to cost you your job, and probably a lot more."

"I don't care. It all went wrong last night."

He described how the band of Chekists had shown up at St. Isaac's Cathedral in place of Irina, and how he had only just managed to slip through their fingers.

Dukes got to his feet and wandered to the fireplace. He poked at a burning log with the toe of his boot. There was something ominous in his studied silence.

"I'm going to tell you this now," he said eventually, turning to face Tom. "Because if you don't hear it from me, you may never hear it at all." He paused. "She was executed last night."

Tom felt a cold hand settle on his heart. His words, when they came, sounded distant, hollow.

"How do you know?"

"Console yourself with the fact that they would have killed her anyway. You see, I never met her myself, but I know of people she helped. We were aware of her . . . predicament."

Her predicament? He made her sound like a debutante torn between two evening gowns in Harrods.

"How do you know?" demanded Tom, more forcefully this time.

"I had it on good authority early this morning."

"Good authority?"

"A very reliable source, I'm afraid."

"Who?"

"I can't say."

"I have a right to know."

"And I have a duty to protect his identity. If you're captured by the Cheka they will make you talk. Don't look so affronted—everyone talks. Do you want him to lose his life too?"

At that moment Katya returned bearing a tray, which she placed on a low side table. She must have been eavesdropping from the kitchen. It wasn't just the misting of pity in her hard eyes; before pouring the tea she handed Tom two tablets and a glass of water.

"Aspirin. For your wrist."

The teacups matched the antique porcelain pot, and Dukes savored a first, warming sip before continuing.

"Look, believe me, I'm sorry. We've all lost friends, good friends, and I daresay we stand to lose many more. But you shouldn't have come here. Markku should not have given you this address. There's nothing we can do for you."

"I didn't come here for me, I came here for you—to warn you."

He explained that Markku had put him in contact with a man named Dimitri Zakharov. It was Zakharov who had organized the escape, Zakharov who had betrayed him to the Cheka.

Dukes and Katya exchanged a brief look.

"I doubt that very much," said Dukes.

"Zakharov gave them a description of me. I overheard them say it."

Dukes hesitated. "If he did, then it was tortured out of him."

"He didn't look too distressed when I saw him leave his apartment an hour ago."

Dukes was clearly taken aback by this news. "Maybe we're talking about another Zakharov."

"How many Zakharovs does Markku know who live on Kazanskaya?"

"Katya . . . ?"

For once she looked shaken. "Anything is possible. We both know that."

Dukes turned his attention back to Tom. "I was wrong. You were right to come here." He handed the revolver back. "I'm surprised there are still six bullets left in the cylinder."

Tom had indeed trailed Zakharov for a good few streets, imagining the moment—the muzzle of the gun planted at the base of the traitor's neck, or maybe a swift tap on the shoulder first with the barrel so that Tom could carry with him the flash of recognition, of terror, in the other man's eyes as a future balm for his soul. In the end, though, he had allowed Zakharov to slip away from him.

Maybe it had been cowardice, the knowledge that retribution would surely come at the cost of his own life, or maybe the calculating pragmatist in him had prevailed over base emotion. Either way, he was alive, and the information he had just handed on might even save lives. It clearly had value; he could see its worth reflected back at him in Dukes's eyes.

"This changes everything," said Dukes. "We can't stay here. Katya, you also have to leave."

"No."

"You must."

"Not if I don't know where you're going."

"Katya—"

"Do I know?" she insisted.

Dukes shook his head solemnly.

"Then go," she said. "Both of you. What are they going to do with an old woman like me?"

Her life had been reduced quite enough already to this: this queer museum of displaced artifacts. The barbarians might be hammering at the gates of the city, but the curator had no intention of abandoning her post.

It took Dukes a few minutes to gather his belongings together, and all the while he was issuing instructions to Tom. Katya accompanied them downstairs as far as the first-floor landing. Pressing something into Dukes's hand, she said, "It was my mother's."

Tom also received a parting gift—a jeweled gold locket on a chain.

"You are a brave boy," said Katya, "and you deserve to live. But remember . . . keep back one bullet for yourself."

She shooed them off down the stairs like a mother sending her two sons out to play.

Tom left the building first, turning up his collar and heading south on Liteiny Prospekt. Dukes went north. Ten nerve-racking minutes later they reconvened, as arranged, in front of a haberdashery on Nevsky Prospekt. There was no acknowledgment; it was an opportunity for each of them to determine if the other was being followed. Dukes had said he would stamp the snow from his boots if he felt they were safe to proceed. This he now did, before setting off once more at a brisk pace. Tom tailed him at a distance, his fingers closed around the revolver in his pocket, unsure of their destination.

He tried to remain alert, but his grief came at him in waves. He had walked this same route with Irina, idly strolling in the summer heat, stopping every so often to peer into a shop window, the scarlet trams rattling back and forth nearby.

He choked back a sob and felt the heat of anger rising in his belly. He didn't fight to suppress it; he let it spread through him, into his chest, along his limbs, warming him.

It came to him quite suddenly what he would do and how he would do it.

It was a religious building of some kind, set well back from the street behind a high wall at the southern end of the Nevsky. Beyond the imposing entrance gate the trees rose tall and bare on either side of the pathway. Dukes cut left almost immediately into the trees, taking a well-trodden trail through the deep snow. It led to a cemetery deep in the wood, a bosky burial ground for the wealthy, sparsely populated with the dead. Large freestanding tombs were scattered around a frozen lake, like temples in some eighteenth-century garden.

The packed snow of the snaking pathways suggested that many others had visited in recent days, possibly paying a final tribute to their ancestors, it occurred to Tom, before fleeing the country for good. Right now, though, the two Englishmen found themselves alone. The purpose of their own pilgrimage was still no clearer to Tom, even when Dukes made for a tomb, pushing foursquare through a deep drift.

No larger than a garden shed, it was maybe twice as tall, its roof crowned with a Russian cross. The pale green stucco of its outer walls had crumbled in parts, revealing the bare stone blocks beneath. Its door was of solid wood and firmly locked.

Dukes was still struggling with an iron key when Tom joined him. The lock finally emitted a rasping groan and the door swung open on rusty hinges. The moment they were inside, Dukes shouldered it shut behind them.

The only illumination came from a small lunette above the door, and it was a few seconds before Tom's eyes adjusted to the gloom, by which time Dukes was already on his knees before the altar. For a worrying moment it looked as though he were praying, but he was working away at one of the flagstones, prizing it up with a pocket knife. Buried in the packed earth beneath was an old cigar box. It contained a wafer-thin package wrapped in waxed paper.

"Here," said Dukes. "Take it with you."

Tom had handled enough of Dukes's coded intelligence reports in the past to know what it was.

"Tell them I need more money—a lot more." Replacing the flagstone, Dukes got to his feet and stamped it down. "Deal directly with Leonard. I wouldn't trust Bayliss with anything more than a cocktail shaker."

"You're staying?" asked Tom incredulously.

"It's not over yet."

"But what about Zakharov?"

"You think he's the first to betray us?"

The weary fatalism of the statement grated. It suggested that the Zakharovs of the world were an unavoidable irritant to be endured, like mosquitoes, or people coughing in the theater.

Tom removed his cap and pulled some banknotes from the lining. "It's all I have left."

Dukes riffled through the money, clearly delighted. "How much do you need?" he asked.

"I'm not sure."

Dukes pocketed most of the cash and handed the rest back. "This should see you back to Helsinki."

These weren't the last words the two men exchanged. As they parted company outside, Tom asked, "How do you live like this?"

Dukes hesitated before replying. "I was here when the Revolution broke, when we turned the Tauride Palace into an arsenal. You see, I once believed in the New Jerusalem. Maybe I still do. But this isn't it. This . . . this is Abaddon."

He touched Tom lightly on the arm. "Tell Leonard from me that it's not too late."

"For what?"

"He'll understand."

As Tom watched the slight, anonymous figure shuffle off down the pathway, something told him that this would be his last ever glimpse of the man.

Abaddon, the place of punishment.

A fitting analogy, Tom reflected, his thoughts turning once more to Zakharov, the betrayer.

2

Toulon, France. July 1935. (Sixteen years later.)

The porters were already in place, ranged along the platform like a guard of honor, when the train pulled into Toulon station. The heat was oppressive, and they fidgeted in their brass-buttoned tunics. A few of them crushed their cigarettes underfoot as the train shuddered to a halt and the carriage doors swung open.

Lucy was one of the last to descend. She had cut her hair short, and Tom might not even have recognized her had she not spotted him and waved.

Seeing her at a distance lent a new perspective. He realized, with a touch of sadness, that although she had lost none of her coltish grace, she was no longer a girl. She had become a woman. It wasn't just her new coiffure, or even her elegant organdy summer frock; it was the way she carried herself, the easy manner in which she proffered her hand to the guard who helped her down to the platform, the casual comment that set the fellow smiling.

Tom fought his way through the throng, arriving as her Morocco traveling bags were being loaded from the luggage car onto a trolley.

She might have changed, but she was still happy to launch herself at him and hug him tight, limpetlike, as they had always done. She smelled of roses.

"Thank you," she said.

"For what?"

She tilted her head up at him. "For the nice man at Victoria Station who showed me to the first-class carriage, and the other nice man in Paris who showed me to my own sleeping compartment."

"An early birthday present. Don't assume I'm setting a precedent."

Releasing him, she looked around her. "Where's Mr. H.?"

It was her name for Hector, his flat-coated retriever, his shadow for the past four years.

"Missing."

"Missing?"

"Since yesterday."

"Oh, Tom . . ."

"I'm sure it's nothing," he replied with as much nonchalance as he could muster. "Maybe he needs a holiday too."

But it wasn't like Hector to go off for more than an hour or so, and only then to scrounge scraps from the customers at the bar in Le Rayol. Hector was a big coward at heart, although, like all the best cowards, he cloaked his fears in bold and boisterous behavior.

"It's not the first time he's done a disappearing act. I'm sure he'll turn up as soon as he knows you're here."

Lucy looked unconvinced but was happy to play along if it spared them both the discomfort of any further discussion.

"So, what do you think?" she said brightly, flicking her fingers through her cropped hair and throwing in a theatrical little pout for effect.

"I think your mother's going to need a very stiff drink."

"That wasn't the question."

"I think," Tom intoned with deliberation, "that you are more beautiful than ever."

Lucy smiled. "Spoken like a true godfather."

Tom's car was parked out front in the shade of a tall palm. The porter set about loading the bags into the trunk.

"A new car," Lucy observed.

"Not new, just different."

"It's a lot smaller than the last."

"Ah, but this one doesn't break down."

"Where's the fun in that?"

She was referring to the previous summer and the day trip with her family that had turned into a two-day trip when the big Citroën had resolutely refused to start, stranding them, just as the sun was going down, at a remote beach on the headland beyond Gigaro. There had been just enough food left in the picnic hamper to cobble together a simple supper and they had hunkered down for the night. Lucy's half brothers, George and Harry, had slept in the car, the rest of them under the stars around a driftwood fire, cocooned in Persian rugs. Leonard had embraced the setback with his usual sunny good humor, and even Venetia, who relished her creature comforts, had entered into the spirit of the occasion, leading them in a repertoire of Gilbert and Sullivan numbers, which had set Hector howling in protest. Remarkably, Leonard and Venetia had gone a whole evening without arguing, although they had bickered like a couple of old fishwives during the long and dusty march back to Gigaro the following morning.

"Don't worry," said Tom. "I've already planned another night at the same beach. It's on the itinerary."

"Ahh, the famous Thomas Nash itinerary."

"Would you have it any other way?"

"Of course not," said Lucy, hugging him again. "I need someone to take command of my miserable existence."

"Oh dear, are the hardships of student life taking their toll on poor little Lucy?"

She pinched his arm and pulled away. "Well, *obviously* you're too old to remember, but Oxford's not all honey and roses."

"Okay, what's his name?" asked Tom wearily.

Lucy looked convincingly aghast for all of a second before her face fell. "Hugo Atkinson . . . although I now have a whole bunch of other names for him."

"Didn't he like your hair?"

"This wasn't done for him!" she protested, a touch too vehemently.

Tom was suddenly aware of the porter regarding their little theater with curiosity. He paid the man off handsomely and opened the passenger door for Lucy.

"You can tell me all about the bounder over lunch, but I think I might have found just the thing to help you get over him."

"Oh, God, please, not another Italian lawyer."

"Francesco, I admit, proved to be something of a disappointment."

They both laughed at the memory of the disastrous dinner last summer. Two cocktails on the terrace at Les Roches had revealed Francesco to be a pompous and pugnacious bigot, and even before their entrées had arrived he was making eyes at one of the waiters.

In the ordinary course of events Tom would have driven directly from the station to the old port, where a stroll along the bustling waterfront would have been followed by lunch at the Brasserie Cronstadt. That was his customary routine when guests arrived on the late-morning sleeper from Paris. But he had others plans for Lucy, and they involved driving straight to Le Lavandou, skirting the hilltop town of Hyères before dropping down through the pine forests toward the coast.

They chatted lightly about the string of parties that had kept Lucy back in London, sparing her the long drive south through France with Leonard and her mother.

"I can't say I missed it. All those detours to cathedrals that Leonard insists on making, the lectures on the transition from Romanesque to Gothic architecture . . ."

"Is that the real reason George and Harry can't make it this year?"

"No, Grandfather really is taking them to Portsmouth for Navy Week."

"And you weren't tempted?"

"I'd rather gnaw through my arm."

Tom laughed. "Well, I'm sorry they won't be here."

"I'm not. They've become insufferable lately."

"You mean big sister can't boss them around anymore?"

"Exactly! The willful little brutes."

Le Lavandou, with its palm-fringed promenade and its port backed by a huddle of old buildings, still felt like a frontier town to Tom. Although he visited it often, it lay at the western limits of his ordinary beat and he rarely ventured beyond it. Whenever he did so, returning there was like returning home, even if home still lay a good few miles to the east, along the twisting shoreline of the Côte des Maures.

The table was waiting for them under the awning at the Café du Centre, and Pascal appeared within moments of their arrival, bearing a bottle of white Burgundy on ice. Nothing had been left to chance. The table, the wine, even the fish they would eat, all had been chosen in advance by Tom when he'd passed through earlier that morning. He wanted the buildup to the big surprise to be perfect.

Pascal was one of the few people in on the secret and he was obviously determined to play his part to perfection. Like a child sworn to silence, though, he found the burden almost too much to bear.

As soon as he had disappeared back inside, Lucy lit a cigarette and inquired, "What's wrong with Pascal? He keeps looking at you in a funny way."

"Really?"

"All weird and wide-eyed."

"Maybe it's lack of sleep. Their new baby's only a few weeks old."

This seemed to satisfy her; besides, they had better things to discuss. It was almost six months since they'd last seen each other—during one of Tom's rare visits to England—and on that occasion there'd been little opportunity to talk openly. In fact, there'd been little opportunity to talk at all, because Lucy's great friend Stella had muscled in on their lunch at the Randolph Hotel. Like Lucy, Stella was a second-year modern history undergraduate at St. Hugh's College. Unlike Lucy, she seemed to think this entitled her to hold forth at length on any subject that happened to pop into her head. And there was certainly no shortage of those: everything from the worrying rise of

Fascism to the latest fashions in women's shoes. In her defense, Stella was well informed and extremely amusing with it, but Tom could still recall the delightful silence of the long drive back to London from Oxford.

"How's the irrepressible Stella bearing up?"

"Oh, dear," sighed Lucy. "Poor Stella . . ."

"What? She's developed lockjaw?"

"Worse. She's gone totally potty on an Irish laborer."

"You're joking!"

Apparently not. St. Hugh's was in the process of putting up a new library, and the college had been crawling with brawny workmen for much of the year, one of whom had caught Stella's eye.

"Nothing's happened," Lucy explained. "I mean, I'm not sure he even knows she exists, but she spent most of last term moping around her rooms like a sick cat. It's all very Lady Chatterley and Mellors."

"What would you know about Lady Chatterley and Mellors? That's a banned book."

"Which is precisely the reason there are so many copies doing the rounds at university."

"As the man who took an oath before God to lead you towards a life of exemplary purpose, I'm disappointed."

"As the man who had Henry Miller's *Tropic of Cancer* lying around his house last summer, don't be."

"Ah, it's not banned in France."

"Well, it should be."

"Oh, God, you didn't read it, did you?"

"Of course I did, the day you all went off to Saint-Tropez."

"Ah, yes . . ." said Tom, remembering now, "the day you were struck down with a bad headache."

"A little trick I learned from Mother." Lucy tapped the ash from her cigarette onto the cobbles at their feet. "How is she, by the way?"

"Eager to see you."

"You really must learn to lie more convincingly."

"Well, I now know who to turn to for lessons, don't I?"

They had been sparring partners for as long as he could remember, ever since Lucy was a small child. With the passage of time, the tickling and romping and mock fights of those early years had been replaced by a battle of wits and a war of words. Tom had always encouraged the playful cut-and-thrust of their relationship, if only because there had never been much of that sort of thing at home for Lucy. Venetia, for all her "modern ways," was a mother cast in a traditional mold, somewhat cold and remote. As for Leonard, when not submerged in his work at the Foreign Office, he leaned far more naturally toward his two sons than to the dead man's daughter whom Venetia had brought with her into the marriage.

Tom no longer feared for Lucy's emotional well-being. She had blossomed into something quite extraordinary: a beautiful, intelligent and amusing young woman who seemed genuinely oblivious of her manifest charms. And if he still sought out her company whenever he could, it was as much for his own benefit as hers, for what she somehow managed to bring out in him. As the conversation continued to coil effortlessly around them over lunch, she was, it occurred to him, one of the few true friends he had in the world.

When the coffee arrived they carried their cups with them to a wooden bench just across the cobblestones from their table. Here, in the drowsy shade of the plane trees, they sat and watched in reverential silence as four old men, tanned to the color of teak, played boules.

"Let's go for a wander," suggested Tom, the moment the match was over.

He led her across the road to the port. On one side of the central quay were moored colorful wooden fishing yawls, one of which had landed their lunch much earlier that day, while the rest of the world was still sleeping. Being a fanatical sailor, Lucy was far more interested in the array of yachts and dinghies bobbing on the gentle swell across the way. They came in all shapes and sizes—there was even an ostentatious gentleman's cabin launch among them—but her eye was drawn to one sailboat in particular.

"Oh, my goodness, look at that!"

"What?"

"That racing sloop."

"Yes, pleasing on the eye."

"I bet she flies."

"I'm not so sure," said Tom. "She looks like she's sitting a little too low in the water."

"That's to fool idiots like you. I'm telling you, she flies."

"Well, let's find out, shall we?"

He leapt from the quayside onto the varnished foredeck, turning in time to see Lucy's look of incredulity give way to realization.

"Don't tell me—the royalties on your last book came through."

Tom was on the point of revealing all—this was exactly as he had imagined it happening—but he held himself in check. "Something like that."

Lucy kicked off her shoes and joined him on the foredeck, barely able to contain her excitement. "She's not French. Where's she from? Where did you find her? What's she called?"

"No . . . Sweden . . . Marseilles . . . *Albatross*."

"*Albatross*—I told you she flies! What is she, thirty feet?"

"Twenty-eight."

"Her skinny lines make her look longer."

Lucy dropped into the deep cockpit, running her hand along one of the benches before gripping the tiller and staring up at the tall mast. "Oh, Tom, you're a lucky man."

"I thought we'd sail the rest of the way to Le Rayol."

"What about the car? My luggage?"

"Pascal's going to drive it over."

She smiled, aware now that she'd been set up. "I'll have to change my clothes first. I can hardly go to sea dressed like this."

"There's a shirt and some shorts down below. No standing headroom in the cabin, I'm afraid, so you'll have to crouch."

The mainsail was already rigged, and while Lucy changed, Tom rigged the jib.

"Good work," came a voice from behind him as he was finishing up. Lucy was barefoot and wearing an old cap tilted at a rakish angle.

"Thanks, Skipper."

Her face lit up. "Really?"

"Take her away. There are winches for both halyards, so any half-decent sailor should be able to handle her solo, even in a blow."

Her eyes narrowed at the challenge.

They slipped the lines and backed the sloop out between the pilings into the harbor. Tom made to paddle the stern around.

"Stand down, bosun, if you know what's good for you."

Lucy raised the tall jib so that the wind brought the nose around and the boat began to make gentle headway.

"So, tell me more about your antidote to Hugo Atkinson," she demanded.

"Well, he's American, and he's a painter."

"A good one?"

"Good enough for Yevgeny and Fanya to take him on."

"That sounds suspiciously like a no."

"He's of the willfully modern school. You know the sort of thing . . . a bowl of fruit can't be allowed to actually look like a bowl of fruit—it has to look like it's been hurled to the floor, trampled by a battalion of the Welsh Guards, scooped up with a shovel and dumped back on the table."

Lucy laughed. "Well, obviously Yevgeny and Fanya see something you don't."

"Large profits, I suspect."

Yevgeny and Fanya Martynov were an eccentric couple, White Russian émigrés who ran a thriving Left Bank art gallery in Paris devoted to the avant-garde. They had summered in Le Rayol for the past four years, following their purchase of a pseudo-Palladian villa up on the headland toward Le Canadel. They operated an open-house policy for artists of all kinds, and the steady stream of painters, sculptors and photographers passing through La Quercia was always a welcome source of entertainment.

"They've put Walter in the cottage so that he can work in peace."

"Walter?"

"He's not as stuffy as he sounds, and he knows how to swing a tennis racquet."

"Have you played him?"

"Four times now."

"Vital statistics?"

"Won three, lost one."

Lucy threw him a look.

"Mid-twenties, although he looks older, probably because he's on the portly side."

"Portly?" said Lucy, unable to mask her disappointment.

"Pleasingly so. Well fed rather than fat. What else? He's not tall, but you wouldn't describe him as short . . . well, some might. And he still has most of his hair, which is dark and rather wiry."

"He sounds . . . intriguing."

"No he doesn't, but he is. I've got to know him rather well over the past couple of weeks."

Lucy brought the sloop about, falling in behind a forty-foot cruising ketch motoring toward the harbor mouth.

Beyond the breakwater, the wind piped up nicely, but Lucy seemed in no hurry to run up the mainsail. Her gaze was fixed on the ketch beating to windward at a fair lick, under full sail now.

"I think that's enough of a head start, don't you?" she said, cranking the winch and raising the mainsail.

The moment the ketch's skipper saw them coming he began barking commands, not that it made any difference. The *Albatross* cut through the chop as if it didn't exist, her big canvas sheets sucking every available ounce of energy out of the air. While the crew of the ketch scrambled about her topsides, trying to trim up properly, Lucy barely moved a muscle. When she finally did, it was only to offer a demure little salute to the skipper as she overhauled him.

"Judging from his expression, I would say he hates you."

"It wasn't me." Lucy grinned, her flushed face a picture of pure contentment. "The helm's so balanced I could have tied off the tiller and taken a nap."

They fell off, running dead before the wind to the eastward, making for Le Rayol. While Lucy put the sloop through its paces, getting to know its limits, Tom sat back and enjoyed the view.

There were any number of spots along the Riviera where the mountains collided with the sea, but for a short stretch east of Le Lavandou it seemed almost as if the two elements had struck some secret pact, Earth and Water conspiring together to create a place of wild, primitive beauty. The high hills backing the coast fell away sharply in a tumble of tree-shrouded spurs and valleys that were transformed on impact with the sea into a run of rocky headlands separated by looping bays. Dubbed the Côte des Maures—a reminder of a time when the Saracens had held sway over this small patch of France—and the exoticism of the title seemed entirely appropriate. The beaches strung out along the shoreline, like pearls on a necklace, were of a sand so fine and white, the waters that washed them so unnaturally blue, that they might well have been transported here from some far-flung corner of the tropics.

"Stand by to jibe!" called Lucy.

"Ready."

"Jibe ho!"

They both ducked the swinging boom as the stern moved through the wind, bringing them around onto a port tack run. Lucy steadied up the *Albatross*. "She feels like a big boat but responds like a small one. How's that possible?"

It was a rhetorical question, and Tom smiled at her wonderment.

Only one thing was missing from the moment: Hector. He should have been there with them in the cockpit, or, as he often liked to do, standing steadfastly at the bow, snout into the wind like some canine figurehead.

Tom had spent the previous evening walking the twisting coast road either side of Le Rayol, checking the shoulders and ditches, sick with fear at what he might find. He pushed the memory from him, steering his thoughts toward a far more pleasing prospect: that Hector had finally found his way home, and that as they sailed into the cove below the villa he would come bounding out of the trees behind the boathouse onto the little crescent-moon beach, barking delightedly.

It didn't happen.

They tied up at the buoy, where the rowboat was already tethered and waiting for them. The *Scylla*, Tom's old knockabout dinghy, lay at her anchor nearby.

"So," he asked, "what do you make of her?"

"What do you think I make of her! She's the closest thing to perfection I've ever helmed."

"That's good, because she's yours."

Lucy stared, unsure if she'd heard him correctly.

"Your twenty-first birthday present. A week early, I know, but I couldn't wait."

Lucy was speechless.

"She comes with free transport to England . . . I might even sail her back myself. Should ruffle a few feathers down at the Lymington Yacht Club," he added with a smile.

Lucy didn't smile. In fact, her face creased suddenly and tears filled her eyes.

"Hey . . ." Tom moved to take a seat beside her, slipping a tentative arm around her shoulders. "What's the matter?"

She shook her head as if to say that she couldn't explain. He thought perhaps he'd made a big error, wildly misjudging the appropriateness of such a gift.

"I don't understand," choked Lucy. "Why me?"

"Because I love you, of course."

This set her off again, worse than before, and it was a while before she composed herself enough to ask, "How can *you* say that so easily?"

She was wrong. He had only ever spoken those words to one other person, a long time ago.

"Does Mother . . . ?"

"Don't worry," said Tom. "She knows."

"But she doesn't approve."

"She thinks I spoil you."

Lucy wiped at the tears with the back of her hand. "She's right—you do."

"Godfather's prerogative. Besides, I don't have anyone else to spoil."

He hadn't intended it to sound so self-pitying, and her response threw him.

"What about your lady friend?"

"My lady friend?"

"The one who lives in Hyères." He glimpsed the familiar spark of mischief behind the watery sheen of her eyes. "Leonard told me about her."

"That's not like him."

"He was defending you. Someone at dinner said he thought you were a homosexual."

"Oh?"

"Leonard put him straight."

"So to speak."

Lucy smiled weakly at the joke. "Do you buy your lady friend boats?"

"She has other admirers for that sort of thing."

Lucy looked at him askance. "You mean you share her?"

Tom hesitated. "That's not how I think of it."

"How can you share her?"

"Get to my age, then see if you ask the same question."

"You're only thirty-nine."

"It feels older than it sounds."

It was a few moments before Lucy replied. "Well, I hope I'm still asking the same question when I'm thirty-nine."

"So do I," said Tom softly. "So do I."

Lucy laid her head against his shoulder, sobbed a couple more times, then said, "Thank you for my beautiful present."

He kissed her on the forehead. "It's my pleasure. Now pull yourself together, Captain—whatever will the crew think?"

They parted company just behind the boathouse, where the path bifurcated.

"Are we seeing you later?" Lucy asked.

"Not tonight. You have houseguests."

"Really? Who?"

"I'm not sure you know them. They're friends of your mother's psychoanalyst."

"Oh, God . . ."

"They're not so bad. I had them over for dinner last night. She speaks as much nonsense as the time allows her, and he perks up no end if you get him onto Phoenician pottery."

Lucy groaned. "Thanks for the tip."

"Until tomorrow."

Lucy set off up the steep pathway through the trees, making for the house that her parents rented every July. Standing proudly on the promontory, just back from the bluff, it was so hemmed in on its three other sides by Tom's land as to make it almost part of his property. With any luck, by the end of the summer it would officially become so. He was deep in negotiations with the owner, a retired thoracic surgeon from Avignon eager to convert his home into hard currency, which he planned to fritter away before he died— anything to prevent it from falling into the hands of his two feckless sons.

He was a charming old boy, but he drove a hard bargain. He knew that the British pound went considerably further in France than it did back home, and he understood the notion that something could amount to more than the sum of its parts. Tom might already own a substantial patch of the coastline directly east of Le Rayol, but the last remaining parcel at the heart of his kingdom must surely be a thorn in his proprietorial side, and therefore worth considerably more to him than the marketplace might suggest.

That was Dr. Manevy's thinking, and Tom couldn't fault it, or even begrudge the old fellow for it. If he'd learned anything during his five years in the country it was that no Frenchman could abide the idea of being taken for a ride. *"Ne pas être dupe"* was the inviolable code by which they led their lives, and Tom had grown to embrace the theater that accompanied most negotiations.

He would continue to play up his role as the impecunious author of travel books, Manevy would bleat on about the scandalously small government pension he received, and eventually they would arrive at an agreement satisfactory to both of them. That was the way of things. One had to remain patient.

As for the house itself, Venetia referred to it affectionately as "the Art Nouveau eyesore." Like the castle in *Irene Iddesleigh*, it was "of a style of architecture seldom if ever attempted": a clumpy, three-floored structure devoid of any obvious charm, which the architect, for reasons known only to himself and his original client, had chosen to orientate facing inland, turning a dumb mask to the stunning sea view. Tom's own house—an imposing Art Deco villa verging on the ostentatious—dominated the other headland flanking the cove, and together they stood like two watchtowers guarding against a seaborne invasion.

A crease in the rising ground ran north from the cove, deepening as it went, bisecting Tom's land from the water's edge almost to the railway line. This was the route he now took after parting company with Lucy.

While most of the fifteen-acre plot was carpeted in cork oaks, pines and palms, the narrow gulley was a shady world bristling with ferns, hostas, Petasites and other plants that favored the dark and the damp. In summer, the ground was dry and firm underfoot, but for much of the year it was positively boggy with springwater. Le Rayol was known for its springs, a rare asset along this parched stretch of coast, and— miraculously, like the widow's cruse—his well never ran dry. It stood at the center of a deep dell near the head of the gulley, where the rocks rose sheer on three sides and the interlocking branches of the trees overhead provided a welcome canopy against the sunlight.

"Hector . . . Hector . . . Come on, boy . . ."

The words echoed back at him, hollow, futile.

Hector would often come here to cool off when the mercury was nudging ninety degrees, but he wasn't here now.

The donkey engine and the water pump were housed in a wooden shed beside the well. Tom cranked the wheel, amazed, as always, when the faithful old Lister *phut-phutted* into life. The water in the big holding tank up top was running low. It would take a couple of hours to fill— more than enough time to complete his task.

He started in the northeast corner, right up by the railway cutting, where the ground vanished in a sheer drop of some thirty feet to the steel tracks below. From here he made his way back toward the sea, working methodically, taking each patch of land between the latticework of pathways in turn and searching it thoroughly, delving deep into the tangled underbrush.

3

___

The man signed for the cocktails and lay back on the lounge chair. As jobs went, he reflected, things didn't get much better than this. He cast his mind back over the other ones and concluded that things didn't get *any* better than this. Talk about mixing business and pleasure: a summer break at a top hotel right on the beach, just one little chore to perform and then he'd be gone. It should all go smoothly enough, now that the dog had been dealt with.

"Why are you smiling?"

She had finished her swim and was toweling herself dry in the sunshine. She was in good condition for her age, although gravity had taken its inevitable toll on her breasts and buttocks.

"Because I'm contented," he replied.

He spoke a formal French, far too formal, but it would have to do. It was the only shared language between them. He barely spoke a word of German, let alone Swiss German, and her Italian was a joke.

"Is that for me?" she asked in her guttural French, nodding at the drinks set on the table between their loungers.

"Yes."

"You're a bad boy."

He was about to reply that she sounded like his mother, but checked himself just in time. She was, after all, close to his mother's age—not so close as to repel him, but close enough for him to feel mildly squeamish at the prospect of seducing her.

"I'm on holiday," he said. "And so are you."

For the first time in their brief acquaintance, he used the familiar "*tu*" instead of "*vous,*" and he could see that this didn't go unnoticed by her.

She adjusted her bathing costume, brushed some imaginary sand from her thigh and lowered herself onto the lounger.

"Well, if you insist . . ." she purred coquettishly, following his lead and using the familiar pronoun.

He knew from their conversation on the terrace after dinner last night that her husband had been held back in Zurich on business, leaving her to travel on ahead alone. He could picture the husband rolling around with his secretary on some disheveled bed, and he wondered if she suspected the same.

"Did you contact your friend?" she asked.

"My friend?"

"The painter in Cannes."

"Oh, him . . . yes."

He remembered now. Stuck with the cover story he'd already shared with a couple of the other hotel guests, he'd embellished it slightly for her benefit, adding a touch of glamour to impress. The painter in Cannes was a childhood friend from Rome who had recently found great success abroad, and was eager to show off his new house on the Cap d'Antibes.

"Have you decided when you're leaving?"

Not immediately after the job was done; that was liable to arouse suspicion. No, he would brave it out for a day or two afterward, as he usually did.

"When is your husband arriving?"

"Saturday."

He glanced around him, but the only people within earshot were two sun-bronzed children, a brother and sister, playing beach quoits nearby, and they were far too absorbed in their game to be listening.

"I was thinking Friday," he said.

There—it was done. He had made his intentions plain. It wasn't the end of the world if she didn't take the bait, but it would be much better if she did. It was always good to have an alibi up your sleeve.

She didn't react at first; she just took a sip of her cocktail and stretched out on the lounger, closing her eyes.

"I've never done this sort of thing before," she said quietly.

"You haven't done anything."

She turned onto her side and looked at him. "No, but I want to."

He saw the way the skin hung loosely on her thighs and around her neck, and he wasn't entirely lying when he said, "Knowing that is enough for me."

"Well, it's not enough for me."

4

Tom was familiar with the sound. The creak of the big old vine that coiled its way up the front of the villa would often carry through the open French doors into his room when the wind was up.

But there wasn't any wind tonight, not a breath of it.

He rarely slept the sleep of the innocent, lost to the world, and he shrugged off his liminal state in an instant, alert now, ears straining.

Maybe he'd been mistaken. All he could hear was the beat of the waves on the rocks below the villa, the ocean's blind purpose to make all things sea.

No. There it was again. And a faint rustle of leaves.

Someone was climbing the vine, and there was only one reason he would be doing that: in order to reach the large terrace that served the master bedroom, where Tom slept.

He cursed himself for his complacency. He hadn't slept with his gun at hand for almost a year. The old Beretta 418 was locked away in a drawer in the study, a symbol of a time when his life had been ruled by fear and suspicion. He prided himself on having finally mastered that debilitating state of mind. As if in affirmation of this, a harmless explanation came to him quite suddenly, taking the edge off his building panic.

Barnaby.

Barnaby wasn't due until tomorrow evening, but he was quite

capable of changing his plans on a whim, especially if he'd landed himself in trouble while motoring down through France, which was quite probable. Trouble and Barnaby had always gone together, and Tom could picture him having to flee some tricky situation entirely of his own making. Turning up unannounced in the middle of night and then pouncing on Tom while he slept was exactly the sort of infantile prank that would appeal to Barnaby's sense of humor.

The moonlight flooding through the French doors and painting the wall beside the bed would allow Tom to see the shadow play of anyone entering from the terrace. Well, he would turn the tables on Barnaby, waiting until the last moment before scaring the living daylights out of him.

Then again, maybe he was stretching the realms of possibility, even by the preposterous standards of his old friend. Maybe it wasn't Barnaby, but a burglar. A small band of Spaniards, professional housebreakers from Barcelona, had passed this way two summers back. Some were still serving time in Toulon Prison.

Whoever it was, the person had now cleared the stone balustrade and was creeping across the terrace. His soft footfalls ceased, replaced by another sound. It was hard to make out, but it sounded like someone unscrewing the cap of a bottle.

Tom exaggerated his breathing to convey the impression of someone deep in slumber, and moments later the visitor slipped silently into the bedroom.

He knew immediately that it wasn't Barnaby, not unless he had shrunk by half a head since April. Everything about the shadow on the wall was wrong. Most worryingly, it moved with a professional stealth, confident, unhurried. It was definitely a man, and as he stole toward the bed it became clear that he was carrying something in his hand, not a weapon—not a gun or a knife or even a cudgel—but something else.

Facedown on the mattress, his head turned to the wall, Tom knew he was at a serious disadvantage. The only thing in his favor was that the intruder seemed set on drawing closer, leveling the odds with every step, bringing himself within range.

It was the familiar, sweet-smelling odor that spurred Tom into action. He exploded from the mattress, twisting and hurling himself at the figure looming beside the bed. Caught off guard, the man was sent crashing to the floor with Tom on top of him, gripping his wrists.

Stay close in, but keep his hands where you can see them. Then finish him off.

He drove his forehead into the man's face. Twice. He was going for a third when the man bellowed and twisted away, slipping Tom's clutches, not big, but surprisingly strong, and with the natural agility of youth on his side. Tom was after him in an instant. He wasn't expecting the leg to lash out, catching him in the midriff, upending him.

Winded, he just managed to suck in a lungful of air before the chloroform-drenched rag was clamped over his nose and mouth. The man held him tight in an embrace from behind, wrapping his legs around him, locking his ankles. Tom knew he had only a matter of moments before the world went black, and he reached back and dug his thumbs deep into his assailant's eyes, threatening to scoop them out of their sockets.

It was an old lesson, long forgotten, but it came back easily enough. It also worked.

The man screamed, and as he released his grip Tom rolled to his right, instinct telling him he needed a weapon.

Springing to his feet, he seized the African carving from the chest of drawers. The naïf wooden figure of a woman had cost him a small fortune from a dealer in Paris, and it now saved his life.

Spinning back, he swung her blindly like a club just as the man was bringing a pistol to bear on him. The carving broke off at the knees and the gun skittered across the floor, beneath the bed. Tom found himself thinking that it was a clean break, and could be repaired seamlessly enough by the right restorer.

This momentary loss of concentration bought the man enough time to pull a knife from his pocket. Tom hurled himself at his young adversary. Welded together, they landed briefly on the mattress before crashing to the floor, jammed in between the bed and the wall.

It wasn't a knife. It was a syringe, and its slender needle glistened in the moonlight as they fought for possession of it.

Tom was dimly aware of the blood from the other man's shattered nose splashing his face, then he found the purchase he was looking for and broke the man's wrist with an audible crack.

The syringe clattered to the floor.

Tom lunged for it.

The man didn't. He took the opportunity to flee.

Tom groped frantically beneath the bed for the gun, but his scuttling fingers turned up nothing. No time to search further. The man was already gone, out through the bedroom door. If he didn't follow now, it would be too late.

He breasted the main staircase in time to see the shadowy figure throw the latch on the front door and disappear into the night. Trusting to instinct, Tom took the stone steps three at a time in the darkness, trying to narrow the lead.

Barefoot, bare-chested, and with his pajama bottoms flapping about his legs, he burst outside into the moonlight. *His* moonlight. It served the hunter, not the hunted.

The man had made straight for the shadows, eschewing the driveway for the thick vegetation on the right. Tom glimpsed him just as the trees swallowed him up.

He set off in pursuit, immune to the sharp gravel tearing at the soles of his feet.

The man was fast, faster than Tom, and he had obviously done his homework. He knew the pathways crisscrossing the gardens and he knew not to head south toward the sea, where he ran the risk of being cornered. Thankfully, he was less sure of himself the farther they traveled from the house. As they skirted the head of the gulley his sense of direction seemed to abandon him completely.

Rather than sticking to the path, which would have seen him safely away, he bore left up the slope, into the trees, crashing through the underbrush. It was a bad mistake, and Tom seized the opportunity to bring the foot chase to an abrupt and brutal conclusion. Something had to happen soon. His legs were all but spent, his bare feet scratched and bleeding.

Suddenly, there was silence ahead of him. The man had gone to ground. Tom dropped into a crouch, falling utterly still.

He won the waiting game. After a few minutes, he heard movement. He crept to his right as noiselessly as possible until he judged himself to be directly down the slope from the man.

Knowing that his adversary was young as well as wounded, he was banking on him being scared.

With a wild scream, Tom burst from his hiding place and charged up the slope.

His quarry broke cover ahead of him, turning tail and weaving blindly through the trees. He gave a surprised gasp as the ground disappeared beneath his feet, and a second or two later, Tom heard a dull thud.

He hurried to the edge of the railway cutting and peered down into the void.

He couldn't make out much in the darkness, but he heard the sounds of a badly wounded beast below. The man was still alive. He had feared the fall might kill him.

It took Tom a while to work his way around to a point where he could safely drop onto the tracks. He approached cautiously, stepping from tie to tie to spare his bare feet, brandishing a branch he'd snapped from a tree.

He needn't have worried; the man lay like a heap of rags where he'd fallen. One leg was grotesquely twisted beneath him.

Tom came and stood over him. "Where's my dog?"

"*Per piacere . . .*" implored the man weakly, raising a hand.

"Where's my dog?" Tom repeated in the same flat tone, switching to Italian.

"The well . . ."

"Where? In the well?"

"Buried nearby."

He only just resisted the urge to swing the branch and administer the coup de grâce.

"Are you alone?"

"Yes."

"Who sent you?" he asked.

"Alfiero."

"Who's Alfiero?"

"I can't move my legs. Am I dying?"

"Maybe."

The young man emitted a deep sob. "I don't want to die."

"Nobody wants to die."

Tom struggled to feel any sympathy. The pathetic, broken figure before him had killed Hector, his companion, and only minutes earlier had tried to send him the same way.

"Tell my mother I love her," pleaded the man pathetically.

Tom crouched so that they were almost face-to-face.

"I'll tell you what I'm going to do. I'm going to find your mother and I'm going to kill her very, very slowly . . . unless you tell me who Alfiero is."

The young man struck out at him weakly. "Don't you touch my mother . . ."

Tom batted the arm aside and seized him by the throat, throttling him. "You obviously don't know who I am," he hissed, "or you'd answer the question."

He allowed time for the words to sink in before releasing his grip. "Who's Alfiero?"

"Alfiero is . . . Alfiero."

The man wasn't being evasive; he was teetering on the brink of unconsciousness now, not thinking straight. Tom slapped his face to bring him around.

"Why does he want me dead?"

"I don't know. He never tells me why."

"Where is he?"

"Rome . . . Viterbo . . . Pescara. He moves around . . ."

The words trailed off, replaced by a deep and tremulous groan, unlike anything Tom had ever heard before.

"What's his surname?"

The man started to slip away. Tom slapped his face again to bring him back. "What's his surname?"

"Tosti . . ." It came out as a low croak. The man then fell slack and silent.

Tom felt for a pulse at his neck. It was there, but weak. He might well be bleeding internally.

Tom glanced up and down the cutting. He remembered the drill: remain focused and deal with the immediate situation. There would be time enough later to weigh the bigger questions.

He had to move the man; he couldn't leave him lying there. But what if he had lied? What if he had an accomplice? What if the accomplice was waiting out there somewhere in the shadows for Tom to show himself? He went with his gut, taking the man at his word. Everything about him suggested a lone operator.

He checked the man's trouser pockets so that nothing would be lost in transit. He turned up a key. It was attached to an oval metal fob familiar to his touch, even if he couldn't see it properly in the darkness.

Shouldering the man proved easy enough, and he tried his best to ignore the unnatural geometry of the shattered limbs bumping against him as he bore the burden back to the villa. For much of the way, he stuck to the level ground afforded by the railway tracks, bearing left into the vegetation just before the crossing that led to the gates of the villa.

Somewhere along the route the man died. Tom couldn't say when, exactly—he had sensed no change in the inert weight—but when he laid his load as gently as possible beside the yew hedge fringing the terrace and felt once more for a pulse, he detected nothing.

So be it, he told himself. It's probably for the best.

He glanced up at the twisted old vine. Probably no more than twenty minutes had elapsed since the dead man beside him had set about scaling the plant, but he knew in his bones that everything had changed in that brief time, everything he had built here.

He had just heard the first resounding trumpet blast against the walls of his private Jericho.

He smoked two cigarettes in quick succession while the bath was running, and he topped up his brandy glass before climbing into the water.

His feet stung like Satan, but there were no deep cuts, just lacerations. His penis, he noted, with a mixture of curiosity and alarm, had shrunk to the size of an acorn.

He dressed in dark clothing, then made a methodical tour of the bedroom, first recovering the pistol from beneath the bed. It was a Browning 1922 with a full clip. Common sense dictated that he dispose of it, but a second weapon was a welcome addition to his limited armory, especially one with more stopping power than his Beretta.

The floor was spattered with blood from the man's smashed nose, as were the sheets and blue twill bedspread, but he could use those to wrap the body in. The person he feared most was Paulette, his housekeeper. She might not say anything about the missing bedspread and African carving, but she would certainly register their absence. Nothing in the house escaped her eagle-eyed notice, and it would be wise to have explanations ready.

The broken carving upset him, for symbolic reasons as much as anything. It was a spirit figure from the Baule people of the Ivory Coast, a woman shaped from wood as black as coal, her skin polished to a silky patina except where it was marked by intricate scarification. She stood on short, flexed legs—now broken off at the knees—her hands resting gently on her protruding belly. Her breasts were full and pointed, and there was something ineffably serene about the gaze of her almond eyes. Even now, they seemed to carry in them the knowledge of what she—his spirit wife, his protectress—had done on his behalf.

She had given her legs for him, and she had taken those of the man outside in payment of her sacrifice.

He pressed the two parts of her together. He would take her to Paris and see her made whole once more, but for now, he carried her downstairs and locked her away in a cabinet in his study, along with the syringe and the small bottle of chloroform, which the Italian had left outside on the bedroom terrace. Returning upstairs with a mop and pail, he sluiced the bedroom floor. It was best to do it now, while the blood was still wet. It would be dried and encrusted by the time he returned.

* * *

The Italian was definitely dead; his body had noticeably cooled. Tom rolled him in the sheets and the bedspread, heaved him over his shoulder and set off down the path to the cove.

He felt painfully exposed as he emerged from the treeline into the moonlit glare of the beach, but a few seconds later he was in the boathouse, safe from prying eyes.

He worked by the light of a lone hurricane lamp. First he took a length of rope and trussed up the bedcover bundle. This he then rolled onto a heavy-duty tarpaulin and laid an anchor on top of it. For good measure, he headed outside, returning with two large rocks, which he also placed on the body. Folding over the tarpaulin, he bound it tightly in place with more rope—around and around, and also lengthwise—until the finished product looked like some monumental Italian salami.

It was a struggle, but he managed to carry it in his arms to the rowboat, staggering across the sand and dropping it into the bottom of the boat. He kicked off his shoes, rolled up his trousers and hauled the rowboat toward the water.

The *Albatross* was the obvious choice but he decided against it, not wishing to curse the sloop by bringing a corpse aboard. This consideration came at a hefty price. He almost capsized his dinghy while trying to haul the package aboard, receiving a crack on the head from the boom for good measure, which almost blacked him out.

He short-tacked into the warm breeze blowing in from the southwest, relaxing a little as he cleared the bay. The sail still gleamed unnaturally white in the moonlight and the dinghy only made sluggish headway, but he was in open water now, the seabed dropping sharply away below the boat. He knew that it plunged to more than four hundred fathoms in the channel between the coast and the islands, six or so nautical miles off, but he would have to content himself with maybe half that if he didn't want to run into the fishing fleet. He could see their lights sparkling on the horizon like a swarm of fireflies.

When he was ready he lowered the mainsail, removed the tiller and the rudder, then heaved the body up onto the transom. After his close call back in the cove, he knew that if he put it over the side, the weight of it might cause the *Scylla* to heel over and capsize.

He eased the package off the aft. It didn't sink at first, buoyed up by the pockets of air inside the tightly bound tarpaulin. However, these slowly filled with seawater, and it finally dipped beneath the waves. Convention dictated that he mark the moment with some words, a token tribute, but he struggled to find the will. The Italian had gambled and lost. If he didn't know the rules of the game he should never have taken to the field of play.

Raising the mainsail, Tom set a course for home.

Sleep was out of the question. His body was weary, aching, clamoring for rest, but his brain danced wildly in open rebellion. He wound up the gramophone and found himself reaching for the *Goldberg Variations*. The rigid, almost mathematical structure of Bach's masterpiece might help lend some order to his thoughts.

It didn't. He knew the piece so well that every cadence ran ahead of the needle in his mind, and he sat hunched at the table on the terrace in stunned immobility. The coffee he had made for himself was cold by the time he even looked at the key in his hand.

It was a hotel key, and the oval metal fob was engraved with a room number: 312. The name of the hotel wasn't marked. It didn't need to be; he'd placed enough surplus guests at the Hôtel de la Réserve over the years to recognize the fob. The hotel was a grand affair that towered over the narrow beach. When alone in Le Rayol, which was most of the time, he would often wander down there of an evening for a cocktail and a bite to eat. He was known to most of the staff, and he could even count Olivier, the manager, as a friend. He certainly shouldn't have any difficulty gaining access to Room 312. He was in possession of the key, and his presence in the hotel was unlikely to arouse too much suspicion.

This wasn't what bothered him, though, and it was a while before he isolated just what it was that jarred at the back of his thoughts.

The man, the Italian sent to kill him, had known exactly where he slept. Moreover, when fleeing the bedroom he had reached unswervingly for the correct door. The door immediately to its right, also shut at the time, would have led him into the blind alley of the bathroom. How had the Italian known which door to select? Surely a man in desperation would have tried both handles at the same time before making his choice. And how had he managed to negotiate the darkened corridors and staircases of the villa with such speed and confidence when making his escape?

Maybe Tom was underestimating the aptitude of his would-be assassin, but he was left with the uneasy feeling that the Italian had come armed with more knowledge than was natural. It didn't make sense, not unless he had somehow managed to scout the inside of the villa before making his move, or he had been briefed by someone who knew the internal layout of the building. The first seemed unlikely; Tom had always been a stickler for security, much to Paulette's amusement and annoyance. The second possibility implied that a friend or close associate was a party to the attempt on his life.

He shrugged this unwelcome thought aside, turning his mind to the larger issues. Who wanted him dead? And why? Unfortunately, there were a fair number of options. He had done some bad things in the name of King and Country over the years, and although that murky world was well behind him now, there was no reason others should have been as eager as he to forget and move on with their lives.

Whoever they were, he had to assume they still wanted him dead, and the moment they realized they'd failed in their mission they would gather themselves to strike again. This gave him a small window of opportunity, maybe half a day, in which to steal the initiative.

He hated them for leaving him no other choice. He hated them for the fear that had returned to his life. He hated them for what they had made him do. He had killed a man, not with his bare hands, admittedly, but as good as, driving him to his certain doom.

This, he realized, was what he really despised them for—for showing him that he was still the same man.

After more than five years, and despite his best efforts to improve on himself, he had barely changed.

5

Lucy woke with a start. She was lying on top of the covers, still in her clothes, and her face was damp against the pillow.

Then she remembered. She remembered why she was dressed, why she had been crying.

She reached for the travel clock on the bedside table. It was early, not yet seven o'clock, but someone was already moving around downstairs, clattering about in the kitchen. It couldn't possibly be Mother; she rarely rose before nine, not even for guests.

Mr. Chittenden, most likely. He had announced over dinner that he was always up with the lark. These were some of the few words he had spoken all evening. For much of the time he had sat hunched in his chair, a look of benign befuddlement on his face, chortling every so often while his wife held forth.

Barbara Chittenden liked to talk. She maundered on and on as if her life depended on it, as if the moment she fell silent someone might put a bullet in her head.

Lucy had been tempted to do just that on a couple of occasions, especially when it had emerged that Barbara was a long-standing member of the Eugenics Society and held strong views on the sterilization of the unfit.

"Although we now prefer to call them the 'social problem group.' The 'unfit' is so very . . ."

"Offensive?" proffered Lucy, with studied innocence.

This brought a little chuckle from Mr. Chittenden and a warning scowl from Mother.

"'Vague' was the word I was searching for."

Apparently, the "social problem group" covered a wide range of hereditary and moral sins, everything from lunatics, idiots and the feeble-minded, through deaf-mutes and the congenitally blind, to tramps, prostitutes, inebriates and epileptics.

"Don't get me wrong. I'm not one of those extreme types calling for compulsory sterilization, although it seems to have worked a treat in the United States and Germany."

"Be careful what you say," Mother cautioned. "Lucy is young and therefore liable to go up like straw if she doesn't agree with you."

Lucy bristled. "I didn't realize you'd been won over to the cause."

Mother fired back a pinched smile that said: You're on your own, darling.

"What's there to disagree with?" Barbara blundered on. "John Maynard Keynes, George Bernard Shaw, even the Cambridge Union all have come out in favor of voluntary sterilization."

"Oh, that makes it all right, does it? The so-called intelligentsia are for it."

"Something has to be done. A biological disaster is looming. Reckless breeding by the 'social problem group' is leading to an irreversible degeneration of the racial stock. The very future of civilization is at stake."

Lucy fought hard to restrain herself. "I know some who would say that civilization has considerably more to fear from the self-interest and prejudice of the privileged classes."

"When she says 'some' she means her godfather," chipped in Mother. "She likes to parrot his opinions."

"I happen to agree with some of them," retorted Lucy.

"You mean Tom?" exclaimed Barbara. "I'm sorry, but I don't think so. I talked with him last night at some considerable length on the subject."

"And what did he say?"

Barbara Chittenden hesitated. "Well, not very much, as it happens. Although I think I can safely say he was persuaded of my argument."

Lucy found that hard to believe. "Oh, really?"

"Absolutely. He said that up until now he had never been fully convinced of the grave threat posed to society by the mentally deficient."

Mr. Chittenden erupted in a loud guffaw, and Mother only just managed to contain her own laughter.

"What, Harold?"

Mr. Chittenden, still chuckling, waved her question away.

"Ignore him," said Barbara. "He's an archaeologist. All he cares about is stones and bones."

The little dinner for four hadn't been the most propitious start to the holiday, but at least it meant that things could only get better. The Chittendens would be leaving immediately after breakfast, motoring west to Spain, and Leonard would be back from Cannes in time for lunch. He liked to sneak off there from time to time with Yevgeny for a round or two of golf at the Old Course, and his return would offer a welcome buffer against Mother, who was in particularly malicious form right now.

The barbed and belittling comments were coming thick and fast, rising to a peak, the usual prelude to one of their explosive confrontations. This would be followed by a tearful reconciliation, which in turn would give way to a lengthy period of calm. Then gradually the comments would begin to intrude again—a small note of criticism here, a gentle reprimand there—the heat building once more by barely perceptible degrees.

This was the fixed pattern of their relationship, the drearily predictable cycle into which they had settled, though not by mutual consent. Lucy dreamed of an alternative future, one without the endless round of highs and lows, of war and peace.

Tom was less hopeful. He had never known Mother to be any different, and not just with Lucy. They all suffered the same treatment at her hands. It was the price you paid for being loved by her. "It's not so bad.

You cry in her arms, you laugh in her arms, and every so often you scream blue murder at each other. I'd take that any day over the indifference I knew as a child."

Leonard had found his own way of dealing with it, somehow managing to remain immune to her moods. Things hadn't always been this way. Lucy could remember the rows when she was younger, the look of quiet satisfaction on her mother's face when she succeeded in piercing his carapace of self-control and getting a rise out of him. Those days were long gone. Leonard now displayed an almost saintly forbearance in the face of her moods. Maybe he had simply been numbed into a kind of stupor. Maybe with time the same thing would happen to her.

Thoughts of Mother precluded any possibility of dozing on for another hour or so, and Lucy swung her legs off the bed, making for the bathroom. The bathtub was still desperately in need of a new coat of enamel, and the crumbling cork mat had disintegrated further since last year, but the water was as hot as ever.

She stripped off her clothes, catching sight of her naked self in the long mirror screwed to the wall beside the sink. She examined the reflection with a cold and critical eye: too tall for the tastes of most men, and still too thin, although she had finally begun to fill out a little in the past year, her narrow hips losing some of their bony angularity.

She cupped her breasts in her hands, weighing them, as if judging between two pieces of fruit at a market stall—small fruit, sadly, oranges rather than grapefruits. There was little hope on that front, if Mother was anything to go by. Only pregnancy might improve on their modest proportions. Ten years behind the times, she mused wearily. Her lean look would have gone down a storm a decade ago. Nowadays, it was associated with poverty and deprivation and all the other unwelcome memories of the Depression.

Thank God for Claudette Colbert, the standard-bearer of small-breasted women everywhere. Only a few years before, she had frolicked naked in a bath of wild asses' milk in *The Sign of the Cross*—a picture that George and Harry had trooped off to watch half a dozen times, ostensibly as fans of Cecil B. DeMille, although Lucy suspected the fleeting glimpse of Miss Colbert's nipples above the milky froth might have had more to do with her brothers' devotion to that particular entry in the director's oeuvre.

She ran a hand down over her pale belly, her fingers curling through the dark arrowhead of hair at the fork of her thighs, darker than dark, as good as black. That she owed to the Spanish blood on her father's side, along with the large eyes and the strong mouth whose lips were a touch too full for beauty.

Fortunately, the swirls of steam rising from the bath clouded the mirror, dimming her unforgiving gaze.

6

Tom picked his moment carefully, arriving at the Hôtel de la Réserve when he judged most of the guests would be taking their breakfast. He knew that breakfast was a case of all hands on deck. The reception area was unlikely to be manned, allowing him to slip inside unnoticed, and maybe even sneak a look at the register in the process.

His instinct proved correct; the front desk was deserted, although the register had been locked away in the back office. It didn't matter too much. With any luck he'd find everything he needed in the room.

He hurried past the doors to the dining room, glancing briefly inside to assure himself that he hadn't been spotted. The hum of conversation and the clatter of cutlery on crockery swiftly receded as he made his way up the main staircase to the third floor.

Room 312 turned out to be at the far end of the corridor, a corner room with views over the sea and to the west, both served by balconies, Tom knew. The Italian had obviously decided to treat himself.

Tom knocked softly and pressed his ear to the door to be sure.

The Italian's failure to show up for breakfast would be noted but was unlikely to arouse any undue suspicion for now. The maids wouldn't be around to clean the rooms until the guests had taken to the beach, which meant plenty of time for a thorough search.

The moment Tom let himself into the room he realized he was wrong. A quick survey revealed that the Italian had lied to him. He wasn't on his own, and his traveling companion appeared to be a woman. Her diaphanous pale blue peignoir lay discarded on the unmade bed next to a wide-brimmed raffia sun hat, and her cosmetics were spread out on the dressing table.

He was going to have to move fast, very fast.

Pulling on his doeskin driving gloves, he started with the writing desk, tugging out the empty drawers and checking that nothing was taped to their undersides. Both bedside cabinets were also empty, although there was a German novel resting on one of them beside a glass of water and a pair of ladies' reading glasses. He checked the first few pages of the book for a dedication, a name, but it obviously hadn't been a gift.

There was nothing under the bed, and the drawers of the dressing table were stuffed with women's underwear, brassieres, stockings and so on. Like the novel, the cosmetics were German, although the perfume was French—Feu Follet by Roger & Gallet. It was hardly the scent of a young woman, and together with the reading glasses suggested someone further along in years than her Italian companion.

A search of the chest of drawers only added to his confusion. Buried beneath some neatly folded men's socks was a shagreen box containing three pairs of solid gold cuff links, bone collar stiffeners, a diamond-set money clip, a pearl tiepin, and some silver and onyx dress studs. It didn't make sense. Who carried such costly accessories with him on a mission of murder? And why so many pairs of socks?

The long drawer below contained some summer shirts in a variety of colors and materials. Tom opened one up. It had above-elbow sleeves and was cut to fit a tall man of some considerable girth, whereas the Italian had been short and compact.

He was still struggling to make sense of this when he heard footsteps outside in the corridor. It was probably a guest returning to one of the other rooms, but he folded the shirt as quickly and neatly as possible and silently slid the drawer shut.

He was right to have anticipated the worst. Someone was now at the door, ferreting for a key in a bag.

His eyes darted around the room. The bathroom was out of the question, as was the built-in wardrobe; he had no idea what lay behind its louvered doors. The key was turning in the lock as he slid noiselessly beneath the bed.

It was a woman—wide navy-blue cotton slacks breaking on tan leather sandals. She made straight for the desk, not bothering to take a seat. He heard her pick up the telephone receiver and dial a three-digit number. It was a while before she spoke.

"Where are you?" she asked in German. This was clearly for her own benefit, because she hung up almost in the same breath.

She skirted the bed, making for the wardrobe. Tom shifted to get a better view, ready to withdraw suddenly if she turned around. Her blond hair was done in a youthful wave and she had a trim figure, but the hands that now removed a man's jacket from a hanger were those of a middle-aged woman. She pulled a key from the hip pocket of the jacket—a key attached to an oval metal fob, just like the one that Tom held tightly clenched in his fist.

This was the last he saw of her. He slunk back as she turned, fearing for a moment that she'd spotted him. She hadn't, though. She made straight for the door and left the room.

He was up and after her in an instant, pausing at the door, listening to her footfalls receding down the corridor. Chancing a quick glance outside, he saw her turn down the main staircase. Easing the door shut behind him, he set off in silent pursuit.

Her destination was a first-floor room toward the front of the hotel, almost directly above the main entrance. In terms of location (and cost, no doubt) it couldn't have been more different from the one they'd just left. She knocked furtively on the door. When no one responded she let herself in with the key.

Tom approached just close enough to read the number on the door: 104. Everything told him this was the Italian's room, and the urge to gain entry to it right now, to force some answers from the woman, was almost overwhelming. Cold common sense prevailed, though. He mustn't do anything to link himself to the dead man. He knew the rules. He had to remain faceless, nameless, at all times. Besides, an idea about the real nature of the woman's role in this affair was beginning to take shape in his head, and he needed to test the hypothesis first.

Olivier, the hotel manager, was making conversation with an elderly couple at their table in the dining room, but the moment he saw Tom enter he made his excuses and hurried over, beaming.

"Mr. Nash . . ."

He pumped Tom's hand.

"After five years, I think you can call me Tom, don't you?"

"I'm on duty."

"You spend far too much time on duty, Olivier."

"What can I say?" Olivier shrugged, an ironic twinkle in his eye. "I'm a consummate professional."

"Then find me a table on the terrace for breakfast."

"Find it yourself, *connard*," Olivier fired back, and they both laughed.

They hadn't seen each other for a couple of weeks, not since Tom had strolled down to the hotel with his book for a quick dinner, only to end up staggering home in the early hours of the morning after a marathon, and rather drunken, bout of bezique. They would probably have played right through till daybreak if Olivier's wife, Nadine, hadn't searched them out in the bar in her nightdress and summoned her husband to bed.

Tom opted for the terrace because he suspected Olivier would come to sit with him, and he knew that the guests were obliged to pass across it when making for the beach below. He selected a table near the head of the wide steps that ran down the bluff to the sand, turning his chair to admire the view while waiting for Olivier to return with his coffee and the two fried eggs he didn't really want.

He almost never dropped by for breakfast, and he'd thought it wise to play up the occasion: the final meal of the condemned man, condemned for the next few weeks to a string of houseguests and other friends in need of near-continuous nourishment and entertainment. This was the still before the storm, and he couldn't exactly mark it with a solitary café au lait—hence the eggs. He had passed up the offer of a fried slice of pork belly to go with them. The eggs were bad enough, the mere thought of them threatening to unravel the tight knot of nausea that had been sitting low down in his belly for the past hours.

He felt bad lying to Olivier, but he could hardly tell him the truth: that he'd killed one of his hotel guests, the man in Room 104, and that the young Italian now lay trussed up in tarpaulin on the seabed somewhere over there.

He squinted out to sea, trying to identify the spot. He realized, with a stab of self-reproach, that he should have thought twice before dumping the body where he had. The exact location might not be visible from where he was sitting, but it certainly would be from the villa, whose terra-cotta roof tiles he could see poking above the pines on the headland around to his left. As long as he lived in Villa Martel he would have a direct line of sight, a constant reminder of his actions.

He should have gone east toward Cavalaire, around the corner: out of sight, out of mind. He rarely sailed that way, whereas he was always beating to and from the islands. He saw himself as an elderly man sitting hunched at the helm, an arthritic hand on the tiller, still tensing and falling silent every time he passed over the watery grave.

This vision of his dotage was, he reflected miserably, the very best he could hope for. It assumed that he would still be around to see out his declining years in Le Rayol; it supposed that he would come through the current situation unscathed, and that, having done so, Le Rayol and the simple life he'd carved out for himself here would not have been irredeemably tainted. It relied on a lot of things, none of which he could guarantee, or even reasonably hope for.

He was stirred from his maudlin trance by a voice behind him.

"What are you thinking?"

It was Olivier with a tray.

"How beautiful it is."

There were any number of sandy bays to choose from along this stretch of coast, but none held a torch to Le Rayol. Some were too narrow, too enclosed, or too expansive and exposed, or the hills pressed in too tightly behind, or, as at Cavalière, their slopes died too far back from the sea. There wasn't one thing at Le Rayol he would have changed: the lazy arc of the white beach, the gin-clear water and the proud thrust of its headlands, which protected the bay from all but the most southerly winds.

"Yes, and you own a nice big piece of it," said Olivier, settling himself down at the table. "I wish I could."

"You can."

"Not on my salary."

Tom didn't say anything, but he decided then that if he ever had to sell up and leave he would parcel off a bit of his land and gift it to Olivier and Nadine. He knew how much they loved this place. He knew that when they shut up shop in November and returned to their native Grenoble they spent the winter months dreaming of April and the new season on the Côte des Maures.

"Why don't you have children?" Tom asked suddenly.

The question just slipped from his lips. It was as unexpected to him as it was to Olivier, who pushed his lank, dark bangs from his eyes before replying.

"We tried. It didn't happen."

"I'm sorry."

"Why are you sorry? You don't have children either, and at least I have a beautiful wife I love."

"Point taken," Tom conceded, reaching for his coffee.

"Actually, we're still trying. I think Nadine might be too old. Don't tell her that, though, or she might want to stop trying."

Tom laughed, and as he did so he caught sight of the woman from Room 312 stepping from the dining room into the glare of the terrace. She was now wearing a light summer frock along with the raffia sun hat he'd seen lying on the bed upstairs. A large beach bag swung from her hand.

He had only ever viewed her from behind, and he saw now that she was in her forties, but wearing the years extremely well.

"Frau Wissmann." Olivier nodded as she passed.

"Monsieur Perret."

Tom waited for her to disappear down the steps before asking, "German?"

"Swiss German. She's a regular, comes every summer with her husband, although he's running late this year, something to do with a business deal back in Zurich."

"She's very attractive."

Olivier lowered his voice. "You're not the only one who thinks so."

"Oh?"

"There's an Italian here who's taken a shine to her. Young fellow. Flash. Struts around like a cock in heat."

Not anymore, thought Tom.

"Hardly her type, I imagine," he said.

"You haven't met Herr Wissmann. Any type would be better than that. He's arrogant, and rude with it. Nadine despises him."

"I've never known you to be so indiscreet about your guests."

"Not just my guests. You should hear what I say about you."

Tom laughed, cutting into the eggs.

The theory held: Frau Wissmann was an unwitting pawn in the Italian's game, little more than a convenient alibi. This was the only logical explanation.

The Italian must have set out to seduce her, to spend the night with her, planning to slip from her room, taking her key with him, and returning after the deed was done. It was no more than a brisk five-minute walk to Tom's villa along the coast path. If all went well, he would have been back between the sheets within twenty minutes. Only it hadn't gone so well for him.

"An Italian, eh?" said Tom. "I think I might have seen him around. Does he drive a fancy roadster?"

"Must be someone else. Signor Minguzzi arrived by train. I know because he insisted on being picked up from the station, even though it's a short stroll."

Minguzzi. And no car to search, just the room, which meant filching a spare key from the reception desk. Or maybe not. With any luck, Frau Wissmann would have left the original back in her own room. She had obviously returned there to get changed for the beach after her visit to Minguzzi's room.

Tom tried to imagine what she was thinking. Undoubtedly confused by the Italian's sudden disappearance, and probably a little insulted, she was unlikely to do anything that would draw attention to their illicit tryst.

He knew he didn't have long before the maids went into action, and he needed a convincing reason to return upstairs. The best he could come up with on the spur of the moment meant spinning yet another yarn to poor Olivier.

"I've got a full house in a week or two, which means boarding a couple of guests here. Is there any chance of viewing one of the rooms on the top floor?"

One of them happened to be free, and Olivier was all for showing it to him. Tom told him not to worry; he was quite happy to check it over on his own.

"I'm sure the consummate professional has better things to do."

"I'm sure the wife of the consummate professional would agree with you."

Nadine had tossed a couple of disapproving glances the way of her husband while scampering around the terrace, attending to the breakfast requirements of the hotel's residents.

Armed with the key from Olivier, Tom made his way back up to the third floor, ignoring the vacant room and making straight for 312. He estimated that he had five minutes, give or take, before he'd be expected back downstairs. It wasn't long, and he'd used up most of it by the time he finally figured out that Frau Wissmann must have taken the Italian's room key with her to the beach. Minguzzi's jacket was still hanging in the wardrobe, but the key wasn't back in the pocket, or on any of the surfaces, or in any of the drawers. This left him with little choice.

Fortunately, the reception area was deserted. Unfortunately, Olivier came hurrying into view just as Tom was about to help himself to the spare key to Minguzzi's room from the bank of cubbyholes on the wall behind the desk. Had Olivier seen exactly what he was doing? Probably not, Tom judged, and he made a show of returning the room key Olivier had given him to its hook.

"Well? What did you make of it?"

"Perfect. How much does it cost?"

"More than most, but a trifle for a man of your means," grinned Olivier.

"Can we check availability for the week of the fifteenth?"

"Give me a few minutes. I have to put an urgent trunk call through to Paris for one of the guests."

While Olivier was unlocking the door to the office, Tom surreptitiously pocketed the key to Room 104 from the rack.

"Take as long as you need—I'm not in any hurry," he said, strolling casually back toward the main staircase.

Minguzzi's room turned out to be half the size of the Wissmanns', if that: a dark, north-facing little box without a balcony. The curtains were closed, the bed made, unslept-in. Minguzzi had obviously been a fastidious type. His socks were grouped according to their color in the chest of drawers, and in the bathroom his bottles of hair pomade (and various other ointments and unguents) were carefully arranged in ascending order of size on the marble-topped washstand.

Tom had been expecting to find the suitcase packed, ready for a swift departure, but the Italian had evidently decided to stay on, which suggested a certain self-assurance.

Pulling out a pen and notebook, he wrote down the name of the tailor in Rome who had cut the lightweight summer suit and linen jacket hanging in the wardrobe. The shoes were ready-to-wear, but the Homburg-style Panama hat on the high shelf in the wardrobe offered up something intriguing. There was a name embossed in gold on the leather sweatband: CESARE POZZI.

Was that the hatmaker, or Minguzzi's real name?

Tom suspected the latter. He couldn't say why, exactly. Somehow it fitted with the man he'd brushed with, briefly and violently.

"Minguzzi" was surely an assumed name, adopted for the job. It's what any professional would have done, and the Italian's professionalism, though not beyond reproach, was palpable. That much became clear when Tom made his way to the desk between the windows.

He had saved the best till last, but soon found himself disappointed. There was no diary, no address book, no checkbook, no incriminating names or telephone numbers scribbled on scraps of paper. In fact, there was nothing of any note in the desk drawer besides a brochure for a hotel in Biarritz—another job?—and a bundle of French francs. Tom thought about pocketing the money, but decided against it. Ideally, he would have searched the room more thoroughly. As it was, he did the best he could within the given time.

Pulling the door shut behind him, he removed his gloves, slipped them into his jacket pocket and made his way back downstairs.

Olivier was loitering in the reception area while a silver-haired woman, seated at the desk in the office, gabbled away on the telephone.

"It turns out all she wanted was to check on her cat," he announced irritably. "I think she's even trying to talk to it."

He was all smiles and kind words, though, the moment the woman had finished her call. While Olivier fussed around her, Tom took the opportunity to restore Minguzzi's key to its cubbyhole. As soon as the woman had wandered off, wet-eyed with emotion after her feline communication, the charade was followed through. The register was checked; a third-floor room with a sea view was reserved for the week commencing the fifteenth.

Strolling home along the narrow coast path, Tom struggled to draw any satisfaction from the success of his mission. Yes, he'd managed to gain access to the assassin's room undetected, but what exactly had he learned? Very little—almost nothing other than that one of Minguzzi's last living acts had possibly been to have sex with a Swiss German woman almost twice his age.

He could envisage Leonard's barely disguised look of disappointment when he got to hear Tom's account of the past hour. For all his skills as a backroom spymaster, Leonard had never been a convincing dissimulator in person; he wore his feelings far too readily on his face. His true talent had always lain in selecting operatives who didn't.

It had been there all along, but Tom became intensely aware once more of the Beretta tucked into the back of his waistband, hidden beneath his jacket. He knew that it would be on his person, or within easy reach, until this thing was over. He found himself wondering if he was being observed even now, and he tried to estimate his reaction time based on a man stepping suddenly from the undergrowth up ahead and pointing a gun at him. He calculated that he wouldn't stand a chance. He would be dead, his blood leaking into the sandy soil before he could even draw his weapon.

He moved the Beretta to the hip pocket of his jacket, closing his fingers around it, narrowing the odds on the imaginary assailant.

It seemed like a deeply symbolic act.

It had taken him a good couple of years to shake off the paranoia that had ruled his life for so long, to learn to walk down a city street without checking to see if he was being followed, to not glance up every time a new customer entered a restaurant where he was dining, to accept the innocent attentions of a stranger for what they really were.

Depressingly, the same paranoia he had come to despise might once more prove the saving of him. He could list the moments in the past when it had come to his aid, just as he could identify the times when, had the other man been more suspicious or alert, things might well have turned out differently for both of them.

Paulette never appeared before ten, which gave Tom a little less than an hour to deal with Hector.

He smoked a cigarette on the terrace, steeling himself to the grim task. He then armed himself with a spade from the toolshed and headed for the gulley.

The low morning sunlight slanted through the trees overhead, dappling the rock walls around him. By noon, the building heat would have silenced the unseen choir scattered about the branches, but for now, the trilling birdsong rang loud and clear, a fitting accompaniment for the occasion.

Buried near the well, the Italian had said, but when Tom surveyed the ground in the vicinity of the brick wellhead he saw no obvious signs of digging. For a terrible moment he feared he might be denied his final farewell, but then he found the spot.

Hector had been hidden in a sloping bank of debris at the base of the rock face, where it had slowly disintegrated over the years. He scraped at the scree and the stones with his hands, revealing the black pelt, usually so lustrous, now dimmed by dirt. He scraped till Hector lay fully exposed, stretched out, lying on his right side, as he liked to do in front of an open fire in winter.

The soil clung to the congealed blood at the back of his head. Tom ran his fingertips along the noble snout, up and over to the wound, feeling the depression where the skull had been caved in.

He could picture the scene. Poor Hector, all bark and no bite, so trusting. An extended hand, even that of a stranger, would have been enough to silence the low, rumbling growl. A few soothing words and he would have drawn closer, tail wagging, panting in anticipation of the tasty morsel contained within the closed and empty hand. His greedy eyes would have remained locked on that hand; they wouldn't even have registered the rock raised high in the other.

Was that how it had been? Maybe not. But probably something close to it.

He gently scooped Hector out of the earth and laid him in his lap, cradling the limp and heavy corpse, rocking him, smoothing his fur.

"I'm sorry, my friend. It was me he was after."

He wanted to say more, but a wave of emotion muzzled his lips. All he could produce was a sudden loud sob.

It seemed for a moment that he had it under control, but he was weeping now, all composure gone, hot childhood tears washing away the last vestiges of his self-possession.

7

Others came and went over the summer months, and some even stopped by out of season, but the two weeks spanning late July and early August—when Leonard, Venetia and family were in residence at Dr. Manevy's house—had always been sacred to Tom.

That sunstruck fortnight was the one fixed point in his calendar. It was also his gift to them, a hopelessly inadequate "thank you" for all their kindnesses to him over the years. There was more to it than mere gratitude, though. Leonard and Venetia had nursed him through the worst of times, and he wanted them to see that their efforts hadn't been in vain. He wanted them to know that he was all right now.

All this, he imagined, was lost on the two boys, if not Lucy. What were they to know of his troubled past? What did they care? Young minds were not inclined to unpick the tangled histories of their elders. Maybe that would come later, but for now Tom was simply an old friend and former colleague of their father's who happened to be much closer to their mother in age, and whose company they were obliged to share for two weeks every summer.

He assumed that they favored their fortnight in Le Rayol over the annual springtime pilgrimage to Aix-les-Bains, where they twiddled their thumbs and took French classes while their mother subjected herself to every conceivable form of water torture, from skin-wrinkling immersions through to high-pressure pummelings. Leonard was spared this annual mortification of the flesh by the "sudden and pressing work commitments" that seemed to materialize as if by magic every Easter, shackling him to his desk at the Foreign Office.

Leonard's devotion to Le Rayol had never been in question. He had fallen hard for the place during their first visit five summers ago, and each year he threw himself headlong into his "annual brush and polish on the Riviera" with characteristic gusto. He was an outdoorsman by nature, surprisingly slim and sinewy for a man just shy of his sixtieth birthday, and although he wasn't averse to a bit of loafing on the beach with a book, he was at his happiest when fishing or boating or bathing. He swam vast distances with no apparent effort, never fearing of currents or cramps. He also spent endless hours prowling the craggy headlands with his fishing rod, as sure-footed as a mountain goat. He had once described life in Le Rayol as "a foretaste of paradise," which wasn't entirely true. Leonard's perfect paradise would have included a grouse moor, a shallow chalk river for fly-fishing and a golf course.

There was nothing to be done about the grouse moor and the chalk river, but the golf course was near at hand, in Cannes, and from time to time he would disappear there with Yevgeny, usually overnighting because they both enjoyed a flutter at the tables, although they always swore blind to their spouses that they never darkened the steps of the Casino Municipal.

In recent years, Leonard and Yevgeny's relationship had transcended the rarefied summer confines of Le Rayol. Whenever Yevgeny found himself in London, usually when buying at auction or courting the custom of some artist or other for the gallery in Paris, he would stay with Leonard and Venetia at their house in Warwick Square. Likewise, on the odd occasion when Leonard's work carried him to Paris, Yevgeny and Fanya would welcome him into their home, an exquisite *hôtel particulier* on the Rue Barbet-de-Jouy. It was compact compared to the buildings just around the corner on the Rue de Varenne, although its main staircase was still broad enough to take a four-in-hand. Over the years, large numbers of wealthy American collectors had trooped up that marble flight to dinner in the salon, and they had brought their checkbooks with them. They knew that Europe, broken by the Great

War and groping to put itself back together, was where it was at. And if they didn't, then Yevgeny was on hand to convince them of that fact.

How many heavyweights could the United States field against the likes of Picasso, Braque, Villon, Picabia, Matisse, de Chirico, Dalí, Dufy, Léger, Ernst, Miró, Mondrian, Kandinsky, Brancusi and Duchamp? Very few, maybe just three: Georgia O'Keeffe, Edward Hopper and Man Ray (who was, to all intents and purposes, a Parisian).

Yevgeny always said, "The French buy with their eyes, the English with their ears and eyes, and—thank the Lord—the Americans with their ears only." He felt no shame at talking himself into a small fortune, convinced that the lofty prices he charged his clients would one day prove to be mere pittances. He was, he genuinely believed, simply assisting the wealthy to become even wealthier.

Tom had a lot of respect for Yevgeny, possibly because he had witnessed the desperate flight of White Russians at first hand all those years ago. Some had even turned up at the embassy in Petrograd begging the British authorities to smuggle their jewels out of the country, convinced that the Bolsheviks would rob them even of these at the border. Yevgeny had lost almost everything in the Revolution, not least of all his parents, dragged from their motorcar by a rampaging mob and beaten to death. He had stepped off the train in Paris in 1918 with one suitcase and a string of his grandmother's pearls sewn into the lining of his jacket. In this respect, his story was not so different from that of many others, but few of his compatriots had managed to turn around their fortunes so swiftly, and those who had were not generally inclined to help out those who hadn't. Yevgeny was an active member of the displaced White Russian community in the French capital, known for his generosity.

Venetia was more circumspect about the "funny little Russian art dealer" and his nervy, wasp-waisted wife, Fanya. She found them far too eager to please, which meant little coming from a woman who made almost no effort whatsoever on that score. Privately, Tom suspected that Venetia was jealous, not so much of Leonard's relationship with Yevgeny, as of Fanya's quite justifiable claim to be even more neurotic than she. Pretenders to that particular throne were never welcome, although Venetia was big enough to rein back her more hostile instincts for one fortnight a year. Why rock the boat when it was such a very fine boat to be aboard?

Summer in Le Rayol moved to a pleasing, if somewhat repetitive, rhythm. They would all gather midmorning at the cove between the two houses for a spot of bathing, boating and leaping off the rocks. The tight demilune of sand was, in effect, a private beach, even if the law said otherwise. Every so often, a sailboat would anchor off the beach and a band of interlopers versed in their rights would row or swim ashore.

They rarely lingered.

It wasn't that they were subjected to a frosty reception—quite the opposite, in fact. They would be showered with attention and offers of food and drink, quizzed to within an inch of their lives, asked their opinion on Schoenberg's atonal *Second String Quartet* blasting from the gramophone (the disc was always at hand for such occasions). If none of this worked, then they would be exhorted to join in a vigorous game of volleyball— "I'm ever so sorry, but you don't really have a choice in the matter. You see, you're lying on the court." On one memorable occasion, Leonard had resorted to stripping off his bathing costume and searching for shells in the shallows. Normally, though, the invaders were long gone before then, convinced that they'd just slipped the clutches of some sinister cult bent on enlisting new members.

Luncheon was usually provided by Venetia and Leonard—a light meal of cold cuts, cheeses, salads and the like, prepared by Paulette's surly sister-in-law, Blanche, and served up at Dr. Manevy's house, beneath the vine-threaded pergola in the courtyard. A hock-induced siesta inevitably followed, which took care of the least hospitable time of the day, when the heat was at its most prodigious.

Around four o'clock, they would all emerge from hibernation, blinking into the sunlight, and congregate once more at the cove for a bracing dip to bring them around. Later, once the heat had subsided sufficiently, the cove would be abandoned for the tennis courts just below the village bar. If they weren't invited elsewhere for the evening, then cocktails and dinner were generally hosted by Tom at the villa.

Numbers fluctuated according to which of the guests had guests of their own staying with them, but there were rarely fewer than ten around the table on the terrace, and often nearly twice that number.

Paulette was a peerless cook with a seemingly endless repertoire of fish and shellfish recipes. Carnivores went hungry; she made no allowances for those who didn't appreciate the bounty of the sea. Tonight, lobster pilaf was on the menu in honor of Lucy's arrival. Lucy had always adored lobster, and in Paulette's eyes Lucy could do no wrong. In fact, aside from her own daughter, who was sometimes drafted in as a sous-chef, Lucy was the only person allowed in the kitchen while Paulette was working her magic. Even Tom was banned, until it was time to start bearing the platters of food to the table.

Paulette was running late today. By half past ten, long after Tom had laid Hector to rest, she still hadn't appeared at the villa. This wasn't unheard of—she relied on her unreliable husband, Claude, for a lift to and from work—but given the recent turn of events Tom felt an understandable clutch of concern.

He was about to lock up and head for the cove when he heard the crunch of tires on gravel.

They had clearly had a blazing row in the car. Claude wore the look of a man still smarting from the lash of his wife's tongue, and he sheepishly mumbled some excuse when Tom appeared from the house.

Paulette didn't speak; she stomped inside, leaving the two men to unpack the provisions.

"She sometimes wonders why you aren't married," said Claude.

"Does she?"

"I don't."

Lucy was alone on the beach, stretched out on a straw mat, reading a book.

"Good morning," Tom called as he approached.

Lucy twisted to look at him. "Morning."

She was a wearing a skintight black maillot, cut high on the thigh and open at the back, the very height of risqué beachwear fashion.

He deposited himself beside her. "I like your new bathing costume."

"Mother hates it. She says it leaves nothing to the imagination."

Venetia's things were laid out nearby, but she was nowhere to be seen.

"Has she gone off and drowned herself in protest?"

"Sadly not. She's taken the kayak out."

"Excuse me?"

It was a preposterous notion.

"She woke up this morning and decided she was fat, so she's resolved to be more active."

"That rather scuppers her theory that all women who take exercise are lesbians."

Lucy smiled, but there was something unconvincing in the curl of her lips, and it very soon became clear that she was carrying something she wanted to say.

Raising herself up so that she was sitting cross-legged in front of him, she reached across and gently took his hands in hers.

"Tom, I know what happened last night. I saw you."

He felt his heart lurch.

"I was here. Well, there . . ." She nodded behind her, up toward the headland. "I couldn't sleep. I kept thinking about the *Albatross*—my wonderful present from you—and I just had to get up and come and have a look. That's when I saw you down here."

He stared deep into her dark eyes, trying to calculate just how much she could have seen from up there on the headland. Enough. Damn the moonlight.

"It was Hector, wasn't it?" said Lucy solemnly.

He lunged at the excuse she'd offered him, an explanation he would never have had the presence of mind to conjure up on the spur of the moment. He lowered his gaze by way of affirmation.

"What happened?" she asked.

He was safe now, working ahead of her, already putting the finishing touches to the story.

"I think it was poison. They lay a fair amount of it around these parts against rats. God knows where it happened. I suppose it's best I don't know who's responsible, or I might just do something I regret."

Don't over-egg the pudding, he told himself.

"Where did you find him?"

The pain in her eyes was palpable, and he opted for the gazebo. If he mentioned the gulley, she was liable to make a pilgrimage there. She might even find the fresh grave he had just dug for poor Hector.

Lucy glanced off at the islands. "A burial at sea . . ."

It wasn't a question, but she sounded as if she was trying to make sense of it.

"You know how much he loved the water."

That was the truth. If Hector had been there now he would have been clawing impatiently at the sand, eager for them to join him in a bout of jumping off the rocks.

"You could have taken the *Albatross,* you know. I'm almost insulted you didn't."

"The thought crossed my mind."

"Why didn't you?"

"I'm not sure. Perhaps because it wasn't a boat he knew."

She nodded, accepting the explanation.

"Our secret, Lucy. I don't want anyone else to know."

"Why not?"

"I don't want his death hanging over the holiday."

"But it is."

"You know what I mean. Promise me. I'm not sure I could cope with all the sympathy."

"Not even from me?"

"Not yet."

She nodded.

"Say it," he insisted.

"I promise."

Her voice cracked as she spoke the words, and he thought for a moment she might be about to break down in tears. She didn't, though; she just gripped his hands more tightly.

"Ahoy!" came a distant cry.

It was Venetia, rounding the headland in the kayak, rocking wildly as she thrashed inexpertly at the water with the paddle.

Lucy released her hold on his hands, discreetly maneuvering away from him.

"Ahoy!" Tom hailed back, waving.

But even at a distance he could see from the shift in Venetia's bearing that she had registered the moment. She knew that she'd caught them unawares, intruding on something private. And Tom had little doubt that he'd be held to account for it before long.

Leonard and Yevgeny returned from Cannes just before midday, having squeezed in a quick nine holes before leaping into the car and racing back. They came bearing gifts and a whole batch of golfing anecdotes. The former went down far better than the latter.

"What is it about golfers?" Venetia declared. "The bribes I can handle—in fact, I thoroughly approve of them—but the stories . . . My father and brothers are just the same. Do you really think that those of us who've never swung a club in our lives care a fig about 'bogies' and 'birdies' and 'drives off the tee'? I can assure you we don't."

Yevgeny ran a hand over his bronzed pate, smoothing down the phantom hair, no longer there. For reasons that still baffled even Fanya, he had chosen to shave the whole lot off back in the spring. Whatever his thinking, it suited him; he had the right kind of cranium to carry it off.

"My dear Venetia," he chirped, "you don't understand. There is no other game like golf—"

Venetia raised her hand, cutting him dead.

"Yevgeny, I don't doubt you're about to say something terribly profound, but it might have more authority if you weren't wearing those ridiculous checkered trousers."

No one seemed sure whether to laugh or shout her down. Her sense of humor sailed perilously close to the wind at times. Yevgeny opted for a third way.

Unbuckling his belt, he let the trousers fall to his ankles.

"Is that better?" he demanded.

There was a stunned silence. And then laughter, wild and uproarious.

Yevgeny's undershorts were adorned with little golf clubs.

Leonard was eager for a swim before lunch. It was the opportunity Tom had been waiting for, and he followed his friend into the water.

"Mind if I join you?"

"Of course not. The headland and back?"

It was maybe half a mile across the bay to the headland separating Le Rayol from Le Canadel—a mere paddle for Leonard, but at the limit of Tom's range.

Ever the gentleman, Leonard slowed his stroke so as not to leave Tom languishing in his wake. At one point he even settled into a lazy but surprisingly effective backstroke. The conditions were perfect—a gentle swell, no chop—and it took them no more than fifteen minutes to make it across, suspended in a turquoise dream.

"Now that's what I call a morning pipe cleaner," declared Leonard on arrival. "Straight back, or a quick breather?"

"Hazard a guess," gasped Tom.

They hauled themselves up into the tumble of large boulders at the base of the bluff. The rock face betrayed a violent past, its layered strata coiled into serpentine patterns, even folded right back on itself in places, like kneaded dough. The trees shrouding the headland clung on tenaciously, their roots like grasping claws, defying the vertical almost to the waterline, where the smooth, sea-washed bones of their fallen brethren lay jammed among the rocks.

"Thanks for holding the fort," said Leonard, planting himself on a flat boulder. "Another evening with the Chittendens would have finished me off."

Tom settled down beside him. "I bowed out, left Venetia and Lucy to fend for themselves."

"Wise man. I could have done with a quiet night too, but Yevgeny had other plans."

"It was anything but quiet," said Tom. "Someone tried to kill me."

Leonard turned and fixed him with a searching stare. He was known for his composure under pressure. He outdid himself now.

"Well, that rather knocks the holiday into a cocked hat," he deadpanned.

"I'm sorry about that."

"Did you get him?"

"Yes."

"Alive?"

"Dead."

"Where is he?"

Tom nodded out to sea. "About two miles in that direction and half a mile down."

Leonard nodded. "Did he talk?"

"Not much. He was . . . damaged."

"Start at the beginning . . ."

" . . . go on till you come to the end: then stop."

Leonard smiled weakly at the memory. It was an old joke of theirs reaching back to debriefings of old: a line from the King of Hearts to the White Rabbit.

Tom spelled out the events of the previous twelve hours, taking it slowly, chronologically, the way he knew Leonard liked it. He also knew that no detail was too small, and he left nothing out. For much of the time, Leonard sat with his eyes closed, building pictures in his head. Every so often, his eyes would snap open, staring at the distant horizon, only for the eyelids to fall once more. He didn't speak a word until Tom had finished his account, and even then a good minute of silence hung between them before he finally found his voice.

The questions came in short, clipped sentences: When exactly did you become aware that Hector was missing? What was the Italian wearing on his feet? Is it possible he had time to fire before you clubbed the gun from his hand? When he fled your bedroom was the light on in the corridor outside? Did you check his mouth for dental work before disposing of the body?

Tom could make out the thinking behind some of the questions, but by no means all of them. It didn't matter. The very fact of sitting there and watching Leonard's analytical mind at work was deeply reassuring. He could feel the shock and confusion loosening their grip on him, leaking away, evaporating through his skin.

"When Olivier greeted Frau Wissmann as she passed by your table on the terrace did she catch your eye?"

"Leonard, I really don't think she's involved."

"Oh, she's definitely involved, wouldn't you say?" replied Leonard, almost irritably. "It's the exact nature of her involvement we're after."

Tom stuck to answering the questions, which kept coming in a steady stream: On the two occasions you headed upstairs at the hotel, are you sure no one saw you? Did you wipe your fingerprints from the Italian's room key before replacing it? Knowing Olivier as you do, how long before he alerts the police to his missing guest?

When Leonard was finally done, he said, "Okay. That's it. For now." He lapsed into a brief silence before adding, "I'm sorry."

"For what?"

"For you, Tom. You walked away from this sort of thing a long time ago. I'm sorry it's sniffed you out."

"Maybe I always knew it would."

"Listen to me," said Leonard firmly. "In our game we all have to live with the things we've done, but it doesn't mean we have to die for them. We'll get you through this and you can return to your life."

"That seems . . . well, unlikely."

"Don't be so bloody defeatist. You never used to be, and it doesn't suit you."

"For God's sake, Leonard, they tried once, which means they'll try again."

"How can you be sure of that? We have no idea who we're dealing with."

"I have a pretty strong hunch," said Tom.

"Oh, really? Let's hear it." The skepticism in Leonard's voice flirted with sarcasm.

"Well, for one thing, he was an Italian. Doesn't that tell you something?"

"Yes, his nationality." Leonard raised a cautionary finger before adding, "Maybe. Did you find his passport? No. If you had, could you be certain it wasn't false? Have you ever traveled to the Ticino? I'm sure you know they speak Italian in that part of Switzerland. In fact, Italian is one of the country's official languages. Maybe he was Swiss, like Frau Wissmann."

"The labels in his jackets . . ."

"I know Englishmen who have their suits tailored in Rome."

"You're playing devil's advocate."

"Of course I am. Never take anything at face value. You know that."

"And *you* know what I mean, Leonard. I'm talking about last autumn. I'm talking about Marseilles."

"Ah, Marseilles . . ." drawled Leonard.

It was often said that a job at the Secret Intelligence Service was a job for life, whether you liked it or not; the organization never relinquished its hold on you. This hadn't been Tom's experience. He had severed all links with the SIS five years ago, at the same time that Leonard had departed for the Foreign Office, cherry-picked by the new permanent undersecretary at the FO, Sir Robert Vansittart, to act as his right-hand man. Both he and Leonard had moved on, one to a job even closer to the heart of the British establishment, the other to a writer's life at the poor man's end of the French Riviera.

Tom had never doubted that their friendship would survive this parting of the ways. What he hadn't anticipated, though, was the overture that Leonard had made to him a few months later. It had seemed a tame enough proposal at the time. In the light of his recent brush with death, he now wondered whether he shouldn't have rejected it out of hand. If he hadn't, it had been more out of a sense of loyalty to Leonard than to his country. The notion of patriotism sat uneasily with him; he would never forget the dark places he had visited in its name.

Leonard had been very clear when spelling out the terms: You now live in France, and you travel widely researching your books. All we ask is that you keep your ear to the ground. If you happen to hear of anything that might be of interest to us, simply pass it on. In return, we'll cover some of your travel expenses, and we'll also place a furnished apartment near the Palais Royal in Paris at your disposal. Dinner parties, as you know, can be hotbeds of indiscretion. I'm sure we can even be persuaded to help out with the catering costs.

The prospect of his own place in Paris had played a big part in his decision to accept Leonard's offer. That first winter in Le Rayol had been extremely unpleasant—nothing compared to the big freeze of 1929, as the locals insisted on telling him, but from November to January the coast had been swept by a bitter Levant wind that fled down out of the east, setting all the world's teeth on edge and bringing clouds and rain. Tom had found himself making excuses for yet another trip to the Bibliothèque Nationale in Paris, anything to break the monotony of the gray, wet, dead days beside a granite sea.

With one book under his belt—an irreverent swipe at the gimcrack Orientalism of the Egyptian tourist trail—and a healthy advance from his publisher for a second in the same vein on Palestine, a base in the French capital had been a welcome antidote against the isolation of his new life as a writer, and he always returned to Le Rayol reinvigorated after his forays north.

At first, Leonard had left him entirely to his own devices, quite happy to receive the reports when Tom chose to fire them off. In the past couple of years, though, as the situation in Europe had continued to deteriorate, Leonard had grown more demanding: Would it be possible for Tom to try to cultivate a relationship with a particular individual at the French Ministry of the Interior? Any chance that he could attend the opera and take note of the comings and goings in a particular box from his seat in the stalls? One time, he had even been asked to eavesdrop on a conversation between an Austrian industrialist and a French journalist in a brasserie near the Place des Vosges.

This sort of activity was a notable escalation from the dinner party tittle-tattle he'd been sending back home, but it was hardly hazardous work and he'd been happy to oblige. He knew that he wasn't the only one at it. With Europe edging its way toward an ever more uncertain future, the stakes were high and information of any kind was at a premium. For the past year or two, rumors had been reaching Tom's ears of certain Parisian individuals, primarily women, whose circumstances had taken a sudden and marked turn for the better, and he had duly handed on their names to Leonard.

Only once had Tom refused a request, when called on by London to take photographs of the French fleet in Toulon harbor. It had felt too much like a betrayal of the nation he now thought of as his home and the people who had welcomed him so warmly. There had been no question of refusing to cooperate, however, when he'd been asked to turn his attention to the assassination of the King of Yugoslavia in Marseilles last October. If nothing else, the incident had disturbing echoes of the murder of Archduke Franz Ferdinand in Sarajevo twenty years ago—the catalyst for the Great War. Leonard had even insisted on traveling to Paris to discuss the affair with Tom in person.

King Alexander I of Yugoslavia had been slain within five minutes of setting foot on French soil. Disembarking from the Yugoslav cruiser *Dubrovnik,* he was greeted on the Quai des Belges by the French minister for foreign affairs, the energetic and formidably intelligent Jean Louis Barthou. The two men then climbed into an open motorcar and set off from the old port along the city's most famous thoroughfare, La Canebière. It was here that a lone gunman burst from the cheering crowds, bounded up onto the car's running board and with a cry of "Long live the King," began firing his automatic pistol.

King Alexander died almost instantly. Barthou was also fatally wounded, as were several bystanders. Others, although struck by stray bullets, survived. The assassin didn't. Hacked to the ground by the sword of a mounted policeman, he was beaten to death by the angry mob. Remarkably, the whole gruesome spectacle was trapped for posterity's sake by a news cameraman, who just happened to be filming at the exact spot.

Europe reeled in shock, though not necessarily surprise. There had been a prior attempt on King Alexander's life the year before in Zagreb, and his reputation as a brutal tyrant was well grounded. In 1929 he had abolished the constitution and declared himself dictator of the new Kingdom of Yugoslavia, since which time he had dealt ruthlessly with those who didn't share his grand vision of a unified empire of Slav peoples under his rule. Supported by the majority of Serbs, whose interests he blatantly favored, he was reviled by other ethnic groups. Both the Croatians and Macedonians had formed revolutionary movements committed to independence from the new Yugoslavia as well as the murder of their despised monarch. Indeed, the Croatian Ustasha had officially pronounced a death sentence on Alexander from the safety of Belgium just a short time before his official state visit to France.

Rumors and counter-rumors were still flying when, ten days after the assassination, Leonard turned up in Paris to brief Tom. By this time the true identity of the assassin had been established. He wasn't Czechoslovakian, as his fake passport suggested, but a Bulgarian national of Macedonian extraction. Vlado Chernozemski was a man with a violent past and close ties to IMRO, the Macedonian revolutionary movement—so close, in fact, that he had once been the chauffeur of IMRO's leader, Ivan Mihailov.

A predictable enough picture of disaffected Yugoslav revolutionaries hell-bent on regicide was beginning to emerge. Nevertheless, certain questions remained unanswered, not least: Why had King Alexander been provided with such a woefully inadequate security detail by the French authorities? And who had assured him that his ninety-strong personal *garde du corps* could quite happily remain aboard the *Dubrovnik*? And why were there running boards on the motorcar, when everyone knew that these afforded a would-be assassin a distinct advantage? And how exactly had Chernozemski managed to lay his hands on a state-of-the-art German machine pistol capable of dispensing death with such efficiency?

Leonard's concerns lay elsewhere. In fact, he was considerably less troubled by the death of King Alexander and what it meant for the future of Yugoslavia than he was by the slaying of the other passenger in the back of the motorcar, Jean Louis Barthou. Leonard had a lot of respect for France's minister for foreign affairs, both personally and professionally. Barthou—like Leonard and his boss at the Foreign Office, Sir Robert Vansittart—had always harbored a deep, instinctual mistrust of Germany's charismatic new chancellor, Adolf Hitler. In this respect they differed somewhat from the British government of the day, who welcomed Hitler's strengthening of the German nation both as a buffer against the Soviet Union and as a counterbalance to France's dominance in Europe. That was often the way of things, though: the Foreign Office and the British government didn't always see eye to eye. Vansittart was still in a rage about Prime Minister Baldwin's capitulation to Hitler over German naval rearmament.

Barthou, meanwhile, had been working tirelessly to hem Hitler in and keep Germany contained, forging pacts, treaties and ententes wherever he could. To the south, he was courting Mussolini to ensure that the Italians never joined hands with their fellow Fascists in the Third Reich. To the east lay the "Little Entente" between Yugoslavia, Romania and Czechoslovakia, and Barthou backed it to the hilt. He had even persuaded the Czechs and Romanians to establish diplomatic relations with the Soviet Union, whose membership of the League of Nations he had championed so successfully just before his death.

On that gray October day in Marseilles Europe had lost its wily and bewhiskered little puppet master, and the only evident beneficiary of Barthou's untimely demise appeared to be Adolf Hitler. What Leonard wanted to know, what he wanted Tom to ascertain, was whether Barthou had been an unfortunate victim caught in the crossfire or whether he had also been an intended target of the assassin.

The French were being very cagey about the specifics of the attack, though not necessarily because they had anything to hide. The country was caught up in a maelstrom of recriminations and accusations, with heads already beginning to roll. The mayor of Marseilles, the minister of the interior, the director of national security—all had been forced to resign. It would be a good while yet before the facts began to emerge, but Leonard wasn't prepared to wait that long—hence his approach to Tom.

Marseilles lay to the west of Le Rayol, beyond Toulon, no more than a three-hour drive away. Tom knew the city well enough, but only to depart from and arrive at by boat; he had never been inclined to linger there. The place had a tough, coarse air to it, an impression reinforced by the natives, who seemed to slink furtively about the streets as if permanently engaged in nefarious activities of some kind or other. This was certainly the reputation of Marseilles, one that it had failed to shake off over the centuries: a city where sailors, traders, adventurers, smugglers and other ne'er-do-wells could happily gather from all four corners of the globe to engage in shady dealings. It was, in fact, exactly the sort of place where a foreign monarch might meet a violent end.

It had been easy enough to pose as a journalist, considerably harder to avoid the pack of genuine British newspapermen who could have fingered him for an impostor. Fortunately, they were staying en masse at the Hôtel du Louvre et de la Paix and rarely ventured forth from the bar, which they'd colonized. Tom took a room at the Hôtel de Noailles and set about his inquiries.

Eyewitnesses to the assassination were thick on the ground and eager to talk, certainly if a drink or a meal was on offer. There were, however, glaring discrepancies in their accounts of the incident. Some said that Chernozemski had not been operating alone and that his accomplices, hidden in the crowd, had also opened fire on the motorcar. Others maintained that the extra shots had come from the police, who had panicked, firing blindly at Chernozemski and hitting innocent bystanders in the process.

There was more of a consensus when it came to the fate of Jean Louis Barthou. The French minister had, apparently, been hit only once—in the upper arm—but the lone bullet had severed an artery. Had the wound been correctly tourniqueted he might well have survived; however, he had been neglected in the ensuing pandemonium and had tragically bled to death. There seemed to be no evidence that Barthou had been directly targeted. Indeed, most were of the firm opinion that if Chernozemski had wanted Barthou dead his body would have been riddled with bullets, like that of King Alexander.

Leonard's suspicion that Hitler might have orchestrated the attack in order to rid himself of the troublesome little Frenchman was not, it seemed, supported by the testimonies of the eyewitnesses interviewed by Tom. Evidence had just come to light suggesting Croatian collusion in the assassination—a sort of joint enterprise with their fellow Macedonian revolutionaries—but there was nothing to indicate that the conspiracy extended beyond the boundaries of the Yugoslav kingdom.

That all changed on Tom's last night in Marseilles, when he fell into the company of an entertaining young Italian. Emilio Nicoletti said he was a journalist for the Catholic newspaper *L'Italia*—a claim that later proved to be true—and he seemed set on drinking himself into a stupor. The reason for this only became clear once the two of them had abandoned the bar in the Hôtel de Noailles for a restaurant down at the old port, where Emilio glumly announced that he was staring at the biggest scoop of his short career, and yet there was absolutely nothing he could do about it. He had no choice but to let it slip away.

When pressed to elaborate on the statement, he explained that the Croatian Ustasha—outlawed from Yugoslavia, and recently implicated in the assassination of King Alexander—had been operating quite freely from bases within Italy for a number of years now. It seemed a preposterous notion that Mussolini should have offered them safe harbor, and Tom said as much. Emilio was adamant, though. He had grown up in Parma, but his family owned a country estate to the south, deep in the hills of Emilia-Romagna. He said he knew for a fact that there was a Croatian camp at Borgotaro, even if the foreigners who came and went always claimed to be Bulgarians. Gunfire could sometimes be heard emanating from the compound of farm buildings, suggesting that military training of some kind took place there.

Tom left Marseilles at first light, briefly breaking the journey at Toulon to fire off a telegram to Leonard:

NO SIGN OF OUR GERMAN FRIEND HERE STOP AM
LEAVING FOR ITALY FOR A SPOT OF HUNTING STOP
ALL BEST TO YOU AND FAMILY

Hampered by heavy rain, it took him two days to drive to Borgo-taro, an unremarkable town set low in a valley, with densely wooded slopes rising sharply to the north and south. On arrival, he made straight for a dingy bar in the main piazza, the sort of place populated with idlers whose tongues might be loosened by a glass or two of grappa. He kept the story simple: a Bulgarian friend had suggested he visit Borgotaro if he was ever passing through. Andrey Vazov. Maybe they knew him? He had spent time in some kind of refugee camp nearby.

It wasn't a camp so much as a large farm. Set amid trees on rising ground to the west of the town, there was one dirt road in and out, lined with sorry-looking cypresses. Tom made two passes before find-ing a narrow lane that wound its way up into the hills behind the farm.

It was an old device, one he had employed before. Few people sus-pected a painter, even a bad one. He was happily installed on the hill-side and about to embark on his second watercolor when he saw the men approaching. He knew immediately that something was wrong. How many people went tramping through the countryside in gabar-dine suits and leather shoes? They were Italian, and they made no bones about their business. They asked him politely but firmly to accompany them.

He was held for three days in a small building at the headquarters of the local carabinieri, a walled and wired compound on the far side of Borgotaro. During that time he was questioned incessantly by the two men: Who is Andrey Vazov? Where did you meet him? Are you sure he's Bulgarian? What does he look like? When did he tell you about Borgotaro? How long did he spend here? When exactly was he here? Where does he live now? How can we contact him?

They were good, never aggressive, just patient and persistent, re-peating their questions every so often, trying to wear him down, fish-ing for inconsistencies. They didn't deprive him of sleep, though, and he was well fed, eating in the cold canteen where the carabinieri took their meals. His frequent requests that he be allowed to place a call to the nearest British legation were politely deflected with the feeble ex-cuse that, unfortunately, all the telephone lines were down at present.

He was released just before noon on the third day. There were no apologies.

"Enjoy your time in Parma."

He had told them he was en route to Parma to research his next book.

"You think I'm going to Parma after this?"

"I can recommend an excellent hotel just off Piazza del Duomo."

"I'm going straight home, and the first thing I'm going to do is register a formal complaint with the British authorities."

"While you're at it you might want to contact the International League of Human Rights. I believe they're based in Paris."

That, in many ways, had been the most revealing thing about the experience: their absolute belief in their ability to behave as they had. The state allowed them to act as they saw fit, and they had complete confidence in the power of that state to protect them.

It had been a chilling insight into the workings of Fascism.

"Ah, Marseilles," drawled Leonard.

"In case you've forgotten, I was arrested and interrogated."

"I didn't ask you to go to Italy. You went at your own initiative."

"I'm not blaming you, Leonard. I'm just saying that they know who I am, where I live. And I'm pretty damned sure they know what I was doing there."

"That doesn't mean they want you dead."

"What about the upcoming trial?"

A trial date had been set for later that year in Aix-en-Provence, at which three members of the Croatian Ustasha were going to have to answer for their involvement in the assassination of King Alexander. "You think Mussolini wants it coming out that he's been harboring the group responsible?"

"I know he doesn't," replied Leonard. "And it's not going to happen. The Hungarians are going to get the blame."

Tom took a moment to digest this statement.

"The Hungarians . . . ?"

"The Ustasha also had a camp in Hungary."

"How convenient. So Mussolini is exonerated."

"Come on, Tom, you know how these things work. We need Mussolini on our side right now."

"Whatever the cost?"

"He wasn't behind the assassination. He was a fool to welcome the Croatians into Italy, but he sees that now." Leonard paused. "Look, Barthou was nudging him towards a new southern pact—France, Italy and Yugoslavia—a sort of Mediterranean Locarno. We're trying our damnedest to keep the thing alive."

"And what does Il Duce want in return?"

"A guarantee that Hitler won't get his hands on Austria."

"Is that all? It doesn't sound like much of a sweetener."

Leonard hesitated. "He also wants Abyssinia."

It was the talking point of the moment—Italy's designs on the East African nation. All the other Great Powers had their kingdoms in the sun, and like some jealous schoolboy Mussolini wanted one too.

"You're going to let him have it, aren't you?"

"I'm not sure we could stop him even if we wanted to."

"It's not yours to give."

"When did you become so bloody holier than thou?" retorted Leonard.

"You're building a monster—you know that, don't you?"

"No, Tom, we're doing our best to contain one. The greatest threat to the world order right now is Adolf Hitler. Have you read *Mein Kampf*? That man's territorial ambitions are laid out plain as day. They're as real as the rock we're sitting on." Leonard slapped his palm against the stone for effect. "Oh, he's changed his tune—he's had to—but Barthou wasn't fooled by him, and Barthou was right: boxing him in is the only way."

Tom stared at his friend. Maybe Leonard was right about Hitler. Maybe empowering Mussolini would bring the Italians into the fold. But Tom's thoughts lay elsewhere. He had never heard Leonard speak in such terms before; he had never seen him so exercised. The cold pragmatism of his words and the fire in his eyes made for an unsettling cocktail.

"Aren't you worried I'll blow the whistle?" Tom asked.

"You'd never do that."

"Not if that fellow out there had had his way last night." He nodded toward the islands.

The insinuation wasn't lost on Leonard. "How dare you!? We would never . . ." He trailed off, not lost for words, but because they both knew that the British government was not above sacrificing its own for the greater good. "Believe me, you couldn't be more wrong."

"So who, then?" Tom demanded. "Who the hell wants me dead?"

"A cuckolded husband, for all I know."

It sounded facetious, but it was said in a spirit of conciliation.

Tom heaved an apologetic sigh. "That's about the one area where I'm entirely innocent."

"Well, let's run through the others and see what we turn up, shall we?"

It was a disagreeable prospect, dredging up past misdeeds long since overlaid if not forgotten.

"After lunch, while the ladies are napping," suggested Tom, glancing across the bay toward the cove. "They'll be wondering where we are."

They clambered down off the rock and eased into the limpid water.

"You should know . . . Lucy saw me last night down at the cove."

"What!? How?"

"Bad luck. She couldn't sleep. Don't worry—she assumed I was dealing with Hector, and I obviously didn't say anything to disabuse her. I told her I thought he'd died from eating rat poison."

"Poor old Hector," said Leonard distractedly, pushing off out into the bay.

8

Lucy hurried along the pathway, all too aware that she was late.
She was always running late. Even when she had time enough in hand, she would inevitably fritter it away until she found herself bicycling like fury across town, bustling breathlessly into crowded lecture halls and tutors' rooms, forever mumbling excuses to friends in pubs and cinema foyers. It infuriated Mother, who was a stickler for punctuality and who ascribed her tardiness to youthful affectation, which it wasn't. Tom didn't seem to care too much. In fact, he had once said she was at her most beautiful when flustered.

As she climbed toward the villa, the welcome shade fell away and she felt the sudden sting of the sun against her skin. She had overdone it on the first day, as she did every year. She should have avoided the cove after lunch. Everyone else had resisted, but she had wanted to take the *Albatross* out again and now she was paying the price. Her bare arms and legs flamed in protest against the white of her tennis outfit.

She arrived to find Tom deadheading petunias on the terrace, making the rounds of the pots spread along the balustrade.

"Sorry I'm late."

"By your usual standards this is positively early." He smiled, pinching off a few more spent blooms.

"That looks like fun."

"You just wait. Gardening makes considerably more sense when you're older."

"As does a team of gardeners, I imagine."

"There are only two of them," came his indignant reply. "And besides, they spend most of their time arguing."

Fernand and Alphonse were two bull-necked brothers from Le Canadel whom Tom had inherited with the house. They'd given him little choice in the matter, simply turning up and setting themselves to work one day as if nothing had happened. They were always quarreling, and Tom had dubbed them Cain and Abel, convinced that it was only a matter of time before one of them dispatched the other with a shovel.

"I don't know why you don't replace them," said Lucy.

"I do—fear."

"Fear?"

"Would *you* want them as enemies?"

"I'm not sure I'd want them as friends."

"Well, there's no danger of that, not since Paulette let slip my nicknames for them the other day."

"She didn't. Oh, dear."

"Actually, I think they were rather amused by it," said Tom. "Although they're still bickering over which one of them is Cain and which is Abel."

Lucy laughed.

"Lemonade?" A jug and two glasses stood on the table beside a couple of tennis racquets. "Paulette made it especially for you."

"Do we have time?"

"A quick glass. We need to talk tactics. Yevgeny and Walter make quite a formidable pairing."

While he poured she filched two of his cigarettes, lit them both and handed him one. It was an intimate gesture—not one she would have permitted herself with any other man. He didn't appear to notice, though, wordlessly placing the cigarette between his lips and raising his glass.

"Tinkety Tonk."

"To victory."

They clinked.

"I hope your backhand's improved since last year."

"Oh, a lot," she replied. "It's almost as bad as your serve now."

He laughed.

She liked it when she made him laugh. He had put over so much of his time down the years to amusing her that it always felt good to return the favor. She could clearly recall the first occasion when she had set off his deep laugh, the real laugh, not the indulgent godfatherly chuckle she'd grown accustomed to. It had been just before her fourteenth birthday—a terrible age for any child, that cruel and uncertain limbo before adulthood, but worse, far worse, she suspected, for girls than for boys. George and Harry had embraced it as a necessary rite of passage that couldn't come too soon. The body hair, the deepening voice, the extra inches of height, even the pustules all were badges of honor to be worn with pride at school. The taller, the hairier, the more malodorous the better, it seemed.

Not so for her. She had been quite happy with the way things were. She had no desire for breasts, and yet they had sprouted on her chest like two malignant growths, declaring themselves to the world, demanding to be seen, entitling people whom one hardly knew to remark upon them as casually as they might point out a pair of swans on the Serpentine. The sheer embarrassment of that first fitting for a brassiere at the little shop in Knightsbridge, where the staff could judge your requirements at a glance . . . the favorite shoes and cherished items of clothing, still with plenty of life in them, which had to be discarded as one's bones stretched out at an alarming rate . . . the face of a stranger in the bathroom mirror every morning, distorted, misshapen. No, for her it had been a catalog of sheer misery, even discounting the monthly cramps and the blood.

By the time of her fourteenth birthday, everything was in place, but somehow none of the parts belonged to her. She felt as if she had been hastily assembled by some mad inventor. This was the rough and gawky creature who had greeted Tom at the door of their house, who had barely been able to look him in the eye, who had dreaded the prospect of spending the day out and about with him for fear of the embarrassment she would inevitably cause him. To make matters worse, he had just returned from a posting in Athens, lean and tanned and immaculately turned out in a cream linen suit, his blond hair bleached whiter than she had ever seen it by the sun.

He hadn't mentioned the swans on the Serpentine, although he must have felt them pressing against him when he took her in his arms and kissed her oily forehead. Maybe he had also sensed her hesitation about venturing forth, because he had swept her off without further ado, bundling her into his motorcar before she could resist.

Her days out with Tom had always been shrouded in mystery; she never knew what lay in store. This one was no different, except that it had soon become apparent that there were to be no boat trips along the Thames, no visits to London Zoo or Madame Tussauds wax museum, no lavish meals at Quaglino's. Only when they had cleared the city limits and were well on the road to Henley had he announced that they were headed for Oxford.

She remembered it as a faultless day: the cloudless skies and the warm, liquid breeze; the young green of the rampant hedgerows as they motored through the Chiltern hills before dropping down into the Vale of Oxford; the lazy stroll through the university colleges scattered about the city center; the gobbets of history and the tales of Tom's wild escapades during his time as an undergraduate. They lunched in the shade of a weeping ash at a riverside pub, and afterward he taught her how to punt. Teetering on her stilt-thin legs at the back of the boat, she gripped the pole and wrestled them up the Cherwell on a zigzag course.

All this, though, was only a distraction to throw her off the scent, a prelude to the big surprise. They were maybe fifteen minutes from Oxford, back on the road again and supposedly heading for home, when he sprang it on her.

The airfield consisted of little more than a rough grass landing strip and a scattering of low huts on the outskirts of a honey-stoned hamlet. Apparently, the airfield had been developed since the Great War, which made you wonder what it must have looked like before. Maybe the limp windsock had been a different color back then; maybe there had once been two tatty airplanes standing around instead of the four now on show. And if she had known that Tom was lying, that he wasn't simply dropping in on an old friend in the Royal Air Force, she would have insisted that they turn the car around and hightail it immediately.

By the time she realized that they were to take to the air, it was too late; an oil-smeared mechanic was shoving some overalls into her hands and waiting for her with a leather helmet, gloves and some goggles. Tom did his best to reassure her: he'd accumulated many hours of solo flying time while in Greece, and the biplane they were going up in was a notoriously reliable beast. In fact, the first solo flight from England to Australia had been achieved earlier that year in an Avro Avian.

"Don't worry—she won't let us down."

"He's right, miss," quipped the mechanic. "She'll take you right along with 'er if she goes."

The moment the tires left the turf her fear vanished, washed clean away by a sudden flood of exhilaration. She was flying! Flying!

They soared and swooped about the heavens for almost an hour, Oxfordshire laid out beneath them like a map, its shallow contours thrown into relief by the westering sun. Every so often Tom would turn and grin at her and give her a thumbs-up, or he would point out some landmark far below, banking the aircraft to give her a better view. On a few occasions they flew so low that she was able to track their hedge-hopping shadow and return the waves of the Lilliputians on the ground.

Eventually, they bumped back to earth, and the eerie silence once the motor had been cut seemed to reinforce her sense of forlornness at returning to the real world.

"Is it a secret?" she asked as they drove off from the airfield. Somehow she couldn't imagine Mother sanctioning such a thing.

"I told Leonard."

"I understand. Mum's the word."

He had laughed, but the real laugh came a little while later, on their way back to London, when they stopped in Thame for dinner. Tom had warned her that the proprietor of the Spread Eagle Hotel was an eccentric character, downright difficult at times, and John Fothergill didn't disappoint. He spent the first five minutes at their table railing against the Royal Automobile Club, which he held unreservedly to blame for the endless procession of motorists looking to use his lavatories for free, and the next five minutes bemoaning the state of British politics. The country needed a leader of Lloyd George's stature and dynamism. Better a randy old Welsh goat than a spineless pencil pusher like Baldwin.

Lucy, still abuzz with the thrill of her time aloft, piped up that she'd heard a funny story about Lloyd George, instantly regretting the use of the word "funny" as Fothergill turned his quelling gaze on her. Mumbling a feeble disclaimer that she only had it secondhand from her step-father, she launched into the anecdote.

Some years ago, when he was prime minister, Lloyd George was driving back late one night from his home in Wales when his car broke down near Epsom. Finding himself right outside Horton Asylum for the Insane, he roused the porter, who demanded to know who was beating on his door at such an ungodly hour. "I'm the prime minister," Lloyd George announced. "Oh, that's all right," replied the porter. "Come on in. We've got eight of you here already."

Fothergill exploded, baring his long yellow teeth like a chimpanzee, and Tom nearly matched him for the loudness of his laugh. The other diners stopped and stared, mainly in bewilderment, Lucy later learned, because the curmudgeonly old innkeeper had rarely been known to crack a smile, let alone sound a laugh.

For a child who had spent her life silently observing the performance of adults, it had been a significant moment, a thrilling step from the shadowy stalls into the bright lights of the stage. Yes, she had gone on to make mistakes, tempted above herself into youthful errors of judgment that still made her blush with shame when she thought back on them, but Tom had always been there, a quiet presence at her side, leading her through the painful metamorphosis into adulthood. Despite the sporadic nature of their friendship, no one had helped her more than he had, showering her with unconditional support and affection over the years.

Would she ever have summoned the courage to go against Mother's wishes and apply for a place at St. Hugh's if it hadn't been for Tom's unswerving (and sweetly misguided) faith in her intellectual abilities? It seemed unlikely. So much of who she was, of what she had become, she owed to him. Maybe she had always known it in her bones, but she was of an age now when she could admit it to herself, acknowledge the debt. In fact, she had determined to do just that on this holiday, to tell Tom for once what he really meant to her.

He, of course, would attempt to silence her with some wisecracking comment—that was his way—but she intended to persevere and tell him just the same. She would have done it yesterday if she hadn't broken down in hopeless floods of tears on hearing that the *Albatross* was hers. And she thought about doing it now, as they strolled together up the twisting lane from the villa to the tennis courts.

It was the wrong moment, though. Tom seemed strangely tense, distracted, his eyes darting around them while they walked and talked.

It didn't matter. She could wait. There would be other opportunities.

The grandly named Club de Tennis boasted three tennis courts, a croquet lawn, a *piste de boules* and a small tea pavilion. Hacked out of the slope just beneath the Maurin des Maures, the main bar in the village, the club was a relic of a dead dream to turn Le Rayol into an exclusive holiday resort for the wealthy. Had the property company behind the scheme not gone bust after the Crash of 1929, the slopes around the bay would now be blanketed with hotels and public parks and endless miles of tree-lined avenues wide enough to take motorcars two abreast, the whole thing topped off by a reconstructed Provençal village.

As it was, all that remained of this ghastly prospect was the Hôtel de la Réserve down on the beach, a wooden pergola up in the village, a monumental stone staircase splashed with flower beds, and a tennis club where one never had any trouble getting a court.

Yevgeny was already there, trading shots on the lower court with a tall and tousle-headed young man who was standing at the net, calmly volleying away.

Puzzled, Lucy turned to Tom. "Where's Walter?"

"That's Walter."

"What happened to short, fat and balding?" she demanded in a whisper.

"Must be the Mediterranean air," grinned Tom. "How does he compare to Hugo Atkinson?"

She wasn't going to allow herself to be drawn that easily, even if she knew the answer at first glance. "Well, he's certainly a better volleyer."

That's when they saw Fanya. She was seated beneath a sunshade by the tea pavilion, nursing a cold drink and idly flicking through a copy of *L'Illustration*. As ever, she was a picture of easy elegance, her patterned chiffon frock tapered to her slender figure, her hair scraped back off her ascetic face.

"*Chérie!*" she hailed.

Rising to her feet, she spread her arms and took Lucy in a bony embrace before stepping back and scanning her catch from top to toe with her large gray eyes. "Yevgeny was right. You are *plus ravissante que jamais.*"

Unlike Yevgeny, Fanya mixed and matched her languages before coating them in a thick Russian accent that was no less pronounced now than it had been four years ago, when Lucy had first met her.

"I could say the same of you. You look incredible."

"*Petite menteuse,* lying to an old lady," Fanya scolded. "Please, don't ever stop."

She gave a short snort, the prelude to her infectious, trademark cackle.

"And Leonard? Where is he? Did you bring me no one to talk to?"

"He had to go to Toulon."

"Toulon?"

"Something to do with work."

Fanya turned her inquiring gaze on Tom, who shrugged. "He said he'd be back in time for dinner."

"Well go and beat them," commanded Fanya, wagging an irritable hand at the opponents. "They have been talking about it all afternoon and I'm bored with them."

"Have they got a game plan?" asked Tom.

"*Bien sûr.* You know Yevgeny . . . he plans to win."

Tom made the introductions. Walter, she noted, stood almost as tall as Tom, and both men shared the same vague air of general shabbiness, although Walter won on account of his unruly mop of auburn hair and the paint on the hand he offered for her to shake.

"Pleased to meet you."

"You might not be saying that in an hour or so."

Oh, God, she thought, *he's American; he probably won't understand the irony.*

His thin smile suggested otherwise, as did his reply. "Oh, I don't know—I'm very gracious in victory."

"You seem very sure of yourself."

"My partner's the most competitive man in the known world. I'm banking on him doing all the hard work."

"We can put money on it, if you want," she suggested.

"You'll have to speak to Yevgeny. I don't have any."

"Yes, I hear he keeps his artists on a tight leash," chipped in Tom.

"Lies!" retorted Yevgeny. "Not true. Now can we please stop talking and play?"

"Let battle commence," said Tom.

And it was a battle, albeit a good-natured one. Yevgeny had always taken the game very seriously, playing at least once a week throughout the year at the Tennis Club de Paris, forever obsessing about his ranking under the incomprehensible French system. Coming late to the game, he wasn't a natural, but what he lacked in style he more than made up for with brute determination, hurling himself around the court, puffing and blowing like a grampus. He was a wily competitor who played to one's weaknesses and approached every rally as if it were match point.

Lucy and Tom quickly figured that they had to keep Walter pinned down on the baseline. He was far too adept at the net, comfortably killing off anything that came his way. For a big man, he was surprisingly graceful, with a long, lazy swing. Fortunately, Tom was on his game, because Lucy was off hers, her timing all out, which began to infuriate her, though not nearly as much as Tom's comment when they changed ends halfway through the second set.

"Relax—you're trying too hard. Just keep the ball in play and let them make the errors."

"Shut up, Tom."

"Just a suggestion."

She heeded it, and after breaking Yevgeny's serve—which had him ranting in Russian—they both served out to force a third and deciding set. By now the sun was well in the west, dropping behind the ridge, and a cooling breeze was rollicking up from the bay. The stage was set for the showdown, and at last there were no bands of tricky sunlight raking across it. They were at four games apiece, and desperately fighting to hold Tom's serve, when they heard a voice from behind them.

"My God, four monkeys in a cage."

It was Barnaby, wearing a crumpled linen suit and a wide grin.

"Bugger off, Barnaby," said Tom.

Barnaby tilted his head at her. "Lucy . . . looking lovely, if a little sweaty. Gentlemen," he added, raising a hand to Yevgeny and Walter down at the other end of the court. "I'll just settle myself down on this grassy bank here with my beautifully cold beer."

"This is the last thing we need right now."

"What you need right now, my dear Thomas," said Barnaby, for their ears only, "is to start knocking the ball short to Yevgeny's backhand; he's lofting his slice."

For all his general hopelessness, Barnaby was a gifted sportsman, and Lucy could see Tom weighing the tip. "Do you mind?" he said irritably.

" 'If music be the food of love . . . ' " chimed Barnaby.

Lucy found herself laughing.

"Don't," scowled Tom. "You'll only encourage him."

It was all over in five minutes, Yevgeny lofting his slice, which they were able to volley away with ease. Yevgeny seemed stunned by the loss, aware that he had been targeted, though not exactly how, and certainly not why. He smacked a tennis ball high off into the trees in frustration.

"Petit-bébé!" chided Fanya from the pavilion, really quite angry at her husband's petulant display.

"No, go for it," said Walter, tossing his partner another ball. "As my father likes to say: 'Show me a good loser and I'll show you a loser.'"

It was a perfectly judged intervention, setting everyone laughing, Yevgeny loudest of all.

9

By eight o'clock, when the first guests began to show up at the villa, there was still no sign of Leonard, and Tom was beginning to wonder if something hadn't gone badly wrong in Toulon. He was only able to relax once Lucy and Venetia appeared. Leonard had just telephoned from the road suggesting that they go on ahead without him. He would change for dinner and hurry over as soon as he was back.

Surprisingly, Venetia didn't seem too annoyed with her husband, although this might have had something to do with the rum cocktail that Barnaby thrust into her hand the moment she stepped onto the terrace. Possibly sensing Tom's distraction, Barnaby circulated like an energetic host, ensuring that glasses were topped up and the canapés given a fair wind, making introductions, pairing people off and generally sprinkling his fairy dust about the place.

Their friendship reached back years, through university to their very first day at boarding school—two thirteen-year-old boys packed off by their parents to a forbidding flint pile on the south coast. It was an improbable match: Barnaby loud, confident, devil-may-care, more than happy to be free of his family; Tom quiet, guarded and resentful at being sent so far away from home. Their shared passion for running themselves ragged on the soccer field had provided the glue, along with an unspoken understanding that the same seam of unhappiness ran through them both.

The friendship had faltered during their first year at Oxford, when Barnaby had turned jester-in-chief to a pride of strutting young peacocks with titles and country estates. He had made them laugh and kissed their rings and they in return had sneered at him behind his back.

Although it no longer stood between them, Barnaby's fascination with the great and the good showed no signs of abating. After many years in journalism he was still little more than a gossip writer, the longest-standing member of the "Londoner's Diary" team, peddling tittle-tattle about the high and mighty to the masses. This allowed him to rub shoulders with those same high and mighty, including Lord Beaverbrook, the proprietor of the *Evening Standard,* who had come to regard him as something of a surrogate (and slightly irritating) son.

Obsessed with money, Barnaby never seemed to have any of his own, and was forever hatching doomed plans to get rich quick. However, what little he had in his back pocket he always shared freely with his friends. It was one of his many redeeming qualities. Last year he had shown up in Le Rayol behind the wheel of a borrowed blinding-white Bentley sedan, accompanied by a monosyllabic but exquisitely beautiful Romanian chorus girl whom he'd met in Paris, two cases of very fine white Burgundy acquired directly from the château while motoring south, as well as the usual treasure trove of gifts for Paulette and her two daughters, which always included a selection of teas from Fortnum Mason and a tin of Huntley Palmers biscuits.

Barnaby had style, and he struck with the force of a hurricane wherever he went, sweeping all before him. More important, he liked his fellow man, actively embracing others' faults and foibles, possibly because he had so many of his own to contend with.

It was good for Tom to have his old friend around at a time such as this, although the idea that he might be placing Barnaby in the firing line didn't sit comfortably with him. He had raised the subject with Leonard during their tête-à-tête after lunch, while everyone else was at siesta. Leonard was of the firm view that no one other than Tom was in danger. Whoever lay behind the attempt on his life had been very precise in their targeting of him and certainly hadn't wished to draw attention to themselves. Chloroform to disable the victim followed by a lethal injection was hardly the chosen modus operandi of someone looking to make a show of things. It would be a little while yet before they knew exactly what the syringe contained, but Leonard strongly suspected that it would prove to be potassium chloride, which brought about cardiac arrest, leading to a likely prognosis of death by natural causes. No, someone had set out to terminate Tom's life in a manner that raised as few questions as possible, and preferably no stink at all.

Leonard had pressed his case forcefully in response to Tom's suggestion that he pack his bags and disappear.

"And how long will you be in hiding for? Will you ever not be in hiding? Do you really want to spend the rest of your life looking over your shoulder? We have to draw a line under this . . . we have to draw them out . . . here and now."

"Easy for you to say—you're not the one being used for bait."

"You're wrong, Tom. I know exactly what I'm asking of you, but I'm asking it for your own sake. And—who knows—maybe we can negotiate with them."

"Negotiate?"

"Maybe we have something they want, something we can trade. It all depends who they are."

They had run through the various alternatives, reaching right back to that first time in Petrograd, all those years ago. Barely a day went by when he didn't think about Irina and her death at the hands of the Cheka, about Zakharov's betrayal and his own bittersweet taste of revenge. But it was a private place, a dark sanctuary of the soul; exploring it with Leonard hadn't come easily to him.

He saw it now, but as a spectator might, pressed up against the wall of the gloomy stairwell. He could hear the weary footfalls ascending the staircase, getting closer, the soft scrape of a gloved hand on the banister rail, and then the jangle of a latchkey as the dim figure breasts the top step. It's a man, and he's pausing to catch his breath when two hands come hurtling out of the darkness, driving into his chest, driving out what little air remains in his lungs. He doesn't tumble down the steps; he flies, looping backward through the air in a graceful arc, like a gymnast. He doesn't die instantly. He lives long enough for Tom to come creeping down the steps and crouch beside his twisted body on the half-landing below, long enough to feel the lips pressed to his ear telling him why this is the end, to feel the hand clamping over his bloody mouth with its broken teeth, cutting off the air.

So young. So reckless. So completely out of his depth. So consumed by a thirst for retribution that nothing else had mattered at the time, not even his own life. After parting company with Dukes in the cemetery, he had made his way straight to Zakharov's apartment building and he had waited there, patient, immobile, hunched in the shadows of the top-floor landing like some avenging imp.

"It's not the Soviets, though," Leonard had insisted.

"How can you be sure?"

"Because there's no way they could possibly have known it was you who killed Zakharov, even if they suspected it. He was a man with many enemies. Second, why on earth would they wait—what?— sixteen years before acting against you? And third . . . third, this just isn't their style. I've never once heard of them using freelancers; they always send their own."

Sound logic, but Tom still felt cheated by it. Irina's death sat unseen at the heart of everything, the central fact of his existence, and he found it strangely comforting that there might be others out there still bound to the same bitter past. It meant that he was not entirely alone in purgatory. It meant that in some small way Irina lived on.

Leonard had been adamant, though, favoring the incident in Constantinople over the other possibilities, chiefly because they knew for a fact that Tom's anonymity had been compromised on that occasion; indeed, he had been lucky to get out of the country alive. Moreover, the Turks had notoriously long memories and a rare gift for revenge.

Leonard had toyed with the idea of returning to London in order to conduct the investigation from there, opting instead to stay at Tom's side and use an intermediary. Apparently, there was an agent in Toulon—"a good man based out of the embassy in Paris"—who could act as their conduit with London. In fact, Leonard had already arranged to meet the fellow in Toulon.

"Just how good is he?" Tom had wanted to know.

"Top-drawer."

"If that's the case, why didn't you use him to look into the Marseilles assassination last year?"

"There's really no need to be quite so suspicious."

"From the man who spent ten years telling me I was far too trusting."

"We didn't use him for Marseilles," intoned Leonard, "because he's only been in Toulon since February."

"A novice, then?"

"Actually, your paths crossed in Egypt in 1928."

"Not Mustapha the camel boy?"

"Very droll."

Before leaving for Toulon Leonard had assured him that the Foreign Office, the SIS and MI5 would soon be bending themselves to the task of finding those responsible. Meanwhile, he was to carry on with life as best he could, while taking the obvious precautions, of course.

Tennis had offered a welcome distraction, his mind flushed free of all dark thoughts as he lost himself in the match, one eye on the little dance taking place between Lucy and Walter, each playing shots that made the other look good. It didn't take a genius to detect the crackle of mutual attraction. What he hadn't anticipated was the mild stab of jealousy.

He had felt it then, and he felt it now, while observing their quiet flirtations on the terrace.

Leonard appeared shortly before the food was served, hot and flustered but in an immaculate cream linen summer suit. He managed to take Tom on one side and say, "He'll be boarding the sleeper to Paris about now. Don't worry—everything's in hand." He then downed his Dubonnet sec in two gulps, the first of three, Tom noted, that he put away before they took their places for dinner.

They would have been fourteen around the big teak table, and two more European nations would have been represented, if Beatriz and

Margot hadn't already accepted an invitation elsewhere that evening. In their early sixties, they lived together in a small farmhouse along the coast near Cap Nègre, and were the cause of endless speculation among the locals. Were the tall Spanish potter and the petite Belgian music teacher more than mere companions? Or were they what polite society called "new women"? Tom was privy to their secret but would never have considered sharing it, because he also knew just how much pleasure it gave them to think of all those wagging tongues. They were about the only other foreigners who lived in the area throughout the year, and they mothered him like a pair of broody hens, which was just fine by him.

He owed their friendship, along with many other things, to Benoît and his impishly attractive wife, Chantal, who had driven over from Le Lavandou for dinner. Benoît was the notary who had overseen the purchase of Villa Martel five years ago, championing Tom's bid with the executors of the estate over those of the other interested parties in a manner that wasn't altogether professional. "The first time we met, you made me laugh, and then when you came to lunch you played with the children," Benoît had explained some years later, when their acquaintance had blossomed into something more meaningful and Tom no longer referred to him as Maître Véron.

The other "local" guests at dinner were new to the area, and possibly not long for it. Klaus and Ilse Straub were brother and sister, he an author, she a journalist. Both had been forced to flee Germany after attracting the unwelcome attentions of Chancellor Hitler's henchmen for their outspoken attacks against the new regime. Nomads for almost six months now, their journey had taken them from Munich to Rome, then briefly to Capri, before depositing them in Le Canadel back at the beginning of June. Poor as church mice, almost entirely reliant on the grace and favor of friends or admirers, they were staying in a house belonging to a Swiss publisher whom they had never met, and whom no one else had ever met, for that matter. Yevgeny and Fanya— fellow exiles—had recently swooped on them, drawing them into their circle of friends.

Tom had always had a lot of time for Germans—certainly since his posting to Berlin in 1927, which had seen him travel the country widely and put to rest any prejudice left over from the Great War—but his admiration for Klaus was close to boundless. He was still struggling to square the quiet, grave-eyed young man he had recently come to know with the extraordinary novel he'd just finished. Somehow, the two just didn't seem to mesh.

The Gardener told the story of an aimless young drifter who finds himself employed as a leaf raker one autumn at a state-run asylum for tubercular patients in Bavaria. Doctors and nurses hold Godlike sway over the establishment, dispensing pleasure and pain according to their increasingly capricious moods, dangling elementary rights as if they were privileges before the noses of the infirm. It was hardly the stuff of humor, and yet the story was laced with the most subtle wit, which both undermined yet somehow heightened the veiled metaphor of a nation's slow slide toward totalitarianism.

It was Klaus's second novel, his most recent, and Tom knew from Yevgeny that it had died a sudden death in Germany, assisted to an early grave by a government quick to take offense. To Tom's mind, the novel was a work of genius, and he had waited until they were all seated at the table before telling Klaus as much, eager for everyone else to hear his verdict.

Klaus was taken aback, unaware that Tom had even read the book. "Where did you get it?" he asked.

"My book dealer in Paris."

"He must be good at his job ... to find one." Klaus's wry and self-effacing smile was typical of him.

"Oh, he is. He also read it before sending it, and you now have a big fan in Paris."

"You see," said Ilse to her brother. "It's not just me."

For some strange reason she had chosen to plait her long blond hair and coil it in two snail shells over her ears—an unfortunate coiffure which blunted her beauty, although it hadn't dampened Barnaby's blatant interest in her.

"Unfortunately," said Klaus, "no critics agree with you."

"Oh, you don't want to worry about them," Barnaby piped up. "The ones on my newspaper can barely read. I mean, they even gave Tom's last book a favorable review."

Tom acknowledged the insult with a smile and a little nod.

Venetia stabbed out her cigarette in the ashtray, her face alight with mischief. "I would say neutral rather than favorable."

"I take it back," conceded Barnaby. "Maybe they *do* know their stuff, after all."

Ilse dimpled in sympathetic effrontery. "Is this how you treat your host in England?"

"No, this is how we treat him in France," said Leonard. "We're far tougher on him back home."

"You must forgive us," explained Venetia. "You see, we're still a little insulted that Tom chose to reject us in favor of a life down here." As often with Venetia's jokes, there was a tang of truth about it.

"But *we*, on the other hand, are honored," declared Benoît. "*N'est-ce pas, chérie?*" he added, turning to his wife.

"Yes, we are honored," parroted Chantal, gripping Tom's forearm in a display of tender solidarity.

Her English wasn't quite up to her husband's, which was impeccable, and not only because his work as a notary brought him into contact with foreign clients. Despite his solid bourgeois air, there was nothing ponderous about Benoît's mind; he was a shrewd man in the liberal tradition, as well as being the most voracious reader Tom had ever met.

"Really?" said Barnaby. "I'd always been led to believe you French didn't have much time for the English. Please don't tell me Tom's the one exception—I'm not sure I could stomach it."

"Oh, no, we have other English friends."

The bit between his teeth, Barnaby insisted on knowing what the French truly thought of the English. "And don't go pulling your punches. We can take it."

Benoît, sly dog that he was, suggested that Tom was probably better placed to answer the question, having a foot firmly in both camps. Strangely, for all their many discussions over the years, it wasn't a subject they'd ever broached.

"Well," Tom began, "you have to remember that France was civilized from the south, and that England was civilized from the north of France. And then you have to remember that Benoît and Chantal are southern French, through and through."

Benoît gave an appreciative chuckle.

"It's not true!" protested Chantal. "He's teasing us."

"Oh, I see," said Barnaby. "While they're prancing around with poets and philosophers we're still daubing ourselves with woad?"

"Something like that," said Tom.

"Sorry, remind me—just how many thousands of years ago was this?"

"Come now, Barnaby," scolded Leonard. "I thought you said we could take it?"

"Exactly," Venetia concurred with her husband. "Why ask for wine if it's water you want? Let's hear Tom out."

They had a rule that there were no forbidden subjects at dinner, and Tom told it as he saw it: that the French looked on England as a gloomy, inhospitable land populated by strange and rather dull-witted people lacking in imagination, who through a happy mix of good fortune and determination had grown prodigiously wealthy yet remained almost entirely unversed in the culinary and amatory arts.

"My God," said Walter. "I hate to think what they make of Americans."

"I'm afraid you would," Tom replied.

Benoît held up his hands in a gesture of conciliation. "These are just stupid prejudices for stupid people. I'm sure you have the same for us French."

"Very few," said Barnaby. "Although I once met a rear admiral who said he much preferred crossing the Atlantic on a French ship because if anything happened there was none of that 'women and children first' nonsense. Does that count?" he asked innocently.

Yevgeny was convinced that French antagonism toward Russians owed less to historical enmity than to a simple question of money. The 1917 collapse of the Russian Imperial Bond Issues had wiped out the savings of countless ordinary Frenchmen.

"They are always telling me this as if it is my fault and they expect me to write them a check."

It was at this point that Fanya announced suddenly, and maybe a little drunkenly, that a French friend of hers in Paris had once offered a definition of all foreigners as *"des types qui ne savent pas baiser."* The person in question was, apparently, a woman of considerable sexual experience, and the English figured at the bottom of her long list.

"Maybe we should change the subject," suggested Venetia. "There are young ears at the table."

Lucy slewed around to her. "Oh, for goodness' sake, Mother, I'm at university, not a nunnery."

"More's the pity."

"My dear Venetia, not if there's half a grain of truth in some of the stories I've heard of convent life," said Barnaby, to much amusement.

Venetia had always had a soft spot for Barnaby, and was quite happy to be disarmed by him, although she avenged herself beautifully.

"I apologize, Fanya. Please continue—tell us why your friend rates Englishmen as such terrible lovers."

"She says they are too quick."

"Oh, is that all? No mention of whips?"

In the uncertain silence that followed, a few pairs of eyes flicked involuntarily toward Leonard. Tom leapt to his defense.

"Venetia's being wicked. What she means is the French have got it into their heads that flogging is a feature of English lovemaking." Out of the corner of his eye he saw Ilse translating for her brother's benefit. "I know a bookshop in the Palais Royal where the window display is entirely given over to titles like *Lord and Lady Lash* and *Miss Floggy*."

"What a load of old rot!" protested Barnaby. And then without missing a beat: "Where did you say this bookshop was?"

They were still laughing when Paulette appeared with the food. As usual, she lingered just long enough to wave aside the tributes to her latest culinary triumph, before hurrying off home to a late supper with her family.

The conversation fragmented over the lobster pilaf as people paired off with their neighbors, but it continued to ripple merrily around the table, punctuated by laughter and assisted by several bottles of a tingling white wine from Anjou. The seating plan was perfect. In fact, everything was perfect—the lambent light of the candles, the soft ruckle of the palm leaves, the bats spinning their invisible webs overhead, the balsamic night scent of the pines carried on a breeze just strong enough to cool the skin—and yet Tom struggled to engage with any of it, a stranger at his own feast, almost an impostor, only there because he had somehow managed to cheat his destiny less than twenty-four hours previously. This one thought lodged itself in his head, poisoning the evening for him.

He sought refuge in the duties falling to him now that Paulette was gone, insisting that everyone else stay put while he cleared the plates and went in search of the next course.

He was tossing the green salad in the kitchen when Lucy appeared noiselessly at his shoulder, startling him.

"What's wrong, Tom?"

"What makes you think anything's wrong?"

"Well, for one, the fact that you've just answered a question with a question."

"Nothing's wrong."

She looked unconvinced but didn't pursue it. "Give me something to do."

"You can grab the cheeses from the larder."

He was cutting bread when she returned with the rough wooden platter that Paulette had already loaded with an array of cheeses.

"Why isn't she here?" Lucy asked.

"Who?"

"Yvette or Sophie or whatever she's called—the mystery lady of Hyères."

"Hélène."

"Hélène. And does she have a face to launch a thousand ships?"

"A good few hundred, maybe."

Lucy smiled. "So, tell me . . . tall or short? Fat or thin? Dark or fair?"

"She's not quite as tall as you, not quite as thin as you and not quite as dark as you."

"God, I hate her already. When can I meet her and scratch her eyes out?"

"You have nothing to be jealous of. One day men will sack cities for you too."

"Don't think you can deflect me with flattery. Tell me about her. Why won't you share her with us?"

"She's very private. She's also in Greece."

This wasn't quite true; Hélène had returned from her travels a few days ago.

"With one of her other admirers?" Lucy probed.

"Possibly. I don't know."

"You didn't think to ask?"

He hesitated before replying. "She lost eight years to a violent and controlling husband." It made her sound like a victim, and that's the last thing Hélène was. "She's learning to live again, enjoying her freedom."

"I think I get the picture—a footloose divorcée, like Norma Shearer in that film."

"More of a merry widow. Her husband had the good manners to die rich and well before his time."

"Are there children?"

"No."

"Will there ever be?"

"If you're fishing for her age, she's twenty-nine."

"What's *cradle snatcher* in French?"

He laughed. "I'm not sure. But *petite effrontée* means 'insolent little girl.' "

Lucy gave a sharp, theatrical intake of breath.

They were standing across from each other at the big pine table in the middle of the kitchen, the one Paulette kept scrubbed as white as paper.

"So, are we done?" he asked. "Is the interrogation over?"

"Not quite. How did you meet her?"

"Through Benoît and Chantal."

A subtle piece of matchmaking, he explained, which had taken place on neutral ground at a party thrown by Charles and Marie-Laure de Noailles at their extraordinary modernist villa high on the hill above Hyères. There had been something wild and reckless in the air that night, stirred up by Salvador Dalí and his coterie of fawning acolytes. A fair number of the women present had looked more like men, dressed in suits and sturdy shoes. Fortunately, Hélène hadn't been one of them.

He described to Lucy his first glimpse of her, carmine-lipped and raven-haired, playing miniature golf in the twilit garden below the cuboid concrete house, putter in one hand, slender flute of Champagne in the other. She had been wearing a long bias-cut evening gown with an open V-back descending to a large bow, which sat invitingly at the base of her spine, clamoring to be undone. She was, she had confessed to him later that evening, exactly the sort of person whom the Spanish prankster and his disciples were looking to shake out of her bourgeois stupor, and together they had smirked and sneered at the studied eccentricity of the occasion, its forced bacchanalian air.

He didn't tell Lucy that they had then left the party early, strolling down the hill to Hélène's house in the old town, where they had stripped each other bare in her living room and made love on the Aubusson rug beside the grand piano. Nor did he detail the two days and two nights he had spent holed up in Hélène's bedroom, hardly moving from the huge four-poster hung with citron brocade; or how, on Sunday evening, when he had climbed back up the steep incline to recover his car from the driveway of Villa de Noailles, he had fully expected Dalí to pop out from behind a bush, jeering and laughing triumphantly at him like some deranged, mustachioed satyr.

"Satisfied?" he asked.

"For now," replied Lucy. "I'm holding back a couple of questions to prolong your agony."

"I don't mind talking about her with you."

"Yes you do."

She was gone before he could reply, turning on her heel and leaving with the platter.

Tom had decanted three bottles of 1920 Cheval Blanc to go with the cheese. Faithful to tradition, whenever they drank one of the wines from the fine cellar that had come with the house a toast was raised to Monsieur Montalivet.

"Who is Monsieur Montalivet?" asked Klaus.

"Was," replied Barnaby. "The poor fool who built this sorry pile."

Tom was more helpful, explaining that Montalivet was the Parisian banker who had bought the land, erected the villa and laid out its gardens. On losing everything in the financial crash of 1929, he had done the ignoble thing and hanged himself from a banister riser in the entrance hall, leaving a wife and three children to tough it out on their own.

Barnaby turned to Ilse. "There's a theory that he didn't really commit suicide but was done in by irate creditors."

"Like most of Barnaby's theories, there's not one shred of evidence to back it up," Venetia clarified.

"Call it intuition," said Barnaby.

"I prefer to call it journalism," retorted Venetia.

Ilse bristled. "I am also a journalist."

"I know, my dear, and it's a pleasure to meet a real one."

"I surrender," said Barnaby, crossing his wrists in front of him. "Lash my hands with rope."

"Never speak of rope in the house of the hanged."

This was Leonard's first contribution for a while, and it drew a hearty chuckle from Walter.

"It's an old Foreign Office expression," Leonard explained.

"Meaning?" Walter asked.

"Tact and discretion at all times. Not two of Barnaby's strongest suits."

"How can you say that? I never breathed a word to anyone when I saw you rolling drunk at the St. James's Club last month."

Ilse clapped her hands together, delighted by the comeback. "Very good," she said. "Very good." When Barnaby beamed at her, Tom recognized the glint in his friend's eye—that of a predator closing in on its supper.

After some senseless chatter about the King's Jubilee, the exact nature of Lady Ashley's role in the divorce suit brought against Douglas

Fairbanks by Mary Pickford, and the recent infestation of rats at the Royal Opera House, the talk turned—as it was no doubt doing all over Europe—to the possibility of another war.

The table was divided among those who thought it inevitable, those who thought it highly unlikely, and Venetia, who opined drily that it wouldn't even be an issue if there were more women as heads of state.

"You mean like Catherine the Great of Russia, who went to war with the Ottoman Empire and annexed the Crimea by force?"

Venetia's eyes narrowed at this challenge from Lucy, but she decided against a public spat with her daughter, turning instead to Leonard and saying, "I told you we should never have let her study history at Oxford."

Barnaby had gone with the views of his employer at the *Evening Standard*, Lord Beaverbrook, who felt that Chancellor Hitler was no longer a man to be trusted, now that he'd started rearming the country. "Although I'm thinking of popping over to Nuremberg in September to see for myself what all the fuss is about."

"Why on earth would you want to do that?" Tom asked.

"Because Unity Mitford is such a pretty thing," quipped Venetia.

"That foolish girl and her silly sister," muttered Leonard.

"Actually, it wasn't Unity's idea. Old Sigismundo, the press attaché at the German Embassy, invited me—all expenses paid, with a trip to Karlsbad thrown in."

Ilse spat something incomprehensible to her brother in German before rounding on Barnaby. "If you go to the Parteitag I will never forgive you."

It was good to see Barnaby rendered speechless for once, weighing the pleasing prospect of a roll in the hay against a free holiday.

"Hitler has started to kill his political enemies," Ilse went on. "Do you think he will stop with them? No. This is just the beginning."

"It is the same in Russia," said Fanya. "Everyone knows Stalin was behind the murder of Sergei Kirov."

"And that monster has killed sixty more of the Central Committee this year," added Yevgeny.

This was news to most of them, but Leonard confirmed that there did indeed appear to be some truth in the rumors leaking out of Soviet

Russia about Stalin's ruthless purge of his opponents within the Party following Kirov's murder.

"My God," said Barnaby. "Do you think the Webbs know?"

"Sidney and Beatrice Webb, like most English intellectuals, are quite divorced from reality. One closely guided tour of the Soviet Union with lots of smiling workers on show and they're running around saying they've seen the future of Civilization."

It was one of Leonard's bugbears: the myopic zealotry of some of the country's ablest minds. Yes, capitalism had been dealt a blow by the financial crisis of 1929, but to blindly lunge for answers in the tyrannies of left and right was little short of madness. Did democracy and freedom count for nothing when set against totalitarian regimes that were revealing themselves to be increasingly homicidal? We were infected with a morbid anxiety—how could we not be when newspapers like Barnaby's had spent the past five years telling us we were all going to hell in a handcart?—but it behooved us to look beyond this collective malaise to the bigger picture; we owed it to ourselves to keep things in perspective.

It was a subject on which Leonard could work himself into quite a lather, but he held himself in check on this occasion, curious to hear from Klaus and Ilse what was really going on in Germany. "Surely the German people don't want another war."

"Read Klaus's book," replied Ilse. "The German people are sick and they are weak. They will go where they are told to go."

Klaus was keen to point out that he couldn't speak for all Germans, but he knew Bavaria well. He and Ilse had been brought up in the mountains south of Munich, near Oberammergau, and he talked with engaging frankness about the hardworking, generous and happy folk of that region, of their fondness for apple wine, their kindness to strangers and their love of children and animals. He offered a touching little tale by way of illustration. Two winters back, when the harsh mountain weather had come early, catching out the late migrating birds, the local people had collected together thousands upon thousands of shivering, weary swallows doomed to die, transporting them in wooden crates to

Munich and paying for them to be flown by airplane across the Tirol to Venice, from where they could continue their journey south to Africa.

His point was this: they were good people, and like good people everywhere, they had fought bravely in wars with almost no understanding of why they were required to slay their fellow man. Their greatest strength was their *Pflichtgefühl*—which Ilse translated for their benefit as "sense of duty"—but it was also their greatest weakness, if hijacked by another.

"Were you in Munich last year," Leonard inquired, "when Hitler had Ernst Röhm and the others rounded up and killed?"

Klaus nodded grimly.

"I would very much like to discuss it with you at more length . . . although now is possibly not the time."

"Now is *definitely* not the time," put in Venetia. "All this talk of dictators and impending war and murder is not only deeply depressing, it's playing havoc with my appetite."

"It is the world we live in," pronounced Yevgeny.

"Is that so? Then what, may I ask, is this?" replied Venetia tersely, spreading her arms to embrace their surroundings. "Is this not life too? A perfect Mediterranean night, a sky sown with stars, delicious cheese and excellent wine laid on by a charming host whom we all love. Does none of this count for anything?"

She was maybe a glass or two off slurring her words, which meant anything could happen. As it was, she raised her wineglass.

"To poor Monsieur Montalivet—victim of the modern age—thank you for the claret you laid down, the terrace you built, the view you cherished. Something tells me that others will one day be sitting here enjoying just the same things long after we are gone and the likes of Chancellor Hitler and his thugs are moldering in their miserable graves."

"Bravo," called Chantal from the far end of the table.

"I'd vote for you," seconded Barnaby. "In fact, I think you should consider standing in the next general election. Baldwin's sure to call one soon."

"And what shall we name our new party?"

"I propose the Ostrich party," suggested Leonard drily.

Venetia turned to him. "My dear, we may have our heads buried in the sand . . ."

"But at least our arses are in the air," chipped in Barnaby.

Walter gave a loud laugh. "Now that's what I call a political slogan!"

10

Tom fought the urge to count the bullets in the Beretta yet again. God only knew how many times he'd removed the pistol's magazine in the past couple of hours, but it was definitely becoming a nervous habit. Best to master it now. Unchecked, it was the sort of thing that could play havoc with your head, like endlessly glancing at the clock on the mantelpiece.

Twenty-two minutes past three.

Less than three hours until sunrise, although it would be light long before then. The first rose glimmer of dawn was probably staining the eastern horizon right now.

It struck him that he was like that poor fool Harker in Bram Stoker's *Dracula,* praying for the new day and the safety it would bring. As if on cue, he felt a sharp prick on his forearm and slapped the mosquito away in a smear of blood.

Maybe he could permit himself forty winks on the divan. The study was secure, the windows shuttered and barred, both doors locked and bolted. He had even jammed chairs under their handles.

The evening had been a ringing success, certainly if the number of empty wine bottles now standing on the kitchen table was anything to go by. True to form, Barnaby had wanted to stretch the night out as long as possible over a bottle of whiskey once all the guests had left, but Tom had pleaded exhaustion after a token glass of single malt, going through the motions of taking himself off to bed, only to creep back downstairs again once the deep rattle of Barnaby's snoring had begun to reverberate through the upstairs corridors.

He had attempted to work, spreading his books and papers out on the desk, only to stare blankly at them, his pinching eyes heavy for sleep. Two hours later, intoxicated with fatigue, he now found himself pacing the room, his thoughts twisting themselves into dark and demonic shapes.

Dinner had taken on the guise of the Last Supper, and seated somewhere at the table on the terrace was his own private Judas. He was more convinced than ever that the Italian had been briefed as to the layout of the villa, which meant that he had been betrayed by someone close to him. Which one of them, though? The distorting glass of suspicion made it possible to construct a case, however improbable, for everyone who'd been present that evening—all except Lucy. He didn't even attempt to pull her into the pattern.

There was definitely something coming off Leonard, though; there had been all day. Tom had worked with him long enough to know that he was holding something back. What, though? And why wasn't he willing to share it?

He struggled with Klaus and Ilse, but even they could be made to fit the mold. It wasn't the first time they had visited the villa; he had invited them for dinner with Yevgeny and Fanya two weeks ago, and on that occasion they'd shown themselves very eager to be given a thorough tour of the house. Too eager? What did he know of them? What did anyone really know of them? They had materialized from nowhere with a convincing tale of hardship and woe, but with no one to vouch for them. Were they even brother and sister? There was no obvious physical resemblance. Ilse was almost as tall as Klaus, and as blond as he was dark.

"Pull yourself together, man," he said suddenly.

He stopped his pacing, lit yet another cigarette and dropped onto the divan.

He had to keep a grip. The nighttime could have this effect on him, inflating his bleakest thoughts until they pressed against his skull.

Things would take on their true proportion come daybreak; they always did.

All he had to do was stay awake for another hour or two.

The bell was attached to a large metal buoy streaked with rust that dipped and curtseyed on a choppy sea.

Tom was alone in a rowing boat, naked from the waist down, wrestling with the oars. Seawater lapped around his ankles, and high overhead gulls wheeled on stirless wings against a windy sky of cerulean blue flecked with cotton-wool clouds. The birds seemed to be circling directly above him, tracking his slow progress toward the buoy.

The bell fell strangely silent, although a quick glance over his shoulder confirmed that the buoy was still rocking wildly.

How was that possible?

Aware that he was shipping water and sinking fast, he pulled harder on the oars, but he might just as well have been rowing through treacle for all the good it seemed to do him.

Desperate, he looked toward the distant coastline with its familiar landmarks, calculating his chances of swimming for shore and dismissing it as an option almost immediately. The buoy was his only hope. And only now did he realize what it was doing there. It marked the exact spot where he had put the Italian over the side of the dinghy.

He could hear the bell again, no longer tolling to guide him in, but to warn him off . . .

Tom snapped awake, sitting bolt upright, wild-eyed.

The doorbell.

And another noise: the Beretta clattering to the floor.

He stared at it, getting his bearings.

He had fallen asleep on the divan, the gun on his lap, and, judging by the sunlight leaking through the cracks in the shutters, he'd been under for quite a while. Almost six hours, according to the clock on the mantelpiece. That couldn't be right!

He stood up, recovering the pistol from the floor. He wasn't expecting anyone, but neither did assassins tend to present themselves in daylight at one's front door. He slipped the weapon out of sight behind a cushion.

A pair of buttocks, white and hairless, confronted him in the entrance hall.

Barnaby, quite naked except for a hand towel clutched modestly to his privates, was reaching for the handle of the front door.

"Barnaby, don't—" Tom called, too late.

Barnaby pulled open the door. "*Bonjour,*" he growled.

"*Bonjour, monsieur,*" came back a male voice. "*Est-ce que Monsieur Nash est là?*"

"He most certainly is. In fact he's right *là,*" replied Barnaby, turning and pointing. "I'm going back to bed," he mumbled to Tom as he shuffled off toward the staircase. "Don't wake me."

Standing on the threshold against the glare of the sun was a small cock-robin of a man, barrel-chested and besuited. What remained of his hair was artistically heaped over his florid cranium.

"May I help you?" Tom asked in French.

"Commissaire Roche, from Le Lavandou."

Not just any old policeman, the commissaire, the top dog—strange enough in itself, but even stranger that he was alone.

"I wonder if I might beg a few minutes of your time."

The words had a ring of bogus cordiality about them.

"What's it concerning?" asked Tom.

"It shouldn't take long."

Tom stepped aside. "Of course. Please . . . come in."

"Thank you."

Closing the door, Tom saw his general dishevelment reflected back at him in the commissaire's quick, appraising glance: the sleep-tousled hair, the creased clothes and probably a creased face to go with it.

"Forgive me—I was working late and fell asleep at my desk."

"I hear you're an author."

"That's right."

"Do you mind if we stick with French? My English is lamentable."

"As you wish," said Tom.

He led Commissaire Roche through to the drawing room, pulling open a couple of the French windows that gave onto the terrace. Sunlight slanted into the room, splashing the yellow Samarkand rug.

"You have a beautiful home," said Roche. "I'm obviously in the wrong job."

"May I offer you a coffee?"

He needed time to think, to gather his wits about him. He also needed his morning dose of caffeine if he was going to get through this.

"Thank you. I had an early start this morning."

"Make yourself at home. I won't be long."

Commissaire Roche took him at his word. When Tom returned from the kitchen with the tray, he found the door to his study open and Roche making a lazy tour of the room. Tom cursed himself. The back of the chair was still jammed under the handle of the door leading to the dining room. It was unlikely that this detail had escaped the scrutiny of the commissaire's alert little eyes, with their curious birdlike blink.

"You have a lot of books. Have you read them all?"

"Most. Some of them are for show."

Roche laughed. "I like that. Honesty's a good quality in a man," he added with a slight barb.

"Shall we . . . ?" suggested Tom.

Tom was pouring the coffee in the drawing room when the commissaire revealed the purpose of his visit. "I'm investigating a missing-persons case."

"Oh?"

"An Italian gentleman who's staying at the Hôtel de la Réserve. That's to say, he was, until the night before last, when he disappeared suddenly."

This is what Tom had been expecting, and he was prepared. "I was at La Réserve only yesterday."

"Yes, I know—for breakfast."

"That's right."

"And how often do you take your breakfast there, Mr. Nash?"

It was clear from the casual nature of the question that he already knew the answer.

"Rarely," Tom replied.

Roche made a show of pulling a black notebook from the leather folder he was carrying, along with a gold drop-pencil. "Rarely," he repeated slowly, writing it down. Then, looking up: "How rarely?"

"I'm not sure. Three or four times a year."

"Three or four?" Roche threw in an apologetic smile. "Forgive me, I'm a very meticulous man—infuriatingly so, my wife would say."

"Three."

Roche wrote it down. "And why did you choose yesterday of all days to have breakfast there?"

Tom repeated the story he had fabricated for Olivier, the manager at La Réserve: that for the next few weeks he was going to be run off his feet looking after houseguests, and he needed a quiet moment alone.

"The gentleman who just answered the door seemed quite capable of looking after himself."

"I'm sorry—I don't understand your meaning."

"No meaning intended. A simple observation. When did he arrive, the naked man?"

You're right, thought Tom, *you are in the wrong job. There are interrogators at the SIS who could learn a trick or two from you.*

"Yesterday evening."

Commissaire Roche wrote it down. Commissaire Roche wrote everything down as he continued to niggle and probe, demanding to know Tom's every move from the moment he had arrived at the hotel.

It didn't make sense. Roche was handling him with a conviction and surety of purpose far beyond any knowledge he could possibly possess. Either he was a genius or he was holding back a trump. As the conversation wore on, Tom began to fear that both were true.

The answer came a short while later, with the trilling of the telephone.

"Do you mind?" Tom asked.

"Please . . ."

Tom made for the console table beside the baby grand and picked up the receiver. "Villa Martel."

"Tom, it's me." It was Olivier, and he sounded agitated. "Is Commissaire Roche with you?"

"Good morning, Leonard," Tom replied in English.

"I thought so. He was here at the hotel asking all kinds of questions about you and the Italian guest who's gone missing. His colleague's still here. I managed to slip away."

"Yes, it was a most enjoyable evening," said Tom.

"Look, I don't know what's going on, but they have a photo of you."

A photo? What photo?

"No, I've only just got up," said Tom.

"I just wanted to warn you."

"Can I call you back? I have the police here right now. . . . That's right. . . . I don't know—I think they suspect I killed one of the guests down at La Réserve." He gave a little chuckle for effect. "I know—I should have covered my tracks more carefully."

"I'd better go," said Olivier, confused by the charade being played out in English at the other end of the line.

"Okay, I'll see you down at the beach later—assuming, of course, that I'm not in jail."

He hung up and turned to Commissaire Roche. "I'm sorry. Where were we?"

As Tom suspected, Roche had not only been listening in on the conversation, he had understood every word of it.

"I'm not accusing you of murder, Mr. Nash."

Tom deposited himself back in the armchair. "I'm pleased to hear it."

"How could I possibly accuse you of murder when there is no body, no weapon and no sign of any struggle?"

"Absolutely."

"I'm just doing my job, gathering together as many facts as possible about Signor Minguzzi, if that indeed is his real name."

"I understand, but I'm still not sure where I fit in."

"I believe Signor Minguzzi's name came up in conversation between you and Monsieur Perret, the hotel manager, while you were having your breakfast on the terrace."

"Did it?"

"That, at least, is what Monsieur Perret told me." Roche flicked back through his notebook, searching for the scribbled entry. "Yes, here it is."

"Now I think of it, Olivier did mention an Italian who had taken an interest in one of the female guests. She was Swiss, I think."

"She still is," joked Roche awkwardly. "Frau Wissmann is her name."

"If you say so."

"She passed by your table when you were talking to Monsieur Perret."

"I remember seeing her—an attractive woman."

"And do you also remember saying to Monsieur Perret that you thought you might have seen Signor Minguzzi driving about the place in his car?"

Christ, Roche had drained every drop from poor Olivier.

"It turned out I was wrong. It must have been another Italian-looking gentleman. Olivier said this . . . Minguzzi . . . arrived by train."

"So, as far as you know, you have never set eyes on Signor Minguzzi."

"No. Never."

Roche sat back in his armchair, scrutinizing Tom. "You intrigue me, Mr. Nash. Either you're very patient for putting up with my tedious questions or you're hiding something from me. I can't decide which it is."

He was right; Tom had mishandled the situation. An innocent man would have shown more indignation at this unwarranted intrusion into his life.

"I'm not hiding anything from you, Commissaire Roche."

"So how, then, do you explain this?"

Roche reached into the leather folder and removed a black-and-white photograph, which he then laid on the low table between them.

It was a photograph of Tom, in profile, seated somewhere outdoors on a sunny day. He was smiling and there was a cigarette smoldering between his lips.

"It's me," he said pointlessly, while desperately trying to place the image.

"It was hidden in the lining of Signor Minguzzi's suitcase."

Tom was furious with himself for having missed it when he searched the Italian's room, but even more angry with Minguzzi for his sheer bloody amateurishness.

"His suitcase? How is that possible?"

"How indeed?"

"It doesn't make sense."

"Nevertheless, there is an explanation—there has to be. It's simply a question of wheedling it out." Roche paused. "Maybe you have an idea of when and where the photograph was taken, and even by whom."

Tom shook his head, but it was coming to him now, coming on a chill, chill wind.

"I would say it's fairly recent, wouldn't you?" prompted Roche.

"Yes, but not this year."

"Oh . . . ?"

"The shirt I'm wearing, I tore it last September and threw it out," Tom lied.

"Last summer, then?" suggested Roche.

"It's possible. But I couldn't tell you where it was taken, or who took it."

"It's a pity the background's out of focus."

If the background was out of focus it was only because the photographer had known exactly what he was doing, narrowing the depth of field to blur out everything other than his intended subject. It was the work of a gifted photographer, a professional, and this was enough to confirm Tom's building suspicion.

He wanted to be mistaken, but he knew he wasn't. He remembered the day vividly—a glorious Saturday back in May.

"I'm sorry I can't be of more help," said Tom, handing over the photograph.

Roche hesitated, skewering him with a look before taking it off him and slipping it into the folder. "Well, thank you for your time," he said, getting to his feet.

Tom accompanied the commissaire to his car.

"I'm sure it'll all become clear once Signor Minguzzi reappears."

Roche stopped and turned. "Something tells me he's not going to. You see, he left everything behind, including a considerable sum of cash."

"Strange."

"Indeed, but I'm sure we'll get to the bottom of it. There's nothing I like better than a good conundrum."

I can believe it, thought Tom, extending his hand. Roche's grip was firm and he seemed reluctant to let go at first, almost as if the physical contact offered him some pathway to Tom's most private thoughts.

"I'll keep you abreast of any developments."

"Thank you—I'd appreciate it."

The moment the black sedan had disappeared down the driveway, Tom made for the terrace and smoked a cigarette, pacing, replaying the encounter in his head, totting up the errors he'd made.

Commissaire Roche had him in his sights—that much was certain—but unless the Italian's body came bobbing to the surface, the investigation was doomed to peter out through lack of physical evidence. It was the only consolation to draw from this unexpected turn of events. The rest was almost too depressing to think about.

That one photograph had changed everything.

It told him that his instinct had been correct. No one was to be trusted, not even Leonard.

And certainly not Yevgeny and Fanya.

He took the Beretta with him, wrapped up in a towel, which he tucked away between the rocks at the water's edge.

His morning swim was an institution, a chance to clear his head and order his thoughts before going to work. Today, it served a far greater purpose than simply priming him for a morning at the typewriter. He needed a plan; he needed to figure out some device for drawing the enemy into the open. Pleasingly, he had settled on a course of action by the time he stepped from the water.

He spread-eagled himself on a flat rock at the base of the bluff and played the stratagem through in his head, testing it, challenging it. Things would move quickly once he'd set it in motion, and he found his thoughts turning to Hélène. If he didn't search her out soon he might not get another chance to for a while. Worse still, he might *never* get another chance to.

If only he could just disappear with her, vanish to some far-flung corner of the country, as they often did. Food had always been a determining factor in their jaunts around France. The last had been back in the spring, to the Charente-Inférieure, in search of oysters. They had taken a small villa at Ronce-les-Bains, and when not making love or gorging themselves on shellfish they had cycled through the pine forests south of the town to a deserted, dune-backed beach that ran straight as a plumb line for six miles or more, and there they had frolicked naked in the wild Atlantic surf, the undertow plucking at their heels like the hands of the sea people.

These trips away had never been conceived as building blocks to something more lasting and meaningful. Rather, they were momentary explosions of indulgence, of sexual abandon, played out in some quiet backwater, anonymously, far from the eyes of their friends back home. He knew there were other men in Hélène's life, just as she was aware that he didn't always sleep alone when he stayed at his apartment in Paris. This was the unspoken understanding that had always existed between them, so why did he now find himself calling into question the terms of their tacit agreement?

Maybe Lucy was to blame. With her probing inquiries and her thinly veiled expression of disapproval, she had held a mirror up to his face and demanded that he take a long, hard look. Had the challenge come from anyone else—Barnaby, say—he would have fought back. Lucy was another matter altogether.

No, he would call Hélène and arrange to see her while he still could.

* * *

He returned to the villa to find Paulette doing battle in the kitchen with the detritus of dinner while Barnaby bounced around her, waiting for the coffee to come to the boil.

"Who was the dwarf in the suit?" Barnaby asked, meaning Commissaire Roche.

"A neighbor. It's an old boundary dispute—the joys of country life."

"Don't knock it. I've decided to shake the city dust from my feet and go rustic, like you."

Tom laughed; it was a ridiculous notion.

"It's true," bleated Barnaby. "It came to me in the bath just now."

"Had you taken one of your pick-me-ups from Heppell's?"

Heppell's was the chemists' in Piccadilly where Barnaby went in search of substances to regulate his moods.

"Annoyingly, Old Man Heppell has become rather snooty about what he's happy to dispense me. No, this was the real thing: a genuine epiphany."

"In a bathtub?"

"I'd take a bathtub over a dusty road to Damascus any day."

Barnaby wasn't joking. The moment Paulette shooed them from the kitchen to the terrace, he was quick to elaborate further.

It began with the usual litany of misery: finances in a hopeless tangle . . . down to absolute bedrock . . . a welter of debts and threats of legal proceedings . . . creditors dunning him from all quarters . . . some bank or other calling up his overdraft . . . prostituting his talents as a hack journalist . . . going off the deep end with drink.

For once, though, this cold shower of self-reproach wasn't a prelude to an appeal for yet another handout from Tom. Barnaby was resolved to turn things around by himself.

"I don't want to end up as a cautionary tale, Tommy."

He only ever called Tom "Tommy" when he was speaking from the heart, when he wished to be taken seriously. It was an old code of theirs, reaching back to boyhood.

"So, you've decided to go rustic?"

"That's right—'a God-wotter in a lovesome thing, rose plot, fern'd grot, whatnot'—as the poet says. It worked for you, didn't it? Obviously,

I couldn't afford anywhere as grand as this; I don't have a wealthy great-aunt eager to assuage her guilt by settling a vast inheritance on me."

"It wasn't quite like that."

"It was close enough," said Barnaby. "No, my shoebox in Hangover Terrace is mortgaged to the hilt, but if I put it on the market I'll have just about enough to rent a place out of town for a year or two, along with a bit of juggling money. I'm thinking Henley—a damp little cottage with an overgrown garden and horny-handed country folk for neighbors."

"Somehow, I can't see you with horny-handed country folk."

"You think I can? I despise horny-handed country folk. That's the point."

"You're losing me."

"I'm going to write a book about it."

"About how much you despise them?"

"Of course not. I'll paint them as engagingly eccentric and bursting with uncommon wisdoms."

"'When the cuckoo comes to a bare thorn, Sell your cow and buy your corn; But if she sits on a green bough, Sell your corn and buy your cow.'"

"Exactly! Complete and utter nonsense, but it sounds likes centuries of wisdom distilled down to a few lines. A city readership will lap it up."

It wasn't a bad idea, not bad at all.

"Got any more like that?" asked Barnaby.

"'A moon early seen, seldom seen.'"

Barnaby chuckled delightedly. "Of course you do—a Norfolk lad from the back of beyond. I'll give you a shilling for each and every one of them."

"And where are you going to pitch yourself in this paean to a lost age?"

"As a hopeless but entertaining scoundrel who finds himself slowly seduced by the pastoral idyll. It'll be a life of unspeakable drudgery, of course, but unsophistication is now the ultra-sophisticated thing. The duller we are, the more amusing we are. I might even get myself a dog—yes, an old bull terrier bitch who hates grass snakes. That's got to be good for a chapter or two. And—who knows—maybe I'll even find myself a girl, some rosy-cheeked wench with honest peasant buttocks who skins rabbits in her spare time."

Tom laughed. "You know, I think you might be onto something."

"Really?"

"Absolutely. It's very timely. Throw in a bit of local history, the more macabre the better—ghosts, highwaymen swinging from gibbets, that sort of thing—and maybe a few seasonal recipes—"

"—learned at the elbow of some toothless old crone."

"You're getting the idea."

"*My* idea," said Barnaby, with emphasis.

"If you're not in Henley by October, it's up for grabs."

"I'll be there."

There was something in Barnaby's voice that suggested this particular fantasy might actually come to life.

"Humor's the key," suggested Tom.

"You managed to be mildly amusing about the Wailing Wall in your last book. I'm sure I can do the same for inglenook fireplaces that don't draw properly and—I don't know—badgers digging up my vegetables."

"Is that what badgers do?"

"Believe me, those bloody badgers will do whatever the hell I tell them to do."

Tom laughed. "There's only one problem."

"What's that?"

"When the first book flies off the shelves, you're going to have to stay on in Henley and write another."

"Oh, fuck," said Barnaby. "I hadn't thought of that."

11

Lucy had fully expected to find Leonard banished by Mother to one of the other bedrooms for the night, but as she made her way downstairs for breakfast she could hear the two of them giggling like naughty children in their bathroom. These sounds of merriment were accompanied by the splashing of bathwater, which brought to mind an image hard to stomach at such an early hour.

The seeds of the argument had been sown during the walk back from dinner at Tom's, when Mother had stumbled in the darkness, falling and grazing her knee. Quite reasonably, Leonard had suggested that it was a little unfair of her to curse the uneven pathway, given the amount of alcohol she had consumed over dinner.

"You're a fine one to talk," Mother had retorted. "Was it three or four Poire Williams you put down at the end there?"

"It's important to cleanse the palate before bed."

"Bugger, I think I'm bleeding."

"Mother, language."

"Oh, don't you go playing little Miss Prissy with me. I saw the way you were carrying on with Walter. That poor boy—he'll probably have nightmares."

"Nightmares?"

"About wild-eyed harpies holding him captive."

"Yes, the poor boy," said Leonard ruefully.

"That might be more amusing if it wasn't so predictable."

It had been one of Mother's more benign argumentative moods, but that had all changed the moment they arrived at the house. Leonard was held to blame for the fact that the tincture of iodine hadn't traveled with them from London, and then castigated for his heavy-handed nursing skills while crouched at her feet with an enamel bowl of water and a roll of cotton.

"Surely they taught you how to clean and dress a wound in the army?"

"Wounds, yes. We spent less time on scratches." His wry smile was intended for Lucy.

"Why on earth are you smirking at her?"

"Okay," said Lucy, "that's it. I'm going to bed."

"Traitor," mumbled Leonard.

She left him there in the drawing room, kneeling before his wife like some elderly vassal paying homage to a feudal lord.

Lucy was brushing her teeth when she heard the piercing scream. Worried that Mother had finally pushed Leonard too far, she hurried naked to the head of the stairs, straining to hear the voices rising up from below through the darkness.

The scream, it turned out, had been brought on by the liberal application of Chanel No. 5 to the graze.

"You enjoyed that, didn't you?" Mother snapped accusingly.

"Well, I had to put something on it."

"Why stop with scent? You'll find a bottle of bleach in the cupboard under the kitchen sink."

"Venetia, please . . . I don't want to have a fight. I want to go to sleep."

Mother was having none of it, though. That scream had cleared her lungs; they were ready for action.

"Tired, are you?"

"A little," Leonard replied.

"A heavy night, was it?"

"Excuse me?"

"You can't have forgotten so soon. Last night . . . in Cannes . . . with your good friend Yevgeny."

"Not especially heavy."

"So where were you when I called your hotel room just before midnight?"

"Playing billiards, I believe, downstairs."

"And at one o'clock in the morning? Still playing billiards, were we?"

"The reception doesn't put calls through to the rooms after midnight."

"Oh, you checked, did you? That's very telling."

She was like a dog with a bone; she wasn't going to release it until she'd picked it bare. First she accused him and Yevgeny of taking themselves off to some sordid little bordello, to which Leonard replied that she couldn't be more mistaken; it had been a large and rather upmarket bordello.

"I knew it!" Mother declared.

"I'm joking."

"Well, I'm not. The two of you were up to something. Did you even see a golf ball during your time there?"

"Oh, for goodness' sake, Venetia!"

"You've shipped her in, haven't you? Your little hussy—set her up in an apartment in Cannes."

A puzzling silence stretched out, and for a moment it seemed to Lucy that Leonard might actually be about to say yes. He didn't, although what he did say was no less shocking.

"I gave you my word I would never see her again, and I haven't."

"Unfortunately, I remember you giving me your word that you weren't having an affair with that slattern when in fact you were."

"I thought we were over this."

"Did she bring one of her floozy friends along for Yevgeny? Is that what happened? Is that why you're so bloody tired?"

Lucy's legs had grown suddenly and strangely numb, and she crept unsteadily back to her room on them, flopping onto the bed and clutching a pillow to her midriff.

While the row rumbled on downstairs, she tried to make sense of what she had just overheard. Leonard had had an affair with another woman, so why didn't she feel more anger toward him? The pain in

Mother's words had been palpable, a living thing buried beneath the bile, so why was she unable to muster more sympathy for her? She struggled to feel anything. Even the suspicion that life as she knew it was over lacked any real sting.

She could no longer look on Leonard as a long-suffering saint; he was also a sinner. Mother didn't just dish it out; she also had her own cross to bear. Lucy's world hadn't fallen apart, she realized as she lay there curled in the darkness—it had simply shifted on its axis, revealing another face to her, an alien aspect. There was nothing to fear from it, though. How could there be when she still had Tom, a fixed point in the universe by which to orientate herself?

This was the consoling thought she had carried with her into her dreams, the thought that had then warped itself malignly while she was sleeping into a torrid fantasy, which had seen her wake with a start just before daybreak, hot, breathless and wet.

It wasn't the first time that Tom had made love to her in a dream. She remembered the first time, the confusion and the guilt that had followed, the blame all hers for having led him astray. It hardly qualified as a recurring dream, if only because the circumstances were always different, but it had caught her out enough times for the shame to have given way to a sort of bemused acceptance of their secret nocturnal trysts.

Last night had been different, though. She had not been relieved to wake from the dream; she had tried to will herself back into his arms, his bed, and when that failed, she had slid her fingers between her thighs and she had finished what they had started together. Afterward, she had fallen into a deep and peaceful slumber, waking several hours later, not at all ashamed of what she had done, but with a satisfying glow still in her belly and a lazy smile on her lips.

Something had changed in her, and she suspected that in some convoluted fashion it had to do with the knowledge she now carried within her. Why else was she feeling so defiant, so empowered? It could only be because she saw Mother and Leonard's relationship in a new light: a flawed and faintly ridiculous pairing of two quite different people, unsuited to each other in so many ways, almost a generation apart in age.

So what if she had indulged in a little private fantasy? She and Tom were not only closer in age, they were closer in almost every other way too.

What she didn't anticipate, when Mother and Leonard finally tripped downstairs to breakfast, was how well disposed she felt toward them. Mother's apology helped.

"Darling, did I make a complete fool of myself last night?"

"Not a complete fool."

"Do you think you can bring yourself to forgive me?" The question was accompanied by a coy little pout.

"What your mother means is: 'Forgive me.'"

"Do I?"

"Yes," replied Leonard firmly.

"Forgive me, darling."

Lucy got up from her chair, wandered around the table to where Mother was seated and wrapped her arms around her from behind. Stooping to kiss her on the neck, she said, "You're forgiven."

"So are you, my darling—for being such a strumpet with Walter."

"Venetia!"

"It was a joke."

If you only knew the truth, thought Lucy.

An almost identical thought passed through her head when she greeted Tom down at the cove.

He and Barnaby were diving off the rocks around to the right, but on spotting them all arriving they both swam ashore, rising from the water onto the sand—one pale, one brown as a Balinese.

"Apologies for the disgustingly white slug flesh," said Barnaby. "Feel free to vomit."

Mother prodded him in the belly. "That wasn't there last year."

"And you won't know it from a washboard by the time I leave."

"Meanwhile, it's good for buoyancy," said Tom.

"Thus speaks the praying mantis," retorted Barnaby.

"I agree," said Mother, spreading out one of the old rugs. "Tom's looking far too thin. Don't you think, Lucy?"

She found herself flummoxed by the question, fearful that her response would somehow betray her. Barnaby came unwittingly to her aid.

"She's hardly the person to ask. Look at her. I assumed she had cancer when I turned up at the tennis club yesterday."

"Actually, I do," Lucy replied quietly, with as much dove-eyed sincerity as she could muster.

Barnaby's jaw almost hit the sand, and he found no comfort in the awkward looks of the others. But as he began to stammer an apology, Leonard caved in, his loud laugh setting everyone else off.

Barnaby leveled a finger at her.

"You, young lady, will pay dearly for that. Before this week is out."

Yevgeny, Fanya and Walter showed up in their sailboat an hour or so later, Yevgeny swimming ashore while Walter rowed Fanya in.

Barnaby was curious to know if Ilse would be joining them.

Yevgeny gave him a slap on the back. "Don't worry—I think she likes you."

Walter passed by with a grin. "Don't worry—I *know* she likes you."

"So where is she, then, this great admirer of mine?"

"Shopping," replied Fanya.

"For new underwear?"

Yevgeny laughed. "For lunch. She and Klaus have invited us all to lunch."

Eight people on the beach meant an obligatory game of volleyball; it was one of the house rules, no excuses allowed. Lucy found herself teamed with Tom, Yevgeny and Fanya—who, like Mother, spent most of her time complaining that the sand was too hot underfoot. Nevertheless, they all made fools of themselves, leaping about the place and working themselves into a sweat before running into the sea to cool off at halftime. The others were leading 8–6 and Yevgeny was all for discussing tactics, but Tom seemed determined to pursue an altogether different conversation.

"Yevgeny, I almost forgot—I spoke to Baptiste earlier. He sends you his best."

"Baptiste?"

"The photographer who stayed with you when you were down briefly back in May."

"You spoke to Baptiste Daumier?"

"A friend of mine in Paris wants some portraits taken of her children. I thought he might be interested."

"I would have thought portraits were beneath Baptiste."

"Well, times must be tough, because he said he was happy for her to call him."

"That's good," said Yevgeny, sinking beneath the water before resurfacing.

"He's a very nice young fellow."

"Yes," concurred Yevgeny. "Yes, he is."

"He reminded me of that day we all spent in Saint-Tropez."

It came across as a strangely pointed statement, because Tom left it hanging so that it required a response from Yevgeny.

"I remember it."

"I'd love to see the photographs sometime—the ones he said he sent you later."

"Yes, of course. I should have brought them from Paris."

"No rush," said Tom. "Although he did say there's a particularly good one of me that I might want to keep."

It was a bizarre exchange, made all the more so by the fact that it took place between two disembodied heads bobbing on the surface of the sea.

"Come on," said Fanya, who had been silently listening in while swimming in circles. "We have a match to win."

They lost it by three points, which gave the victors control of the gramophone for the rest of the morning—another house rule. No one complained. Walter had come armed with the latest discs from America, which his younger brother in New York sent over on an almost weekly basis.

"He's worried about me, thinks I'm falling behind on real culture over here."

Even Mother, whose taste in modern music didn't extend much beyond Lew Stone and Cole Porter, declared, "You know, I think I might be coming round to this American 'swing' thing. What did you say his name was?"

"Benny Goodman."

"A Negro, I assume."

"White as salt, actually."

"Even better," said Yevgeny, looking for a cheap laugh.

He didn't get one from Tom. "I don't understand. Better than what? Better than black?"

There was a distinctly hostile edge to his tone, not something Lucy had ever heard before from him.

"You have to remember that Yevgeny is a *White* Russian," joked Leonard, ever the diplomat, looking to smooth things over.

Tom's eyes remain fastened on Yevgeny. "Yes, that must be it." The words were accompanied by an unconvincing smile.

Yevgeny didn't look shocked by this public challenge from Tom, or even angry. He looked scared.

Walter followed Leonard's lead, swiftly changing the disc on the gramophone, shortening the uncomfortable silence as best he could. "If you like Benny Goodman, wait till you hear him on this."

It was a bouncing little tune, a duet between a clarinet and a piano, but nothing remarkable, not for the first minute. Then the voice kicked in—a female voice, raw and worldly, yet somehow innocent, perfectly suited to the intriguing lyrics, which hold the tale of Emily Brown, an alluring young woman about to blow into some nameless town.

She sang just behind the beat, but in control, almost as if she were teasing the musicians accompanying her. When she fell silent and the band took up again at the end, they played too vigorously, eager to assert themselves, but even they must have known that the battle had already been lost. It was her song and hers alone.

The record ended with a click and scrape.

"We have to hear that again," said Barnaby. "Immediately. Who is she?"

"Her name's Billie Holiday. Hard to believe she's only twenty, just a kid."

As a fellow twenty-year-old, Lucy's instinct was to take issue with this last statement. She decided against it, though, not wishing to sour the mood with yet more friction; the voice had enchanted everyone, banishing the awkward business between Tom and Yevgeny.

They all lay there on the scattering of raffia mats and threadbare Turkish rugs, transfigured by the sun, and listened three more times to the story of the mysterious Miss Emily Brown coming to town, before Leonard requested some Al Bowlly.

It was Tom who reminded Lucy of her promise over dinner to take Walter for a spin in the *Albatross,* and it was Tom who offered to row them out to the sailboat. It seemed almost as though he were trying to get rid of them, to spare the youngsters any more adult nastiness that might be about to unfold. She voiced this suspicion to him while they were dragging the rowboat into the shallows and Walter was gathering together his things.

"Don't be silly," Tom replied brightly. "You're imagining it."

"So what's going on between you and Yevgeny? I didn't imagine that."

"Maybe I've traveled more widely than Yevgeny. Maybe I don't think it's funny to make demeaning jokes about people based on the color of their skin." He held out his hand so that she could steady herself as she climbed into the rowboat. "Would you prefer it if I laughed along with that sort of nonsense?"

"No, of course not," replied Lucy. "But it's not like you to be so . . ."

"Vocal?"

"Aggressive."

Tom glanced over at Walter, who was approaching across the sand, almost within earshot now. "I'm sorry if I upset you," he said quietly. "Next time I'll find a more subtle way to make my point."

*   *   *

Tom helped them rig the *Albatross* before rowing off with a mock salute and a cry of "*Bon route et bon vent.*"

"Where do you want to go?" Lucy asked as the *Albatross* picked up headway.

Walter reached into his pocket and pulled out a tatty cotton sun hat that looked like it had been fought over by two dogs. He tugged it over his unruly locks. "How about the islands?"

"We'll be late for lunch. We might even miss it altogether."

"I've got a hunch there'll be others we won't miss." He leaned back on the bench, elbows on the deck, his long legs stretched out in the cockpit. "Nice ride."

"This is nothing. Wait till the wind picks up in the channel."

"Are you going to let me drive it?"

"You *drive* a motorboat. This is a sailboat."

"Oh."

"I might," said Lucy. "If you promise not to crash it."

Walter threw back his head and laughed.

There were any number of reasons why she loved sailing, but up there near the top of the list was the intimacy of the conversations that seemed to flow so effortlessly while out at sea. Maybe it was the abstraction from quotidian realities, or simply the cry of the elements, but people seemed inclined to a free exchange of confidences—like two strangers thrown together in a train compartment who end up baring their souls to each other.

She and Walter were, after all, little more than strangers. The fate of Lucy's real father certainly hadn't come up as a topic of discussion between them the previous evening, although it soon emerged that Walter knew the story.

"Tom told me," he explained.

"What exactly did he say?"

"Only that he died in France toward the beginning of the war. And that your mother doesn't like to talk about it."

"No, she doesn't. She was very young. I think it almost destroyed her. I mean, it comes up, of course. It can't be avoided. We still own the house where he grew up. Mother wanted to sell it, but Leonard persuaded her not to. We go there in the summer for weekends. It's on the coast, just across from the Isle of Wight—Lymington. It's where I learned to sail. He loved sailing."

She was rambling now, as she often found herself doing when speaking about her father.

"You didn't know him, did you?"

"No, he died just after I was born."

"That must be tough."

"I don't know." Lucy shrugged. "Maybe not as tough as knowing him and then losing him."

"No, I guess not," replied Walter. He stared up at the mast before looking back at her. "I lost two uncles in France—later, of course, toward the end of the war—one to a firing squad, one to influenza. Not very heroic."

"A firing squad?"

"Uncle Freddie turned out to be a coward. At least, that's what they told us at the time. Others came home with a different story. Seems he suffered some kind of nervous collapse under fire. Whatever it was, it was enough to get him shot by his own people."

"That's awful."

"That's war." Walter shrugged. "An officer must set a shining example to the ranks at all times." There was a sardonic edge to his words.

Lucy was seized with a sudden urge to tell him how her father had died. She had never told anyone before, but she was even able to describe the field of battle to him, the lazy rise and fall of the land around the small village near the Belgian border, with its canal and its sturdy little church and its narrow high street fringed with old lime trees. She was able to render the place in such detail because Tom had paid a visit there a few years ago. It had been his gift to her—a secret pilgrimage on her behalf—knowing that the subject was strictly off-limits at home, and suspecting that she might be curious to hear more about the exact circumstances of her father's end.

"Only, I didn't want to hear it, not at first. It was almost a year before I let him tell me."

A sudden German advance had seen the Royal Fusiliers fighting a rearguard action, and her father had been shot four times while firing a machine gun near the swing bridge over the canal. It was the fifth bullet that killed him.

"Tom even found his grave. One day we're going to visit it together."

Walter shifted on the bench. "Your mother should be there too."

"That's never going to happen. She'd murder Tom if she knew what he'd done."

"What he did for you," said Walter with quiet deliberation, "was a wonderful thing."

"He's a wonderful man."

"He is. Even if he doesn't like my paintings," he added with a wry grin.

"He told you that?"

"He didn't have to."

"You were working this morning, weren't you? The paint on your hands . . ."

Walter glanced down at his hands. "Up with the sun. Yevgeny's a tough taskmaster."

But he didn't want to talk about himself, or painting, or even Yevgeny; he nudged the conversation back to Tom. "There's something mysterious about him."

"Mysterious?"

"Don't you think?"

"It's hard for me to judge. For as long as I've known him he's always been coming and going, disappearing off to exotic places. The only difference now is that he does it for himself, his writing, instead of the government."

"Yevgeny says he used to work for Leonard."

"That's right, but they've always been friends, right from the first. He even came to live with us once, when I was very young, soon after Leonard and Mother were married. He's still about the only colleague of Leonard's Mother will have in the house."

"Somehow I can't see it—Tom in an official capacity. I mean, I've hardly ever seen the guy in shoes, let alone a tuxedo."

Lucy smiled. "I don't think embassy life abroad is all dinner parties."

"It is in the trashy novels I read."

"You'll get over the disappointment."

Walter kept up the conversation about Tom with a string of casual questions, which after a while began to feel more and more like an interrogation, as if he were casting about for some secret to which only she held the key. At a certain point, she'd had enough and batted one of his questions straight back at him.

"*You* tell *me*," she insisted. "Why *does* a man suddenly up sticks and move to France?"

"Because he's running from something. Or searching for something. Probably a bit of both."

She wasn't sure if he was speaking of Tom or of himself, so she left him no choice.

"And what are you searching for?"

Walter hesitated. "A better way of life."

"And have you found it?"

"What day is it today? Thursday? Yes. By rights I should be sitting at a desk in the family brokerage firm on Wall Street, wearing pressed trousers, a stiff collar and a suitable necktie. That office is where my life was headed for as long as I can remember. Instead, I'm here—skimming across the waves with a beautiful girl." He paused. "Yes, I think I've found it."

She registered the compliment, but ignored it. "What happened?"

"My father would say that I lost my marbles, or that I fell in with the wrong crowd at Harvard, or that he always knew I didn't have the backbone for 'real' work. But in the end, Mark Twain's to blame."

"The author?"

"He's always been a hero of mine, ever since I was a kid. Then in my sophomore year I read something he wrote, an observation, just a few lines."

"Come on—out with it."

"He said: 'Twenty years from now you will be more disappointed by the things that you didn't do than by the ones you did do. So throw off the bowlines. Sail away from the safe harbor. Catch the trade winds in your sails. Explore. Dream. Discover.'"

"A fitting metaphor, under the circumstances."

He smiled. "It changed everything. Not immediately. But it got lodged in my head. I couldn't shake it off. I saw the rest of my life laid out in front of me, mapped out for me by others. I mean, no one had even bothered to ask me. Not once. Then here was Twain, my hero, telling me that I didn't have to do it, not any of it. And if I didn't do it, I'd be happier for it. Well, he's right—I am. The sun's shining, the wind's in my face, I've got paint on my hands. I'll take those three simple things any day over stocks and shares and bonds."

It was quite a speech, and she wasn't sure how to follow it, so she said, rather inanely, "I can't imagine Wall Street's the place to be right now."

"Don't you believe it. My father made a mint anticipating the Crash. And since the market bottomed out in '32, it's been business as usual for him and his kind. My cousin assures me there's a fortune to be made in defaulted railroad bonds, which seems rather unnecessary, as he already has several fortunes. New York Central's the hot tip, by the way."

"I'll be sure to cable my stockbroker the moment we make landfall."

Walter laughed.

"Here," she said, handing over the tiller and switching places with him. "In the spirit of Mark Twain—explore, dream, discover."

He teased the tiller.

"If you start heading over there," Lucy warned, "you're going to have to come about onto a starboard tack."

"Ready about."

"*Ready,*" she replied. "Just remember to release the jib sheet—"

She didn't get a chance to finish as Walter pushed the tiller away from him with a call of "Hard alee!"

That's odd, she thought, as the bow moved through the eye of the wind. The term she'd been using was "Helms alee." They both ducked the boom, crossing to the other side of the boat. Walter was already trimming the jib by the time she was settled.

"That's good," she said encouragingly.

It was more than good; the trim was perfect, and when he nonchalantly sheeted in the mainsail she realized he'd been having her on all along.

"Beginner's luck."

Walter grinned. "Must be."

He looked so completely at home helming her boat that it was almost irritating. No—it was extremely irritating.

"She handles like the Herreshoff S-Class I used to race when I was younger. That's another sloop with acres of canvas." He stared admiringly up at the pregnant mainsheet.

"Where did you learn to sail?"

"Cape Cod. We have a summer place there. One of the privileges of being a Poor Little Rich Boy." He paused, thoughtful. "That house is one of the few things I'll miss. You can't begin to imagine how beautiful it is."

"I doubt it's going anywhere."

"No. But I won't be visiting." He hesitated. "My father cut me off without a cent and swore never to speak to me again."

"That seems a little . . . extreme."

"He thought it quite reasonable."

"I'm sure he'll come round."

"You don't know my father." He visibly brightened. "Enough of that. Tell me where to point this thing before I drown us both in self-pity."

"Have you ever been to Héliopolis?"

"Sounds Greek."

"Put it this way: the people there wear about as many clothes as your average Greek statue."

"Nudists?"

"A whole community of them. You can't see it from here—it's round the corner at the western end of the Île du Levant there." She pointed into the far distance. "They even have their own beach."

"Hang it," said Walter. "Let's go join the other boats drifting slowly by just offshore."

12

It was the first time since their arrival that Ilse and Klaus had entertained, and they outdid themselves, laying on an impressive feast for lunch, which was served at a long table in the shade of a towering holm oak near the foot of the garden.

Tom made his excuses the moment the main course plates were cleared, claiming that Benoît had a batch of papers requiring his urgent signature, legal documents relating to the upcoming purchase of the "Art Nouveau eyesore."

"As long as you're back in time to mix the potions before supper," said Venetia.

It was good to hear her make a jest. She'd spent much of the meal fretting about Lucy and Walter, convinced that they must have drowned. "It's just not like her to go off like that."

"Well, it's just like Walter," Fanya had reassured her.

The house in Le Canadel where Klaus and Ilse were staying, the house belonging to the mysterious Swiss publisher whom no one had ever met, was a bland brick-built affair embowered in tall pine trees and set on the rising ground between the beach and the coast road. The property gave almost nothing away about the owner. It was sparsely yet adequately furnished, and there were even some competent watercolors of Mediterranean coastal views on the walls. However, there was none of the usual telling clutter: no books, no photographs, no restaurant menus, no knickknacks from foreign travels sprinkled about the place.

Tom might have been more suspicious had he not been so fixated on Yevgeny. And Fanya. Yevgeny made all the noise, but Fanya was the power behind the throne, the one who steered and regulated their lives. It was inconceivable that she wasn't also involved.

It had been a bluff; Tom hadn't spoken to the photographer Baptiste Daumier. The operator had done a grand job of tracking down the number in Paris, but the telephone had gone unanswered. It didn't matter. He knew in his bones that the talented and painfully shy young man he had met back in May was not part of the conspiracy. Baptiste had snapped a photograph of him in Saint-Tropez and passed it on in all innocence by way of thanks to his Russian hosts. The real question was how that photograph had then found its way into the hands of an Italian assassin.

On that score, Yevgeny had confirmed his own guilt, unable to mask the slight tremor of alarm in his eyes at the mention of Baptiste's name. In trying to recover, he had then overcompensated, adopting an exaggerated air of indifference to their conversation. Tom's impulse had been to swim over and throttle a confession out of him right there and then. Had they been alone, he might have done just that. Fortunately, his head had mastered his heart.

He didn't mind alerting Yevgeny to his suspicions; that had been his intention. He wanted Yevgeny to know that he was onto him. He wanted to turn the heat up under him. The enemy was more likely to stumble if coerced into action. He would, of course, have to be more vigilant than ever, but at least the game was finally afoot. Anything was better than the maddening uncertainty of the past thirty-six hours.

These were the thoughts that had been swirling around his head over lunch. The need to keep up appearances around the table, to keep up with the babble of speech, meant that he wouldn't be able to weigh the bigger questions until he was alone and heading for Le Lavandou.

Klaus had shown himself to be a gracious and attentive host, and he now insisted on seeing Tom to his car.

"Thank you for what you said about my book . . . last night, at dinner."

"I meant every word," replied Tom.

"It is nice to hear good things. I am not a confident writer."

"That could be why you're such a fine one."

Klaus gave a self-deprecating smile as he held open the garden gate for Tom to pass through. "In Germany we say a writer is only as good as his next book. And I don't have one."

"No ideas, even?"

"One. Forgiveness."

"Forgiveness?"

"Did you fight in the last war?" asked Klaus.

"Yes. Briefly."

"France?"

Tom nodded. "Near Bouchavesnes."

"Our brother—Gustl—he was in France."

"Did he make it back?"

Klaus shook his head. "And yet here we all are . . . having lunch." He paused. "People amaze me."

Maybe it was the memories of the futile carnage dressed up as military expediency, of the mud and the fleas and the foot-rot, or maybe it was simply the need to remain focused on his immediate predicament, but Tom found himself anxious to terminate the conversation.

"Well, as long as they do, you'll always have something to say." He extended his hand. "Thank you, Klaus, and I'm sorry I have to rush off."

At this hour of the day the sun was a furious ball and the hills seemed to tremble in the searing heat. Everyone was either at lunch or sleeping it off, and the twisting coast road was as deserted as the communities he passed through, although he still kept a wary eye on his rearview mirror.

If, as the photograph suggested, Yevgeny and Fanya were involved in the plot to have him killed, then he had to discard all thoughts of the firm friendship that had sprung up between them in recent years. He couldn't allow sentimentality to cloud his judgment. He also had to lay aside everything he thought he knew about them. Evidently, they weren't all they purported to be. So who were they?

That Yevgeny was an art dealer of some considerable renown was beyond any doubt. That both were Russian could also be relied upon; he knew from Parisian friends that they were respected pillars of the large community of Russian émigrés in the French capital. But that's where the verifiable certainties broke down. Who had they been before they showed up in Paris in 1918, displaced victims, supposedly, of the Bolshevik Revolution?

Was there any truth in Yevgeny's story of wealthy parents slain by a rampaging mob, of stitching family jewels into the hem of his jacket before fleeing abroad? It was well known in intelligence circles that the Bolsheviks had attempted to infiltrate the White Russian exiles in Paris right from the start, fearing the influence they might bring to bear on foreign powers to intervene back home. Some of these Soviet agents had been exposed; others, presumably, had gone undetected. Did Yevgeny and Fanya fall into this last category? If so, had they been working for the Soviets all along, or had they been recruited at some later date?

Either way, Leonard's misgivings still held: how could the Soviets possibly know for sure that it was Tom who had done in Zakharov in that darkened stairwell in Petrograd in 1919? And why had they waited sixteen years to exact revenge for his murder? He knew there was an explanation; he just couldn't see it yet.

He turned his mind back four years to the moment when Yevgeny and Fanya had first appeared in his life, drifting into the cove below the villa on one of the Hôtel de la Réserve's pedal boats, coming ashore and spending the whole afternoon on the beach. There had been no reason at the time to doubt their story: that they were staying at La Réserve while searching for a house to buy.

A few days later, they had invited Tom, Leonard, Venetia, Lucy and the two boys to drinks and dinner at the hotel, repaying the hospitality that had been shown to them. And they had then gone on to buy La

Quercia, high on the headland toward Le Canadel, a house that, though not officially on the market, Tom had tipped them off to, knowing that the owners were in tight financial straits. He had even accompanied them on their first visit to the property, delighting in their wild enthusiasm for the place, as well as his own good fortune that such an unusual and entertaining couple might soon become his near neighbors.

There was no avoiding the stark truth: that he'd been played for a fool from the beginning, that there'd been something altogether more contrived about their seemingly chance appearance on a pedal boat that sunny, windblown afternoon. But assuming he'd been targeted by them, why had they followed through with the charade of buying La Quercia, and why had they then waited four years before acting against him?

The answer came to him suddenly as he was dropping down toward the long white sweep of Cavalière's pine-trimmed strand.

He was a bloody fool—so blinkered, so besotted with the notion of his own victimhood that he had failed to grasp the bigger picture.

Yevgeny and Fanya hadn't turned up in Le Rayol looking to cultivate a relationship with him; they had come for Leonard!

Leonard was the real prize: a high-ranking official at the British Foreign Office, right-hand man to Sir Robert Vansittart himself. How much was such an acquaintance worth to the Soviets? How much information about British foreign policy had Yevgeny already managed to inveigle out of Leonard under the guise of innocent friendship? Leonard had hardly been discreet during the discussion over dinner last night about the looming clouds of war. How much more candid was he when alone with Yevgeny?

It was a devilishly simple idea. Exiles of a Communist regime reviled and feared by the major Western powers, intensely vocal critics of Stalin, Yevgeny and Fanya were beyond suspicion.

Tom's instinct was to turn the car right around, but something stayed his hand. It was an uneasy feeling, low down in his gut, difficult to diagnose at first.

Leonard's insistence that the Soviets couldn't possibly be behind the attempt on his life had struck him as strange at the time; Leonard wasn't known for closing off any avenue until the matter was well and truly settled. And as for his assertion that it made no sense for them to have waited so long before moving against Tom, well, he was right.

But what if they hadn't been waiting all this time? What if they had spent the past sixteen years in complete ignorance?

Christ, it was so glaringly obvious now.

If the Soviets hadn't acted before now, it was only because they hadn't known the truth about Zakharov's death. Which meant that someone had only just told them.

How had he missed it? Was he really so far off the pace after only five years out of the game? Clearly. Or maybe it was something else. Maybe his unconscious mind had denied him access to the realization, knowing that the only logical conclusion to be drawn from it was too painful to bear consideration.

His conscious mind, however, had no difficulty in settling on another thought, more of an image: Leonard and Yevgeny far away in Cannes together, conveniently absent, the night the Italian assassin had come visiting.

Benoît operated from the first floor of a stuccoed building adjacent to the town hall, right in the heart of Le Lavandou. The rooms were large and light, their fireplaces of white marble, their lofty ceilings trimmed with elaborate stuccowork.

Tom fully expected to cool his heels for half an hour or so before Benoît and his minions returned from lunch, but the door downstairs was unlocked and he let himself in.

Benoît's office ran the entire width of the building at the front, with three tall windows offering a far-reaching vista over the crowns of the lime trees to the sea, and the islands beyond. His monumental desk was backed by a wall of books, as was the seating area at the other end of the room. Objects and curios of all sizes and descriptions littered every available surface, which, together with the books, lent a distinctly scholarly whiff to the place.

Benoît was at his desk, poring over some papers. He removed his spectacles and rose to his feet when Tom entered.

"Thomas . . ."

"Am I disturbing you?"

Benoît fluttered a disdainful hand at the papers on his desk, the same papers that had, presumably, kept him from his lunch. "It's nothing."

"I was passing through."

"That's good, because I was just about to pour myself a small Cognac."

Untrue, of course, but Benoît was never one to let urgent business get in the way of the important things in life, such as friendship and fine Cognac, of which he kept an unrivaled selection. Tom allowed himself to be ushered toward the divan and armchairs, the uneven parquet creaking beneath his feet.

In large towns, notaries were little more than scriveners. Out here in the provinces, they wore a variety of different hats: financial adviser, usurer, banker, land agent, house agent, even marriage counselor. The roles were rich and diverse.

Benoît, it seemed, had recently added "dealer in antiquities" to the list. As soon as they were settled with their tulip glasses, he pointed out a polychrome figurine on the table behind Tom, maybe two feet in height.

"What do you think it is?" he asked.

It was a woman of Asian appearance with gently composed features. She stood tall and slender, dressed in long flowing robes that descended to her bare feet.

"Is it Chinese?"

"Bravo. It's Quan Yin, the Buddhist goddess of mercy."

"Where did you find her?"

"She found me. A sailor came by a few days ago, just back from the Far East. He wants me to find a buyer for her. He thinks she's worth a fair bit, maybe even two thousand francs. I told him I'd look into it while he's visiting relatives down the coast. He'll be back tomorrow."

"Okay," said Tom. "Why the big smile?"

"Well, yesterday I had a wealthy gentleman in here. He's looking for a large property to buy in the area. Yours would be ideal for him, by the way. As you know, prices have picked up considerably since you bought. You'd clear a very tidy profit."

Benoît was ribbing him; he knew that Tom would never consider parting with Villa Martel.

"Tell him twenty million francs."

Benoît laughed at the exorbitant sum. "He might just say yes. I have the feeling money is no object to Monsieur Dufresne."

He offered Tom a cigarette, lighting it for him.

"Anyway, while we were talking, he spotted the Quan Yin standing there and he became very excited. I said I was holding it for the owner, who was considering selling it, at which point he became really quite agitated. What do you think she's worth to Monsieur Dufresne?"

"I have no idea. More than two thousand, though."

"More than ten times two thousand. He said he would be happy to pay twenty-five."

Tom nodded, impressed.

"I said I couldn't do anything without first speaking to the owner. Monsieur Dufresne then produced three thousand francs as a sign of good faith."

"And to secure the piece for himself."

"Exactly. He's going to be back in a few days."

"I see your dilemma," said Tom. "How much do you offer the sailor?"

"He'll be happy with two thousand francs, but I don't think I can do that."

"Ahh, I see—what price your conscience?" Tom teased.

"I was thinking of offering him ten thousand."

"Which still leaves you a profit of fifteen."

"What do you think?"

Tom sat back, working it through in his head from all the different angles.

It was brilliant.

"I think," he said eventually, "that your beautiful Quan Yin is worthless."

"Worthless?"

"It's a scam, Benoît. The sailor and Monsieur Dufresne are in on it together."

Tom could see the cogs turning, but Benoît wasn't ready to relinquish his easy rewards just yet. "But he left me three thousand francs . . ."

"That's the genius of it. That's the reason you're happy to hand over ten thousand to the sailor. But it still leaves them with seven thousand."

"My God . . ."

"The moment you've paid the sailor, you're never going to see Monsieur Dufresne again."

"Okay, okay," said Benoît irritably, "I'm with you now." He got to his feet and stomped to the window.

"Don't be angry. They didn't get you."

"I'm not angry," snapped Benoît.

"Anyhow, I'm sure we can figure out a way for you to keep your hands on the three thousand."

Benoît turned, intrigued.

"Revenge," Tom went on, "plus a nice consolation prize. Did you give your Monsieur Dufresne a receipt for the money?"

"Of course."

Tom took a sip of Cognac. "Give me a moment to think."

It took him a good few minutes, because he was trying to find a way to work Commissaire Roche into the conversation at the same time. Meanwhile, Benoît sucked the life out of another cigarette.

"Okay, here it is. Tomorrow, when the sailor returns, you tell him the good news that his Quan Yin is worth twenty-five thousand francs. Not only that, but you have a buyer lined up who has already put down three thousand francs. He won't be expecting that."

"No, he'll make some excuse and take the Quan Yin back."

"Ah, but you can't give it to him."

"Can't I?"

"No, because you no longer have it in your possession."

"No?"

"No, because the moment you established its true value you placed it in the safekeeping of your good friend Commissaire Roche—who has kindly agreed to oversee the transaction once the prospective buyer returns."

A ghost of a smile appeared at the corners of Benoît's mouth.

"Somehow, I can't see the sailor demanding to head right over to the commissariat to reclaim it," Tom continued.

"No."

"He'll disappear."

"But Dufresne will be back for the three thousand. It's a lot of money."

"Yes, but the trouble is, you don't have it anymore."

"No?"

"No. You tell Monsieur Dufresne that the seller was eager for a quick sale and you proudly announce that you managed to negotiate a price of three thousand francs with him, thereby securing Monsieur Dufresne the most extraordinary bargain. He'll know you're lying, of course, but what can he do about it? If he kicks up a fuss, you suggest he take up the matter with your good friend . . ."

" . . . Commissaire Roche."

"They'll cut their losses and run; they won't have a choice. Besides, they'll make the money back off some other greedy fool before long."

Benoît scowled at the insult but seemed pleased with the overall proposal. "You're a dark horse, Thomas. One day you're going to have to tell me what you really did for the British government before you became a writer."

Tom smiled. "It might be wise to alert Commissaire Roche to the presence of two con men in the area. I'm sure he'd appreciate it."

"So you're acquainted with Roche, are you?"

"A little. An easy man to underestimate."

"Not if you've known him as long as I have." Benoît swirled the Cognac in his glass, then came and sat back down opposite Tom. "I may be a greedy fool, but I'm not a complete idiot. What is it you want to know about Roche?"

It would have been insulting to keep up the charade. "How good is he at his job?"

"Put it this way: he could easily have made a name for himself in Toulon or Marseilles."

"Why didn't he?"

"He likes it here," Benoît said with a shrug.

"That simple?"

"No, he has a wife who doesn't like it here. I think she's finally accepted that they're not going anywhere else, though."

"When he gets his teeth into something, does he ever let go?"

"No," said Benoît. "Never."

Tom nodded.

Benoît looked concerned. "I don't know what's going on, and I don't want to know." Tom made to speak, but Benoît silenced him with a raised hand. "No, just listen. You are a friend of mine, and I'll do whatever I can to help, whatever you ask of me. It may surprise you to know that I don't have much in the way of religion, or even morality, when friends are in need."

"Thank you," said Tom.

"Remember what I said."

"I shall."

"Another glass of Cognac?"

"Maybe a finger."

Remarkably, that was that. The matter was closed and the conversation moved on seamlessly to a postmortem of dinner the night before. Benoît had been very taken with Klaus, especially his story of the Bavarian mountain dwellers boxing up the weary swallows and shipping them to Venice, and he was very keen to borrow the German's latest novel. Tom promised to drop it off the next time he was passing.

"You mean, you really were passing?"

"I'm on my way to Hyères, to see Hélène. She's back from Greece."

"Yes, I know. Chantal had lunch with her two days ago."

It was strange that Chantal hadn't mentioned it over dinner last night, even stranger that Benoît's nervous eyes seemed incapable of meeting his gaze.

"What is it, Benoît?"

Benoît leaned forward and stubbed out his cigarette before replying. "Hélène has met someone."

Tom understood the words; it took a little longer to absorb their meaning.

"Where? Here?"

"In Greece."

"Who?"

"I don't know, exactly . . . some Polish count."

Tom nodded, taking it in. "It must be serious or you wouldn't be telling me."

"It would certainly be very serious for me if Chantal knew I had told you."

"Don't worry."

"Forewarned is forearmed, and all that."

Forewarned proved to be hellishly distracting. Tom reached the outskirts of Le Lavandou in a daze, barely aware that he'd been driving. The last of the houses fell away on either side as the road climbed lazily toward Bormes-les-Mimosas.

There had been nothing in Hélène's voice when they'd spoken that morning. She had seemed delighted at his suggestion that he drive over to see her after lunch. Maybe two years of complacency had dulled his hearing—complacency and presumption. He had always supposed that if she were ever to seek someone more constant in her personal life, he would be the man she chose. She had even intimated as much on a couple of occasions; at least, that's how he'd taken her words at the time. Incorrectly, it now seemed. She had found herself a Polish count while on holiday in Greece, and her small stable of admirers back in France was for the chop.

With Hector gone and Leonard's rocklike presence in his life under serious question, the thought of also losing Hélène bit deep. But what right did he really have to be upset? She wasn't to know that his world was crumbling around him. And, for God's sake, it had taken Lucy in the kitchen last night during dinner to point out to him that he was missing her. Lucy had detected it in him, so why on earth hadn't he? If he was so out of touch with his own feelings, how could he possibly hope to keep track of Hélène's?

He heard it before he saw it: a building roar above the throb of the wind blustering through the car's open windows. The rearview mirror revealed a snub-nosed black sedan gaining from behind, powering up the slope as if to pass him on the straight. A quick glance back at the road told him that the other car wasn't going to make it before the bend up ahead. That's when he realized that the driver had no intention of making it. He also became acutely aware of the steep drop-off to his right, the ground disappearing beyond the graveled shoulder into a deep valley of scrub oak, rocks and scattered pines. If he ended up down there he could go undiscovered for weeks, even longer.

He dropped a gear and stamped on the accelerator. The Renault responded, but not urgently enough. The sedan had stolen the advantage while he wasn't looking and now swung out wide to overtake him. Tom yanked the steering wheel to the left, foiling the maneuver. Before he knew it, the bend was upon him—a sharp left-hander, almost completely blind—and he was still on the wrong side of the road. If there was any doubt that the driver of the other vehicle had it in for him, that vanished as he caught sight of the sedan over his right shoulder, looking to undertake him, to keep him boxed in against any oncoming traffic, to force him into a head-on collision.

He swerved to the right, bracing himself for the impact, but the sedan's driver had anticipated the move, hitting the brakes and dropping in behind once more. They were bumper-to-bumper as they hurtled around the next bend into a long climbing straight. The Renault was woefully underpowered in comparison with the sedan, but the incline played in Tom's favor, the sedan unable to pick up enough speed to pass him just so long as he kept veering from side to side to obstruct it. He knew that would all change when they breasted the rise and the road leveled off once more.

The occupants of the sedan seemed to know this too. Tom could just make them out in the rearview mirror: two men sitting as still as department store mannequins. Strangely, it was their inhuman composure that brought him to his senses. His brain began to function once more, a cold and clinical reasoning coming to his aid, reasserting itself after years of softer pursuits.

He had to accept the inevitable—that he was outnumbered and in an inferior vehicle. There was no point in pretending otherwise. But what did he have going for him? Not much: the Beretta, which he now removed from his jacket pocket and placed on his lap. He had to assume the two men were also armed, but it didn't necessarily follow that they were prepared to use their weapons. The Italian sent to kill him had intended to complete his mission while leaving no signs of foul play. In all likelihood, the two men in the car behind were under the same instructions. Forcing him off the road was one thing, peppering him with bullets another altogether. They might have the upper hand, but they were limited in their options. This was the nub of the strategy beginning to take shape in his head, a plan of action that he executed the moment the road leveled off.

He spun the steering wheel hard to the left and the Renault slewed toward a narrow dirt road that struck off obliquely into the scrub and trees. Too close to its prey to abandon the chase, the sedan instinctively followed. They weren't to know where he was leading them; he barely knew himself. All he had to go on was an unwelcome memory of once trying to work his way north to the main road from the remote beaches around Brégançon and swearing never to attempt such a thing again. He had found himself hopelessly lost in the rugged landscape just back from the coast, and it had taken detailed directions from two old men stripping cork from an oak to see him out of the labyrinth of winding valleys shut in by high, ridged hills.

His pursuers must have doubted the wisdom of following him, finding themselves smothered in a dense pall of dust thrown up by the speeding Renault. Chickens scattered as a farmhouse whistled past on Tom's right, after which the road noticeably deteriorated before plunging down the side of a narrow valley—the gateway to the violent tumble of hills that lay like a choppy sea across his path. He knew he had little chance of making it through to the coast. Given the speed at which he was traveling, the guts would be ripped out of the Renault long before then. Whatever was going to happen was going to have to happen soon.

The Renault danced and leapt over the ruts, grounding its belly every so often. He had no way of determining if the sedan had abandoned the chase; all he could make out in the rearview mirror was a billowing cloud in his wake, talcum-powder-white in the blazing sunshine. Only when he slowed to negotiate a T-junction at the foot of the valley did he glimpse the vehicle over his shoulder. It had dropped back, content to pursue from a distance. This wasn't what he wanted. He needed it tight in, close on his tail, if his plan was to work. He also needed to gain height.

He bore left at the junction, barreling along on loose gravel, the trees thickening around him, his eyes scanning ahead, searching for a turn that would lead him back up the hillside. Twice he slowed, only to reject the side tracks as too steep to negotiate. At last he saw it: a slender thread working its way diagonally up the side of the escarpment on his left.

Winter rains had scored deep runnels in it, and for a moment it seemed that the Renault wasn't up to the task. But the tires finally bit, spitting dust and stones, and he regained speed on the ascent. By the time he soared over a bald crest into the adjacent valley, the needle was nudging sixty miles per hour on the dial.

The dirt road dipped sharply before leveling off and worming around a deep bowl in the hills, a vast corrugated amphitheater, like a Japanese fan, which fell away to his right. The road had been crudely hacked out of the slope—sheer rock on his left side, an unparapeted drop on the other. It was almost perfect, certainly close enough to what he had envisaged, and it would have to do. The Renault was beginning to suffer, one of the rear wheels thumping in protest, its suspension gone.

He checked to confirm that the sedan was still on his tail, estimating that it was four or five seconds behind him, and after the road veered to the left, hiding him beyond an outcrop, he hit the brakes as hard as he dared. The Renault skidded and shuddered to a halt, the rear end swinging out and blocking the path. For a foolish moment, he imagined flee-ing the vehicle, but he rapidly calculated that the best he could hope for was to recover the Beretta, which had long since bounced off his lap onto the floor, staying low and preparing himself for the impact.

He saw nothing. He heard almost nothing; the blood was beating so loudly in his ears. There was a dim whistle, followed by a brief silence, then a more distinct sound of shattering wood. He saw it in his mind's eye: the sedan tearing around the bend, the driver finding his path blocked and instinctively yanking the steering wheel to the right. He couldn't go left, into solid rock. It had to be right, into the void.

This is exactly what Tom had hoped for, and yet he stepped from the car a little stunned that he had managed to turn the tables on his pursuers so suddenly, so completely. They were down there some-where, lost in the thick tangle of oaks and underbrush blanketing the slope. He could make out the spot where the sedan had left the road, shearing off a young tree close to its roots and gouging a path through the undergrowth. The sun beat down with a biblical heat and the cica-das kept up their pulsating chorus, undaunted. The rest was silence.

Tom checked the Beretta and set off down the slope. One whole side of an oak tree had been stripped clean of its bark by a glancing blow, but there was still no sign of the sedan. For a moment, he imagined the driver expertly working the wheel, picking a path through the trees, the persistent tug of the dense undergrowth gradually slowing the car's passage until it drew to a halt. In which case, the two men were out there and on the move. They might even have him in their sights right now. A sudden fear felled him, dropping him into a crouch, and it was a good minute or so before he was confident enough to continue on his way.

He needn't have worried. The sedan had indeed come to a halt, but with its front end concertinaed against the trunk of a large and gnarled oak. The tree seemed to have lost none of its grip on the thin soil with the impact. It rose straight and proud and defiant. The two men, by contrast, lay twisted in their seats.

The driver was dead, impaled on the steering column, his hands still clasping the snapped-off wheel. The passenger was slumped to one side, his face a crimson mask. Whether he had forced open his door or it had burst open on impact was hard to say. Either way, he was alive and struggling to come to his senses, like some collapsed drunk in the street. Aside from the deep gash on his forehead, he appeared to be intact, and Tom was figuring out how best to remove his bulk from the crippled vehicle when the gasoline ignited, sending a carpet of blue flames dancing through the sandy soil beneath the engine.

His instinct was to extinguish the fire immediately. No man, whoever he was, however evil his intentions, deserved to die such a hideous death—immolated alive. Dropping to his knees, he scooped handfuls of soil onto the licking flames. Sensing that he was losing the battle, and fearing that an explosion was imminent, he turned his attention back to the passenger, who was regarding him with vacant, pleading eyes. Tom scrambled to his feet and wrestled the man out of the car as best he could, falling back, winded, under the dead weight. He hooked his hands beneath the man's armpits and hauled him as far from the vehicle as his strength permitted, propping him up against the base of a tree.

A deep-rooted pragmatism kicked in. What if the dead driver was in possession of identity documents? What if the car contained other essential evidence? He had to prevent the vehicle from going up in flames, if only because the plume of smoke would act as an unwelcome summons to all who saw it. He still needed to contain the situation as best he could.

Hurrying back to the sedan, he yanked open the crumpled hood. There were flames playing around the engine block, but he extinguished them swiftly enough with handfuls of soil. A branch was brought into action to break up the spread of fire beneath the sedan toward the fuel tank at the rear. He then scrabbled around the vehicle on all fours, sweeping more dirt beneath it, and when finally satisfied that he'd doused the blaze, he stamped out a few smoldering shrubs before they could ignite in earnest.

Only then did he turn his attention back to the passenger. He hadn't moved from the base of the tree, but he now had his arm raised, a pistol leveled straight at Tom. He was blinking the blood from his eyes, but the hand holding the weapon was surprisingly steady. There was certainly no question of Tom making a move for the Beretta in his hip pocket.

He was dead meat.

"Go in peace," said the man in Russian.

Tom stared, disbelieving. It was a phrase layered deep into the beaten gold leaf of his memory. He saw a baby-faced priest in a side chapel in Petrograd, and he saw himself, gun in hand, uttering the same words to a terrified young agent of the Cheka with whom he had collided after fleeing the cathedral. The intervening years had filled out his frame considerably, but the same lean and handsome face lay beneath the gore. It had to be the same man he had spared all those years ago.

"I won't say it again." The man spoke in French now, and he wagged the barrel of his pistol up the slope to make his point.

"You need a doctor."

The man snorted dismissively. "I need a priest."

He wasn't dying, but he obviously believed he was as good as dead. And he was probably right. The NKVD, as the Soviet intelligence organization was now known, didn't look kindly on failure. They'd pin the Order of the Red Banner on your chest one day, then shoot you in the same chest the next, as an enemy of the people.

Tom could have walked away, and maybe he should have, but he found himself saying, "I know a place with both—a place where they won't ask questions and no one will ever find you."

The man wiped the blood from his eyes with the back of his forearm. The gun remained trained on Tom. "Where is this place?"

"Up in the hills."

The man hesitated before replying. "Why should I trust you?"

"I don't know. Because you don't have a choice?"

The man placed the muzzle of the pistol against his own temple and regarded Tom inquiringly.

"That's not a choice—that's cowardice."

"It's a better death than the one waiting for me."

"I got out."

"Really?" replied the man, skeptically. "So what am I doing here?"

"Maybe you should ask yourself that same question."

It was a few moments before the man lowered the pistol and said, "Help me up."

Tom approached warily and hauled him to his feet. "Can you walk?"

"I think so."

"Put your arm round my shoulder."

"Is it a bad wound?"

Tom peered at the man's forehead. It was a T-shaped wound just below the hairline, deep, and pulsing blood.

"Not as bad as the one you were about to inflict upon yourself," he said.

The man laughed weakly.

They didn't speak again until they had struggled back up the slope to the Renault and were on the move, wending their way slowly back through the hills toward the main road.

"Who was your friend?" Tom asked.

"He wasn't my friend. I only just met him."

He said he had been summoned from Paris with instructions to take a room at the Grand Hôtel in Le Lavandou, where he was to wait until contacted. That contact had occurred less than an hour ago, when the man now skewered on the sedan's steering column had knocked on the door of his hotel room. They had sat in a parked car and they had waited and watched a building. He claimed to have recognized Tom immediately, despite the passage of the years, and when Tom had emerged from the building and driven off in his car, they had followed him.

Tom knew better than to take this account at face value, but now wasn't the time to dig out the exact truth. He did, however, need to establish one thing that hadn't been made perfectly clear.

"You saw me enter the building?"

"Yes. And we followed you when you came out and got into your car." The man turned and looked at Tom with a groggy, unfocused gaze. "They'll send others. You know that, don't you?"

"How long do I have?"

"They'll come from Paris, like me. Maybe twenty-four hours."

"You live in Paris?" Tom asked.

"For a few years now."

"Hunting down White Guards and Trotskyists?"

"If I'd known I was going to get a lecture, I would have shot you. I still might."

"What's your name?" asked Tom.

"Pyotr."

"Well, in case you hadn't noticed, Pyotr, you no longer have your pistol—I do."

13

The moment Hélène opened the door her face fell. "My God," she gasped. "What happened to you?"

Tom gave a furtive check over his shoulder and slipped inside, pushing the door shut behind him and bolting it.

"It's a long story," he said. "Although I don't have long to tell it."

He had parked the car in Place Massillon, the main square in Hyères, traveling the rest of the way on foot, taking a circuitous route through the streets, doubling back on himself every so often to ensure that he wasn't being followed. He had also scoured Hélène's street thoroughly, checking each of the parked cars in turn to establish that the house wasn't under surveillance. Only then had he mounted the front steps of her stolid late-Victorian villa.

He had been so distracted by the events of the past two hours that it didn't occur to him until he tugged on the bellpull that the new man in Hélène's life, the Polish count whom Benoît had mentioned, might actually be inside.

But Hélène was on her own, and looking more beautiful than ever. A month in Greece had darkened her skin to the color of light mahogany and her hair, pinned back behind her dainty little ears, had the luster of black silk about it. He searched for signs in her appearance of the news she was about to break to him, but her pale lemon summer frock was tight and alluring, cut low at the front to reveal the necklace he had bought her during their trip to Saint-Jean-de-Luz. She was also wearing the perfume she knew he loved.

Maybe she was intending to sleep with him one more time, a courtesy to their long and slightly bizarre relationship. The devil on his shoulder told him to take what was on offer; after brushing with death twice in the past few days, the urge to lunge at anything life-affirming was almost overwhelming. He repressed the impulse, though. He wanted her gone, far away, as soon as possible, until the storm tossing his life had blown itself out.

He had drained the tall glass of water she gave him long before his story was finished. Hélène sat in stunned silence while he spoke, perched demurely on the divan in the drawing room, and for the first time he told her the truth of his past, of his involvement with the Secret Intelligence Service, Britain's equivalent of her own country's Deuxième Bureau. He left out the more sordid details, but he couldn't hold everything back, not if he was to convince her of the seriousness of the situation, of the very real danger in which he had unwittingly placed her. He had to make clear there was a strong likelihood that the people bent on killing him knew of her existence, and that they might well use her to get to him.

When he was finished, she rose silently and approached the overstuffed armchair in which he was seated, a look of compassion in her eyes. The notion that she might be about to stoop down and hug him was swiftly dispelled by the stinging slap across his cheek.

She walked to the window, crossing her arms in front of her and staring outside. Without turning, she said, "You should have told me before."

"All this has only just happened."

She turned now. "You should still have told me before."

"I know. I understand."

"No, you don't," she fired back firmly. "How can you possibly know what's in my mind? I don't care that you lied to me. I don't even care that you've placed me in this situation. I *care*," she said with a bitter emphasis, "that things could have been very different between us if I'd only known who you really were." She paused. "It explains so much about you. About us."

Benoît would suffer for it, but he had to say it. "I know you've met someone—someone important to you—and I understand."

It took her a moment to process his words. "Oh, such magnanimity!"

Tom felt his own anger rising. It even carried him to his feet. "What do you want? You want me to fight for you? Is that what you want? Believe me, you're far better off with your Polish count."

"I don't doubt it. At least he's a man who wouldn't tell me what's best for me, a man who might allow me to make up my own mind."

"I'm not sure you've quite grasped what's happening here. Your life is in danger. You have to pack a suitcase and you have to disappear—immediately."

"I'm not sure you've quite grasped that I find that idea rather thrilling."

Tom heaved a conciliatory sigh and took a couple of steps toward her. "Hélène, listen, I haven't been entirely honest with you."

He held up his hands, the hands that had held her, caressed her, wiped the tears from her cheeks, pulled the splinter from her foot in Avignon . . .

"These hands have taken the lives of two men in the past two days. They've also killed before that. They are soiled, defiled. They will always be defiled. That may not bother you now, but one day it will. And I would think less of you if it didn't."

He could see that his words had struck home. Fear clouded her expression.

"I thought I'd buried the man I used to be, but others have dug him up again . . . and I'm going to have to call on his services if I'm to get through this."

Hélène stepped close, took his hands in hers and raised them to her lips, kissing each of his palms in turn, anointing them. It was such a tender and unexpected gesture, but there was also something final in it.

"I'm so sorry."

She shook her head, dismissing the apology. "Where shall I go?"

"Somewhere obscure."

She thought on it for a moment. "My sister has a friend who's a painter. She lives in the Corrèze. Saillac. It's a small village in the middle of nowhere."

"The middle of nowhere is good. We'll find you a train in Toulon to get you as close as possible."

"I'll go and pack," she said quietly.

What I wouldn't give to be going with you, he thought forlornly as he watched her leave the room. *Carefree, unencumbered, without fear—the way things used to be.*

He didn't know the Corrèze intimately, but he had motored through the *département* on a couple of occasions, and he could picture himself there with her: feasting on foie gras and *magret de canard* in some medieval village beside the Dordogne River, walking in the humped hills scattered with stout stone farmhouses, coiled damp and spent on a lumpy mattress beneath the crooked beams of some ancient *auberge*.

It was never going to happen. Not now. Not ever. He had deceived her, lied to her. But would things really be different between them now if he had come clean with her before? He doubted it. For all her words, she would have been horrified by the revelation. His honesty would have shattered the strange spell that bound them together.

He took a cigarette from the jade box on the side table and lit it, holding the smoke down before exhaling.

He could see what he was doing; he was already writing the obituary of their relationship, growing a great scab of indifference, because if he stopped to really think about the gaping wound that had just appeared in his life, he was liable to find himself swallowed up by it.

The dried blood on his shirtsleeve wrenched him back to the present and the hard realities hedging him in on all sides. However, like the stains on the famous shroud he had visited in Turin two winters ago, it also held the promise of some deeper salvation.

Pyotr's blood, the blood of his enemy, a man whose wounds were now being attended to by Carthusian brothers at their sprawling monastery high in the hills near Collobrières. There was an almost mystical circularity to the chain of events, a cycle that had started with a few words of kindness uttered by a young priest in a Russian cathedral. Tom had taken those words and had handed them on to another, who in turn had carried them with him over the years, before handing them back and taking refuge in a community of holy men.

If he hadn't lost his faith long ago he might have been tempted to detect some divine purpose at play, but all belief in God's providence had died with Irina back in Petrograd, hurling him into a darkness from which he had finally dragged himself, years later, by sheer force of will.

Yes, he had spared the young Pyotr beneath that streetlamp in Petrograd, but the following night he had dispatched Zakharov without so much as a flutter of conscience. With cold pleasure, even. And when fleeing the country by the northern route, he had killed again, quite effortlessly. The guide he had paid to see him safely through the snowy wastes and across the border into Finland had chosen instead to hand him over to the Bolsheviks. Tom had put two bullets into the man's head as he was shouting to attract the attention of a border patrol.

My life, or your life? He hadn't even hesitated. That's how easy it had been.

Had there been regrets later? Had he been tormented by thoughts of the dead man's daughters mourning their father's murder? None that he could recall. In fact, he would have been quite happy to search out the two sour-mouthed sisters with whom he had briefly shared soup in front of a spitting cedarwood fire and inform them that their father had met a violent end entirely fitting to his low treachery and that the world was a far better place without him. Such had been his state of mind at the time, the blind malignity of his thinking.

He had anticipated far harsher treatment at the hands of the Secret Intelligence Service on his return to Helsinki; after all, he had stolen a sizable sum of money from the organization in order to fund his failed rescue mission. But when shipped out to Sweden to face the music, he found himself treated like a returning hero at the embassy in Stockholm.

This had been his first encounter with Leonard, whose sympathy and solicitude never once wavered during the two days of his debriefing. On the third day, Leonard invited him to luncheon at the Grand Hôtel, and over the cheese course offered him a permanent post with the SIS. Tom was dumbstruck. It didn't make sense. He had expected a traitor's death at the end of a hangman's noose, or a long spell in jail, at the very least, certainly not a job offer. Still reeling from his ordeal, he lunged unquestioningly at the lifeline before it could be snatched away.

It was a good few months before he fathomed the true motive behind Leonard's surprising offer. At the time, the Secret Service Committee was preparing to make its first report on the performance of the respective intelligence agencies during the Great War. MI5, Military Intelligence, Special Branch and the SIS were all under close scrutiny, and there was worrying talk of cutbacks and mergers to avoid "overlapping." Consequently, the SIS was doing everything in its power to boost its reputation and set itself apart from the other agencies. It just so happened that Tom's actions in Petrograd squared nicely with this agenda.

His rogue mission was swiftly dressed up as an undercover operation sanctioned by SIS Stockholm, and for which Tom had bravely volunteered. At great personal risk, he had exposed (and then disposed of) a Bolshevik double agent closing in on Britain's last remaining agent in Soviet Russia: the near-mythical ST-25, Paul Dukes. It was entirely due to Tom that Dukes was still at large in Petrograd, channeling home invaluable information.

Irina might have been written out of the doctored tale of derring-do that found its way through to the Secret Service Committee, but Leonard had not forgotten her, or the devastating impact of her death on Tom. On their return to London, he insisted that Tom move in with him and his new bride at their house on Warwick Square, a temporary arrangement while he searched for an apartment.

A month slipped by unnoticed, then another, then a third. It wasn't a case of Tom abusing the kindness and hospitality shown him by Leonard and Venetia. Every time he identified a suitable flat to rent, Venetia would insist on casting an eye over the place, only to dismiss it as some "bolting-hutch of beastliness" or "not fit to trap a rat in." She successfully kiboshed all his efforts to move on, and Leonard appeared quite happy to play along with her, not in the least threatened, it seemed, by the close friendship springing up between his young wife and Tom.

For Tom, it was an uneasy ménage à trois—or, more precisely, ménage à quatre, Lucy being a precocious four-year-old at the time— though not so uneasy that the prospect of life on his own in a scrap of a flat south of the river held any real allure. The spacious basement apartment at Warwick Square was effectively his, and although he took most of his evening meals with Leonard and Venetia, they weren't exactly living out of each other's pockets. Moreover, after a few months he began to realize that his presence in their lives also suited their needs. With the Secret Intelligence Service's future still trembling in the balance, Leonard was working improbably long hours, often hurrying straight from the office to some club or other for an official dinner. Far better for Venetia to have company of an evening than to be knocking around a large town house on her own and possibly wondering just what she had got herself into. Instead, she had a lodger at hand who was happy to mix her a cocktail and play with her daughter and watch the stove while she lounged in the bath with a novel.

It was a taste of domestic life so very far removed from his own experience, and so very much more appealing. Whereas his father would berate his mother for her profligacy in lighting a second candle at the dinner table, Venetia insisted that the house be permanently ablaze with electric light come nightfall. And then there was the music. Venetia required classical music, always loud, selected according to her mood. She sat him down and made him listen to the end of the slow movement of Brahms's *Fourth Symphony* ("for clear beauty"), to the fanfares in Berlioz's *Requiem* ("for fervor"), and to all of Liszt's piano music ("for its aquarium brilliance").

She had just turned twenty-five at the time, which made her his senior by a mere two years, and yet her self-possession and sophistication left him feeling like a stripling by comparison. In truth, he was slightly in awe of her, and possibly a little in love with her too.

One evening, when they found themselves alone together yet again, he made the mistake of hinting as much. She put him smartly back in his box, like a plaything she'd grown bored of. He wasn't in a position to trust his feelings, she told him, not after what he'd just been through in Russia. He didn't know his own mind and wouldn't for a while yet.

She wasn't patronizing him; she was speaking from hard experience. She too had suffered the distress of having someone she loved cruelly snatched from her before his time. She understood the toxic effects of despair. She knew exactly what he was going through.

This wasn't quite true. Yes, she knew about Irina's death at the hands of the Cheka—she even knew that Irina had been pregnant at the time—but the details of the revenge he'd exacted on Zakharov had, unsurprisingly, been kept from her by Leonard. Tom certainly had no intention of telling her. She would never have permitted him to romp around on the drawing-room rug with her young daughter if she had known.

The offer to become godfather to Lucy was put to him eight months after his arrival at Warwick Square, and just as he was preparing to vacate the basement for a cramped top-floor flat on the border of Waterloo and Kennington. One of Lucy's two godfathers, an old childhood friend of Leonard's, had died in captivity in Mesopotamia following the Siege of Kut, and it was put to Tom that he fill the dead man's shoes. He suspected the proposal was made more from fear for his welfare than anything else, their thinking being that he was less likely to stick his head in a gas oven if given some kind of responsibility for a small creature.

Maybe they were right. He was already devoted to Lucy, but nothing quite prepared him for the flood of emotion he experienced when he agreed to act as life mentor to her. Having ruthlessly taken two lives within the last year, he was hardly equipped for such a role. Evidently this wasn't a problem for Leonard, though, so he put those reservations from his mind and threw himself into the task, marking the occasion with a trip to the London Zoo, where Lucy devoured so much ice cream that she threw up vigorously all over the rear seat of the taxicab on their way back to Pimlico.

* * *

Tom crushed out his cigarette in the ashtray.

These were more than idle reminiscences. He was scavenging for clues, resonances of which might have carried down through the years to the present day. Only now was he being held to account for his actions back in 1919, and there had to be some kind of causal chain at play behind the scenes.

The obvious link in that chain was Leonard: the man who had raised him up and welcomed him into his home, his employer, his controller at the SIS, the man who had determined his existence for more than a decade, dispatching him around the globe to deal with "matters of some considerable sensitivity"—that phrase, always that same phrase—but never prescribing how best to tackle the problems in question. He left that side of things to Tom's discretion. He didn't wish to know the more unsavory details of how the issue had been resolved, just so long as it had been. Blackmail, bribery, intimidation or worse, the various coercements were never recorded in official files.

For years, Tom had rationalized his actions as playing dirty in the best interests of the nation and the Empire. Besides, everybody else was at it, not just the British. It was an ongoing war, one hidden from the public gaze and with its own rules of combat—a secret war that never slept. He found the work challenging and invigorating. Moreover, he seemed to have a natural gift for it. Even after the debacle in Constantinople, he had bounced back full of enthusiasm.

Then one day, inexplicably, he'd had enough. He'd done enough. Any more, it seemed to him, and his soul would be permanently, irreparably blackened. If he descended any deeper into the murky chasm of immorality, he would never be able to rise once more into the light. Such high-flown thinking, framed in religious concepts he'd long since discarded, was the first indication that his sanity was also at stake, not just his soul. He was, he realized, beginning to lose his grip, flirting with a serious nervous collapse.

The news that Leonard was soon to move on, vaulted from the Secret Intelligence Service to the Foreign Office by Sir Robert Vansittart, cleared the way for his decision. After spending ten years together as a team, the thought of working for anyone else was inconceivable, even if the desire had been there. Leonard understood this, and one of his last acts before being kicked upstairs was to secure Tom an honorable discharge from the service on psychiatric grounds.

Leonard. His friend. The man who knew more about him than any other person on the planet. If Leonard was involved, then Tom was dead and done for. Leonard permitted no failures, no loose ends. He harbored a quiet ruthlessness that the young men assigned to do his bidding found hard to square with the relaxed, even jocular, air that hung about him.

Had Leonard been turned? Had he gone over to the Soviets? If so, he wouldn't be the first. Special Branch had been penetrated by Soviet intelligence toward the end of Tom's time at the SIS, and he'd heard rumors since leaving the service that a couple of cipher clerks at the Foreign Office had been exposed as spies. Did the tentacles of Soviet influence extend higher up that organization? Leonard's close relationship with Yevgeny hardly amounted to a guilty verdict, but his overeagerness to dismiss the Soviets from the picture when their involvement in the plot now lay beyond any possible doubt suggested a degree of professional incompetence quite uncharacteristic of the man.

No, Leonard was definitely up to something, and the temptation was to go for a direct confrontation—possibly even a gun in the face—and see what came out of it. A bit impulsive, maybe, but it was a tactic that had served him well enough in the past.

Meanwhile, though, there was other work to be done.

Tom checked his wristwatch: half past three in London. With any luck Clive would be at his desk, following a lazy lunch at the Cavalry Club and his statutory twenty-minute doze, stretched out on the floor in a corner of his office, a book for a pillow.

Tom made for the telephone on the desk, gave the number to the operator, then replaced the receiver on its cradle.

Clive was one of the few people at the Secret Intelligence Service with whom he'd remained in contact—a short, bluff bulldog of a man with a foul mouth and a face like a clenched fist. They had first met at the Teheran Legation in Persia back in 1924, when Clive was still working for Military Intelligence. It was a critical time for Britain's diplomatic and commercial interests in the country, a time of violence and uncertainty. Reza Khan, the prime minister, had risen to office on the back of a British-backed military coup two years earlier, suppressing the power of the clergy and the tribal leaders in the process. The Anglo-Persian Oil Company's considerable operations in the south of the country appeared secure. But then Reza Khan had opened negotiations with the United States over oil concessions in the north.

Tom was dispatched to Teheran in August, a month after the American vice consul, Robert Imbrie, had been beaten to death by a two-thousand-strong mob of fanatics. Tom's mission was, essentially, a damage-limitation exercise. Rumors abounded that the British had stirred up the mob violence, resulting in Imbrie's death, with a view to scuppering the passage of the pro-American oil bill through the Persian Assembly. Tom was charged with quashing these rumors . . . while employing whatever means he deemed advisable to scupper passage of the oil bill through the Mejliss.

The complexities of Persian politics lay far beyond the ken of the average Persian, let alone a young Englishman. Fortunately, a slightly older Englishman was at hand to educate him. Clive had been kicking around the country when Reza Khan was still a Cossack colonel in Qazvin. He knew the ropes. He knew where the bodies were buried. More important, he knew whom to bribe and just how much to pay them.

It was quite possible that Clive hadn't got wind of what was unfolding down here in France—not everyone in the organization would be drawn into the loop—but he could be relied upon to discreetly ferret out just how the matter was being handled back in London. He could also be trusted to keep his mouth shut.

The phone rang, startling Tom. He picked up the receiver to find that his call had been put through successfully.

"Good afternoon," came a very proper female voice down the crackling line from London, pleasant but guarded.

"Clive Jopling, please."

"Who shall I say is calling?"

"Reginald Meath-Butterworth."

It was a pseudonym Tom had employed in Teheran, chiefly because no one would be able to remember it, let alone repeat it.

After a few moments there was a click on the line and a voice said in Farsi, *"Goh bebareh roo gahbret."*

This roughly translated as: "May shit rain down upon your grave."

"Goozidam too chesmet," Tom replied.

"I fart in your eye."

Clive's deep laugh was followed by a question. "How are you, you old dog?"

"Fair to middling," said Tom.

14

Lucy had just changed into her tennis gear when the telephone shrilled through the house.

It was Tom.

"Where are you?" she asked.

"Le Lavandou."

"Still?"

He'd had a problem with his car, something to do with the suspension, which a mechanic was still trying to fix. He wouldn't be back in time for tennis, and suggested that Barnaby stand in for him.

"If I can detach him from Ilse," she said. "They're still down at the cove."

"Tell him it's an order from me. And he's also in charge of the cocktails. With any luck I'll be back before we leave for the restaurant."

"And if you aren't?"

"I will be."

He was. Just.

Lucy had assumed he was lying, that he'd taken the opportunity to sneak off to see Hélène in Hyères, but he was covered in dirt and grime, and there was even some blood on his shirt where he'd cut himself trying to fix the suspension by the side of the road.

He didn't want to talk about his wasted afternoon, though; he was far more eager to know how the tennis had gone.

"Six–four, six–three," said Barnaby, handing him one of his lethal rum concoctions.

"To you two?"

Barnaby rolled his eyes. "Of course."

"You should have seen it," said Mother. "Barnaby was prancing around the court like a man possessed."

"Ilse was watching," added Lucy, with a teasing grin.

"You men are so deluded. If you only knew how little store the female of the species sets by sporting prowess."

"What, we'd hang up our tennis shoes for good?" asked Barnaby.

"I was going to say, you'd take up the cello or learn how to paint."

Lucy saw the glint in Barnaby's eye and guessed what was coming next.

"Is it true, Lucy? Does a man who knows how to paint set your heart racing?" Barnaby turned to Tom. "Walter insisted on 'showing her his etchings' this afternoon."

"First of all, he didn't insist—I asked. And second, they're not etchings, they're oil paintings."

This drew a few chuckles.

"It's a euphemism, my darling," explained Mother. "Barnaby was trying to be funny."

"Well, give me a bit more warning next time and I'll try to remember to laugh."

"Ignore them," said Tom, planting a kiss on her cheek and handing her the rest of his cocktail. "And finish this. I need a swim."

Mother glanced pointedly at her wristwatch.

"If I'm not out front and ready to leave in fifteen minutes, dinner is on me," called Tom as he hurried off, snatching a beach towel from the line slung between the two tall palms beside the terrace.

Lucy found her eyes tracking him as he made off down the pathway, already pulling the shirt from his trousers and tugging it up over his head.

When she turned her attention back to the chatter on the terrace she saw that Mother's eyes were on her. They lingered, expressionless, but just long enough to let her know that her momentary distraction had been registered.

She would always remember the first time she dined at Les Roches. It wasn't her first night in France—they had taken two days to motor down from Calais—but it was her first ever night on the Mediterranean. And it didn't disappoint.

This was hardly surprising. After the unseasonal rain that had done its best to foul their passage south, and the detours to visit the cathedrals so beloved of Leonard, it would have taken a very strange child indeed to be disappointed by the cloudless skies and scented heat and crystal-clear waters of the Côte des Maures. The exoticism of the place was immediately captivating. Even the palms, with their feathery top-knots, seemed to speak of a secret lotusland.

It was Tom's first summer in Le Rayol, and although he had completed the refurbishment of Villa Martel, installing new plumbing as well as electric light, he was still in the process of filling its large and echoing rooms. There were beds for all, a big table to eat at with benches, the odd armchair here and there, a picture or two on the walls, but that was about the extent of the furnishings. His study contained one old desk, home to every worm ever born, along with a mountain of books still in their packing cases. Surprisingly, Mother had not balked at the prospect of the simple living, so taken was she by the Art Deco house, which held the memory of a high style she aspired to.

Dinner at Les Roches that first time was Tom's treat to them all after a tiring day on the road. It was to become their canteen over the following week; that's how good the food had been.

The hotel was proudly perched on dark rocks that rose sheer from the water, and its restaurant occupied a vast terrace, like the deck of an ocean liner, overlooking the wide expanse of the sea. Lucy could remember sitting at their table, drinking in the twilit fragrance, and scampering around on a small patch of sand with the boys in between courses. But her strongest recollection of the occasion was the story Tom had told them toward the end of the meal.

Maybe he embellished it for the benefit of George and Harry, who were ten and eight years old at the time. If he did, it was worth it. The two boys sat in rapt silence, listening to his account of how he first became acquainted with this stretch of coast that was now his home.

The story started simply enough. Soon after his eleventh birthday, he had come south one Easter to Hyères with his parents. The year was 1907, and the town had long been a popular winter resort with the British. Robert Louis Stevenson had sought a "cure" there, and since the visit of Queen Victoria, many of the shopkeepers had taken to advertising their wares in English as well as French.

The event in question, though, took place on the coast, just to the east of where they were all sitting, a short walk from Les Roches, around the headland.

An associate of Tom's father's, a missionary recently returned from the wilds of central Africa, happened to be staying at that time with friends in Cavalière. Invited to luncheon, Tom and his parents took the train over there from Hyères. During the course of the meal it became clear that the poor missionary had been traumatized by his experiences in the Congo, and Tom was excused from the table with instructions to make himself scarce. He strolled off along the beach to the rugged little headland west of town, and was happily foraging through the flotsam at the rocky waterline when a boat hove in view around the point.

He had never seen a sailing vessel like it.

Long and sleek, it was painted pink and green and blue, and was driven by a vast lateen sail, which the crew now furled. The boat glided gracefully toward the small beach west of the headland and nosed into the sand.

Tom's view was obscured by an outcrop. Unable to approach along the shore for fear of being spotted, he took to the pines at the top of the bluff, creeping stealthily closer, wincing with every crack of a twig underfoot.

They were working so silently that he thought at first he must have imagined the whole thing. But then he saw them down below: half a dozen men shoveling sand by hand into large reed baskets, which they then heaved onto their shoulders and humped up a crude gangway laid from the prow of the strange multicolored boat to the beach. In appearance, they could have stepped directly from the pages of *The Arabian Nights*. Their heads were bound with colorful kerchiefs, they wore loose, high-waisted cotton breeches, more like skirts, and their shirtless backs were browned to a deep umber.

To Tom's young mind they were, of course, pirates, possibly a raiding party sent to snatch a small white boy off into slavery. If there was any doubt, he now saw their captain, supine on a flat rock, turning a shiny knife in his hands, as if he might hurl it at any moment at one of his crew. There were thick gold hoops in his ears, an ancient pistol was tucked into the crimson sash around his waist and his head was tied with a colorful foulard.

Tom lay on his belly, as still as a toppled statue, barely breathing. The minutes ticked agonizingly by, but still the barefoot crew kept loading the ivory-white sand, padding quietly up and down the gangway.

His parents would already be wondering where he was, and yet he risked discovery if he moved. He was caught on the horns of a terrible dilemma. Was it to be his father's volcanic temper, and a near-certain thrashing, or a lifetime of slavery in some distant land? There wasn't much to choose between them, but he was spared having to cast his lot.

A barked order sent the crew scurrying aboard. The captain then rose to his feet and slowly surveyed the wooded slopes backing the beach, his chin raised, as if sniffing the air. If he detected the smell of a terrified young boy, he didn't react to it. Rather, he turned and strode majestically across the sand and up the gangway.

They used the anchored line they'd dropped off the back of the boat to haul themselves off the beach. A light breeze filled the sail and the felucca slipped silently away, making for the islands.

Only when Tom calculated that he was out of range of a pistol shot did he break from cover and begin to run.

George was eager to hear if Tom had been beaten on his return. Harry, although younger, had always been far more pragmatic in his thinking, and he wanted to know why the pirates had been stealing sand. Was it very precious sand, perhaps with gold dust mixed in?

Tom explained that he had got away with an ear-bending from his mother, having stumbled breathlessly into the house in Cavalière to find his father still deep in prayer with the troubled missionary. As for the sand, well, he now suspected that the men weren't pirates after all, but traders. Having offloaded their cargo along the coast, they were filling the empty hold of the vessel with ballast for the long slog back to North Africa.

Both boys overcame their respective disappointments as Tom turned back the Wheel of Time, bringing to life a distant era, a thousand years ago, when the Côte des Maures—the Moorish Coast—fell into the hands of the Saracens, where it remained for almost a century until a Christian army commanded by Guillaume I, Count of Provence, expelled the foreigners for good. This chapter might have been written out of French history, but maybe the pirate captain was acquainted with it. Maybe he hadn't been sniffing the air at all, but taking a long hard look at the land of his forebears before heading for home.

The Mediterranean, Tom continued, was littered with such tales of conquest, colonization and eventual displacement. Since time immemorial, the Middle Sea had been fought over by the various peoples inhabiting its shores. It was a vast crucible of disparate cultures and conflicting religious beliefs, a place where East and West collided. And although our own land lay far to the north, the Mediterranean still sat at the heart of our civilization. To ignore its rich history was to blinker ourselves against our true place in the world.

Lucy hadn't been aware of it at the time, but this was also a statement of intent on Tom's part. Yes, she knew he no longer worked with Leonard and was writing a book on Egypt, where he'd spent time as a cultural attaché, but that was about the extent of it. The pattern had only begun to emerge with the release of his second book—an account of his travels in Palestine and Transjordania—which, like the first, offered an unusual mix of history and personal anecdote, spiked with a dry and irreverent humor.

Having explored the eastern reaches of the Mediterranean, Tom had now turned his sights west, to an island at its very center. Lucy knew very little about the twelfth-century Norman kingdom of Sicily other than what Tom had told her when he last visited Oxford, but this slice of the past sounded far more like an adventure story than a history–cum–travel book.

The terrace at Les Roches was jammed with diners. To make matters the worse, the maître d' had reneged on his promise of the large circular table requested by Tom, assigning it instead to a party of loud Americans.

"You're losing your clout, old man," joked Barnaby.

"You obviously didn't tip him enough the last time you were here," said Mother. "Give me a few minutes with the regrettable little man and I'll have him dancing to our tune."

She was persuaded to let the matter drop, although she only began to relax once her wineglass had been filled. Fanya arrived with Walter, Klaus and Ilse as the first bottle of the evening was being poured. Yevgeny wasn't with them.

"He sends his apologies," explained Fanya. "He's not feeling well."

"A bad case of two defeats on the tennis court in two days?" wondered Leonard aloud.

"Tell him we'll let him win tomorrow," said Barnaby.

"Hey, we don't need your charity," Walter fired back, taking the empty seat next to Mother, rather than the one beside Lucy.

This was surprising, almost insulting. Was he trying to send her a message? Did he think they'd spent quite enough time together today? Could it be that he was already bored of her? Or maybe it was something else . . .

A sudden flush of embarrassment warmed her cheeks as she

thought back to her behavior out at the islands earlier that day. Walter had seemed quite happy to play along at the time, but it had obviously been a grave error of judgment on her part. Not that judgment of any kind had featured in her thinking. She had fallen foul of pure impulse.

They had approached Héliopolis from the north, sailing slowly past its cluster of whitewashed houses set among the pines on the rising ground beyond the low cliffs. Disappointingly, they had not spotted one naked person by the time they drew level with the small harbor, and even that appeared deserted. They were on the point of abandoning their voyeuristic mission and beating across the narrow strait to the island of Port-Cros when they saw the beach: a crescent of sand lapped by a turquoise streak of sea. There were a fair few people in view, and not one bathing costume among them.

"It looks like a seal colony," observed Walter, even as Lucy dropped the anchor over the side.

He turned at the sound, then promptly averted his eyes.

"Come on," she said, removing her striped singlet. "It'll be fun."

"Lucy . . ."

"Don't be an old sobersides."

And she was gone, into the water.

Walter stripped off and followed her, though not with any great enthusiasm. On swimming ashore, they lay on their backs, talking nonsense and studiously staring at the sky while the seawater dried on their skin.

It had hardly been fun, although they had joked about it afterward, when they were back aboard the *Albatross* and making for the mainland.

What in God's name had possessed her? Some distant memory of childhood and running around stark naked on the beach at Southbourne? It had made complete sense at the time, but none whatsoever now. With her paranoia in full flow, the events of the day were taking on a disturbing new complexion.

She had shamelessly coerced Walter into removing his clothes, which he had done only out of politeness to her, to spare her the humiliation of finding herself alone and naked in the sea. And later, when she had requested to see his paintings, she'd taken his lack of enthusiasm as the natural coyness of an artist, riding roughshod over it, whereas he'd probably just been trying to get rid of her.

Well, now he was seated next to Mother, never the easiest of dinner companions, as he was discovering.

"Compatriots of yours," she said, nodding at the table of braying Americans. "Any ideas on how to turn the volume down?"

Walter bent his ear toward their table. "New Yoikers," he said. "Not a snowball's chance in hell."

Barnaby had moved seats to position himself between Klaus and Ilse. "I'm happy to have a word," he offered.

"How chivalrous," replied Mother. "And how completely out of character. I can only imagine you've taken too much sun today."

Even by Mother's standards, this seemed an unreasonably hostile comment. She also fixed Barnaby with a round glare that defied him to retaliate.

Barnaby seemed to consider it for a moment, but turned his attention to Ilse instead.

15

Tom had suspected that Yevgeny might not show up at Les Roches. Fanya's attendance surprised him, though, as did her behavior toward him. Like Venetia, she could blow hot or cold according to her own native law, but tonight she was neither withdrawn nor neurotically overanimated, just full of flashing charm.

It was an extraordinary performance, ingenuously coquettish, and he admired her for making such a fine fist of it. If he hadn't caught her glancing at him with a basilisk eye on a couple of occasions he might even have fallen for it.

But it was a sham. She was guilty, guilty as sin itself. She was there to keep up appearances and also to learn a thing or two.

She must have known by now that Pyotr and the other Russian were unaccounted for, that they had surely failed in their mission. But whether they were alive or dead, being held captive somewhere by him or in police custody, she couldn't possibly say. She had come to Les Roches and, like a seasoned poker player, had taken her seat at the table with a view to discovering just what cards Tom held in his hand.

It showed great nerve. It showed great experience. It suggested she was the prime mover in the partnership rather than Yevgeny, who evidently wasn't up to the high-stakes game.

Leonard was far harder to read. Assuming he was involved in the plot, then he would be aware by now of the photo—Yevgeny and Fanya would have told him—and he would be wondering why Tom hadn't mentioned it to him. Tom was quite happy to alert Leonard to his suspicions of him; he was far more likely betray himself if he knew Tom was holding out on him.

But Leonard had given him nothing to go on. In fact, they had barely spoken since that morning. Leonard had taken him aside briefly when they arrived at Les Roches, saying that he had news and they needed to talk, but that was it.

Tom stared at his old friend across the table—laughing with Klaus as they recalled their favorite moments in Charlie Chaplin's films—and he tried to imagine him as a traitor. He just couldn't see it. Leonard didn't have a Communist bone in his body. He had despised the new regime in Russia from the moment of its brutal birth. This meant nothing, of course. One would have been hard pushed to find more vociferous critics of that same regime than Yevgeny and Fanya.

It surprised him how quickly he was changing. Like a snake, he had sloughed his old skin, the one browned and dried by five years in the French sun, and he was beginning to enjoy the fit of the new one beneath. The senses and instincts he'd worked so hard to blunt were still there, and they seemed to be sharpening themselves by the hour. Yesterday he had been reeling in shock and thinking about fleeing. There was no longer any question of that.

Yevgeny's absence spoke volumes. The enemy was worried. Twice they had tried to kill him and twice they had failed. He should have been a footnote in a long-forgotten saga by now; instead, he could sense the wind beginning to shift in his favor. They knew he was onto them and they presumably knew what he was capable of. They were right to be worried.

Tom forced himself back to the conversations unfolding around him. On his right, Barnaby was telling Ilse, somewhat pompously, that it was hard to be a journalist in England and remain a gentleman. Across the table, Venetia was addressing herself to Walter.

"Lucy tells me you studied at Harvard."

"That's right—Class of '33."

"Excuse me?"

"It means he graduated in 1933," interjected Leonard. "Which house were you in?"

Walter seemed surprised by the question. "Adams House. You know Harvard?"

"A little."

"Hardly at all," said Venetia. "He visited once."

Leonard ignored her. "Remind me where Adams House is."

"On Bow Street," replied Walter. "Well back from the river."

"And what did you study?"

"History and literature."

"Then you must have been taught by Matty," said Leonard.

"Matty?"

"Francis Matthiessen . . . ?"

"Oh, yes, of course."

"I thought everyone knew him as Matty," Leonard persisted, a little unnecessarily.

"Not me."

Venetia emitted a little gasp and gave Walter's wrist a playful slap. "Not *I*," she corrected. "And you a literature graduate!"

Was she flirting with him? If so, it didn't suit her.

The conversation turned to President Roosevelt—a Harvard man—and the New Deal he was in the process of pushing on the American nation.

"I can't imagine his ideas are going down too well at the old alma mater," said Leonard. "All those wealthy sons of wealthy men . . ."

"I imagine not."

"And where do you stand, Walter? Are you a New Dealer? Are you also a traitor to your class?"

It was unlike Leonard to adopt such a challenging tone, but Walter took it in his stride, weighing his words carefully before responding.

"My class brought the nation to its knees . . . the greed of a few. I re-member the day Roosevelt took his oath of office. Every bank in the country was closed that day. Every single one. You couldn't touch your savings, assuming you were lucky enough to have any left by then. Unemployment had climbed twenty percent in four years and prices had fallen by the same." He paused. "So much for the old maxim Let the government take care of the rich, and the rich will take care of the poor."

Barnaby, like everyone else, was listening in now. "I say, you're not a Communist, are you?"

He was joking, but Venetia wasn't when she rounded on him. "Oh, shut up, Barnaby. You *do* talk a lot of rot."

Walter, maybe out of sympathy, made a point of replying to Barnaby's question.

"No. Not to my knowledge. But something had to give. In two years Roosevelt's shown that the government can take care of the poor, and the rich can take care of themselves—even with the regulations he's put on them."

Klaus had been silent for much of the meal, but he now said in his thick accent: "Roosevelt has saved capitalism . . . from the capitalists."

Tom and Ilse were the first to laugh, possibly because they were the only ones present acquainted with the delicious irony of Klaus's writing.

Leonard insisted on paying for the meal. Tom then insisted on splitting the bill with him.

"As you wish," said Leonard.

It was the excuse they'd both been waiting for: a chance to be alone together. As they made their way inside to settle up, Venetia shot a sour glance at her husband for not putting up more of a fight, but she kept her tongue behind her teeth.

The moment they were out of earshot, Leonard said, "You had me worried this afternoon when you didn't reappear."

"I should have called earlier, but I assumed you were all down at the beach."

"We were. I hooked four very respectable bream off the rocks. I was thinking we could have them for lunch tomorrow."

If he knew how Tom's afternoon had really gone, he was doing a very good job of hiding it.

They took themselves out the front of the restaurant while the bill was being drawn up.

Leonard didn't waste any time.

"Well, by rights you should be dead. It's as I thought: the syringe contained a concentrated solution of potassium chloride, enough to kill you several times over. Even then, an autopsy wouldn't have picked it up because it breaks down into potassium and chlorine, both of which are naturally occurring compounds in the body. It would have looked like a heart attack."

"The perfect murder . . ."

"Except he's the one who's dead," observed Leonard drily. "We've had our people in Rome looking into him. Minguzzi wasn't his real name."

"How do you know?"

"Because the name you found on the sweatband of his hat came up trumps."

"Cesare Pozzi . . ."

"A known criminal, suspected of a string of murders in Naples, where he worked for a certain Michele Greco. Say what you like about Mussolini, but he's come down hard on organized crime. About a year ago Pozzi showed up in Rome because Naples had become too hot to hold him. The description you gave me fits with what we know of Pozzi."

"Short and dark? I would have thought that covers most of the male population of Italy."

"True, but since arriving in Rome Pozzi has become a known associate of Alfiero Tosti."

It was the name Tom had extracted from Pozzi in the railway cutting just before the Italian lost consciousness.

"Tosti's a small-time criminal, a racketeer, a fixer."

Tom tried to contain his excitement. For all he knew, it was a pack of lies served up to appease him, to convince him that the investigation was moving in the right direction. Had Leonard even been in touch with their people in Rome? He made a mental note to tell Clive to look into it when they spoke again tomorrow.

"Can we bring Tosti in?" he asked.

Leonard's answer did nothing to reassure him. "Under the circumstances, I'm happy to do far more than simply bring him in. The only trouble is, we don't where he is. He's disappeared off the map."

"Pozzi mentioned Viterbo and Pescara."

"And they're on it. I don't know what else to say."

"So we wait."

"I'm afraid so."

They broke off their conversation as an attractive young couple emerged from the restaurant. They looked so joyously devoid of anxiety that it almost hurt to watch them weave off into the night, arm in arm.

"No news from London?" Tom asked.

"None so far. Soon, I hope."

Tom lit a cigarette, buying himself a little time to think.

"There's something you should know. I had a visit from the police this morning, a Commissaire Roche from Le Lavandou."

Only this morning? It seemed like an eternity ago.

"What did he want?"

"He's investigating Pozzi's disappearance from the hotel. He seems to have got it into his head I know more than I'm letting on."

"This morning, you say?"

"He came by the villa."

"And you wait until now to tell me?"

"I've been trying to make sense of it."

Leonard didn't look particularly convinced by the response. "And what did you conclude?"

"That Roche is no fool. He heard I took breakfast at the hotel—something I hardly ever do. He's just being thorough."

"It sounds like there's more to it than that. Maybe you were seen leaving Pozzi's room."

"I'd be in custody right now if that were the case."

"True."

"I asked Benoît about him. Roche is a terrier, a pit bull; once he latches on he doesn't let go."

It made sense to mention Roche; he was letting Leonard know that, should anything happen to him, the matter would be far from closed. Also, he needed Roche off his back.

Leonard understood this immediately. "I'll see if I can't prize his jaws open."

Tom dropped his cigarette on the gravel and crushed it out underfoot. "We should be getting back."

"Walter . . ." said Leonard, trailing off.

"What about him?"

"Keep one eye on him."

"Walter? Why?"

Leonard hesitated before replying. "I don't know. There's a false note in there somewhere."

"Thus spake the overprotective stepfather."

Leonard gave a weak smile. "You're right—it's probably nothing."

Barnaby was all for motoring over to Saint-Tropez and dancing the night away at the lively little *boîte de nuit* in the upper town that he remembered so fondly from last year.

"Or even L'Escale. The band doesn't knock off there until two."

His heart went out of the idea the moment Ilse announced she was "*hundemüde*" and ready for bed. Besides, as Fanya pointed out, they all had to conserve their energy for her party tomorrow night.

"I hope Yevgeny's feeling better by then," said Lucy.

"If he isn't, *tant pis*. The party goes on without him."

"If he isn't," said Barnaby, "I might have something to help him through the evening."

"*Mais, toi, t'es incorrigible!*"

Tom also reminded them that they had the scavenger hunt tomorrow afternoon, immediately after lunch, and they were going to need their wits about them. A few years ago this might have elicited a few groans, but the scavenger hunt had become one of the high points of the summer.

When they parted company out front, Tom searched for some veiled meaning in the kiss Fanya planted on his cheek. However, there seemed to be as much genuine warmth in it as the others she distributed so freely. She even gave his hand an affectionate squeeze before clambering into the back of the car with Ilse.

Christ, she was good.

It was a short run back to Le Rayol from Aiguebelle, but Venetia managed to smoke two cigarettes in that time.

She was pulling a third from her cigarette case when Barnaby remarked from the rear seat, "Do you have to? It's like a gas attack at Ypres back here."

Venetia launched a poisoned look over her shoulder. "As if you'd have any idea what that was like."

"Palestine wasn't exactly a walk in the park," bridled Barnaby.

Venetia didn't light the cigarette, though; she tossed it out of the window. The other cigarettes in the case followed.

"Happy now?"

No one said anything. They all knew better—all except Barnaby.

"Not as happy as the old man bicycling past first thing tomorrow morning."

Venetia snorted, amused, in spite of herself.

Leonard insisted on dropping them at the front steps of the villa. Tom slipped his pack of cigarettes into Venetia's hand as he clambered out of the car after Barnaby.

"Thank you, darling—you're a mind reader."

"Nightcap?" Tom asked once the taillights had disappeared back down the driveway.

Barnaby brightened. "Ooh, a small glass of Calvados might hit the spot."

They carried a couple of armchairs from the drawing room onto the terrace and sat out there beneath the spangle of stars, lapped in the strange liquid tranquillity of the night.

"You like her, don't you?" remarked Tom.

"Who's that?"

"Ilse."

"A bloody Kraut. Who'd have believed it?"

"It might be best to keep that particular moniker to yourself."

"Too late. I've already told her she's a bloody Kraut."

"You old romantic. What did she say?"

"Something offensive, I imagine. I caught the word *engländer* in there somewhere."

"Sounds like the beginning of a beautiful thing."

"You know what?" said Barnaby, thoughtfully. "I think it just might be. She's certainly shaped exactly for my taste, blond and slim and—"

"Big-breasted?"

"Aren't they magnificent? I managed to brush against one of them today."

"Really? Left or right?"

"Left."

"Congratulations."

"Thank you—it took some pretty deft maneuvering, I can tell you."

Tom laughed.

Barnaby had always been far more brazen than he when it came to girls. At school he'd made a shameless play for their housemaster's daughter, and when that had failed to yield dividends (Barnaby's father was a stockbroker), he had turned his sights on one of the girls who worked in the kitchens, detailing his clumsy progress for the edification of his peers in the dormitory after lights-out. He wasn't bragging; he always painted himself as an inept fool. He was simply consumed by a curiosity for the opposite sex, and not in the least concerned about submitting to his baser impulses. In fact, the baser the better. While they were at university he was always trying to drag Tom down to London, to his seamy netherworld of Soho cabarets and chorus girls and basement bars with postage-stamp dance floors. He saw it as his mission to release Tom from the harmful strictures of his upbringing: the lonely childhood in the wilds of East Anglia, sequestered in a damp rectory with a tyrannical priest of a father whose severe religiosity was matched only by his barefaced hypocrisy.

That wasn't exactly how it had been, but Barnaby had always had the journalist's eye for the big story. If the details couldn't be made to serve the argument, then one was entitled to ignore them.

"I've fallen behind in life," said Barnaby, lighting a cigarette and staring up at the firmament. "I'll be forty in three months. It might be time to ditch the old motto."

"Which one is that? You generally have several to hand, most of them contradictory."

"Melius nil coelibe vita."

"The bachelor's life is best."

"Maybe it's time for you to ditch it too," continued Barnaby. "Make an honest woman of Hélène."

Tom was impressed that he'd remembered her name. "If you'd met her you'd know that's the last thing she wants." Not true; she'd set her heart on a Polish count.

"Why *haven't* I met her?"

"Oh, God . . ." said Tom wearily.

"What?"

"I had Lucy on to me about the same thing last night."

"And you're surprised? Of course she's fascinated; she carries a big bloody torch for you."

"Don't be ridiculous."

"Whenever you're about it's all she can do to keep her tongue from hanging out, poor thing."

"Oh, for goodness' sake—"

"Don't pretend you don't know. And don't pretend you haven't thought about it."

"I'm not even going to dignify that with a response."

"Afraid I'll see through the lie?"

He looked Barnaby clean in the eye. "I've never thought about it."

"Not bad," said Barnaby. "Almost convincing. But I'm not falling for it."

They talked the subject into a corner and found Venetia lurking there.

"I can tell you what Venetia thinks, if you like."

"She talks to you about it?" Tom asked.

"She doesn't need to; it's written all over her face. I can safely say it's her worst nightmare, the thought of you and Lucy together. I think she might even kill you."

"Well, she's not going to have to. Anyhow, she seems to have her sights set on you right now."

"Me?" said Barnaby.

"Come on—she's been at you from the moment you arrived."

"You think?"

"You haven't noticed?"

Barnaby hesitated. "No, I've noticed."

"Have you offended her in some way?"

"Worse," said Barnaby, staring at his glass as he swirled the alcohol around it.

"Is there something you want to tell me?"

Barnaby drew on his cigarette and exhaled. "There's something I *don't* want to tell you," he replied finally, with a look that hovered between coy and contrite.

"You didn't?" groaned Tom. "You haven't?"

"Did. Have. But not anymore. It barely lasted a month. That's how significant it was."

"Well, obviously Venetia doesn't agree with you."

"She ended it. Come to think of it, she also started it."

"How very polite of you to play along," said Tom. "So why is she out for your blood?"

"For God's sake, Tom, don't be so naïve. When has Venetia ever needed a reason to do anything? Maybe she sees me and Ilse getting on and it irritates her. Who knows how that mind of hers works? She's certainly not interested in me anymore; I'm not sure she ever was."

"Enough to commit adultery with you."

"I don't think she saw it as adultery. She was only getting her own back. It was revenge."

"Revenge?"

"For Leonard's infidelity."

Tom was too shocked to respond.

"Do you remember Diana Bevan?"

"No . . . yes . . . vaguely. What are you saying? Leonard and Diana Bevan . . . ?"

"Venetia got wind of it and confronted Leonard. He broke it off immediately, but she was pretty upset, as you can imagine, what with it coming on the back of the whole money debacle. Look, I know I shouldn't have done it—"

"Hold your horses," interrupted Tom. "What money debacle?"

"You don't know?"

"Evidently not or I wouldn't be asking."

"Leonard's run through a small fortune on the cards."

He couldn't see it. Leonard had always liked to gamble, but soberly, with restraint.

"How much?" Tom asked.

"I don't know—Venetia didn't say. Enough to make a difference, though. Yevgeny had to step in and bail him out."

Tom tried to find the words. "He's in hock to Yevgeny?"

"Up to his neck, apparently."

So that was it—the missing link. It explained everything. He had been coming at it all wrong. Leonard's involvement had nothing to do with Communist sympathies; he was clearing his debt to Yevgeny.

Barnaby took his silence as disapproval. "I'm not proud of what I did, but I'd be lying if I said it wasn't enjoyable while it lasted. She's a vixen between the sheets."

"I don't want to know."

"I always thought you did already, but she said there'd never been anything between you two."

Tom was taken with a sudden urge to change the subject, and not only because he needed information from Barnaby. It would have been an awkward matter to raise at the best of times. Following on from the shocking revelations, there was no way of folding it casually into their conversation. In the end, he came straight out with it.

"Barnaby, I need to ask you something."

"Fire away."

"At lunch today did anyone make a phone call after I left?"

"A phone call?"

"Yes."

"How on earth should I know?"

"Because you were there. I need to know if anyone made a phone call soon after I left."

"Why?"

"I can't tell you. Not yet. But there's a lot riding on it."

There certainly was. The dead Soviet had been tipped off in good time that Tom was on his way to Le Lavandou—more than enough time to collect Pyotr from his hotel room and for them both to then take up a position in front of Benoît's office before Tom arrived. Given that he'd revealed he was off to visit Benoît's only as he was leaving lunch at Klaus and Ilse's place, and given that it had taken him twenty minutes at the most to drive from Le Canadel to Le Lavandou, he could safely conclude that someone had put a call through within ten minutes of his departure.

"Not good enough," said Barnaby. "What's going on? I thought you'd given up all that cloak-and-dagger stuff."

Barnaby could be an obstinate bugger once his interest was piqued. Dangling a carrot seemed the best method of proceeding.

"Okay," conceded Tom, disingenuously. "There's a story in it."

"What kind of story?"

"The kind that lands up on the front page."

Barnaby regarded him closely before speaking. "It's not your fault, I know—I'm entirely to blame—but you must have an extremely low opinion of me if you think I can be bought off that cheaply."

Tom tilted his head by way of apology. "I don't know what to say. I need your help and I can't tell you why."

"Then ask me as a friend, Tommy."

"As a friend . . ."

Barnaby hesitated. "Soon after you left, you say?"

"Within ten minutes or so. Could it have been Klaus, after he walked me to my car?"

"No, I heard you drive off and he reappeared immediately." Barnaby played the scene through in his head before adding, "It can only have been Ilse."

"Ilse?"

"Or Fanya. She offered to help Ilse bring the dessert out. No one else went inside the house."

"You're sure?"

"Sure as God made little green apples. Talking of which, another glass of that Calvados would slip down a treat."

16

Tom was ready for sleep. He urged it on, willing it to take him, to draw him into oblivion, but it lapped at his ankles like a neap tide, before retreating.

It wasn't the fear. He knew he had more reason to feel secure in his bed than at any other time in the past two days. Pyotr had warned him that others would be dispatched from Paris to deal with him, but at worst these faceless replacements had taken the night train from the capital and wouldn't be here before midday at the earliest. Almost twelve hours' grace. If ever there was a time to catch up on lost sleep, now was it.

His mind, though, had other plans for him. It took him to the Toulon station to see if he could identify the men in question as they stepped from the train, allowing him to steal a march on them. It carried him off to Sicily, where he'd spent much of last autumn researching his book, and where he now constructed a new life for himself, a new identity, a secret existence somewhere remote—Noto, maybe, or Lipari—a place where no one would ever find him, no enemies, no friends. It would mean severing all ties if he was to guarantee his safety. There could be no exceptions. Was it Blaise Pascal who had said that all the misfortunes of men arise from one single thing: that they are unable to sit quietly in a room alone? Well, this time he would heed the lesson of those wise words and do it properly. He would learn to shut himself away.

He knew he could survive the upheaval. He had been cast adrift before, thrown back on himself, forced against his wishes into a new existence far from home, and his mind now hurled him back through the years to that moment and the incident that had triggered it.

His father had always been a man of rigid routine, never more so than on Sunday mornings, when preparing to face his flock. Tom would generally wake to the smell of frying bacon and the sounds of his father pacing around in his study below, putting the finishing touches to his sermon, rehearsing his lines. Notes in a pulpit were anathema to him. What sort of preacher was it who required props? In his opinion, one who had no faith in the Lord's guiding hand. This uncompromising view was typical of his domineering self-assurance.

His father was in a particularly good frame of mind on the Sunday morning in question, having received word the previous day that the bishop would be unable to attend the morning Eucharist due to illness. The bishop's annual visit irritated his father no end, chiefly because it obliged him to temper the language of his sermon to satisfy what he perceived to be the bishop's "Roman" inclinations.

As ever, breakfast was cooked by Olive and served by her niece Kitty. Tom loved Olive—stout and brisk and with her soft, dimpled face—but he adored Kitty with the blind devotion of a neglected twelve-year-old. It wasn't that his parents ignored him—they didn't—but he had never been of any real interest to them, it seemed to him. He hoped that that would all change as he grew up; meanwhile, though, he had Kitty on hand to smother him with attention and occupy his hours during the school holidays.

She would call him Master Thomas around the house, but whenever they were off on one of their wild walks or striding the streets of Norwich together he was "Tom Thumb" or "Ho Hum" and sometimes "Skinny Bum." Kitty opened his eyes to another world, another way of being far removed from the muted, cloistered existence of the rectory.

She also taught him to lie, to look his father in the eye and say that he had enjoyed his visit to the cathedral, when really Kitty had taken him to see the death masks of the murderers in the Norwich Castle Museum, or to watch the eels being skinned at the old fish market in St. Peter's Street.

It was Kitty who introduced Tom to Baint, an elderly tenant farmer who lived in a neighboring village. He was a distant relative of Kitty's father and his real name was Joseph, although Kitty called him Baint because he was always moaning that "Things bain't what they was." Baint had been born with his hands in the soil. There wasn't one thing he didn't know about the countryside, or one thing he wasn't happy to share with a curious boy. Kitty always claimed that he was wiser in the ways of horses than any other soul, living or dead.

Baint proved her right one warm day in spring. Officially, Kitty and Tom were in Cromer, far to the north of Norwich, taking a healthy dose of sea air. Instead, they had headed south with Baint to the races at Bungay. The bookmakers had nothing to fear from Baint that day, and Tom could feel his faith in the old man's equine expertise beginning to waver. Then came the penultimate race of the day.

The leader pulled away from the rest of the field right from the off, flying the hurdles, and was maybe six or seven lengths clear when it popped over the last and came galloping up the slope toward the stand. People were cheering wildly, not least of all Tom, because it looked as though Baint had finally backed a winner.

Baint wasn't so sure. Raising his hands to his mouth, he bellowed: "Get off him—he's a dead 'un!" Several people threw amused glances Baint's way. They weren't smirking when the horse dropped down dead right in front of the stand, sending the jockey tumbling to the turf.

Tom barely slept that night, troubled, though not by Baint's mystical prophecy. He was thinking about Kitty and the double life she had led him into. The lies were getting bigger—betting on horses instead of building sand castles on the beach—and so were the risks. He loved Kitty for her reckless streak, her surefooted lawlessness, but he couldn't help feeling he was being drawn out of his depth, that it would all end in tears.

And so it did, a few weeks later, on the Sunday the bishop showed up for the morning Eucharist.

The fixed routine after breakfast required Tom to squeeze himself into the starched tissues of his "Sunday best" before accompanying his mother and Olive to the church for choir practice. Olive sang in the choir, a tremulous alto, and his mother liked to sit and watch, offering a few kind words of guidance to ensure they were at their best for the service. Meanwhile, back at the rectory, Kitty would be setting the table in the dining room for lunch while his father robed up. Ordinarily, they would arrive at the church together, with five minutes or so to spare.

The routine was shattered that day by the unexpected arrival of the bishop soon after the bell ringers had gone to work. He offered his apologies to Tom's mother; his fever had broken quite suddenly during the night and there had been no time to send word. Tom's mother bowed and scraped and showed him to a pew at the front. She then took Tom aside and instructed him to hurry home and warn his father. Under the circumstances, an alb, chasuble and stole might be more fitting than the humble cassock and surplice his father generally favored.

The rectory was hard by the church, a short walk through the churchyard, beneath the lych-gate, over the footbridge spanning the brook and across the back garden. At a run, Tom covered the distance in less than a minute. He entered the house silently through the back door, not wishing to disturb his father, who he knew liked to give himself to prayer right up until his departure for the church.

Sure enough, Tom heard murmurings from the study. The door was ajar and he stole across the hallway, waiting for a break in his father's devotions before presenting himself. When none occurred, he peered through the crack in the door.

His father was standing in a gloomy corner of the room, beyond his desk. His head was tilted back, his eyes were closed and Kitty was kneeling before him. Although Tom couldn't make out the words, his father's hand was resting on Kitty's head and he was clearly administering a blessing of some kind. But as his eyes adjusted to the thin light from the window Tom realized with horror that quite the reverse was true.

He now saw that his father's cassock was hitched up to his waist and that Kitty's head was bobbing back and forth with an urgency suggesting far more than simple benediction. When her hand rose into view and her nails traced a slow path down his father's long pale thigh, Tom turned and crept away.

He made every effort to be silent, but it was hard to judge, with the blood drumming so loudly in his ears. As soon as he was through the kitchen and out of the back door he began to run. Halfway across the lawn he realized his error and stopped dead. He hadn't delivered the message. How could he possibly explain his failure to do so? His father would know immediately. Then it came to him: he must return and make a lot of noise this time, slamming the back door as he entered, maybe even knocking over one of the chairs in the kitchen. Yes, that was it!

When he turned back to the house he saw his father observing him from one of the kitchen windows.

He tried his best, but lying, he discovered, was much easier when he'd been briefed by Kitty beforehand. This time he was on his own, and after he'd broken the news about the bishop's surprise appearance he was brought down by one simple question.

"Why were you running away from the house, Thomas?"

Nothing came to mind. Nothing at all. He just stood there, hopelessly mute, staring blankly up at his father's grave face.

"Thank you, Thomas. Please tell your mother I'll be right over."

A dismissal. And confirmation that he knew Tom had seen them together. He would normally have repeated the question until he got an answer.

One of the readings that morning was from the First Book of Kings. It told of the death of Ahab at the Battle of Ramoth-gilead. This was a gift from his father, who would throw in a passage from some bloody Old Testament saga every so often for Tom's entertainment. It was their secret. Tom would drop out of time as he listened to the ancient stories of gathering armies and racing chariots and skies blackened with arrows. And later, he would watch with amusement as his father struggled to link the reading to the theme of his sermon that week. He always managed it, though, and when he did he would catch Tom's eye from the pulpit and give him an almost imperceptible wink.

There was no wink that Sunday. In fact his father was barely able to look him in the eye for weeks, even after Kitty had moved on. Nothing was mentioned, but everything had changed. A few months later, his father took him into his study and announced that Tom would not be taking up his place at King Edward VI School in Norwich the following September, but would instead be continuing his education at a school near Brighton—way, way to the south, far beyond London, another world. No reason was offered, and none was required.

With time, his upset gave way to anger and resentment at his expulsion. He no longer blamed himself (for snooping), or the Devil (for leading his father astray), or Kitty (for being, well, Kitty). No doubt his father had squared himself with his God, if not his conscience, but he had made no such efforts with his son. Their relationship was worse than dead; it was a living lie. Only during his last year at school, while they were both preparing for the Oxford entrance exam, did Tom finally pluck up the courage to tell Barnaby about the incident, and only then because it seemed no more scandalous than many of the confidences Barnaby had shared with him about his own family over the years.

"Holy moly," said Barnaby, "that's a hard one to top—no pun intended. But think of it this way: if young Kitty hadn't licked his lollipop, we would never have met each other."

Tom found himself swinging his legs off the bed and pulling on his clothes. He knew he had drunk too much and wasn't thinking straight. He knew that his violently restless mood was too tied up with the past to be let loose on the present. But the memories were coming at him now from all four quarters of his life, reaching for him, clutching at him, drawing him down into the dark world he had vowed never to visit again.

*   *   *

Yevgeny and Fanya's house had shouldered its way into an awkward kind of beauty over the years. Given how little remained of the original farmhouse—a few thick stone walls at the heart of the property—it would have made more sense for the previous owners to have pulled it down and built the Italianate villa of their dreams from scratch. They had put up the guest cottage in the grounds, where Walter was now staying, and its delicacy of touch stood as an unfortunate testament to what might have been achieved with the main house.

The setting, though, was hard to fault. La Quercia occupied a prominent position near the tip of the high headland, with an uninterrupted view down onto the bay of Le Rayol. This was why Tom was able to determine that someone was still up and about. Stalking along the beach, he could make out a couple of lights still burning on the ground floor.

At the western end of the beach the sand gave way to sheer rock, but a narrow pathway cut inland, winding its way up the wooded slope toward the coast road. This was the route he would normally have taken, a route he had often trod: joining the coast road for a few hundred yards before turning down the long dirt road that served as a driveway to La Quercia and the handful of other houses occupying the headland. Tonight, though, he wasn't coming with friendship in his heart and a gift for the hostess in his hand. He couldn't run the risk of being spotted, and as soon as he judged it safe to do so, he bore left off the pathway, scrabbling from tree to tree across the vertiginous slope that ended just below him with a long drop onto the rocks.

It took him five anxious minutes to work his way around to the end of the headland. He knew that the anger still burning inside him was a confused thing, fired by memories of his father. He knew that he should master it, separate out the strands, before deciding how to proceed. But he was in the grip of something that left little place for such prudence. He needed to know if the man who had filled his father's shoes had also failed him, betrayed him.

Somehow, he couldn't bring himself to blame Leonard, even now.

Leonard had been targeted, patiently cultivated, manipulated into a corner. Tom held no such sympathies for Yevgeny and Fanya. God only knew what other evils they'd been party to over the years, but they were about to discover that most things we strive for in life come at a price that is duly exacted. He didn't plan on harming them, but the prospect of calling them to account, of terrorizing them into some truths, was really quite agreeable.

The main terrace was awash with pale moonlight and he kept to the shadows at the rear of the cottage, stepping gingerly through the trees on a blanket of pine needles. The smell of pine sap grew strangely intense on the still night air, as if his senses were heightening in anticipation of the looming confrontation. It was the odor of turpentine, he realized. One of the cottage's windows was open—the window serving the small room that Walter used as his studio. The French doors to the bedroom were also open, he noted, and he crept more carefully than ever toward the main house.

They were in the drawing room, and they seemed to be having a heated discussion of some kind. They were speaking in Russian, but even when he edged closer to the window it was hard to make out the words, muffled as they were by the closed curtains. He needed to be sure they were alone, so he waited there awhile, ears straining for the sound of another voice. Satisfied, he made off around the side of the house, trying the windows as he went. The lights he had seen from down on the beach belonged to the study and the kitchen, and he skipped quickly past both, momentarily caught in the glare.

The back door was locked. So was the front door. And all the downstairs windows were latched from the inside. Yevgeny and Fanya weren't taking any chances, but they had made one mistake: their bedroom window was open. Tom knew where they kept the ladder because he'd helped Yevgeny hang the Chinese lanterns in the trees around the terrace for last year's summer party. He hadn't noticed as he'd skirted the terrace, but the lanterns were probably hanging there now, ready for tomorrow night's festivities, and with any luck the ladder would be back in the toolshed.

It was. Tom lifted it free of the wall hooks and maneuvered it carefully out through the door.

He had taken no more than a couple of steps toward the house when something pressed into the nape of his neck.

"Shhh," soothed a voice from behind him.

He was hamstrung, his hands full with the ladder, the muzzle of the gun cold against his skin. A practiced hand searched him, pulling the Browning from his hip pocket.

"Put the ladder down. Slowly."

The voice was unmistakable.

"It's me—Tom."

"I know," said Walter. "Now put the goddamn ladder down."

As he lowered the ladder to the ground, Tom thought about going for the Beretta tucked into his sock. The odds were against him, though. And besides, he didn't yet know just where Walter fit in the thing.

"It's not what you think," said Tom, rising.

"Oh? And what do I think?"

A sharp shove between the shoulder blades propelled him forward, though not toward the main house.

Neither of them spoke until they were inside the cottage and seated opposite each other in the living room. The fact that Walter left all the lights off said something. The darkness, pricked by a few stray shafts of moonlight, also provided Tom with the opportunity he'd been waiting for.

"What are you doing here?" said Walter.

"Do you have to point that thing at me? It might go off."

Tom heard the click of the hammer being cocked.

"There's always that danger, I guess," replied Walter.

There was another audible click as Tom drew back the slide, cocking the hammer of the Beretta, now secreted in the shadows around his lap and pointing straight at Walter.

"It's a Beretta 418, in case you're interested."

Walter shifted uneasily in his armchair. "I believe this is what's called a Mexican standoff."

"I believe so," said Tom.

"It's a first for me. What happens now?"

"I like you, Walter, and I really don't want to have to shoot you, so why don't you give me a good reason for putting my gun down."

Walter hesitated before speaking. "I work for American intelligence."

"Oh?"

"The MID."

"Which stands for . . . ?"

"Exactly the same thing it stood for when you were in the business," said Walter pointedly.

"The Military Intelligence Division wasn't running its own agents abroad when I was in the business."

At best, they sat at their desks in Washington collating whatever scraps of hearsay trickled home from their embassies and consulates around the world. The British Secret Intelligence Service had always regarded America's MID as something of a joke.

"In case you hadn't noticed," said Walter, "a lot's changed in the past five years. Germany's a one-party dictatorship and the Soviets are more active than ever."

"So much for American isolationism."

"You and I both know if there's another war we'll end up crashing the party like last time."

Tom held up the Beretta and made a show of laying the weapon on the arm of his chair.

"Well, I suppose it explains your paintings," he said.

Walter also laid his gun aside. "You think they're that bad?"

"Bad enough to convince Yevgeny they might be good."

"That's the idea."

"How long have you known about them?" asked Tom.

"Quid pro quo," said Walter. "You go first."

"Only if you give me a cigarette."

Walter tossed over his cigarette case and a lighter. Tom fired up a cigarette, calculating just how much to reveal and how much to hold back.

"Okay," he said finally. "Two nights ago, someone tried to kill me in my bed. An Italian. A professional."

"Christ . . ." muttered Walter.

"He had a photograph of me in his possession. He can only have got it from Yevgeny and Fanya."

"Are you sure?"

"Do you think I'd be messing around with ladders in the middle of the night if I wasn't?"

Walter reflected a moment. "Why you? Are you still active?"

"No. It's an old story, I think, something going back years."

"Petrograd?"

"Is there nothing you don't know about me?"

"Not much," said Walter. He rose from his chair, wandered over and took his cigarettes back. Lighting one, he asked, "An Italian, you say?"

"I know—it doesn't make sense."

"So maybe you're wrong about the Soviets."

"Tell that to the two NKVD men I met this afternoon."

Walter didn't react. Tom liked that. It showed a maturity far beyond his years: absorbing the information, filing it away, no need to comment or to satisfy his curiosity about the fate of the Italian and the other two. The boy had prospects. The MID was lucky to have him.

Walter moved to the window and peered out into the night. "They're still awake, still arguing, I guess. I could tell something was up these past days. I didn't know what, though." He turned and announced suddenly, "You have to leave them be."

"Yevgeny and Fanya?"

"There's way too much at stake. You have to leave them be."

"I'm sorry," said Tom, not quite snorting at the absurdity of the notion, "but I can't see that happening."

"At least hear me out."

17

Lucy was woken by the sound of the wind singing in the pine tops outside her shuttered windows.

Her first thought was of the *Albatross* and the fine sailing to be had before the early-morning blow dwindled to just a satisfactory breeze. She lingered a moment in bed, though, eager to pin down the dream she'd been having, to prevent it from fading forever into the ether of wakefulness.

It wasn't really a dream so much as a gem snatched from the treasury of her childhood memories. For some reason, she had written out the other characters, although she saw them clearly now, just as she saw the large house in its leafy square south of Vauxhall Bridge. She would stay there sometimes with her best friend from school, Amelia, whose father was a horticulturalist attached to the Royal Botanic Gardens at Kew. He had a greenhouse of his own to prove it: an enormous lean-to affair that ran almost the entire length of their garden against the high north wall.

It was here that Lucy saw her first night-blooming cereus. In many ways it was an unremarkable plant, even ugly: a gangling mess reaching to some five or six feet in height, its long rubbery leaves sprouting, then drooping from a stem so spindly that it had to be staked in its pot to stop it from collapsing. What set it apart, though, what made this ungainly member of the cactus family the very finest plant in the known world, in the expert opinion of Amelia's father, were its blossoms. Some said that they appeared only once every hundred years, which wasn't true, but they *were* temperamental. If they graced you with their presence at all, they only ever bloomed at night, and then for a single night before they withered and died. Lucy happened to be staying when the four enormous trumpetlike blossoms adorning the plant that year were set to perform. The girls were summoned from their beds toward midnight and brought downstairs in their dressing gowns to witness the rare spectacle.

In her dream, Lucy was alone, not dwarfed by a tribe of twittering adults who had turned up for dinner and stayed on for the occasion. She stood there on her own in her nightdress, candle in hand, watching in wonder as the long waxy-white blossoms, tinged with pink at their tips, slowly unraveled, baring themselves to her. The pointed petals folded back in snowy sunbursts as big as dinner plates, and the stamens clustered at the base of the slender stigmas seemed to quiver in the candlelight like the tentacles of a sea anemone. The odor was intoxicating, a rich vanilla, almost obscene in its heady complexity.

Then night became day and Lucy found herself standing in the low dawn light of the greenhouse, staring at the blooms hanging limp and lifeless from their stiff purple stems. Their job was done—the moths had been and gone—and they were happy to give themselves over to pulpy decay.

Why on earth had she dreamed of the night-blooming cereus? Mother was all for interpreting dreams, or rather, all for getting Dr. Feinstein to interpret them for her. Maybe that's why Mother had been so on edge lately. More reliant than ever on the good doctor, she had no choice but to make do without him when on holiday. She openly referred to him as her "guru," which last year had drawn the response from Barnaby "Well, I suppose it's easier to spell than 'charlatan.'" Even Mother had laughed. In many ways, that was her downfall—her sense of humor. An amusing comment, correctly timed and applied, could banish her mood in a moment and bring back the best of her.

Why the cereus, though? There had to be a reason. Maybe it had something to do with the brief flowering of youth and her imminent birthday, which would see her step officially across the threshold into adulthood. Yes, it was probably that. She was painfully aware of her own anxieties about the future. She had never felt the need to ignore them or cloak them in bold statements of intent, as some did, although she knew that many of her contemporaries at St. Hugh's regarded her as confident to the point of haughtiness. Her friend Stella had once been kind enough to tell her so, while adding: "Ignore them, darling. For all the opportunities Oxford has given them, most will leap at the chance to raise a horrid little brood with some dreary solicitor who takes the train in from Dorking every morning. They'll be desperately unhappy all their lives and will go to their graves never knowing what an orgasm is."

"Whereas we . . . ?" Lucy had inquired skeptically.

"Whereas *we* are going to change the world: for all, not just for womankind."

"And if we fail?"

"Well, then, at least we have the orgasms to fall back on."

It was bad enough having a friend who talked with such certainty, far worse when that friend then fell hopelessly, inexplicably, in love with a jug-eared Irish laborer whose name she didn't even know.

Lucy wanted to believe in Stella's dream, but when she looked at her life there seemed very little cause for optimism. This time next year university would be over and yet she still had no clear idea of what career, if any, she wished to pursue. She had toyed with the possibility of doing the civil-service exams, or even teaching, but these were plans she'd voiced in order to satisfy others, not herself. As for men, she seemed doomed to be drawn to the worst possible kind, the Hugo Atkinsons of the world, with their blustering charm, their promises and their lies. Even when one like Walter came along—handsome as a prince, considerate, amusing—she ruined it all through poor judgment.

The thought of another year at St. Hugh's, endlessly discussing men, mothers and maidenheads, was hardly an enticing prospect, but she had to face the sad truth: she wasn't yet equipped for anything else.

Except sailing. She was good at sailing.

Maybe that's what she should do with her life, become an Amelia Earhart of the waves. The first woman to sail across the Atlantic single-handedly . . .

A foolish dream. And besides, she could think of only one person who would support her in it.

The wind had ebbed a touch by the time she crept from the sleeping house. The treetops still bowed in obeisance but she could sense their heart already going out of it as she hurried down the pathway toward the cove.

She was dragging the rowboat toward the waterline when she heard the whistle.

Tom was watching from the top of the bluff, the villa looming just behind him. He waved a greeting. Lucy waved back, gesticulating for him to join her.

It took him a couple of minutes to work his way down to the cove. Despite the deep tan, there was a pallor about his face, and his blue eyes, usually as bright as broken water, seemed glazed and without life. He didn't just look tired, he looked exhausted.

"Bad night?" she asked.

"You aren't exactly looking your best, young lady."

"That's because Leonard was up till God knows when talking on the telephone."

"Oh?"

The telephone had rung intermittently for a good couple of hours after their return from the restaurant.

"Work, no doubt."

"No doubt," replied Tom.

She nodded toward the *Albatross*. "Do you want to blow away a few of the cobwebs?"

It was the opportunity she'd been waiting for.

Tom glanced up at the white clouds in full sail against a sea of blue before looking back at her. "Why don't we talk about it over breakfast?"

*   *   *

He rowed her there, just around the corner, and they pulled the boat up onto the beach right below the Hôtel de la Réserve, where two young men in tight blue-and-white singlets were putting out the sun loungers and the beach umbrellas.

She and Tom were hardly dressed for the occasion, both of them in baggy shorts and *espadrilles*, but it didn't seem to bother Olivier, possibly because most of his guests had yet to appear from their rooms. He pretended to be insulted that Lucy hadn't shown her face before now, then surprised her by recalling the exact sequence of piano pieces she had played last year—Debussy followed by Chopin followed by Satie. The embarrassing episode had taken place after a long dinner on a night when the regular pianist had failed to show up due to illness. Forced by a slow hand-clap to take a seat at the old satinwood grand in the hotel bar, Lucy had banged out the pieces as best she could, the Satie from memory.

"Poor Lambert," said Olivier. "He sulked for weeks when he heard someone else had touched his precious piano."

"Well, you can tell him not to worry. He has my word it won't ever happen again."

"And Satie—he hates Satie—and then all he has when he comes back is people asking for Satie."

"Oh, God . . ." she groaned.

"Ah," said Olivier, "but guess who his favorite composer now is?"

"Satie . . . ?"

"No, Brahms. He still hates Satie."

Tom laughed. "Olivier, leave her alone."

"How is that possible?" said Olivier. "Look at her, look at what she has become. Her face has found itself finally. How do you say in English?"

"We say double-handed compliment. We say two coffees and two orange juices, please, and don't spare the horses."

They installed themselves at a sheltered table on the windblown terrace and examined the breakfast menu while the awning flapped and bellied above them. Tom disappeared to place their order before the coffees and juices had arrived, which seemed unnecessary. When he hadn't returned after a few minutes, Lucy poked her head inside the dining room.

Tom and Olivier were deep in discussion near the counter. For all the jocularity of their opening exchange, there was now something decidedly serious, almost furtive, about Olivier's expression. That all changed when he caught sight of her out of the corner of his eye. He beamed at her and laid a hand on Tom's shoulder, dispatching him back outside.

"Is everything okay?" she said, once they were settled back at the table.

"He asked me where Hector was."

"Did you tell him the truth?"

Tom nodded grimly. "I'm dreading having to break it to Paulette. She'll be devastated."

"If it's any consolation, she already assumes the worst."

"You think?"

"That's what she said. She also told me to persuade you to get another dog."

"One day. Maybe."

She almost came out with it there and then. Not wishing to be interrupted, though, she held off until a surly waitress had delivered their food.

"Tom, I've never said this before, and I haven't really thought about how to say it, so I'm sorry if it comes out all wrong. It's something I have to do—no, that's wrong—it's something I *want* to do, I mean, something I've *wanted* to do for years. Oh, God, I'm rambling, aren't I?"

"If you've waited this long, I'm sure I can wait a few more minutes."

Lucy poked at her half-eaten scrambled eggs then put her fork down and looked him in the eye. "Thank you."

"Don't mention it," he replied.

"I mean it. Thank you for being there ... for always being there ... for as long as I can remember ... and for making me laugh ... for always making me laugh ... and for making me feel beautiful even though I'm not . . . and for treating me like an adult even when I was a child . . . for never telling me what to do or what to think . . . for letting me be . . . for letting me be me."

"Lucy . . ." Tom said softly.

"Shut up, I'm just hitting my stride."

"Oh, dear."

"You're a good man, Tom Nash. I don't know a better man and I doubt I'll ever meet one. I can't imagine what my life would be like without you in it. I think about it sometimes and it scares me. No. It makes me feel sick. Like I'm falling. Spinning in the darkness."

Tom was no longer looking at her, but down at the tabletop.

"I'm sorry if I've embarrassed you," she went on, "but I wanted you to hear it. I'm glad I've finally said it."

He reached over and took her hand, and when he looked up there was a sheen to his eyes. And a sadness.

"I'm not embarrassed. But you're wrong. You don't know me."

"I know you well enough."

"Just enough to keep the dream alive."

Lucy frowned, confused. "Why are you saying this?"

It was a moment before he replied. "You said it yourself just now—for letting you be you. You were always you, Lucy, long before I showed up on the scene."

She could feel a panic beginning to swell in her chest. "Why are you saying this?" she repeated.

"I have to go away."

"Away? Where?"

"It doesn't matter."

"Why?"

"It's complicated."

"Tell me."

"I can't. And you mustn't breathe a word of this to anyone."

She gave a derisive little laugh. "How can I, when you're not telling me anything?"

"You have to trust me it's for the best. Do you think you can do that?"

"No. Yes. If you insist."

He gave her hand a squeeze. "Do you remember the time I took you flying?"

"No," she replied sarcastically.

"The following day the engine seized on that Avro Avian—the same plane we went up in. An oil leak. Two young men died in a field near Woodstock. I've never told anyone that."

She felt a chill run through her.

"These things happen, of course, and no one is necessarily to blame—it's just the way of things. *Sic transit.* But that's how fragile life is. That's why we have to be thankful for what we've got . . . for what we've had . . . for making it this far."

She glanced down at her hand, smothered by his, safe, encased. She saw the pale scar like a small smile near the base of his thumb and the way the thick hairs curled around the tan leather strap of his wristwatch. They were details of him she'd noted many times before, and she refused to believe they wouldn't always be there.

"If you leave me I'll never speak to you again."

Childish, petulant words. Worst of all, they were undone by a logic that made them sound more like a statement of the obvious than a threat.

"I'm sorry," she added quickly. "That was pathetic. I understand."

"No you don't," he replied. "But one day you will."

18

Tom felt terrible, torn between thinking he'd told her too much and feeling he should have said more. It was the same tension that sat at the heart of all his relationships: a benign duplicity, a fine balancing act of half-truths and white lies. Much harder to pull off now, though, after Lucy's moving tribute to him.

Distracted by his brief conversation with Olivier about the progress of Commissaire Roche's investigation, he had been caught completely off guard by her heartfelt eulogy when he'd returned outside to the terrace.

Lucy must have seen the tears pricking his eyes, and he hoped that was enough. It would have to do for now. He couldn't risk reciprocating the feelings she'd voiced. If he set off down that path he was liable to start coming apart at the seams.

Ideally, he would have forgone the jaunt on the *Albatross*. The sands were fast running out. The train from Paris pulled into Toulon just after eleven o'clock, and in his mind he was safe only until about lunchtime, at the latest. After that, anything could happen. Before that, he had a host of things to do that would determine how he proceeded. Chief among these was putting a call in to Clive in London to see if he'd managed to turn up anything that might corroborate what Leonard had told him last night.

He decided the call could wait, painfully aware, as with so many other things over the past couple of days, that this might be the last chance he ever got to sail a boat with Lucy.

It was the right decision.

The conditions were ideal, the wind firm but steady, and the *Albatross* rose effortlessly to the challenge, making five or six knots close-hauled on a starboard tack, which carried them out toward the islands. Lucy insisted on Tom bringing them home, surrendering the helm to him.

They flew before the wind on a broad reach, jibing a few times to see them back to Le Rayol. It wasn't just exhilarating; there was something restorative about the sloop's poise and balance even in the heavier air. She was completely undaunted by the testing conditions, and he could feel some of her fearless spirit bleeding into him, up through the tiller and into his arm, filling his chest.

He didn't realize Lucy was watching him closely until she said, "That's the look of a man who's kicking himself for his generosity."

"You might have to let me play with her from time to time."

"That could be tough, what with you *going away.*"

The emphasis and the slight curl of her lips told him she wasn't being snide; she was ribbing him.

Good girl, he thought. *So strong. So resilient. So completely unlike your mother.*

Some of Tom's own resilience deserted him as he eased the *Albatross* toward her mooring in the cove. He saw a figure standing on the terrace of the villa, observing their return from on high. It was a man, short, besuited, stoop-shouldered.

Commissaire Roche was readily identifiable even at a distance.

They rowed ashore to find Venetia and Barnaby already installed on the beach, still wet from a recent swim. Tom could tell from Venetia's body language, the way she lay sprawled on her raffia mat, that Barnaby had been working his charm on her. Or maybe, it occurred to him, they had been discussing their short-lived affair, building bridges, moving on.

Either way, Venetia chuckled when Barnaby declared, "Oh, look, it's the merry buccaneers. Ahoy there, mateys!"

"Where's Leonard?" Lucy asked, possibly sensing something.

"Where do you think?" replied Venetia. "On the telephone. Again."

"Anyone would think that a war had started," sympathized Barnaby.

"And one might well, if he doesn't learn that a holiday is a sacred thing."

There was something overly eager in Barnaby's laugh that must have grated with Lucy too.

"He's not a milkman—he works for the Foreign Office. The world doesn't stop when he goes on holiday."

"We're a little tetchy this morning, aren't we?" purred Venetia. "Did we 'heel over' or 'broach to,' or whatever it is you sailors do?"

Don't react, Tom urged silently, to no avail.

"If you must know, we had a wonderful breakfast at La Réserve and then we went for a very fine sail in a very fine boat."

It was the first time he had seen Lucy exploit the closeness of their relationship against Venetia.

"I'm thrilled for you, darling. What's the world coming to if a girl can't go for a very fine sail in a very fine boat?"

Exquisitely and obliquely barbed, as was to be expected.

"I think I've got a visitor," Tom interjected, calling for a truce.

"You do," said Barnaby. "The same fellow as yesterday. Not your neighbor, as it turns out, but an officer of the law."

"A commissaire, no less," added Venetia with relish. "You must tell us what you've done."

Tom opted for the truth, knowing they wouldn't believe it. "He thinks I murdered someone."

Venetia laughed. "I do hope you've disposed of the evidence."

"It's very important to dispose of all the evidence," parroted Barnaby.

"Dorothy L. Sayers wouldn't have a thing to write about if people only disposed of all the evidence."

Lucy couldn't take any more of the double act. "I'm off to change."

"I'll come with you." Tom fell in beside her, waiting until he judged they were out of earshot before saying, "You have to learn not to react."

"Maybe I want to react. Maybe I'm sick of stepping on eggshells. Maybe things would be better if I'd learned to react a long time ago."

An awkward silence settled on them as they passed by the boathouse and into the trees, Tom fully aware that he was to blame for a good part of her state of mind.

When the path divided, Lucy mumbled, "I'll see you later."

"Lucy . . ."

She turned back, her eyes hard, defiant.

Tom stepped toward her and took her in his arms. She didn't resist. She clung to him as if she would never release him.

"Good morning, Commissaire."

Commissaire Roche was seated at the table on the terrace, peering through pince-nez spectacles at a book.

"Mr. Nash."

"I see Paulette has made you a coffee."

"Not with any great enthusiasm."

Tom was pleased to hear it.

"I hope you don't mind," added Roche, meaning the book. It was a weighty tome plucked from the shelves of the study: Montaigne's *Essays*, beautifully bound in half-vellum and marbled paper, a gift from Benoît.

"Was there ever a wiser man? Or a more honest one? Who else was writing about his impotency back in the Renaissance? Who writes about such things now?" Roche closed the book and removed his spectacles. "He had great respect for the common man, great respect for Nature."

Tom took a seat across the table, wondering where all this was leading. He didn't have to wait long.

"He even suggests that true wisdom is a return to Nature. I imagine you would agree."

"Why do you say that?" asked Tom.

"Well, that is what you have done here, is it not?" The sweep of Roche's arm took in the trees, the sky, the sea.

"I'm not sure I'm any the wiser for it."

Roche smiled, revealing his uneven teeth. "And I, unfortunately, am not much wiser than when I last visited you."

"Still no sign of the Italian?"

"Nothing. Gone. Like dust in the wind." Roche fluttered his fingers above the table, but his pebble eyes remained locked on Tom's, even when he reached for his coffee cup and took a surprisingly dainty sip. "You must be a very important man, Mr. Nash."

"Excuse me?"

"To have friends in such high places."

"I'm sorry—I don't understand."

Roche scrutinized him closely before settling back into his chair. "No, you don't, do you. And yet you must have spoken to someone, or I wouldn't have received the telephone call."

"What call?"

"The one suggesting that I leave you out of my investigation."

"I don't know anything about a telephone call. From whom?"

"Someone I can't refuse. Someone at the Ministry of Foreign Affairs."

So Leonard had done it, as promised.

"Ahh," said Roche, "I see you get my meaning now. Well, you needn't worry. I've never lived down my schoolboy bashfulness when it comes to my masters. I won't be bothering you anymore. Although I'd be lying if I said I wasn't extremely curious. For a simple policeman like me the idea that some international intrigue might be unfolding on his doorstep, right under his nose, well, you can imagine . . ."

"I'm not sure a missing Italian hotel guest qualifies as an international intrigue."

"It does if his disappearance is somehow connected to another as yet unidentified foreigner found dead in a car just off the road to Hyères."

You wily old fox, thought Tom. Had Roche detected anything in his eyes? Possibly. But even if he hadn't, the moment for shaping an innocent-sounding response had passed.

"I suppose you wouldn't know anything about that either?"

"Nothing at all, I'm afraid."

"Well, somebody does. The evidence suggests there were two other men present at the incident, one of them wounded, bleeding."

Tom got to his feet, ending the conversation. "I'm sorry I can't be of more help, Commissaire."

Roche remained seated. "Well, maybe I can be."

"Excuse me?"

"Take it any way you wish, Mr. Nash, but I think you get my meaning." Roche finally rose from his chair. "If my superiors believe you to be on the right side of whatever's happening here, that's good enough for me."

He offered his hand, and there was something in the firmness of his grip that seemed to both reinforce his words and wish Tom well in whatever lay ahead.

"Thank you for your time, Mr. Nash, and please don't trouble yourself. I'll see myself out."

Leonard's prompt intervention with Roche put a new complexion on things. A guilty man would be looking to limit and contain the situation, not flag its existence, along with his own involvement in it, to the French authorities. It proved nothing either way, but Tom took it as a pleasing development nonetheless. With any luck, Clive would have dug up enough to clarify the matter still further.

He hurried to the phone in his study, closing both doors for privacy.

This time, the receptionist with the drawling Home Counties accent at SIS headquarters didn't even attempt to put him through to Clive. "I'm afraid Mr. Jopling is unavailable."

"Unavailable?"

"I'm afraid so, sir. Would you like to leave a message?"

He hadn't revealed much to Clive, but he had certainly made clear the seriousness of the situation. If Clive had said he'd be at his desk at eleven o'clock, he would be at his desk. So why wasn't he?

"No. Put me through to Quex."

"Quex" was the nickname of Sir Hugh Sinclair, chief of SIS, also known as "C."

Miss Home Counties faltered. "Quex, sir?"

"Tell him it's Tom Nash."

"What happened to Reginald Meath-Butterworth?"

"Just tell him it's Tom Nash. He knows me."

There was a click, followed by silence, then Miss Home Counties came back on the line. "I'm sorry, sir—you'll have to call back later."

"I know you're only doing your job, but this is a matter of national security."

"I'm sorry, sir—you'll have to call back later."

She had clearly gone into stuck-record mode, so Tom said, "Marry me."

"I'm sorry, sir—" came back the automatic reply, before she realized her mistake. "Good-bye."

She hung up, unamused.

Why had they shut him out? He sat at his desk, pondering the possibilities. Then he took up the receiver once more.

Hélène had scribbled down the number for him before boarding the train in Toulon. The painter answered. Brigitte was older than he had imagined, judging from her voice, and she informed him that Hélène had arrived by taxi less than an hour ago, having been forced to spend a night in a hotel near the station in Brive-la-Gaillarde.

A sleepless night, it turned out, when Hélène came on the line. "It was the most awful place, dirtier than a hovel, and I was devoured by fleas all night."

"I'm sorry."

"So you should be."

He tried to detect something in her tone that suggested she was joking, but her anger at him had obviously erased all memories of what had passed between them in her bedroom. She could hardly hold him to blame for that. It was she who had called to him from the up-stairs landing, requesting that he carry her suitcases down, she who had then led him gently by the hand to her bed and said, "I want you inside me."

They had made love wordlessly, fully clothed, Hélène straddling him, reaching behind her to feel where they were conjoined, like a blind person building a picture through touch.

There had been little tenderness at the time, and there was certainly none in evidence now. He could hardly hold it against her—cast into sudden exile through no fault of her own—and he took what she hurled at him.

"I'll call again tomorrow, when you're in a better mood."

"I wouldn't bank on it," she replied, hanging up.

He stared at the mute receiver in his hand, wondering if the opera-tor had been listening in, and if so, what she had made of the frosty exchange.

He lit a cigarette and strolled through the French doors onto the ter-race.

Was that really it? Was Hélène to play no further part in his life? Was all of this to play no further part?

He turned, taking in his surroundings, looking up at the villa, then down over the treetops toward the cove. His place of safety. His fool's paradise. The unearthly beauty of it all. Too good to be true: the whis-pering suspicion that had always taunted him, from the moment he'd first set eyes on the villa. Who would ever have believed it, the son of an Anglican vicar living such a life?

He owed it all to his great-aunt Constance. She was the only mem-ber of his mother's side of the family he had ever met—and only then, on one occasion, when he was thirteen years old—although many years later he had set eyes on two uncles across a courtroom when Constance's will had been contested.

The Boltons were a dyed-in-the-wool Quaker family who had made a considerable fortune as merchants during the Victorian era, banish-ing forever the ring of the cash register with their purchase of a Jaco-bean pile to the northwest of Norwich. This was the privileged world of his mother's youth, a world abruptly closed off to her when she lost her heart to a young and lanky Anglican curate on his first posting in a nearby parish. The moment she "went over," her parents refused to have anything more to do with her, and she was shunned by the rest of the family. She endured this rejection with equanimity, rarely speaking about it, other than to say that her family's reaction said far more about them than it did their faith, and that Tom was never to think unkindly of Quakers because of it.

He, of course, was fascinated by the idea that he had a whole host of relatives out there, possibly cousins his own age, and not so very far away. Great-Aunt Constance must have been experiencing something of the same curiosity, because soon after her husband's death she wrote a letter to Tom's mother asking if she could meet her only sister's only grandson.

It was the first time Tom had ever heard his parents raise their voices to each other— not that they knew he was eavesdropping, shivering in his pajamas on the staircase landing. His father must have backed down, because a few days later the situation was presented to him. He went through the motions of weighing his decision before agreeing to go along with Great-Aunt Constance's request.

He had been in a motorcar before, but never one as grand as the Britannia landaulet sent to pick him up. It was a brisk spring morning and he felt sorry for the uniformed chauffeur exposed to the elements up front while he sat warm and cocooned in the cabin behind.

There were cows swinging their tails in the pasture beside the avenue of towering limes that led up to the house. He knew it was foolish to imagine a phalanx of long-lost relatives waiting to greet him warmly, and what he got was a lone footman, who showed him through to an enormous drawing room, where an elderly woman, shrouded in the full weeds of early widowhood, sat perched on a divan. He was barely able to make out the features of her face beneath her mourning veil, although she folded it back the moment the footman had retired. She also rose to her feet and greeted him warmly with a firm hand-shake. She seemed improbably old, her face as creased as crumpled paper, but she looked on him with kind, lucid eyes, as blue as pimpernels. He knew from his mother that Great-Aunt Constance now presided over the family, and although she was a redoubtable character, she didn't possess the same streak of tyranny in her that had marked her dead husband out for the monster he had been.

Tom couldn't recall much of their opening exchange, distracted as he was by the solemn gentility of the setting, the orderly sprinkling of pictures, lamps, china ornaments and other odds and ends that covered the walls and shelves and tabletops. It seemed to him that there wasn't one object in the room that had shifted its place in fifty years, and he said as much when Great-Aunt Constance asked him what he was thinking. This brought an amused chuckle from her. When she suggested that they take a turn around the gardens, he was surprised by her nimbleness, as well as her passion for the plants and trees lining the paths and alleys she led him along.

The outdoors was his world, and he was glad of the opportunity to shine in her eyes. He knew the names; he knew the cycles of life and of the seasons; he knew that the unseen bird *roo-hoo*ing in a tall oak was a collared dove, not a wood pigeon, despite the similarity of their songs. When they arrived at the kitchen garden, with its lean-to greenhouse and hothouse, Great-Aunt Constance became engaged in a discussion with one of the gardeners about whether it was safe yet to put the geraniums and fuchsias out in their tubs. They concluded that there was still a risk of a late frost.

Tom waited until they had moved on before saying, "The mulberry tree in your rose garden has just started to leaf."

"Has it? Well, it's that time of year, I suppose."

"It means there won't be any more frosts."

"Oh, really?" she replied, skeptically.

"Baint says the mulberry is a nonesuch tree and it knows these things."

"Does he, now? A nonesuch tree? And who, pray, is Baint?"

He told her. He must have told her a lot, because he was still talking when they returned to the drawing room.

"Well, I must say, this Baint of yours sounds a remarkable character."

"Oh, he is. He sees things other people don't." And then he foolishly blurted out the story of the horse dropping down dead in front of the stand at the Bungay races.

He realized his error only when she said, "Interesting. I wouldn't have thought your father was a racing man."

He was trapped. To lie would be to cast his father in an unfair light, which was the last thing he wanted to do. So he told her the truth.

She was horrified by his story of bunking off to the horse races with Kitty when the two of them should have been playing on the beach in Cromer. At least, that's what he took her silence to mean. But then suddenly she laughed. She laughed long and she laughed loud. She couldn't stop herself. Even when she tried to suppress it, it came bubbling back out of her. He began to wonder if she wasn't mad, possibly with grief. She finally recovered, though, dabbing at her eyes with a black chiffon handkerchief plucked from her sleeve.

"Well, I must say, your education has been conducted under far ampler skies than that of your cousins."

He never saw her again.

She warned him that this would be the case, and she said he was not to be insulted. There were silly grown-up matters at play that one day he would understand. After that, he received a card every birthday, and they wrote to each other once or twice a year until she was well into her nineties and her eyesight failed.

The next communication he received from that hemisphere of his life was a letter from the Bolton family solicitors in London, informing him that he had been remembered in her will. It was a considerable sum of money and it couldn't have come at a better time. The cerebral hemorrhage that had paralyzed the left side of his father's body and turned his mother overnight into a full-time nurse had occurred just six months previously. Tom suspected that these two events—his father's stroke and the amendment that Great-Aunt Constance had subsequently made to her will—were not unconnected. Either way, after he had won the bitter legal battle instigated by his uncles, Tom was in a position to see his parents set fair for life. He was also able to rescue his own faltering sanity and resign from the Secret Intelligence Service.

A new beginning. And now, it seemed, another might be required. It all hinged on how he played out his weak hand.

Paulette was upstairs, cleaning Barnaby's room. It was in a terrible state, with clothes strewn all over the place. This wasn't the reason for her dark mood, though. She was annoyed with herself for failing to resist Roche, for not turning him away at the door. She was convinced that she'd somehow let Tom down.

She brightened a little when Tom assured her that she hadn't. She brightened even more when he told her she could have the weekend off.

"But how will you cope?"

"We're out and about for most of it."

This wasn't true, but he didn't want Paulette fussing about the place just when things looked set to come to a head.

He showered and changed for lunch. Pocketing the Beretta, he then went and concealed the Browning beneath the driver's seat of his car.

They were eight for lunch at the big table under the awning in the courtyard. The flagged yard sat to the side of the main building and was about the only pleasing feature of the "Art Nouveau eyesore."

Yevgeny and Fanya couldn't make it, too caught up in the preparations for their party that evening. However, Walter had been released from his duties, and he turned up with Klaus, Ilse, two bottles of hock and the scavenger hunt cup, which Yevgeny had won last year in a record time of three hours and four minutes.

"He's pretty upset he can't defend his title," explained Walter.

"Mortified, I imagine," said Venetia.

The rules of the scavenger hunt were fairly straightforward, in that there weren't really any. By fair means or foul, the teams of two had to search out and bring back six unusual items that had been chosen for the occasion by a disinterested third party. This year, it was Benoît who had drawn up the list, and the envelope had been grandly sealed with wax to prevent anyone from tampering with it.

"He obviously knows you better than we do," observed Lucy.

"How can we be sure it wasn't Tom who sealed it . . . *after* he'd examined the contents?" demanded Barnaby.

Venetia turned to him. "My dear Barnaby, that says far more about you than it does Tom."

Tom went to join Leonard, who was cooking the big bream he'd caught yesterday over a low fire he'd cobbled together near the entrance to the courtyard. He might lunch at the Berkeley Grill and dine at Boulestin but he was never happier than when out in the wilds preparing his own food, freshly caught, over an open fire. The sight of him crouched there—all knees and elbows, that intent expression on his face—brought to mind fond memories of their trout-fishing trips near Hungerford in the old days.

"Remember Hungerford?"

Leonard looked up at him. "Of course."

"Do you still fish there?"

"Not as much as I'd like to. I keep up my membership, though. We can go there when you're next back in England, make a weekend of it."

"Assuming I get through this."

Leonard glanced over at the table before rising to his feet. "You've been in tighter corners than this," he said, for their ears only.

"Have I, Leonard?"

His astringent tone wasn't lost on Leonard. "And what's that supposed to mean?"

"It means you've been holding out on me. It means we need to talk."

It hadn't been Tom's intention to forfeit the element of surprise so cheaply, but he was worn down, beyond caring.

The fish were done to perfection, the flesh barely coming away from the bone, and the moment they were served Tom announced that this year they would not be pulling the names randomly from a hat to determine the teams for the scavenger hunt.

Klaus, Ilse and Walter, relative newcomers to Le Rayol, were at a disadvantage, and it was only fair that each of them be paired with someone better acquainted with the area. The teams he therefore proposed were: Klaus and Venetia (acceptable), Ilse and Barnaby (more than acceptable), Walter and Lucy (ditto), and Leonard and him (which drew a swift, knowing glance from Walter). Four teams, four cars and almost four hours to complete the mission. The deadline was six o'clock, when they would all reconvene on the terrace at Villa Martel for well-earned refreshments and the prize-giving. It only remained to open the envelope, and Tom broke the wax seal.

"A horseshoe," he read from the list.

"Easy enough," declared Venetia, the others nodding in agreement.

Tom smiled before reading out the second entry. "A lady's whalebone corset."

"What?" groaned Barnaby.

"An ashtray from the bar of the Hôtel des Bains in Cavalaire. Twelve Madonna lilies. A postcard of Place Victor Hugo in Collobrières. And finally . . . oh, Benoît, you wicked man . . ."

"What?" demanded Ilse.

"Three male *préservatifs*."

There was a puzzled silence.

"Does that mean what I think it means?" inquired Venetia.

"I fear so," said Walter.

Venetia squirmed. "That's not just wicked—it's disgusting."

"It's also impossible," put in Barnaby. "France is a Catholic country. Where on earth are we going to get three . . . ?" He waved his hand about, unable to bring himself to say the word.

"Le Lavandou, apparently," said Tom, distributing the typewritten lists. "Benoît kindly provides the name of a pharmacy where they can be bought under the counter, with a little persuasion."

Klaus was smiling broadly. "The poor pharmacist," he said in his thick German accent. "What will he think of us foreigners after today?"

Half an hour later, Tom and Leonard were zigzagging their way up the hill behind Le Rayol, the car's engine straining against the incline. The sun beat down on them, and the back of Tom's shirt was already lacquered to the leather seat. The tacky asphalt beneath the tires seemed on the point of melting clean away and trickling off down the slope, through the trees.

So far the conversation had valiantly been kept to the question of which route they should take. Benoît had them heading in three quite different directions, and there was a case to be made for both a clockwise loop and an anticlockwise one. A little disingenuously, Tom had argued that they should instead make a headlong dash northward to Collobrières.

It was a picturesque village buried deep in the hills of the Massif des Maures, well back from the coast. Though it was known for its chestnuts, there was little chance they'd be picking up a box of marrons glacés today along with a postcard of Place Victor Hugo. In fact, Tom couldn't see them returning with any of the items on Benoît's mischievous list.

The Col du Rayol was a barren outlook set high on the hill above the village. They would sometimes come here after a day on the beach to fly big box kites in the offshore evening breeze. It afforded an unrivaled panorama of the looping coastline and the islands laid out like stepping-stones in the far distance. It was an extraordinary view, more Theocritan than anything Tom had come across during all his time in Greece, and yet he didn't even glance over his shoulder as they cleared the summit.

Ahead of them, the wild, ridged hills of the Massif des Maures rolled off, wave on darkening wave, into the distance.

"Interesting," said Leonard, as Tom guided the car off the metalled surface onto a dirt road.

"A shortcut," Tom lied.

He knew that the road petered out after a mile or so, giving way to a rocky footpath that wound its way down into the valley. It was the perfect spot to be alone with Leonard. As the ruts grew deeper and the vegetation pressed in more tightly on both sides, Leonard seemed to sense this.

"What's going on, Tom?"

"You were right about Walter. There's more to him than meets the eye."

"Would you care to elaborate?"

"He's with the U.S. Military Intelligence Division."

It was a moment before Leonard replied. "How do you know?"

"He told me."

"And you believed him?"

"Yes, I believed him. There was no reason not to."

"There's always a reason not to."

"For God's sake, Leonard, don't be so bloody abstruse!"

"You're angry."

"Yes, I'm angry."

"Why?"

"Because you lied to me. You've been lying to me all along."

Tom slammed his foot on the brake and the car skidded to a halt at the end of the road. "Get out."

When Leonard didn't react, Tom pulled the Browning from beneath the driver's seat and pointed it at him.

"You're right," said Leonard. "I haven't been entirely honest with you."

"I said get out."

Tom felt strangely calm as he clambered out of the car, keeping the gun trained on Leonard all the while.

"Do you want me to raise my hands?" asked Leonard, facetiously. "Like this?"

"No, I want you to take your jacket off."

Leonard did as requested, tossing it onto the hood of the car. There was no thud as it landed, but Tom still felt for a weapon. "Now raise your hands and turn around." He frisked Leonard thoroughly before stepping back.

"Tom, I can explain."

"Go ahead. Tell me about Walter."

Leonard slowly turned to face him, lowering his hands as he did so. "I can't explain that. I didn't know about that."

"Then why don't I fill you in?"

Tom spelled out what he'd learned from Walter: that the Americans had recently become aware of concerted Soviet efforts to infiltrate some of their key government departments, and although they didn't yet know the true extent of the penetration by Communist moles, the evidence they'd been able to gather from two recent arrests had led them to a man in Montreal, who had provided both of the individuals in question with the fake Canadian passports on which they'd entered the United States. From Montreal the trail then led back across the Atlantic to Paris, to Yevgeny and Fanya. This was why Walter had been tasked with insinuating his way into their circle.

"You don't seem too surprised."

"But I am," replied Leonard. "It's unusual for our American friends to take such a bold initiative alone."

"I meant about Yevgeny and Fanya."

"No, not entirely surprised."

"Walter thinks you've been compromised by them. In fact, he's convinced of it."

"I'm pleased to hear it," said Leonard. "If the Americans believe I've gone over to the Soviets then I've done my job well."

Tom could see what Leonard was intimating: that he, like Walter, was part of some counterintelligence ploy directed against Yevgeny and Fanya.

"Don't lie to me!"

"Calm down, Tom. I'm not lying to you."

"But the gambling debts . . . the money you owe Yevgeny . . ."

Leonard looked impressed. "My, you *have* been busy behind the scenes, haven't you?"

"I didn't have much choice."

"You've also been theorizing ahead of your data." This was a particular hobbyhorse of Leonard's, one he had always ridden hard with his subordinates. "Those debts were run up with the personal sanction of Sir Robert Vansittart. They're underwritten by the Foreign Office. We have to make the Soviets think they have a hold on me."

"Why should I believe you?"

"Because it's true. And because it's me. Look at me, Tom. I'm as susceptible to flattery as the next man, but I'm also more skeptical than most. Yevgeny's interest in me rang alarm bells almost from the first. What does a man like that really care about a civil servant? Yes, there's some common ground, but not nearly enough of it to warrant his eagerness for a friendship. I've played a very long game with him, waiting to see when the approach would come. It hasn't yet, but I believe it's close, now that I'm financially beholden to him."

He paused to pinch the sweat from his eyes.

"People say information is power, but so is disinformation. We'll have an open channel to Stalin. We'll be able to tell the Soviets everything we want them to hear. Think about it . . . they'll have their own man in the British Foreign Office."

"And for that you're happy to throw me to the wolves."

"I don't know what you're talking about."

"Yes you do, Leonard. You've been protecting your baby ever since I told you about Pozzi, trying to persuade me the threat was coming from some other quarter. But it's been the Soviets all along, and Yevgeny and Fanya are up to their necks in it."

"You don't know that."

"Pozzi had a photo of me hidden in his suitcase. He got it from them."

Leonard fell silent, digesting the news, his expression similar to that worn by Walter last night, on realizing that all his good work might have been in vain.

"It's over, Leonard. They're directly implicated. The truth about them is out."

Leonard's response, when it finally came, was telling.

"Who else have you told?"

"Already thinking of ways to salvage the situation?"

"Who else have you told?" demanded Leonard.

"Walter."

"Why on earth would you want to do that?"

"He seemed like the only person I could trust at the time."

Leonard conceded the point with a small nod. "I should have been more open with you."

"And I'm still wondering why you weren't."

"Tom, I'm telling you the truth."

"No you're not. They're just words. Since when have you cared about the Soviets? I thought Hitler was the devil of the moment."

"Don't be fooled by Vansittart's rhetoric, or mine. It's all part of the theater. Yes, Hitler's a dangerous lunatic, but we're already under attack from the Soviets. They've never understood why the Revolution didn't spread beyond their borders. They've never accepted it. And they're doing everything in their power to change that. This is highly confidential, but we've intercepted and deciphered enough Comintern radio transmissions from Moscow to know they're behind the recent subversion in our navy as well as several acts of sabotage at the Devonport dockyard. God only knows what else they're up to."

When Tom didn't reply, Leonard spread his hands and said, "Come on—put the gun down."

"I've got a better idea."

He tossed the Browning to Leonard, who, in his surprise, almost dropped it.

"If you're lying to me, I'm as good as dead anyway."

Leonard regarded him with something approaching pity.

"Do it!" Tom insisted. "I don't care anymore."

"You poor boy," said Leonard quietly. "What's happened to you?"

"Nothing that two attempts on my life in three days can't explain," Tom replied bitterly.

It was a trap, the point in the discussion he'd been steering them toward: a passing mention of the second attempt. If Leonard was innocent he would know nothing about it.

"Two?"

One small word, but it rang like music in Tom's ears.

"Is it true?" Leonard persisted.

"Yes, it's true."

"So why are you smiling?" Leonard's able brain figured it out before Tom could reply. "Oh, I see—I've just passed your test."

"Unless you're a damned good actor."

"Which I might be."

"Which we both know you aren't."

Leonard released the magazine on the Browning. It was empty. So was the chamber. "Very good," he said. "You really weren't sure, were you?"

"I learned my skepticism from a master."

Tom settled himself on a rock in the shade and lit a cigarette.

"What's going on, Leonard? Why do they want me dead?"

"Zakharov had a younger brother—Ivan. He was fighting for the Bolsheviks in Estonia at the time you . . . well, disposed of his brother in Petrograd. He's still in the military, a general now. It's said he's one of the few people Stalin trusts implicitly . . . which probably means he's not long for this world," he added wryly.

So that was it. Revenge. A cycle of violence set in motion by Tom in a darkened stairwell sixteen years ago.

"We can't be certain he's behind it," Leonard went on, "but it's looking that way."

"How does he know?"

"Aye, there's the rub. Who knew? You, me, Sinclair, the members of the Secret Service Committee." Leonard waved a fly from his face. "We think we might have narrowed it down to a leak within the SIS, a Soviet mole, someone instructed to access your file."

"Who?"

"Sinclair's working on it, closing the net. The files of retired agents are stored off-site, which helps."

That would explain the brush-off Tom had received when he'd telephoned earlier. The Secret Intelligence Service had shut up shop while they searched for the traitor in their midst.

The weight of his suspicions about Leonard might have been lifted, but another dead load had replaced it immediately. He could feel it pressing down on him; he could see his future fading out of focus, blurring into oblivion.

For General Ivan Zakharov this was personal, a question of honor. He would never let up, not until he'd avenged his brother's murder. Life as Tom knew it was over. Le Rayol was over. As long as Zakharov was alive Tom would have a sentence hanging over him.

"You've done us an enormous service."

"Have I?" Tom replied, distractedly. Whatever it was, it was meager consolation.

"Think about it. It's the reason they wanted it to appear as though you'd died of natural causes. Making a show of your death would have alerted us. They were protecting their source. If you hadn't killed Pozzi we would never have known they'd infiltrated the SIS. Now we do."

"Why Pozzi? Why send an Italian to do their dirty work?"

Leonard came to sit beside him. "I can only imagine they wanted to put as much distance as possible between you and them."

Even from Leonard's lips, it had a faintly hollow ring.

"Well, as from yesterday afternoon it's a policy they've abandoned."

"Tell me what happened."

Tom flicked his cigarette away into the dust.

"I can do better than that," he said.

From a distance, the Chartreuse de la Verne looked like an ocean liner tossed on an angry green sea. The ancient monastery lay to the east of Collobrières, occupying the upper reaches of a narrow spur lost in a tumble of hills smothered in chestnut forests. Its location spoke volumes about the order of monks who had chosen this remote spot as their home back in the twelfth century. Unlike the Benedictines and the Cistercians, the Carthusians wished to have little or no contact with the outside world, choosing instead to lead simple, ascetic, silent lives. In effect, the Chartreuse de la Verne was a community of hermits who rarely gathered together to worship, and whose meals were passed to them through a hatch in their cell doors by lay brothers.

Times had changed, and so had the Chartreuse. Ravaged by fire, re-built, abandoned, it was now occupied by a bare handful of monks who had restored one small part of the sprawling complex to serve their immediate needs, while doing their level best to stem the decay elsewhere, stripping back ivy, shoring up walls and patching roofs. They dreamed of a time when the monastery would be returned to its full and former medieval glory.

Tom had heard all of this from the mouth of Prior Guillaume during his last visit, when handing Pyotr over to his care. The monks hadn't hesitated to take the Russian in, and Prior Guillaume had shown no curiosity whatsoever as to the cause or circumstances of Pyotr's injuries. The fact that one of God's creatures was in need of succor was reason enough to open their arms to him.

The main entrance to the monastery bore witness to a violent era when even men of God had to defend themselves against attack. It might just as well have been the entrance to a castle or a prison, with large wooden doors set in a high, blank wall over one hundred yards long. The only clue to what lay behind this forbidding façade was the marble statue in the niche above the doors: Mary cradling the Baby Jesus on her hip.

This time, it took even longer for someone to respond to Tom's hammerings. He and Leonard stood out there for almost ten minutes beneath the tawny, sun-baked stonework, and were on the point of resorting to the car horn when they heard a voice.

"Who is it?"

"It's me—Thomas."

"Are you alone?" said Prior Guillaume, switching to English.

"I've brought a friend."

"Another invalid?"

Prior Guillaume had a sense of humor.

"Not this time."

The prior was Belgian by birth, a short man with a sallow complexion and large pouches beneath his eyes. Despite his considerable age, he had a full head of white hair shorn close to a frosty furze, which made him look like he'd been dipped in flour. He didn't walk so much as glide along, almost as if he were wearing roller skates beneath his hooded white habit.

He led them far deeper into the monastery than Tom had penetrated during his last visit.

"How is he?"

"Better," replied Prior Guillaume. "Talking. Always talking. I don't think he knows we are a silent order."

"I'll mention it."

"No, please. The silence is not easy for the young novices. It is good they have a reason to speak."

They found themselves in a dilapidated cloister that gave onto an overgrown courtyard.

"He has told me your story. *Vade in pacem*." He touched Tom lightly on the arm. "I like this story. It is a good story."

He asked them to wait in the cloister and disappeared through a wooden door.

"*Vade in pacem?*" inquired Leonard.

"It's not important."

The door swung open and Prior Guillaume beckoned them inside. "Please . . ."

It was a monk's cell, simply furnished but surprisingly large and light. There was also a crude wooden staircase leading to another room above. A door on the far side of the room opened onto a small garden enclosed by high walls for privacy.

"He is outside," said Prior Guillaume. "I'll wait for you in the chapel."

He withdrew, pulling the cell door shut behind him.

Pyotr was seated at a table in the shade, reading, but now rose to his feet to greet them. His head was heavily bandaged and he was wearing a long white linen nightshirt and leather sandals. The last time Tom had seen him he had been dangerously pale, but there was color in his cheeks now and his eyes were sharp, alert. They darted warily toward Leonard as he pumped Tom's hand.

"This is Leonard," explained Tom in French. "He's from the Foreign Office."

"That was quick," said Pyotr acidly.

"It's not what you think. He's a good friend of mine who just happens to be here on holiday. He might be able to help you."

Leonard extended his hand. Pyotr shook it guardedly. "And what does he want in return?"

"Nothing," replied Leonard, also in French.

"Why do I find that hard to believe?"

"Because you don't know him," said Tom.

Pyotr pulled a couple of wooden stools from beneath the table and invited them to sit.

"Do you have a cigarette?" he pleaded. "I'm dying for a cigarette. I suspect Prior Guillaume smokes—I can smell it on his breath—but he swears he doesn't."

Pyotr savored the first lungful of smoke before exhaling.

"How are you feeling?" Tom asked.

"Better now." Pyotr touched the bandage on his head. "Father Nicolas is very pleased with himself. Apparently he's a dab hand with a needle and thread."

Tom smiled. "I didn't get a chance to thank you yesterday. You were almost unconscious by the time we arrived here, talking nonsense."

"My wife would say there's nothing new in that."

"You're married?"

"Until a year ago. She hated Paris, but grew to hate me more for dragging her there. She returned to Russia."

Leonard leaned forward. "Tom says you have been living in Paris for a few years."

"Before you ask, let me say that I'm not going to betray my comrades. What happened is between me and him." He nodded at Tom. "A private affair."

"I understand, but if you can think of anything that might help Tom stay alive . . ."

"I told him yesterday—I don't know anything. I was ordered to come to Le Lavandou and wait for instructions. No reasons were given. They never are."

"Does the name Ivan Zakharov mean anything to you?" asked Leonard.

"General Ivan Zakharov? I know him by reputation, of course. Why?"

"There's a possibility he's involved."

"I can't say."

"Can't or won't?"

Tom interceded to defuse the palpable tension springing up between the two men.

"Pyotr, a couple of days before you arrived here an Italian called Cesare Pozzi tried to kill me."

"An Italian?"

"We've never heard of the NKVD using foreign operatives to do their dirty work."

"It's rare."

"But it does happen?"

Pyotr nodded. "Especially since . . ." He trailed off.

Tom leaned forward. "Anything you feel you can offer would be gratefully received."

Pyotr hesitated. "Since last year there's a new department of the NKVD in charge of foreign operations. They do things differently."

"Any chance we could have the name of this new department?" inquired Leonard.

"It's not important," said Tom.

Leonard shot him an exasperated look that said: It bloody well is!

Tom ignored it. "Have you decided what you're going to do?"

"Run . . . disappear," snorted Pyotr.

"You can still go back, you know. It's not too late. You can make up some story about crawling away from the crash, finding help . . ."

"I'm never going back," said Pyotr, with dark conviction.

Tom pulled an envelope from the inside breast pocket of his jacket and handed it to the Russian. Pyotr examined the contents: a thick bundle of high-denomination French franc notes. He looked up, speechless.

"I think Spain's your best bet. You should be able to cross the border without papers. There's any number of routes through the Pyrenees at this time of year. If you can get yourself to the British Embassy in Madrid then I'm sure we can provide you with a new passport."

Tom looked for confirmation of this from Leonard, who nodded his assent.

"Maybe even a ticket for your passage across the Atlantic."

Leonard nodded again, with less enthusiasm this time. "We might not be able to stretch to first class."

That amused Pyotr.

"It didn't seem right to bring your gun in here. There are two cypress trees across from the main gates, a large rock between them. I'll hide it under the rock."

"Well, at least you didn't actually give him his gun," said Leonard sardonically.

They were making their way back through the monastery to the chapel.

"You know, I've never thought of you as a sentimentalist before," Leonard continued.

"He spared my life."

"From what you say, he was in a pretty bad way after that smash. Maybe he needed you to get him out of there. Maybe he's still using you now."

"Maybe."

"How much was in that envelope?"

"Enough to give him a fighting chance."

"Well, I don't trust him."

"You don't trust anybody, Leonard."

"And it's served me perfectly well up until now."

Tom found himself pushing Leonard up against the rough stone wall and pinning him there with a hand on the chest. "What do you know about people like him, people like me? We're the ones who do your bidding, but even then you can't bring yourselves to speak the words, to actually say it . . . nothing to trouble your conscience. You sit at your desk and you pull the strings and the puppets dance. What do you *really* know about people like us?"

"Are you quite finished?" asked Leonard calmly.

Tom released him but seized his wrist and slapped an envelope into his palm.

"This is for Prior Guillaume. You can tell him it's from an old sentimentalist."

*   *   *

To his credit, Leonard handled the situation impeccably, even when Prior Guillaume at first rejected the money.

"Thank you, but we have everything we need."

"And a few things you don't," countered Leonard, glancing heavenward.

A corner of the chapel roof had been rigged with tarpaulin to stop the rain from coming in.

Tom had held back a single cigarette from the packet he'd left with Pyotr, and the moment Prior Guillaume closed the main gates behind them, he lit it. He then went and recovered Pyotr's handgun from the car and secreted the weapon under the rock between the two cypresses, as promised.

Leonard joined him in the tight patch of shade thrown by the trees.

"You have to disappear."

"I know."

"I'd already arranged for a couple of our chaps to come down from Paris and keep a discreet eye on you. They'll be here tomorrow, but I'm not sure you should wait."

"You mean, leave right now?"

"Stay out of sight until tomorrow. Then they'll see you safely off."

"What, and miss the party?"

"It's just a party."

But it wasn't. It was a chance to close off this chapter of his life. All his friends would be there, all the people he had come to care for, to love, in some cases. Was he really going to pass up the opportunity to rub shoulders with them one last time?

19

<hr/>

They owed much of their victory to Yevgeny's fancy new Citroën, which Walter had been allowed to borrow on the strict condition that he didn't beat Yevgeny's winning time of last year.

The car was low, fast and very agile, and if Walter had been less of a gentleman they could easily have smashed the record. Instead, they had tootled back from the pharmacy in Le Lavandou, the final stop on their circuit. It had been clear from the pharmacist's expression that they weren't the first people that day to turn up in search of three male contraceptives, which suggested that the other teams had opted to head west first.

Lucy and Walter had instead made straight for Cavalaire, where, with great initiative (and with an ashtray stolen from the bar in his pocket) Walter had asked the concierge at the Hôtel des Bains where they might be able to hire a whalebone corset for a fancy-dress party. Like concierges the world over, the man had discreetly palmed the proffered banknote and made a couple of telephone calls, and twenty minutes later they were driving away from the house of a retired stay maker with a turn-of-the-century white silk overbust corset bouncing around on the rear seat of the Citroën. It was a propitious start, two out of the six items in under an hour, and they never looked back.

Tom and Leonard, on the other hand, had hardly got going before the suspension on Tom's car gave out again. They were the last ones home, limping back from Collobrières with a postcard of Place Victor Hugo and a horseshoe.

"It was the most perfectly wretched afternoon," said Leonard. "Make mine a very large vermouth citron, will you, Barnaby?"

Mother was on sparkling form after her time alone with Klaus, who, she was now convinced, was a genius of the first order. "And so very funny with it. Surely we can find someone to publish him in English."

She spoke as if Klaus weren't there, and kept on and on about it until Tom finally confessed, "I've already sent a copy of *The Gardener* to Bob Howard at Jonathan Cape."

"Thank you," said Klaus, surprised and clearly touched.

"I didn't want to say, in case nothing came of it."

This was accompanied by a quick glance at Mother.

"Jonathan Cape? I would have thought Chatto and Windus was a far better house for him. They did such a fine job with Proust."

It was pure Mother.

When it came to the presentation of the trophy, Walter insisted that Lucy keep the cup.

"I couldn't have done it without my map reader," he announced, somewhat self-importantly.

Lucy handed the cup straight back. "And I couldn't have done it without my chauffeur."

"Bravo," called Ilse.

Walter looked suitably contrite. But it was Tom's quiet smile that gave Lucy the greatest satisfaction.

With the party looming, they lingered on the terrace just long enough to drain the magnum of vintage Champagne that had also gone to the victors. Uncharacteristically, Mother opted to walk back to the house with her while Leonard drove the car around.

Lucy knew what this meant.

Sure enough, as the pathway dropped down through the trees toward the cove, Mother asked, "Have you always been that abrasive with young men?"

"You're so predictable."

"How tiresome for you, but someone has to say it."

"Really? No one else seems to feel the need to."

"I'm your mother, and I'm telling you—behavior like that isn't going to do you any favors when it comes to finding a husband."

"My, how very Jane Austen. I had no idea you were so set on marrying me off."

"You facetious little beast!"

"Well, you know what they say: the apple never falls far from the tree."

Mother stopped dead, her eyes ablaze. "How dare you!"

"No, Mother, how dare *you*! I refuse to be dragged into a fight with you."

Lucy walked on, only to find her arm seized in a viselike grip, which spun her around.

"Don't you turn your back on me, young lady!"

Lucy wrenched her arm free. "I'm not going to let you ruin my evening! Not when it might be Tom's last!"

Tom had asked her not to say anything, but she blurted it out instinctually, in self-defense, knowing that it would throw Mother off balance.

"What on earth are you talking about?"

"He's going away," said Lucy.

"Since when?"

"Since this morning. At least, that's what he told me. He wouldn't say where or why."

Mother recovered quickly.

"Oh . . ." she said, with an insinuating smirk, "so that's why Lucy's so on edge."

20

Yevgeny and Fanya liked to bill their summer party as a low-key affair, but nothing was left to chance. The caterers were shipped in from Cannes, the band from Saint-Tropez and the harpist (along with her instrument) from Paris. Every year a small army of workmen stood by with a truckload of tents, should the weather turn suddenly and a summer downpour threaten to spoil the alfresco festivities.

Most remarkably, the ratio of serving staff (always young and beautiful) to guests was as low as you could ever hope to find. This meant that your glass was never allowed to fall empty and there was never any need to queue for food. You simply had to sit yourself down at one of the many candlelit tables scattered through the trees around the terrace, and within moments you would be pounced upon by some discreetly uniformed waiter or waitress who would reel off the available dishes, take your order and then disappear into the darkness. If eight of you happened to sit down together, your food would always arrive at the same time.

This year, the chefs toiling away behind the scenes had outdone themselves: *consommé madrilène, pâté de canard du Périgord,* langoustes, *soles cardinales, poularde en cocotte,* salads, cheeses, *tarte au citron,* and roasted quinces with verjus and vanilla. Served up without ceremony beneath a cloudless Mediterranean night sky, it was a flawless feast.

Yevgeny and Fanya were rarely to be seen together at their party. They circulated independently of each other through the eclectic mix of guests, oiling the wheels. Yevgeny tended to gravitate toward the wealthier types, many of whom were clients, and Tom knew for a fact that he used the event as a showcase for his wares, shipping in works of art from the gallery in Paris and scattering them about the house as though they were part of his private collection. Last year, Tom had witnessed Yevgeny hook and reel in a Norwegian countess with an exquisite Bonnard painting of a nude in a bathtub, which Tom had helped him hang on the drawing-room wall just the day before. No doubt the profits from that one transaction had covered the cost of the party many times over.

Leonard wasn't particularly happy about Tom's decision to attend the party, and he had done his best to appease him beforehand, fearing that he might make a scene with Yevgeny and Fanya.

"Don't take it personally, Tom. They're not so very different to you and me. They're only doing their job. I mean, it's not even as if we're at war with the Soviets. It's a game, and everyone's playing it."

"How very magnanimous of you."

"All we know is that they were asked to provide a photo of you. It's quite possible they never knew why."

Tom had tried to carry this charitable thought with him into the evening, but it riled him that Yevgeny and Fanya might come through this unscathed, unpunished. How hard would it be for Leonard to turn them? He would certainly try to, having worked so patiently to cultivate them. No, Yevgeny and Fanya were too accustomed to their high life to give it up on a question of principle for a spell behind bars.

It can't have been coincidence that Leonard's first act on arriving had been to search out Walter and wander off with him for a private chat. They had probably discussed how best to proceed, how to pool their resources, how to protect and share the asset. Tom's first act on arriving had been to wonder if, among the many guests already gathered, there might be a couple of characters who had turned up that morning on the train from Paris with murder in their hearts.

When it came to the meal, he orchestrated things so that he was sandwiched between Beatriz and Margot. He rarely went more than a few days without seeing them, often dropping in at their farmhouse unannounced whenever he passed by Cap Nègre, but the quick fall of recent events had kept him from their company. As he sat there, enveloped in the warmth of their motherly attentions, he tried to imagine life without them: no more winter walks through the hills, with Beatriz and Margot nobly encased in matching tweeds, no more impromptu dinners eaten off laps in front of their roaring fire, no more pots thrown on Beatriz's wheel in the shed, no more duets with Margot at the old harmonium while Beatriz pumped the bellows . . .

A hand settled on Tom's knee beneath the table. "What is it, Tomàs?" asked Beatriz, leaning close. "You look sad."

"I think you mean drunk," countered Margot from his right, in her distinctive Belgian accent.

"No, he grins like an idiot when he's drunk."

"You're right, he does. So what can it be?"

"Are you having problems with your little friend?"

Hélène was always referred to as his *"petite amie."*

"You must tell us if you are."

"We'd be more than happy to go have a word with her."

"Maybe he *is* drunk—he's grinning like an idiot now."

It was the thought of Hélène answering her front door to find two leathery sexagenarian lesbians scowling on the threshold.

If there hadn't been others within earshot, Tom might have said more—he wanted to, and maybe one day he would get that opportunity—but he contented himself for now with brushing aside their concerns and broadening out the conversation to include Benoît, Chantal and a lively old boy who talked in cannonades and turned out to be a conductor. There was little chance of involving Barnaby and Ilse; they were far too engrossed in each other to even register their dining companions.

Coffee and *friandises* rounded off the meal, and the moment the band piped up he took his glass of Château d'Yquem and strolled off for a solitary smoke, planting himself on the squat stone wall at the edge of the terrace. The moon was low in the night sky but he could just make out Villa Martel on the far side of the bay, crouched above the cove like a toad over a pond.

Could he ever bring himself to sell the place? It seemed inconceivable. But if forced to, how could he arrange it without leaving a trail for Zakharov to follow? Just how difficult was it to trace the movement of money, even to some distant corner of the globe? And if he asked Benoît to supervise the transaction, would he be endangering his friend's life? Considerations such as these would be ruling his life for the foreseeable future, and he might as well accept that fact now. There was nothing to be gained from pretending otherwise.

Despite the dire turn his life had taken in the past few days, looking down on his property, his tiny slice of the French coast, he was still overwhelmed with a sense of his extraordinary good fortune.

He raised his glass to Great-Aunt Constance, whose generosity had enabled him to patch up the tattered shroud of his life. His efforts might have suffered a serious setback, but thanks to her he was still in a position to give Zakharov a good run for his money.

"Are you ignoring me?"

It was Venetia, in her dazzling dress of white satin slashed with blue. The band was playing "Honeysuckle Rose" and he hadn't heard her creep up on him.

"Like the plague." Tom smiled up at her.

"Where were you just now?"

"Oh, you know, lost in the long ago."

"Mind if I join you?"

"Only if you bring some distant memory to the table."

She sat herself down beside him on the wall. "Warwick Square, the summer of 1919. Do you remember?"

"What do *you* think?"

She took her cigarettes from her clutch bag and lit one. "We were so young."

"You mean, we aren't any longer?" he joked.

"Some of us carry on as if we still were. Others are more realistic."

Tom felt his sinews stiffening for battle. He hoped he was wrong. If she came at him now, he was liable to give her both barrels.

"Lucy tells me you're leaving us."

That surprised him. He had asked Lucy to keep it to herself.

"Is it true?" Venetia went on.

"Yes."

"When?"

"Tomorrow."

He had a story prepared to explain his sudden departure, one he had hatched with Leonard earlier. It wasn't required.

"Were you going to tell me?" asked Venetia.

"Of course."

"Well, that's something, I suppose."

"Meaning . . . ?"

"Does it have to mean anything?"

"It usually does."

Venetia drew on her cigarette, exhaling slowly before speaking. "I don't know, Tom . . . you're more of a son to my husband than my own boys are, and more of a father to my daughter than my husband is. I suppose I'm wondering where I fit in."

He knew what he should say, but he couldn't bring himself to shower her with the words of comfort she sought.

"Anywhere you want to fit, Venetia, which seems to be nowhere right now."

She skewered him with a long look. "I wouldn't take that from anyone else."

"I'm flattered."

"No you're not. And you shouldn't be. It means you don't get to me in the way that others do."

"I'm not trying to get to you," he sighed. "I'm concerned for you."

"My, how very pompous of you. Something about splinters and planks springs to mind."

Venetia had settled on her course. There was only one direction they were headed in, and it wasn't a place he wished to go.

"I think we should end this conversation now."

"Why, afraid of a few home truths, are we?"

"I'm going to join the party," he said as evenly as he could, rising to leave.

"Just be sure to leave my daughter alone."

"Excuse me?" he said sharply, turning back.

"Don't think I didn't see you the other day down at the cove, holding hands and staring into each other's eyes like long-lost lovers. It's not dignified, and it's certainly no way for a man your age to be carrying on with a young girl."

He was tempted to point out that there was less of an age gap between Lucy and him than Leonard and her, but she would only have taken it as proof of his intentions toward Lucy.

"If you really want to know, we were talking about Hector."

"Is that so?" Venetia replied skeptically.

"Lucy had seen me burying him at sea the night before."

He assumed this would be enough to stop her in her tracks.

"I'm sorry . . . about Hector. But I stand by what I said. I'm not the only one who finds your behavior towards her unnatural."

"I assume you're talking about Barnaby."

"Why, has he said something?"

"Oh, yes—quite a bit, as it happens."

He laid on the knowing tone with a trowel, but Venetia ignored it.

"Actually, I was referring to Dr. Feinstein."

"Oh, please . . ." he scoffed. Was she really about to quote her Freudian psychoanalyst at him?

"Why are you so keen to dismiss a man you've never met?"

"Because I hardly think a man I've never met is in any position to pass judgment on me."

"Don't be so defensive. He wasn't passing judgment, merely making an observation."

"Well, let's hear it, if only to see what you get for your money."

That annoyed her, which was satisfying.

Dr. Feinstein's theory, in a nutshell, was this: that Lucy was now the same age as Irina had been at the time of her death, and that Tom's feelings for Lucy were inextricably bound up with the feelings of guilt he carried about his failure to rescue Irina in Petrograd all those years ago.

"Utter tripe. And you can have that from me for free."

"I think there's truth in what he says."

"Well, that's good for him, or you wouldn't keep going back for more of his nonsense."

"It's very telling that you're so threatened by him."

"I'm not threatened by him—I'm angry with him. Look what he's done to you."

"I feel better than I have in years."

"And there's the real tragedy of it, Venetia. I, I, I . . . You're so utterly absorbed in yourself that there's no space for the rest of us. We're all just pillows for you to punch into."

He didn't wait for her to get off a reply.

"Excuse me if I withdraw beyond your range for now."

It took him a good twenty minutes and two stiff drinks to calm down. The dancing helped, the slow tightening of intimacy that came with friends and music. Lucy was there, swaying like a reed in the breeze just beyond the clutches of a tall young man with a goatee who was clearly set on monopolizing her. Tom would normally have stepped in and asked her for the next dance, but he feared Venetia's reaction. Lucy was set to suffer enough already without him rubbing her mother's face in it. He had fully expected Venetia to make an immediate scene, demanding to be taken home by Leonard, and dragging Lucy along with her. The fact that she hadn't was a bonus not worth jeopardizing.

God, he had wanted to scream at her, to tear into the pettiness of her neuroses when compared with his own predicament. It was partly the shock of it. In all the years they'd known each other he had never been directly targeted by Venetia; he was possibly the only close friend of hers who hadn't been. At least he wouldn't have to go through the tedious process of a drawn-out reconciliation. Tomorrow he would be gone.

This thought prompted him to search out Barnaby. He was easy enough to spot in the crowd, having opted for a light blue shantung silk suit, which struck a dapper if slightly tropical note. He was at the bar, loading up with more drinks.

"By God, Tommy, there's nothing to touch the pursuit of pleasure, is there?"

His spirits were running high because Ilse had just offered him the spare bedroom at her place, ostensibly to spare him the walk back to Villa Martel.

"That's very considerate of her."

"And I fully intend to make my gratitude felt."

Tom explained that he'd received some bad news from home. His father had taken a sudden turn for the worse, and he was leaving the next day for England. He was likely to be there for some time, which would mean closing up Villa Martel before he left.

"Leonard says he's more than happy to have you move in with them."

"I'm sorry to hear that," said Barnaby, giving Tom's arm a reassuring squeeze. "How terrible for you. Would you like company? We can tear back to Blighty in my car. Come on—why don't we?"

"What, and have you break off your crusade?"

"Ilse's not going anywhere. Besides, it might fool her into thinking I'm a dashed good sort."

He would have done it too, if Tom had taken him up on the offer.

Many of the guests had long drives ahead of them, and the party began to thin out shortly after midnight. The locals proved far more resilient, as they always did. Leonard, Venetia and Lucy were the first of their gang to leave, despite Lucy's plea to stay on a while longer and walk home with Tom.

"And how do you propose to do that, my darling, when you can barely stand upright?"

There was truth in Venetia's words; Lucy was looking pleasantly sozzled. Tom was quite prepared to be ignored by Venetia but she not only kissed him good night on the cheek, she whispered an apology in his ear as she did so: "Forgive me—I'm a hateful old bitch."

Strangely, this made him feel worse, almost wretched, but the band wasn't ready to down tools yet and he lost himself once more in the melee of the dance floor, the spinning solar system of friends. It felt like an hour filched from a fairy tale, unreal, unsettling, more *Alice in Wonderland* than "The Princess and the Pea."

His last dance was with Beatriz, who moved beautifully, betraying her upbringing, the formal dance lessons of her childhood in Barcelona. As with his mother, that privileged world was now a distant memory to her, a leaf from a forgotten chapter, although in the case of Beatriz it was her son and daughter who had cut her adrift, vowing never to see her again. They had accepted the separation from their swaggering bully of a father, but not her decision to then set up home with an attractive blond Belgian music teacher.

It was the right way to round off the evening. Beatriz's story gave him hope for the future. No amount of dislocation could keep a person from living a full and proper life if he set his mind to it. Not wishing to sour this thought, he said his farewells swiftly, saving Yevgeny and Fanya until last.

"Thank you both for the most wonderful evening. And good luck."

Yevgeny froze. Fanya didn't; she gave a little laugh and said, "Good luck . . . ?"

"Silly me . . . I meant good night."

He didn't offer his hand to Yevgeny, as he would normally have done, and he didn't plant a kiss on Fanya's bony cheek.

As he made off into the shadows he turned to check that neither of them was making for the house, for the telephone. They weren't, but he did see someone following him.

It was Walter, as arranged. Tom had asked him earlier if he wouldn't mind covering his back on the walk home.

"Let me get my gun," said Walter. "I'll be right back."

They both knew the drill. Walter tailed him at a distance, ensuring that they didn't present a lone target. The path down through the trees to the beach was the spot Tom would have chosen for an ambush. There was an abundance of cover and the darkness was almost complete. He held the Beretta at the ready, the safety off, his finger curled around the trigger, his ears straining to pick up the slightest sound.

The rhythmic hiss of the waves breaking on the shore grew reassuringly louder, and suddenly there was sand beneath his feet and polished moonlight washing around. He opted for the water's edge over the deep shadows shrouding the trees at the back of the beach. Although exposed, the sand was firm and the sea offered an escape. He could disappear into it in a moment.

The Hôtel de la Réserve loomed on his left, dark and silent, brooding over the bay, its long jetty, raised on tall stilts, spanning the beach and thrusting out into the water from the top of the low bluff.

Tom slowed as he approached. There was something beneath the jetty . . . something strange . . . not a rock . . . not a shadow . . . a person sitting on the sand. He was about to level the Beretta when he saw who it was and swiftly tucked the gun away in his pocket.

"Lucy? What are you doing here?"

"Waiting for you," she replied, getting to her feet. Her shoes lay abandoned nearby and she was still wearing her green satin evening dress.

Tom glanced over his shoulder: no sign of Walter behind him on the beach, but he was probably tracking him from the tree line.

"I had to see you. Leonard says you're leaving tomorrow."

"Here . . ." He removed his jacket and slipped it around her bare shoulders.

"I'm not cold. Actually, I am."

She pressed herself against him.

"You should be in bed."

"And you should have danced with your goddaughter, knowing you were leaving tomorrow."

"I was open to being approached."

"No you weren't." She looked up at him. "Why weren't you? I don't understand. Leonard said your father's ill, but I know it's not that. You would have told me at breakfast. It's something else."

"It's complicated."

"Try me," she purred. "My tutor says I have a first-class brain."

She wasn't using it now, though; she was using her body. Her hand snaked around his waist, drawing him closer so that her hips pressed against his. He was silenced by the sensation.

"If we were shipwrecked . . . a desert island . . . just the two of us . . . alone together . . . do you think we would become lovers?"

"Do you think you might still be a little drunk?"

"I think we would enjoy being alone together quite a lot."

Thankfully, a quick glance established that Walter was approaching around the rocks, or he might have been tempted to bow his head toward the lips now presenting themselves to him.

"Come on—let's get you home."

"One kiss. I won't tell anyone."

"You won't have to. Walter's here."

He gave a little tilt of his head, and Lucy turned to look.

"That's not Walter," she said.

She was right; it wasn't. The man was Walter's height but a touch broader in the shoulders. He wore an ill-fitting suit, and as he drew closer he reached inside his jacket and pulled a long-barreled handgun from its holster.

The Beretta was a popgun by comparison, but Tom would still have taken his chances with it if Lucy hadn't been there.

It was the right call. A fleeting look over his shoulder revealed another man, much shorter than the first, closing in on them from behind.

"Tom, what's going on?"

She was scared now, sobering up fast at the sight of the Beretta in his hand.

He tossed the gun away onto the sand.

"Don't resist," he said. "Don't scream. Don't do anything."

21

After half an hour on the road, the mental map Tom had been sketching in his head began to break down. He would have to satisfy himself with the knowledge that the car had traveled west—beyond Le Lavandou, but not quite as far as Hyères—before bearing north. The fact that the driver lost his way several times didn't help. Neither did the heel of the other man's shoe pressing down on his neck, forcing his face to the floor.

He and Lucy had been made to lie down between the seats, side by side, head to toe. They had done everything asked of them unquestioningly, and because of this neither of them had been harmed so far. The heel against his neck hurt like glory, but he knew that if he protested he would do himself no favors. A policy of abject compliance was most likely to lead the two Russians to drop their guard, not that he was thinking about making a move against them. He didn't hold out much hope for himself, but Lucy stood a far better chance of coming through this alive if he didn't aggravate them.

Their abductors were unflustered, professional. On the few occasions the driver took a wrong turn, his small companion in the back showed no irritation. They had obviously been briefed that Tom spoke Russian because they gave away nothing of any significance when they talked—no names, no place-names, no indication of their plans.

Lying there, squeezed in beside Lucy on the floor, clasping her hand to comfort her, he could not ignore the probability that Walter had betrayed him, steering him into the trap. He was still working back through all his dealings with the American, searching for the signs he'd missed, when the road surface suddenly deteriorated.

They were bumping along a dirt road, or possibly over a field. Either way, their journey was almost ended and the evident remoteness of their destination didn't bode well for their prospects. Tom pictured a moonlit oak wood and a shovel being pulled from the trunk of the car and thrust into his hands.

He decided it was time to speak. "Leave her out of this. She's the daughter of an important British Foreign Office official. You can use her."

The heel pressed deeper into his neck.

When the car finally pulled to a halt both Russians got out and waited for them to extricate themselves from the vehicle. There was no oak wood and no shovel but there was moonlight, just enough to pick out the low mass of a farmhouse set in a grove of bony olive trees.

It was a large building arranged around three sides of a dirt courtyard, at the center of which stood a stone wellhead. The house was locked, shuttered, and in contrast to the still warmth of the night, there was a close, cold odor in the interior, suggesting that it hadn't been properly aired in a good while.

The Russians made no mistakes, working in expert unison as they moved through the house, the taller one leading the way, while the other kept his gun trained on Tom from behind. They never once allowed themselves to fall within his range. When they reached the room, the big man in front pushed open the door, then retreated, wagging them inside with his revolver.

The swath of electric light from the corridor revealed a single bed in one corner of a beamed room devoid of all other furniture.

"We have orders to kill you if you even try to escape," said the small Russian.

He had a curiously sensitive face, with large, doleful eyes, but the words were all the more menacing for being delivered in such a bland and businesslike fashion.

Tom's jacket was tossed to the floor and the door was pulled shut, plunging them into darkness.

Tom reached for Lucy, drawing her close.

"Good girl . . . for not reacting."

"Who are they? What do they want?"

He could hear the fear in her voice, and she was all ashiver in his arms, not from the cold but the ordeal.

"They want me," said Tom.

"Why? What have you done?"

"Did . . . a long time ago."

When he released her, she called desperately, "Don't go."

"It's okay—I'm right here."

He groped for his jacket on the floor. His cigarettes were still in the pocket, along with his lighter, which he sparked into life. He made a quick tour of the room, trying the electric light switch before noticing that there was no bulb in the overhead light. Both windows were securely barred and there was nothing beneath the bed, which was made up for use.

He asked Lucy to hold the lighter while he yanked free one of the wooden slats supporting the mattress. As weapons went, it was better than nothing, though not by much.

"Cigarette?"

"Definitely," Lucy replied.

They sat beside each other on the bed, not speaking at first, just smoking. She didn't push him to explain; she knew he would when he was ready.

"There's a lot you don't know about me . . . a lot you wouldn't like . . . a lot I don't like."

He had struggled to find a way to say it to Hélène, and had ended up giving her a doctored version of the truth, just enough to persuade her to leave. This was worse, far worse. This was Lucy. Of all the people in his life, she was quite possibly the one with the highest opinion of him, which meant she had the farthest to fall. He was also fearful for himself, though, because hers was the only opinion that had ever truly mattered to him, and he was about to destroy it.

Sensing his hesitancy, she said, "Tom, if things are as bad as I think they are, then now's the time for some plain speaking."

He gave a short laugh.

"What?"

"Dear, sweet Lucy. Ever since I've known you you've knocked me for six with the things you say."

"Don't change the subject."

He didn't know where to start, so he picked a point in the story and launched himself in.

"Your first night here, when you couldn't sleep . . . that wasn't Hector you saw me burying at sea."

She listened in silence, and he surprised himself by the details he revealed to her. He told her how he had ruthlessly shepherded the Italian assassin off the edge of the railway cutting, and how he had then seized the dying man by the throat and threatened to kill his mother if he didn't offer up a name. He told her everything, sparing neither of them, and when he was finished she said quietly, "Go on."

So he did. He spelled out everything that had happened to him in the past few days, and his efforts to make sense of it. He broke off only three times, twice to light more cigarettes for them both, the third time when he was telling her about Petrograd. She knew nothing about Irina or his failed attempt to free her, and when he reached the point in the story when he'd heard of Irina's death, he suddenly faltered.

They were only words, but he found himself transported back to that apartment stuffed with the incongruous trappings of a lost age. He saw Paul Dukes poking nervously at the logs on the fire with the toe of his boot, then turning and breaking the news to him.

The iron hand of the past clawed at his insides, and to his horror, he found himself choking back sobs. She held him tight while he cried. She held him tighter, and even cried a little herself, when he told her about the child Irina had been carrying.

"I'm so sorry . . . no one told me."

"I didn't want you to know," he said.

"You're such an idiot."

"What good would it have done? And if you knew, I would have had to tell you the rest of it."

As before, he didn't hold back any of the unsavory details about the revenge he'd taken on Zakharov, describing it exactly as it had happened, as well as the sweet satisfaction he'd experienced.

By now it was very late, and Lucy suggested they lie down. They kicked off their shoes and pulled the sheet and blanket over themselves. They lay there on their sides, Lucy tucked in behind him while he talked to the room.

He wasn't sure if she was listening—she didn't react—but he needed to say it anyway, to purge himself. It was, he realized, his final confession: a catalog of his worst sins. He began with his killing of the guide who had tried to sell him out to the Soviets when he was fleeing the country, and he went on to detail some of the more shocking things he had done while working abroad for the Secret Intelligence Service under the guise of "cultural attaché." He tried to leave Leonard out of it, not wishing to tar him with the same brush. Besides, more often than not he had acted entirely on his own initiative.

He told her far more than he had ever told anyone, laying himself bare to her, methodically listing the deeds that had pushed him to the brink of insanity.

At a certain point Lucy said, "Shhh . . . I think that's enough for now."

She sounded completely unruffled by his rambling litany of self-hatred. She even stroked his forehead, like a mother soothing a child.

"Zakharov's brother's coming for me. It's the only reason I'm still alive—he must have decided to settle the score himself—but I promise I'll do everything I can for you."

She kissed the back of his neck. "I know you will," she said sleepily.

He didn't want to sleep—time was too precious to fritter away on unconsciousness—but with the warmth of her lean body against his back and her arm draped over him, he felt as though he were enveloped in a dream, and soon he was.

He had no sense of how long he was under, but he was drawn slowly back to wakefulness by the sound of her quiet sobbing. She was still pressed tightly against him, and he could feel the ebb and flow of her breath at his neck.

When he twisted to face her, she clung to him.

"What a perfectly hateful situation," she croaked. "I don't want to die . . . I'm only just becoming acquainted with myself."

Tom found himself smiling at her words.

"I'm not going to let you die."

He reached up, smoothing away her tears with his thumb.

They lay there in the darkness, sightless, nose to nose, listening to each other's breathing. And when Lucy gently pressed her lips to his, he didn't resist.

"One kiss," she had said down at the beach. They must have been thinking the same thing, because they stretched it out for more than a minute before they finally drew apart.

Lucy stroked his face and ran her fingers through his hair. "I knew I was right."

"What's that?" he replied, drugged by the experience.

"About the desert island."

They laughed and held each other close.

He didn't hear them enter the room. He was awakened by the beam of a flashlight trained on his face from a few feet away. His left arm was trapped, wrapped around Lucy, but he raised his right hand to block the glare.

He was quite ready to be hauled from the bed, but nothing happened. Nothing was even said. The light was extinguished, and, judging from the sound of the footfalls, two people then crossed the room and left by the door.

For a moment he thought they'd forgotten to lock it, but then he heard the key turning.

Lucy stirred against him. "What is it?" she asked groggily.

"Nothing, Go back to sleep."

She did, he didn't.

22

The last thing either of them expected was breakfast.

Its arrival was announced by a loud thumping on the door, which was then unlocked and pushed open. Tom slipped from the bed and wandered warily over.

There was a tray outside in the corridor: buttered baguette, a jug of coffee, two cups and a candle burning in a brass holder. Both Russians were also there, guns drawn.

"Did you get some sleep?" asked the small one, with a knowing leer.

Tom ignored him and picked up the tray.

"Big mistake. We didn't know she was your girlfriend."

"She isn't my girlfriend."

"Big mistake."

Lucy laid a blanket on the floor as if for a picnic and placed the candle in the middle of it.

"It's good to see your face again," said Tom.

He was wary about the coffee, but it tasted innocent enough, and besides, the Russian's comments outside in the corridor suggested that a more sinister end was planned for them than a straightforward poisoning.

They heard a telephone ring twice while they were eating, and they also heard a car driving off. They studiously ignored these sounds of activity, just as they went out of their way to avoid all mention of what Lucy had rightly described as their "hateful situation."

They spoke of other things, of her mother and the deep unhappiness she seemed doomed to always carry with her like a curse, and of her father, whose bones would always lie in French soil. Tom also told her his mother's story, a tale of displacement that he suspected lay at the root of his own peripatetic existence. They listed the five people they disliked most in the world, as well as the five they most admired; the five places they wished they'd visited, and the five they wished they hadn't.

They found more things to list, things that allowed them to laugh and to speak of other places and other times. It was escapism, but of a limited kind. They both knew there was something final, something definitive, in the nature of their lists that acknowledged the coming cataclysm.

They would not be allowed to remain there forever—Lucy stretched out on the blanket, her head in his lap—talking by the guttering light of a candle.

When it finally happened, when the key turned in the lock and the door swung open, it was Tom they wanted, and Tom alone.

Lucy clung to him.

"It's not over yet," he whispered in her ear. "And if it comes to it, fight like a hellcat."

He kissed her hard on the lips then left.

Only one of the Russians, the taller of the two, was waiting for him outside in the corridor.

"Where's your boyfriend?"

"Shut up."

"Did you have an argument? Has he left you?"

Tom saw the fury flaming in the big man's face, which was just what he wanted to see. If he could only goad him into making a mistake . . .

There were no mistakes, though, as Tom was shepherded back through the farmhouse and out into the courtyard.

The heat struck his face like the blast from an open furnace, and his eyes struggled to adjust to the blinding sunshine. It was another glorious day, a span of unclouded blue overhead.

Rounding the wing of the farmhouse, Tom plucked a sun-cracked fig from the tree trained against the end wall. This brought a futile reprimand from the big Russian, which Tom ignored. A short distance from the farmhouse a handful of cypresses stood sentinel over a low grassy rise. There was a person seated at a table in the shade cast by the cluster of tall, tapering trees.

It was a woman, and although her back was turned, a simple gesture unmasked her: the way she took her coffee cup between the thumb and middle finger of her left hand before raising it to her lips.

It was enough to stop Tom dead in his tracks.

"Keep moving," ordered the big Russian.

But he couldn't move. He daren't move closer, in case he was right.

A sharp shove in the back propelled him forward, and the woman turned to face him.

He had often wondered what she would look like now, but the mental pictures he had painted of her had done her a disservice. The intervening years seemed barely to have touched her features. Her hair, though shorter, was still as black and lustrous as a lump of anthracite, and the large, dark eyes that met his incredulous gaze were unlined.

"Take your time," said Irina, gesturing to the chair opposite her.

He wanted to make sense of it, but his mind was emptied of all activity. He stared like a halfwit while she poured him a coffee, adding a dash of milk and half a spoon of sugar—the way he had always taken it.

She slid the saucer over to him, along with her cigarettes and a lighter. She then said something to the big Russian that Tom didn't catch. The man backed off, out of earshot.

"You look well," said Irina. "It must be the Mediterranean lifestyle. Or maybe it's the young company you keep."

Her English had always been good. Now it was impeccable, with barely a trace of an accent.

"How old is she, Tom?"

"Don't tell me you're jealous."

Irina smiled. "I am a little. She's beautiful."

So that had been her behind the flashlight.

"Yes, she is. She's also intelligent, kind and above all . . . true."

The emphasis wasn't lost on her. "Oh, please, don't be so dramatic."

"Dramatic!?" He gave a mirthless laugh. "Under the circumstances, you might have to allow me a bit of latitude."

He could see it now, not all of it, but enough of it to know that everything he had always taken for granted could now be discarded as untrustworthy, everything that had passed between them, reaching right back to their first meeting at the embassy party in Petrograd, when Irina had spilled her drink in front of him, splashing his shoes with wine. Mortified, apologizing for her clumsiness, that was the moment she had hooked her fish—a small fish, the most junior member of the special diplomatic mission dispatched from London to negotiate with the Bolshevik revolutionaries.

He had never once thought to doubt her. Why should he have, when others who knew her far better hadn't? Her credentials were beyond reproach. She had even worked as a volunteer nurse alongside Ambassador Buchanan's daughter at the British Colony Hospital on Vassili Island. That's how thorough the Bolsheviks had been in their preparations.

"You're upset," said Irina. "Of course you are. I understand."

"How can you possibly understand? I was shedding tears for you just a few hours ago." She looked shocked by his words. "I've been living a half-life because of you."

"But at least you're alive," she countered. "Others weren't so lucky . . . like Dimitri."

"Remind me . . . ?" said Tom, knowing full well.

"Dimitri Zakharov, the man you killed."

"To avenge your death. Now there's an unfortunate irony."

"More than you think," said Irina. "Dimitri was my lover."

Tom reached for a cigarette. It wasn't the added betrayal that shocked him—nothing could top the grand deceit he was still groping to come to terms with—it was the lengths to which she had been willing to go.

"And how did he feel about you offering up your body for the cause?"

A part of him wanted her to say that Zakharov had never known, that she had never told him, that she had done it for herself.

"He understood."

"Christ . . ."

"We were fighting for a new world, a better world. Nothing else was important. Your navy was in the Gulf of Finland. If you had joined the Whites you would have destroyed us. The Revolution would have been for nothing. We all did what we had to do to stop that."

Baint had once said that the only feature a man could make for himself was his mouth. If this was true, then Irina's betrayed a hardness of the soul he had never associated with her.

"And was it worth it—your better world? How many of your own people have you massacred since then? How many have starved to death? How many have you locked up and forced to work like slaves?"

Irina hesitated. "It has been a long and hard road."

"You don't seem to have suffered too badly from the look of you." His gaze settled on her chain-link bracelet. "Solid gold . . . ?"

Irina glanced at her wrist before looking up. "From a man who lives alone in a palace by the sea large enough for five families . . . ?"

She took her cigarettes back and lit one, pleased with her riposte, and not without justification.

"Why me?" he asked. "Why trick me back to Petrograd? I was nobody."

"Don't be offended, but we weren't after you. We were after ST-25. We were after Paul Dukes."

The plan, she explained, had been hatched by Dzherzinsky, the head of the Cheka, who was obsessed with tracking down Britain's last agent in the capital. They knew he was there, just not where. If Tom could be persuaded to return from Finland, then he would be obliged to use the underground network already in place; he would lead them to Dukes.

"I didn't think it would work," said Irina. "I didn't think you would come for me. When you did . . ." She trailed off.

"What?"

"I still can't believe you came for me."

He hardened his heart against her words. "A tribute to your professionalism. You were very convincing. And the pregnancy was a nice touch. Was that Dzherzinsky's idea too?"

"Yes."

But there had been a moment's hesitation, a brief tremor in her eyes, which now seemed determined to avoid his.

"Irina . . . look at me."

When she finally did, he saw both the lie and the truth written in her face.

"I promised myself I wouldn't tell you."

"A child . . . ?"

She nodded. "A boy. Such a beautiful boy."

When he saw the tears starting to her eyes he felt a chill qualm run through him.

"He died?"

"Died? No."

A boy. A living boy.

"Is he mine?"

"I don't know. Maybe Dimitri's."

"Surely you can tell. He must be—what?—sixteen by now."

"In ten days."

"Surely you can tell."

"How," she demanded, almost aggressively, "when I haven't seen him since he was a baby? I don't even know where he is."

"What do you mean?"

"I mean, think what it was like for me. I was on my own. Dimitri was dead. You were gone. I didn't know who his father was, and yes . . . I wasn't ready to be a mother. Dimitri's family wouldn't take him in case he was yours. No one wanted him." She paused. "He went to an orphanage in Moscow."

"Which orphanage?"

She shook her head and looked at him with sadness. "I shouldn't have told you. Why do you think I'm here, to have coffee with you and talk about the old days?"

"No, I know why you're here. You're here to finish a job."

"It's not a job I asked for, and I couldn't say no."

"I'm touched," he replied sarcastically.

"You should be. Why do you think I sent the Italian? To give you a chance, Tom. You should have disappeared as soon as you'd killed him. I assume you *did* kill him."

Tom nodded.

"I'm sorry, but I can't help you anymore. If you knew the man who gave the order, you would understand that."

"General Ivan Zakharov—Dimitri's brother."

That surprised her, that really surprised her, and Tom glimpsed an opportunity. Under other circumstances he might not have risked it, but now wasn't the time for professional discretion.

"We know more than that, Irina. We also know about your spy in the Secret Intelligence Service."

"I don't know what you mean."

He believed her, not because she had no reason to lie to him, but because she looked worried.

"Zakharov didn't tell you, did he? That's how he knows I killed Dimitri—your man on the inside accessed my file. That's also why it had to look like I'd died a natural death. You say failure isn't an option, but you've already failed, Irina. You shouldn't have given me a chance, you shouldn't have sent the Italian. It was because of Pozzi we knew we'd been infiltrated." He let her absorb his words before continuing. "What's General Zakharov going to think about that when you return home?"

"You're trying to save your life."

"I'm trying to save both our lives."

"You're forgetting Lucy."

That chilled him: the confirmation that Lucy also had a death sentence on her head.

"Irina, listen. Stalin's on the rampage—everyone knows it. No one's safe. You think Zakharov's going to cover for you? He's going to throw you to the wolves to save himself."

"I'll take my chances with him."

"Then you're a fool, because you don't need to." He leaned closer. "Come over to us. We can protect you."

When she looked to her left he thought at first she was checking to see that the big Russian wasn't listening in, but her eye had been drawn by a motorcar approaching along the road to the farmhouse, throwing up a plume of white dust in its wake.

Turning back to him, she asked, "And did you make the same offer to Pyotr?"

"Pyotr?"

How in heaven did she know?

She smiled wistfully. "You're a good man, Tom, too good for all this; you always were."

He watched the car pull up by the farmhouse, the same car that he and Lucy had been transported in. The short Russian appeared from behind the steering wheel and moments later Pyotr unfolded himself from the passenger seat. He was instantly recognizable from the white bandage around his head. Both men made their way over.

Irina rose to receive them, her authority evident in the little bow Pyotr gave as he greeted her in Russian. "It's an honor to meet you, Comrade."

Tom was struck limp and lifeless by the spectacle. Leonard's skepticism about Pyotr had been entirely justified. He had needed Tom to get him away from the car wreck, and now that he was on his feet again it was business as usual.

"Did he tell you about the money I gave him?"

Irina turned to him. "Yes."

"Did he tell you how much?"

Pyotr pulled an envelope from his pocket and handed it to Irina. "This much."

Tom could see from the thickness of the envelope that it was the full amount.

"You bastard," he spat, with as much venom as he could convey.

Pyotr took a few steps toward him, an amused, sardonic light in his eyes. "You're so naïve it's pathetic," he replied in French.

Tom pushed back his chair and launched himself at Pyotr, catching him off guard and bringing him down. He was vaguely aware of Irina issuing an order not to fire, but all his other senses were devoted to one cause: inflicting as much pain as he possibly could on the man beneath him. He managed to land a couple of sound punches to the face before he was hauled off and hurled aside like a rag doll. A well-placed boot to the midriff left him crippled and curled up on the turf, gasping for breath.

Pyotr pulled himself to his feet and dusted himself down. Pleasingly, there was blood streaming from his nose.

"Go and get cleaned up," ordered Irina. "You, show him where."

Pyotr glowered down at Tom, then made the sign of the cross over him.

"*Vade in pacem*," he said.

"What's that supposed to mean?"

"What it's always meant," replied Pyotr, spitting on him as he made off with the small Russian.

Tom saw it now.

It was the hand of Leonard at work, pulling the strings.

Pyotr had played his part to perfection. Tom's only worry was that his own performance would now ruin the show.

He glared up at the big Russian standing over him and found himself staring into the muzzle of a revolver pointed directly at his head.

"Sit down," said Irina.

He had to banish all nostalgic sentiments. She had made her choice. She was the enemy. But he also needed her alive. He needed to know the name of the orphanage.

The moment he was seated again, he groped for another cigarette, lighting it with a trembling hand, which had nothing to do with play-acting.

"It means 'Go in peace.' "

"I know what it means," replied Tom. "I wanted to know what he *meant* by it."

The temptation to glance off into the olive trees was unbearable. Were they here? Had they followed the car? Or had Pyotr agreed to handle the situation on his own? Either way, he had to be ready to move at the first sign of trouble.

"What happens now?" he asked.

"General Zakharov wants to meet you."

"He's coming here?"

"Italy."

"Where?"

"We'll know when he telephones. It won't be long."

Tom fought to hold his thoughts in check. Was it too much to ask? The balance of the game had just swung in his favor, but could he really expect to turn the tables entirely on Zakharov and end the matter once and for all in Italy?

"Irina, you have to let Lucy go."

"He wants her too."

"Is this what you fought for—a man who can have anything he wants, even an innocent life? What do you think would happen if a British general demanded such a thing for purely personal reasons? He'd be court-martialed and shot, and rightly so.'

"The British military has more to answer for than one innocent life."

"Words, Irina—indoctrination. Your beautiful experiment has become a homicidal mess, and you know it."

"Enough!" she snapped, slamming her hand down on the tin tabletop.

The big Russian took a couple of steps closer, and as he did so Tom caught a glimpse of movement out of the corner of his eye. He didn't dare to look but he hadn't been mistaken. A shadow had just flitted between two olive trees beyond the dirt road.

He swiftly spread his hands in a gesture of apology. "I'm sorry."

Irina nodded a wary acceptance.

He looked at her, puzzled. Was this really the woman who had ruled both his waking thoughts and his dreams for the past sixteen years, the woman he had sanctified?

She shifted uneasily under his gaze. "What are you thinking?"

"You don't want to know."

He had to keep her talking, though, keep her looking at him, because behind her there were now two men converging on the farmhouse.

It sounded like the crack of a whip, but muted, muffled. The shot had been fired inside the farmhouse.

Something had gone wrong.

As Irina and the big Russian turned, another shot was fired, louder than the last. One of the men moving in on the farmhouse took cover behind an olive tree, clearly visible from where they were sitting.

It was Commissaire Roche.

The big Russian wasn't an option—there was too much ground to cover—so Tom hurled the table aside and launched himself at Irina. She was pulling a pistol from the pocket of her linen jacket, but he was on her before she could bring it to bear on him, seizing her wrist and twisting her around in front of him as a shield. The big Russian drew a bead on them but couldn't fire for fear of hitting her.

Irina managed to toss her pistol aside, unable to use it herself and determined to deny him a weapon. She barked an order and the Russian advanced on them. Tom backed away. It was hopeless, just a matter of time. He glanced frantically behind him, but although the air was now ringing with gunfire there was no sign of any assistance from that quarter. He did the only thing open to him: he stopped retreating and he charged, lifting Irina from her feet.

The big Russian was caught unawares, not prepared for the sudden impact. As he fell backward Tom released Irina and rolled aside, rising rapidly to his feet and scooping up her discarded pistol. He darted behind a cypress tree as the Russian got off his first shot, taking a piece out of the trunk.

Tom slipped the safety catch forward. He couldn't wait. The farmhouse was under siege and he had to get to Lucy. He rolled left, then immediately right, dropping into a crouch as he did so. The first maneuver drew another shot; the second gave him a hairline advantage over the big Russian, who had to adjust his aim to the other side of the tree trunk and down.

Tom put two bullets in his chest. The third was intended as a head shot, but he missed.

Irina didn't hesitate; she lunged for her comrade's weapon.

"Don't do it, Irina."

When she ignored him he fired, winging her in the thigh, bringing her down.

He hurried over and recovered the Russian's revolver. The big man lay on his back like a felled oak. He was wearing a perplexed expression, bleeding badly, but still breathing.

He wasn't going anywhere, but Irina might, even with her leg wound.

Tom punched her hard in the temple.

It was good to have the excuse.

He rounded the wing of the farmhouse at a sprint to see Leonard pinned down behind the wellhead in the middle of the courtyard. There was another man crouched beside him. It was Walter, which didn't make any sense.

Suddenly, the American was on his feet and running toward Tom, Leonard covering him with a volley of shots directed at a window to the right of the main entrance.

"The car," shouted Walter.

The key was in the ignition, and as Walter fired the engine Tom dropped into the passenger seat. They both kept low, Walter flooring the throttle, not bothering to move up through the gears as he swung the vehicle in a wide arc across the courtyard, its engine screaming. A shot from the farmhouse disintegrated the driver's side window. Others punched into the bodywork as the car straightened up, bearing down on the front entrance.

The impact winded Walter against the steering wheel, but the solid wooden doors were breached, one ripped clear of its hinges, the other left hanging limply.

A figure flashed by in front of them across the entrance hall, loosing off a wild shot that shattered the windshield and showered them both with glass. Tom had a good idea where the little Russian was headed, and he was out of the passenger door in an instant, scrabbling up and over the crumpled hood and into the farmhouse.

He couldn't make sense of the pounding at first, but then he remembered that the big man outside with two bullets in his chest had pocketed the key after locking the door on Lucy.

Tom careered around the corner into the corridor just as the door gave way and the Russian lurched into the room.

He was too late. He waited for the gunshot . . . waited . . . waited . . . and then he was there in the doorway.

The Russian was on his hands and knees and Lucy was swinging something in her hands. She was beating him around the head and the back with the wooden strut that Tom had removed from the base of the bed. It wasn't solid enough to do any real damage and the Russian lashed out with his foot, sweeping Lucy's legs from under her, leveling his gun to finish her off as she crashed to the floor.

Tom fired once—a shot to the head—the muzzle flash illuminating the room, freezing the action in a momentary, blinding flash of light.

The Russian didn't collapse; he seemed to deflate, slowly, unwillingly.

Tom wrenched the gun from his twitching fingers and dropped to his knees beside Lucy.

"It's okay, it's okay, it's me," he said, stroking her face and smoothing her hair.

"Tom . . ."

He felt the bite of her fingernails through his shirt when she clung to him.

"My little hellcat."

Pyotr was alive, but only just. He lay on the floor of the kitchen, bleeding from a stomach wound.

"He saw them coming," he mumbled apologetically. "He was too quick for me."

Walter tore off his own shirt and pressed it to the wound, stemming the flow of blood as best he could.

Commissaire Roche had one of his men bring the car up to the farmhouse and they loaded Pyotr into the back. The nearest hospital was in Hyères. Roche insisted on driving.

"Call the hospital and tell them we'll be twenty minutes."

"Don't let him die."

"Just make the call, Mr. Nash."

"Consider it done, Commissaire."

After the sudden eruption of violence, there was something surreal about the silence that blew in on the back of Roche's departure. There was certainly no elation, no punching the air in victory. They stood there for a moment in the courtyard, spent shell cartridges glinting at their feet, then Tom led them off around the building to the cluster of cypresses.

The big Russian had expired. Irina was still unconscious, her white cotton slacks now stained a bright crimson above her left knee. Tom checked for a pulse.

"Who is she?" asked Walter.

"Irina Bibikov."

"You're not serious," said Leonard.

"It's her."

Lucy stared, unbelieving.

"Sorry to bust in," said Walter, "but who the hell is Irina Bibikov?"

"Someone I knew a long time ago."

"We thought she was dead," added Leonard.

"She will be if you don't stop that bleeding."

Tom was rigging up a tourniquet with the dead Russian's belt when they received a visitor: the local *garde champêtre* on his bicycle. He had been alerted to the gunfire by some residents of the nearby village and had come to investigate, though not with any great enthusiasm. Roche's deputy took the matter in hand, sending the man away with instructions to return with the local doctor as quickly as possible.

Irina still hadn't come around by the time Tom scooped her up in his arms and carried her into the farmhouse, out of the heat.

"Jeez, you must have really clouted her," said Walter.

Tom was laying her on the sofa in the parlor when the phone rang.

"Don't answer it!" he shouted, remembering now that Irina was waiting on a call from General Zakharov.

He was too late. Leonard had already picked up the receiver in the entrance hall. Tom snatched it from him.

"Who is this?" came a man's voice in Russian, calm and authoritative.

"General Zakharov, Comrade Bibikov asks that you call back in twenty minutes."

Twenty minutes to bring Irina around and persuade her to play along. If Zakharov could only be persuaded to keep the rendezvous in Italy, Tom could finish it there.

There was a drawn-out silence on the other end of the line. When the man spoke again, it was in English.

"She isn't Irina Bibikov anymore . . . not since 1919."

There were to be no long years of unshadowed happiness, free of fear. That realization rendered Tom mute.

Zakharov filled the void. "You are a hard man to kill. Don't stop running."

It was the easy hubris in the voice that spurred him to respond.

"There's a difference, Zakharov . . . I know where you are. And you'd better hope I don't find you first."

Zakharov dismissed the threat with an amused grunt.

"Your brother didn't see it coming, but you will," said Tom darkly. "Because I want you to know it was me."

The speed with which the line went dead offered a degree of satisfaction.

Less gratifying were the expressions that confronted him when he hung up the receiver. Leonard, Walter and Lucy were all regarding him with an unsettling mix of surprise and concern.

The metamorphosis, he realized, was almost complete.

There was barely anything left to distinguish him from the man he used to be.

Walter dug up a bottle of cheap brandy in the kitchen, "to settle my goddamn nerves."

They drank it out of teacups, raising a toast to Pyotr and a prayer to God.

Walter made Tom feel the lump on the back of his skull where he'd been clubbed senseless in the trees while trailing Tom home from the party. On coming to, he had hurried to Villa Martel. Finding it deserted, he had then gone to wake up Leonard. Venetia had become hysterical, inconsolable, when it became clear that Lucy was also missing.

Leonard's contact at the French Ministry of Foreign Affairs wasn't too pleased about being roused from his bed in the middle of the night. Neither was Commissaire Roche, when he received the call from his superior in Paris telling him to hightail it over to Le Rayol with as many men as he could muster.

An hour later, Yevgeny and Fanya were also woken—by six armed men bursting in on them. Commissaire Roche was happy to let Leonard and Walter conduct the interrogation right there in the bedroom while he and his men retired downstairs.

"I thought Leonard was going to shoot them both," said Walter.

"So did they, which is why we were sure they weren't hiding anything. They didn't know where you were being held."

Leonard had figured that Pyotr was their only hope, but it would mean persuading him to play a very dangerous game. Pyotr hadn't hesitated, apparently, and they had worked out his story during the short drive from the monastery to Collobrières, where he had called his controller in Paris from a bar.

"He was adamant that the lie had to contain as much of the truth as possible," said Walter. "And whatever he said, it sure as hell worked. There was a car there to pick him up within the hour. All we had to do was tail it without being spotted."

Leonard laid his teacup aside and took Lucy in his arms, just holding her for a moment before saying, "I know someone who would be very happy to hear from you."

"Mother . . . where is she?"

"At Klaus and Ilse's house. I imagine she's sitting right beside the telephone."

"And an overflowing ashtray," said Tom.

Lucy said she didn't want privacy, so they were all present in the entrance hall when the operator put her through and the receiver was snatched up at the other end.

"It's me," she said simply, quite calmly.

But her face suddenly crumpled and the tears came.

"I know," she sobbed into the phone. "Me too. Me too . . ."

23

The hospital was a grand Victorian building, a former private residence put up by some duke or other just south of Hyères on a pine-clad slope facing the sea. Long verandas took up two of its four floors at the front, and these were ideal when it came to giving the less mobile of the patients a dose of sunshine and a breath of salt air. Those more able to get about had access to the manicured gardens, whose main pathways had been laid with tarmac to smooth the passage of wheelchairs.

Irina was permitted no such luxuries. Her room was on the top floor of the hospital at the back, and there were two gendarmes seated on chairs flanking the door.

Lucy remained outside with them in the corridor when Tom entered the room.

Irina was dozing, propped up on pillows. She looked pale and remarkably peaceful, despite the livid bruise on the side of her head, which had leaked around and discolored her eye. In repose, her mouth had lost its iron anatomy.

She stirred as he pulled up a chair, focusing on him with tired eyes. The bullet had passed clean through her thigh, but it had carried a small piece of cotton from her trousers deep into her leg, where it had gone undetected until the infection had started to rage. The surgeon had assured Tom that all was well now, that there was nothing to fear.

Irina held out her hand, palm upward, inviting him to take it. After a moment's hesitation, he did.

"What's going to happen to me?"

"Well, you're not going to lose your leg."

"Just my head?"

He smiled. "Only if I have my way."

"I mean it, Tom. Am I going to be . . . killed?"

He leaned forward in his chair. "You've spent too long with the wrong people. That's not how we do things. Anyhow, you're too big a prize."

Leonard had grown quite excited at the possibilities opened up by Irina's capture, so much so that Tom had begun to wonder if he hadn't been used as bait by his old friend over the past days to draw out such a valuable Soviet asset. He certainly wouldn't put such skulduggery past Leonard.

"So?" Irina asked. "What happens?"

"It's not for me to say, but you know how these things work. It's a horse trade. Your government has people we want back."

"Were you lying about our man in the Secret Intelligence Service?"

"No. We have him now."

"Then use him to get them back. You can't send me home—they'll execute me."

"I thought you were quite happy to take your chances with Zakharov."

"Not now. Not after this." She paused. "If you send me back you'll never know about Alexei."

"Alexei?"

"Your son. Our son."

"Oh, so now he's definitely mine, is he?" He didn't attempt to conceal his skepticism. He also released her hand.

"Of course I couldn't say before—it would have been too cruel."

"This is desperate stuff, Irina."

"What's your middle name?"

Tom hesitated. "Alexander . . ."

Irina's dark eyes bored into him, and the hardness had returned to her mouth. "If you let them send me back you will never know where he is."

"You can tell me now."

"And why would I do that?" she replied.

He'd had enough of her threats and her games. Getting to his feet, he said, "I'll come and see you again."

"I would like that. Maybe we can talk about . . . nicer things."

"I very much doubt that. Good-bye, Irina, or whatever it is you call yourself now."

"Natalya."

It suited her; it had something of the dark prophetess about it.

He was placing the chair back against the wall when she asked, "What happened to Pyotr?"

Tom turned to face her. "He didn't make it."

There was nothing in her expression to suggest what she felt about this.

He knew Lucy could see that his time with Irina had unsettled him, but she didn't probe, quite happy to walk with him in silence back through the building.

They left the main staircase at the first-floor landing and made for the administration offices. Here they found two more gendarmes on guard by a door. This time, Lucy didn't wait outside.

They had visited Pyotr together before, but this was to be the last time.

"Why?" asked Pyotr.

"Because you're officially dead."

"Oh."

"There's going to be a burial and everything."

"Can I come?"

Lucy laughed.

"I'm afraid you'll be in Marseilles by then. They're transferring you to another hospital there tonight."

"So this is good-bye?"

"And it's going to be quick. I hate good-byes."

"He does," confirmed Lucy.

"I've brought you something."

Tom handed over a small package wrapped in gift paper. Pyotr tore off the paper and prized open the box. He frowned. "It's Russian?"

"Yes. It was given to me by a woman the day after you and I first met."

Pyotr held up the jeweled locket, dangling it before his face on its gold chain. "What happened to her?"

"I don't know. But the man she was with that day went on to be knighted by King George V for bravery . . . so it seemed appropriate."

Tom found a route through the tubes running in and out of Pyotr and stooped to hug him. "Thank you," he said.

Lucy was next, kissing the Russian on both cheeks. "I owe you my life."

"Maybe one day I will come and see what you have done with it."

"I hope so."

Pyotr clenched the locket in his fist and shooed them away with his other hand. "Go on, go . . . I have to practice being dead."

Tom was following Lucy from the room when he remembered something.

"Oh, any particular epitaph you want on your headstone?"

"Take a guess," replied Pyotr.

It was an unusual sight: Leonard and Venetia arm in arm. They were strolling across the lower lawn of the hospital gardens.

Lucy avoided the main steps, steering Tom toward a pathway that looped down through a scattering of palm trees, buying them a bit more time alone together.

"Are you all right?"

"She says he's definitely mine and his name's Alexei."

"Do you believe her?"

"It makes no difference. Even if she changes her story and swears he isn't, I still have to know for myself. I can't not know."

"If he is, he's going to be as handsome as a god. Yes . . . and almost my age," she added wickedly.

"Do you really think I'd let my son fall into the hands of a young hussy like you?"

"You're a fine one to talk . . . seducing your own goddaughter in her hour of need!"

"A little louder," said Tom. "I'm not sure your mother quite caught that."

Lucy glanced through the trees at the lawn below them, where Leonard and Venetia were now examining a flower border. "Oh, God, imagine . . ."

"I'd prefer not to."

"Don't worry," she said. "Our secret."

"And a very fine one it is."

Lucy smiled and slid her hand under his arm.

It was such a simple gesture, and yet it seemed to carry with it the full weight of their history. She was, he realized, the only true constant in his life. Even when he had revealed the worst of himself to her, his rotten core, she had barely flinched. It gave him hope for his uncertain future. *She* gave him hope.

"It's my birthday on Thursday."

"I know," Tom replied.

"Leonard says you'll be gone by then."

"There'll be other birthdays I won't miss."

"You know," said Lucy, "I really didn't think I was going to make it through to this one."

"I'm insulted," joked Tom.

"You came back for me."

"Of course I did."

"And you killed him."

"I'm sorry you had to see that."

They walked on a short way in silence before Lucy spoke. "In China they say that if you save a person's life you have to care for them forever."

"Really? I heard it was the other way around."

"Either way is fine by me," she replied, with just enough emphasis to make her meaning clear.

He didn't want to tell her—she would come to realize it herself before long—but the events of the past days had changed everything. The world could never be as it once was, not for any of them, not while General Ivan Zakharov was at large. To dream of future times was foolish when the present offered little hope of certainty.

With any luck the Soviets would solve the problem for them. Stalin didn't tolerate failure, and Zakharov's private vendetta had cost the country dearly: four agents apprehended, four killed, to say nothing of the humiliation, the public loss of face.

Leonard would do everything possible at his end to ensure that the blame for the disaster fell squarely on Zakharov's shoulders, but if by some miracle he survived Stalin's wrath . . .

At that instant they cleared the palms and the view opened up before them: the salt marshes of the Presqu'île de Giens, with its twin sandy spits thrusting out to sea, where the islands shimmered in the brassy glare of the high-noon sun.

It was an ageless vista that cared little for the foolish ways of men, and for a moment it laid a finger on the lips of all that was wrong with the world.

Acknowledgments

Not for the first time, my thanks go to my peerless agent, Stephanie Cabot, and to my editors, Jennifer Hershey and Julia Wisdom, whose unwavering encouragement is a vital tonic. Many thanks also to Amy Edelman for her scrupulous copyediting.

I would also like to thank my good friend Ben Airas, who not only suggested that I read *Operation Kronstadt* by Harry Ferguson, he then went and bought the book for me. This expert and gripping account of Britain's involvement in Russia around the time of the Revolution proved invaluable in my research.

MARK MILLS is a screenwriter and the author of *The Information Officer*, *The Savage Garden*, and *Amagansett*. *Amagansett*, his first novel, was published in a dozen countries and received the British Crime Writers' Association John Creasey Memorial Dagger award, and *The Savage Garden* was a #1 bestseller in the United Kingdom. A graduate of Cambridge University, he lives in Oxford with his wife and their two children.

About the Type

This book was set in Albertina, a typeface created by Dutch calligrapher and designer Chris Brand. His original drawings, based on calligraphic principles, were modified considerably to conform to the technological limitations of typesetting in the early 1960s. The development of digital technology later allowed Frank E. Blokland of the Dutch Type Library to restore the typeface to its creator's original intentions.